# The Judgment

Patriots or terrorists?

A novel about taking back America.

Patrick Michael Alaggio

Avid Readers Publishing Group
Lakewood, California

*In loving memory of my mother, Elsie.*

Who suffered the loss of two young husbands to cancer

and still found the strength to raise her three children alone.

*My special thanks to Mark Lowe*
*for the lovely cover art!*

*If these words ring true to you then this*
*novel will speak to you as well...*
Patrick Michael Alaggio

*"If tyranny and oppression come to this land,*
*it will be in the guise of fighting a foreign enemy."*
**James Madison**

*"The limits of tyrants are prescribed by the*
*endurance of those whom they oppress."*
**Frederick Douglas**

*"I see in the near future a crisis approaching that unnerves me and*
*causes me to tremble for the safety of my country. As a result of the*
*war, corporations have been enthroned and an era of corruption in high*
*places will follow, and the money powers of the country will endeavor*
*to prolong their reign by working upon the prejudices of the people until*
*all wealth is aggregated in a few hands and the Republic (Democracy) is*
*destroyed. I feel at this moment more anxiety than ever before, even in*
*the midst of war."*
**Abraham Lincoln (1864)**

*"The world is a dangerous place, not because of those who do evil,*
*but because of those who look on and do nothing."*
**Albert Einstein**

*"Those who make peaceful revolution impossible*
*will make violent revolution inevitable."*
**John F. Kennedy**

*"We should never forget that everything*
*Adolf Hitler did in Germany was legal."*
**Martin Luther King, Jr.**

*"The most effective way to restrict democracy is to transfer decision-*
*making from the public arena to unaccountable institutions:*
*kings and princes, priestly castes, military juntas,*
*party dictatorships, or modern corporations."*
**Noam Chomsky**

*"Another world is not only possible, she's on her way.*
*Maybe many of us won't be here to greet her,*
*but on a quiet day, if I listen very carefully,*
*I can hear her breathing..."*

**Arundhati Roy**

**The Judgment**

The opinions expressed in this manuscript are those of the author and do not represent the thoughts or opinions of the publisher. The author warrants and represents that he has the legal right to publish or owns all material in this book. If you find a discrepancy, please contact the publisher.

**Avid Readers Publishing Group**

**http://www.avidreaderspg.com**

**ISBN-13:978-1-61286-078-7**

**Printed in the United States**

# (1960)

## *"A Mother's Worst Fear"*

Ruth Stanton was preparing dinner when David's screams of terror reached her. Instinctively she flew down the two outside flights of stairs faster than any forty-three year old should have. As she raced for her son her mind was paralyzed by visions of horror. ***"Dear Lord, not again."*** A few moments later she was beside him. Her heart pounded brutally as she approached him.

There he was kneeling on the ground, sobbing uncontrollably. He looked to be in one piece. *"Perhaps he cut himself."* She thought. What Ruth couldn't see was the tiny sparrow that David had just shot with his brand new bow and arrow. Never in a million years did he think he could hit it, after all he was only six and the target had been so small. ***"MOMMY, I KILLED IT!"*** he screamed. David had never experienced the guilt of killing anything so senselessly before. All he could see over and over again was his arrow as it hit the tiny bird and dragged it mercilessly across the ground.

Ruth held him in her arms for a very long time as the boy sobbed and convulsed in pain. They buried the tiny creature behind the garage of the four-family apartment building where they had just moved. Ruth Stanton helped her son build a cross out of twigs and together they mourned. They placed the cross on the grave and it was there, behind the garage, that Ruth Stanton taught her son how to pray. *"Dear Lord, please forgive me for killing this little bird. Please take good care of him in your home in heaven. Amen."* As Ruth gathered her senses she too said a prayer. *"Dear God, thank you for sparing my son."*

David visited that grave every day for what seemed to be an eternity. For many days thereafter he would pray and ask the sparrow for it's' forgiveness, but he never did forgive himself and he never forgot the exact spot where they had buried the tiny creature.

## *"WIQR, 103.5 FM - Baltimore"*

"Richard, from Gaithersburg… you're on the air. Speak to me."

"Hello Mr. McManus, thank you for taking my call."

"You're welcome Richard, what's on your mind?"

"I've been listening to your show for a few months now and I don't understand how you expect us to change the world. I like what you're trying to do but what can one person really do when we have so little power?"

"That does seem to be the question now doesn't it Richard? How can we change this country for the better? Make the world a place where life is considered sacred and war no longer rules our economies, our governments and our lives."

"Yes, sir… what can I do? I'm just a plumber with a wife and three children and a mortgage to meet."

"Well Richard, you're doing something right now. You've gotten off your gluteus maximus muscles, picked up the phone, swallowed your embarrassment and called us. That's SOMETHING, now isn't it?"

"Well, I guess so… but it's not much."

"There's over three-hundred million of us here in America and if everyone does something, ANYTHING, to effect a positive change then that's quite a bit more than *not much*… don't you think?"

"Well I guess so, but still, I'd like to do more."

"Fair enough… I'm going to dedicate the rest of this hour to Richard's very important question. What can a single person do to effect change in a country where the power seems to be in the hands of the few or in

2

the grasp of multi-national corporations who are hell-bent on keeping us engaged in wars all over the world in order to stuff their coffers with even more loot than they already have?"

"Mary from Annapolis, you're on the line."

"Hello Tim. Alice Walker once said; *"The most common way people give up their power is by thinking they don't have any."* And I think that's a very important first step… for people to realize that they CAN make a difference."

"That's quite a powerful quote Mary. Could you tell us a little more about who Alice Walker is?"

"I'd be glad to. Alice is a novelist, the author of The Color Purple. She's written broadly about the African-American struggle, the environment and is actively engaged in the fight for equal rights and economic justice. She also said; *It just seems clear to me that as long as we are all here, it's pretty clear that the struggle is to <u>share the planet</u>, rather than divide it.*"

"She's obviously a very bright and considerate individual and thank you for sharing her insights with us this evening."

"Mark, from right here in Baltimore… you're on the air."

"Hi, uh… I'd like to do something too but it gets a little frightening with everything going on the way it is and the police becoming more militarized everyday and with the surveillance that keeps creeping into our lives. I mean it's really scary sometimes."

"I'm sure many Americans feel your concerns Mark. But are we to hide away and do nothing? Or take a stand somewhere and make a difference?"

"(sigh) I don't know."

"That's okay, asking the question is the first step and that's an important one. Does anyone out there have an answer for Mark?"

"Hi Tim, this is Beverly from Washington DC and I'm a single black woman with two children under thirteen and it **IS** frightening out here. I take solace in a quote that I've posted to our refrigerator, it says: *"Courage is not the absence of fear, but rather the judgment that something else is more important than fear."*

"That's a wonderful quote Beverly. Do you know who wrote it?"

"Why yes, it was Ambrose Redmoon. But I don't know anything about her."

"I like what you've done by putting up that quote on the refrigerator for you and your children. That's something we could all do to help educate our families. I remember my friends' house where his parents had done that and I loved coming over and reading all the jewels they had posted there. I called it; *Refrigerator Wisdom.*"

"Yes, we've done that too and the children seem to enjoy it."

"Thank you for your call Beverly. Keep on teaching them that they can make a difference too."

"Line two? Caller you're on the air."

"Hi Tim, this is Jim from Rutgers University in New Brunswick, New Jersey."

"Welcome Jim, I didn't know we reached that far north."

"Not always, but the conditions seem nice and clear tonight. I'm happy to be able to tune in to your show."

"Thank you, what's on your mind?"

"I'm an eighteen year old sophomore and I just wanted to tell you about one of the things we're doing to make a difference."

"GREAT, let's hear it!"

"We've begun a campaign to lower the voting age to sixteen so that we could have a say in political issues **before** we're affected by them and drafted off into some unholy war."

"That's very interesting. Tell us more."

"We've drafted a letter and sent it off to Senators, Congressmen, newspapers, activists, schools and who ever we thought might be able to help us push our issue."

"I'd like to read that letter and perhaps share some of it on the air when we have more time… if that's okay with you?"

"WOW! That would be fantastic!"

"Okay then Jim, stay on the line and Jack will give you the number that you can fax it to. Thanks for your call!"

"That wraps up another night here on our *"Door to Door"* show at **WIQR, 103.5 FM, Baltimore**, every **Sunday night at 10pm**. We're looking forward to hearing from you either by the phone, or e-mail at: tim@wiqr.com. Thanks for listening, dream well, goodnight."

## *"The Letter"*

"Hey Tim, I just got done reading the letter the kid from Rutgers sent us and it's pretty damn good."

"Let's see it Jack."

(Pause reading…)

"Do you know who wrote it? Did the kid do it alone or was there a group of them?

"I don't know but I can sure find out. Why?"

"It might make an interesting show… to have them down here, especially if it was the kid who composed this. How old did he say he was, nineteen?

"He's eighteen and already a sophomore, sharp kid."

"Okay Jack, get on it and keep me posted."

The next morning Jack headed for his booth across from the on-air studio that the radio personalities shared and picked up his phone.

"Hello, this is Jack Bennett from **WIQR, 103.5 FM, Baltimore** and I'm looking for one of your students. His name is James Thoreau and he's a sophomore there at your New Brunswick campus. Can he be paged or do I need to leave a number? I'd like to speak with him about the fax he sent us."

"Just one moment Mr. Bennett and I'll check his class schedule. (slight pause) He's in his Calculus class now but I'll leave a message for him to call you."

"Thank you, my number is **410….**"

## *"The Invitation"*

"Jim, there's message for you on the board, looks like it's from a radio station."

"Thanks Chrissie, I'll go check it out. I can't believe they're calling me back so quickly."

"Is it about your voting age paper?"

"Yes, I only faxed it to them late last night!"

"That's great! They're obviously interested in what you had to say."

"You think so? WOW… I'm getting really nervous about this call."

"Don't be, I can come along if you'd like while you make the call."

"Would you? That would really help."

"Sure, no problem, it's not everyday I get to see my friend quake in his boots! (mutual laughing.) Let's do it from my room, Susie and I have a phone."

A few minute later they were in Chrissie's room and Jim was dialing.

"Hello, may I have extension 237?"

"Hello, Jack Bennett here."

"Hello Mr. Bennett, this is Jim Thoreau from Rutgers University."

"Yes, hi James thanks for calling back so quickly. I wanted to let you know that we were all very impressed with your activism letter concerning the voting age and I wanted to ask you a few questions."

"Go ahead sir."

"You can call me Jack and do you prefer Jim or James?"

"Whatever you like, sir… uh, I mean Jack."

"Okay, then James it is for me. Who actually wrote the letter?"

"Why I did Jack. Why?"

"You alone or did you have others that helped you."

"No, it was just me."

"I want you to know that we were all very impressed with your reasoning and the arguments that you raised. They were very persuasive."

"Thank you sir."

"You're very welcome and I do mean ALL OF US. Tim McManus would like to have you as a guest on his show to discuss it. We'll pick up your travel expenses, meals and hotel if you'd join us."

"Are you kidding? I'm stunned!! Give me a moment would you?"

"Sure James, I'll wait."

"Chrissie, they want me to be a guest on the *Door to Door Show* with Tim McManus!"

"Fantastic, you have to do it! You'll be great!"

"But I don't want to go alone. It's too nerve racking."

"If you'd like I could come with you."

"Really, you'd do that for me?"

"Sure, you're fun to watch when you're nervous." (laughing)

"Mr. Bennett, um, I mean Jack. Would it be alright if I brought a friend?"

"I'll double check but I'm sure that will be fine. Is next Sunday night alright?"

"Let's see. No, we have exams most of that week and there's no way I could do it then."

"How's the week after?"

"That should be good. Can I verify that with you tomorrow just to be sure?"

"Absolutely, for now I'll speak with Tim and pencil you in for two weeks from now. We'll bring you down by Amtrak on Sunday afternoon. You and your friend can have dinner in town and just take a cab to get around. Don't worry, we'll reimburse you. You'll be staying in a real nice hotel downtown that's only a five minute walk from us and you can take the train home anytime you'd like on Monday. We'll meet say around 9:30 pm and the show runs from 10:00 to 11:00. How does that sound?"

"It sounds GREAT! A bit scary but other than that... GREAT!"
"Don't worry, you'll do fine and we're all behind you. Okay then. Give me a call as soon as you're certain and I'll look forward to meeting you in a few weeks. Enjoy your day James."

"Thanks Jack... you too."

"Chrissie, I can't believe it! I'm going to be interviewed by Tim McManus and *you're coming with me*. **UNBELIEVABLE! ABSOLUTELY UNBELIEVABLE!!**"

# "The Profiteer"

Maxwell Dreyden had inherited his fortune along with the family business when he was only thirty-one. His father's great grandfather had created one of the most successful tobacco companies in America and although it was now superbly diversified it was still at its core the black heart of death.

His father was one of the seven liars who stood before Congress in 1994 and swore under oath that nicotine was not harmful or addictive. Their own secret documents were made public to reveal their lies and more evidence emerged that they were not only aware of these facts but that their R&D departments had been actively engaged in manipulating tar and nicotine levels to make their cigarettes even more addictive than their competitors.

On another occasion a tobacco executive admitted to authorizing the shredding of over one million documents that could have aided the lawsuits of numerous plaintiffs. Much earlier on, his fathers' marketing department had deciphered the facts concerning early addiction and the long term effects on their customer base. In effect, the younger they could be hooked with the addiction the more likely that person would become a lifetime user of their product.

The fact that five million people died every year of cancer and related illnesses such as heart attack and stroke did little to dissuade the company's insistence that mock science was at work and that the link back to tobacco could not be proven with absolute certainty. This had been the company's stance for generations. Of course science finally did prevail and the awful truth became common knowledge despite the billions of dollars spent on public relations and advertising to convince us otherwise.

Seeing the writing on the wall and the fateful events looming just over the horizon had been one of the crowning achievements of Maxwell Dreyden short tenure as CEO. Beyond the PR campaigns he had successfully diversified their assets into consumer friendly product lines and reduced the overall exposure that the company had faced.

Then came the multi-million dollar contributions for hospital wings and drug and aids clinics for the underprivileged. Those were his wife's ideas and they worked much better than he had hoped to help hold back the onslaught of negative opinion. They had paid their blood money to a handful of victims, lawyers and government fines and had regained a level of respectability. Once again they were on the top of a mountain looking down on a world full of ants.

From his fortress he grew the family empire and although he had to trod gently on American soil he felt no such qualms in maximizing profits throughout the rest of the world with the same ruthless tactics that his family had discovered decades earlier. So now the children in underdeveloped countries throughout the world would start smoking earlier than ever before and start dying at ever increasing numbers, year after fateful year, making even Hitler's six-year holocaust seem like an annual event. Pay enough to the PR propagandists (and to the Devil himself) and you can bury the projections that calculate that tobacco will cause **TEN MILLION DEATHS EVERY SINGLE YEAR** by the year 2025.

Maxwell Dreyden understood all of this very well, but those deaths were in direct proportion to his profits. After all, he hadn't started the business, or been the one who lied under oath. He had only run the company as a good CEO should, to maximize profits while minimizing public outrage.

The **SIX BILLION DOLLARS** spent every single year by big tobacco was a great investment and he had learned the formula well; *Risk = Hazard + Outrage*. The significant fact that twelve-hundred Americans were dying <u>every single day</u> never caused him a moment of lost sleep. The fact that underdeveloped countries were about to start dying at a rate seven times greater than ours caused him even less concern.

# "The Threat"

WACO had become a public disaster nightmare for the FBI and law enforcement officials. The propaganda spin had worked for a while until those infrared images came out and proved that the "good guys" had fired first and that they had lied to the American people about what had happened in that tiny town in Texas. Once the video analysis was proven and the film released: *"Waco: The Rules of Engagement"* there was no stopping the backlash that would occur from the incineration of 86 men, women and innocent children by the law enforcement agents of the good ole USA.

That was enough for tens of thousands of Americans to start buying weapons and a host of surveillance and survival equipment to protect themselves and their families. The FBI data had shown that the weapons being purchased in this latest escalation weren't the normal variety of home protection hand guns. No, they were more powerful semi-automatic assault weapons, sniper-rifles with infrared scopes and all sorts of munitions from the black market, including grenade launchers, hand-held SAMs, incendiary devices and night vision goggles. They were the weapons of war and not of self-defense.

The number of fringe groups and survivalists grew exponentially and the threat assessment and surveillance required by the government was being stretched to the breaking point. For every five agents that had penetrated any of these groups three had been discovered and killed and the other two were working with extreme limitations scared for their lives. Two men had died within the last week while on what was supposed to be a routine surveillance mission of a mid-Western group known only as *"Deep-Six"*.

The combined efforts of the NSA and FBI had determined that there were no fewer than 25,000 heavily armed militia involved in activities that were deemed "suspect" and posed a direct and immediate threat within the United States. Conventional wisdom told many of them that this was a conservative estimate and they argued that the number could be many times greater than that. One agent remarked; *"All you have to do was walk through any hunting area during deer season and listen for semi-automatic rifle fire to get an indication of how serious this problem is."*

The agencies had guestimated that there were at least five-hundred to a thousand of these militia groups in North America alone. When Mexico, Central and South American enemies were included the conservative estimate immediately doubled. Add to that the Middle East, Eurasia and the Far East and the storm on the horizon seemed too dark to imagine. Defending America in the 21ˢᵗ Century was going to be a Herculean task. Even our European allies warned us that our foolhardy rush to develop and deploy "strategic nuclear weapons" was a waste of time in the new world and that our efforts only exacerbated the problem for the rest of the world by forcing them back into an arms escalation of their own.

Mark McNulty knew these things all too well but as a regional department head of his FBI task force there was only so much his team could do. He was tasked with stopping terrorism throughout the Mid-Atlantic region and he and his six counterparts hadn't even been able to synch up the seven regional databases and computer systems yet. That minimum prerequisite was essential before the National Security Agency was going to let them tie into any of their data. Meanwhile, the turf battles continued as each entity fought for resources that simply didn't exist. The need to protect informants and other sources made this a more daunting task and the battle being waged seemed as much bureaucratic as it was real.

## *"The First Step"*

Sunday, June 17th was a beautiful spring day in the Northeast with no hint of rain and temperatures in the mid-70s. Jim and Chrissie hopped aboard an Amtrak out of Metro Park at 11:10am and began their three hour journey to Baltimore passing through the less scenic areas of New Jersey, Delaware and Maryland.

Arriving in Baltimore at 2:20 pm they proceeded to the cab stand and caught a taxi to the hotel. A few minutes later they were checking into a beautiful suite at the Intercontinental Harbor Court Hotel, which had been reserved for them by **WIQR**.

The room was luxuriously appointed and had a spectacular view of the Inner Harbor waterfront. The single King sized bed made Jim a little nervous because they hadn't discussed sleeping arrangements and he laughed out loud when he saw the hot tub in the bathroom. He blushed when he saw Chrissie looking over his shoulder in the mirror with her beautiful green eyes and coy smile staring back at him.

"I'm starved Chrissie!" was the best he could muster to ease the embarrassment of the moment. "Let's check out room service."

"Sure, I saw a menu on the table when we got in. Hey cool, they have TWO award winning restaurants right in the hotel! What are you in the mood for?"

"A nice roast beef sandwich would be great and then maybe we could check out their fitness center later. Jack told me it was a great facility."

"Sounds good to me and then we can try the other restaurant for dinner since we don't have to be at the radio station until 9:30."

"Sounds like a plan. What are you going to get?"

"Hmmm…. Crab cakes and a bowl of onion soup!"

14

"Put me down for the soup too."

(dialing)

"Hello room service? This is room 704 and we'd like to order lunch. We'll have two orders of your French onion soup, one roast beef au jus sandwich and one order of crab cakes. Jim, what would you like to drink?"

"Milk is fine for me Chrissie."

"Okay and two glasses of milk. How long will that take? 20-minutes, great! Thank you!"

"Now I'm really hungry! Check out the fitness center it even has a heated pool! We've got to take advantage of that while we're here."

"But I didn't pack a swim suit."

"Me neither Chrissie but they must sell them here and everything else is free so let's splurge!"

"That sounds great."

"Look at the size of this TV, man what a nice room. Don't let me forget to thank those guys for picking out such a great place. Look at this, we should have flown... we're only twelve miles from BWI."

"Really, that would have been easier. Come check out this great view Jim, wouldn't it be nice to have one of those sail boats out there?"

"Yeah really, I've only done it once but what a nice way to spend a day, it was so peaceful." Jim said as he picked up the remote control and turned on the TV.

"Why don't you turn that off and let's put on some music instead. I don't want to be a spectator today its way too nice for that. Let's just eat, get our swim suits and go play in the gym for a few hours. Then

we can go have a nice dinner before going to the radio station."
"That sounds great Chrissie, maybe we can check out some sights since we're so close to everything."

"Sure, we'll even have some time tomorrow before we have to leave." She added.

"Do you know what time checkout is?" Jim asked.

"No, but it's easy enough to find out. Give me a sec. Hello, what time is your checkout? 11:00am? Um, we're guests of **WIQR** and I was hoping you might be able to offer us a later time? 1:00pm? Yes, that would be much better. Thank you very much. Yes, we're in room 704. Thanks again!" Chrissie said and then hung up the phone.

"Did you just get us two more hours Chrissie?"

"I sure did!" She said laughing to herself. "My dad taught me that one when we went to Boston. He said these places depend on their repeat clients and they almost always do that unless there's a convention in town or something."

"Well then, that settles it… I'm just going to have to bring you along on all of my famous interviews!"

"Deal!" She said with a smack to his raised palm.

(knock, knock.) "Room service."

"Hi, could you put that over there near the window? We want to enjoy this great view of yours."

"Of course sir."

"And this is for you…" Jim said as he tipped the waiter two dollars.

"Um… Jim this smells so good."

"It really does, I'm starving!"

"Slow down boy you're going to finish before I even have my soup!"

"Ha ha, now you sound like my mother!"

## *"The Marksman"*

For nearly two hours a day during the last six years David Stanton had been practicing with his bow and arrows. First at a home made target against the wall of the two-family rental home where he and his mother had moved. Then, when he finally stopped hitting the side of the house, he was given a real straw target that rested upon a wooden tripod. The landlord almost evicted them when he saw the hundreds of puncture marks but settled for damages paid instead.

By the age of twelve David never met a person he couldn't outshoot lefty or righty. He had grown from a 25 pound-pull child's bow, to a 35 pound-pull long bow, to a 46 pound Kodiac Magnum recurve, which was a short stature hunting bow that went from shoulder to knee. It wasn't the most accurate design but it did allow him to easily reach the farthest 50-yard target at the YMCA summer camp that he usually attended. Unfortunately, that bow was designed for right-handers, which took away his more natural lefty shooting.

As a small boy he easily ran through all of the awards at 15, 20 and 30 yards, both lefty and righty when he was only 8, 9 and 10 of age. When he returned to the Catskills at the age of 12 he qualified for all of the awards at 40 yards except for the hardest one, which was 160-points using only 30 arrows. The 35 pound longbow was simply not strong enough and he scored 156 and 158 with alternate hands by aiming at an imaginary point far above the target. This meant he could not yet qualify for the easier Expert Award, which was 50 yards away but required only 120 points with those 30 arrows. In practice he had easily scored 137 and 134-points ambidextrously with the weak bow but it couldn't be counted with the 160 target uncompleted.

The next year, at age 13, he KNEW he was going to lick that 160-point forty yard target with his new 46 pound recurve. *So what* if it was only righty, he wanted that EXPERT award that he should have already won! His first attempts were close but still only in the low to mid

150s as he grew accustomed to the jerky nature of that small bows release.

Then, while playing and walking atop five foot canvas "cage ball" one of the wilder kids at camp kicked it out from under him and he fell… landing on his left elbow and tearing every ligament in his shoulder. His arm was totally useless and when he tried to pull the bow back it would be too weak lefty or collapse when shooting righty.

Knowing that he was heartbroken his cabin counselor brought him up to the rifle range for the first time. Another counselor who ran the range was an expert shooter and he found David to be an eager and competent student. Within a few weeks David had qualified for Pro-Marksman, Marksman, Marksman 1st Class, Sharpshooter 1st and 2nd Bars. He had flown through all of the prone and sitting positions as if they were child's play, which to David, they were.

The following year David returned to camp and immediately went to the rifle range, ignoring his previous life as an archer. Within a few weeks he had made Sharpshooter 3rd, 4th, 5th and 6th Bars, which were all of the awards in the kneeling position, leaving him only the standing position awards to reach expert. He was elected "Captain" of the new rifle team and his camp traveled to a distant camp to compete in three events, soccer, basketball and riflery.

David sighted in his Winchester 75 22-long shot rifle before hopping into the back of an open truck for the two hour trip. He carried the gun gently trying not to let the sights misalign during the bumpy ride. Once at the distant camp everyone had three shots to sight in their rifles. Uncustomary David didn't shoot a tight group and scored three nines at 12:00, 6:00 and 9:00 o'clock positions. His coach told him to leave the sight alone and not to worry since he was probably just nervous.

The two camps were pretty evenly matched. The soccer teams tied and then David's camp lost the basketball game. In the third competition David led his ten-member team to an impressive 80-point victory and shot the highest score of 91 out of a possible 100. One of his team mates tied for the 2nd highest score with the other camps best shooter with 86-points. The next morning at the flag raising Camp Director Dave King led the entire camp in a cheer to celebrate the victory and point out the child's accomplishment. David, although painfully shy was overcome with joy at the recognition they gave him.

## *"The Interview"*

The walk to the radio station was brief just as Jack Bennett had explained a few weeks earlier. A good workout, superb dinner and easy evening of walking and sightseeing had brought Jim and Chrissie to the radio station relaxed and in great spirits.

"What floor are they on Jim?"

"Seventh according to this… let' grab that elevator."

(Receptionist) "Hello, may I help you?"

"Yes, hi… I'm Jim Stanton and I was supposed to meet Jack Bennett at 9:30. I'm being interviewed by Tim McManus on his show at 10:00."

"Okay. Thank you. Just one moment please. (Dialing) Jack, this is Mary at the front desk, Jim Stanton is here to see you. Okay, I'll send him right in. Mr. Stanton, you and your guest can go through those doors and Jack's office is the second door on the left."

"Thank you Mary."

"Hello Jim? I'm Jack Bennett."

"Hi Jack, this is my friend Chrissie Edwards."

"Nice to meet you both, we're really glad to have you here tonight."

"Thank you Mr. Bennett."

"Jack, please Chrissie… just Jack."

"Now let me explain how all this works. It's simple really. Tim will introduce the topic to the audience and all of the audio controls are being managed by me and Tim so all you'll have to do is talk to him and have a good time. Do you have any questions?"

"Can Chrissie join me in the studio?"

"Jim, I'd rather not… it's your paper and I wasn't expecting to do that, please don't ask me to go on the air."

"Sure, that's okay I can handle it… you've been so great helping me relax up until now. Now you can just relax and laugh at me while I stutter all over the place and make a fool of myself!" (Laughing)

"Don't worry Jim, Chrissie can join me in the sound booth and give you moral support from there. How's that sound?"

"That's fine as long as she doesn't start making me laugh!"

"Don't worry Jimmy Boy I will!" (All laughing)

"Okay, we've got five minutes to show time. You'll meet Tim McManus in another minute or so and then you two can have some fun."

"Hi Tim, I'd like to introduce you to Jim Thoreau and his friend Chrissie Edwards."

"Hey guys, how was your trip so far?"

"Fantastic, easy ride, great food and yeah, who arranged for that great suite we're in? I wanted to thank you all for that."

"It's our pleasure and we're very happy to have you with us. We've gotten a lot of e-mails asking us about this show so I know there are people looking forward to hearing what you have to say. You ready to rock?"

"I think so… I'll do my best anyway."

"You'll be fine. Just talk to me and try to relax so you can enjoy yourself, that's the most important part. Ready? Let's go…"

"Good evening ladies and gentlemen and welcome to **WIQR, 103.5 FM, Baltimore**. I'm Tim McManus and this is the *Door to Door* show.

We have a very special guest here for you this evening and I know many of our listeners have written in wondering when this interview was going to take place. Please hold your calls until the second half of the hour so we can hear what our guest James Thoreau has to say."

"Hello Jim and welcome to *Door to Door.* We're glad to have you with us tonight."

"Thanks Tim, thank you for having me."

"A few weeks ago you called us and spoke about a movement that you are involved with to try and get the voting age reduced. Could you tell us a little bit more about why you're focusing on this and not something else, like global warming for instance?"

"I'd be happy to. I guess the idea started when we were talking about the drinking age and how a lot of kids didn't think it was fair to make us wait until we were twenty one to have a drink when we could be sent off to war and die as young as eighteen."

"Yes, I remember that debate from a long time ago… so how did the voting age debate come up?"

"Well, my friends and I went from debating drinking and driving deaths in kids under 21 to the devastating effects of advertising that alcohol and tobacco companies use to target us to get our business, to the military and how they are doing the same thing with their advertising even though it was deemed illegal in the other two industries. The voting age is our way of effecting positive change across the board in all issues."

"That's an interesting point. If I understand you correctly there have been successful lawsuits and new laws to prevent advertising dangerous substances to children and yet our military industrial complex, as President Eisenhower once categorized it, is doing exactly the same thing."

"That's the point. It is the exact same thing. Now I'm only eighteen and I don't consider myself a child. I know a lot of 21 to 29 year olds that still act like children."

"I agree, I know a few 40 year olds that fit that description as well."

(Laughing)

"I guess the question is this; How can we define a person as a child for alcohol and not for war? Are we children until we're 21 or are we adults at 18? You can't have it both ways without discriminating against us in one way or the other."

"And the voting age argument that you're raising is for what purpose?"

"It's so we can have a say in our Country's future BEFORE we have to go off and fight and perhaps even die for it. It's that simple."

"So when should kids be able to vote?"

"We can die in battle at 18, 17 with our parents permission. If we're kids for the purpose of alcohol consumption until we're 21 then that should be true for having to serve in the armed forces as well. First things first, "adulthood" should be defined and the laws applied equally across the board. Second, if I can be told I have to fight when I'm 18 then I want to have a say in the matter at least two years earlier so I can help find a peaceful solution and perhaps even prevent the war."

"So let me get this straight, you're not against war itself?"

"War is ugly and should be an action of last resort but I do believe that some wars are justifiable."

"Do you think Viet Nam was justifiable?"

"No, I don't… but I do believe we were right to take Hitler out and stop him from exterminating the Jews. I only wish we had been smart enough to see it coming and to have done it years earlier. That's another conversation though."

"You said you'd like to lower the voting age to sixteen… how did you settle upon that age?"

"I believe it should be earlier but I also believe there should be no argument about sixteen. At least at sixteen we'd have some say in issues before we were forced to go fight for them. I actually believe that some children may be smart enough to vote intelligently by the time they turn thirteen."

"Now I know that will raise quite a few more eyebrows. Thirteen is just too young for most kids, don't you think so?"

"The way we currently teach children about politics, history and world affairs, yes, I'd have to agree with you. But then I'd have to raise the point that most Americans don't have an accurate picture of what is going on in the world. They don't use the internet like the young do and our so-called "free press" helps to propagandize the issues. The water is so badly muddied that most people are unaware of what the facts are no matter how old they are. That's why I suggested that kids under sixteen should be able to vote if they could pass an exam that would prove their knowledge of world affairs. I don't know how that plays out legally but…"

"It would never fly Jim, how can you make one age group test and not another?"

"I see your point. Perhaps a grade point average of B and above could earn a student the right to vote as early as thirteen. I don't know all the answers I just feel that the younger the voting age the more likely it is that we will seek out peaceful solutions to issues instead of military ones. Especially if we can get the military from telling kids how fun and exciting war can be… Just like the tobacco and alcohol companies telling kids how cool they would be using that garbage."

"Okay, I see your position Jim and I'd like to invite our audience to call in and discuss these issues with us. Sherman from Chevy Chase, you're on the air."

"Hi Tim, I just wanted to ask Jim if he is a conscientious objector?"

"No sir, I thought about that question long and hard but as I understand it claiming that status means that you can't believe in killing under any circumstances and I don't feel that way. I would have shot Hitler myself if I knew what he was doing."

"Do you think lowering the voting age to sixteen is really going to make any difference?"

"I think it could Sherman, especially if we plug the gaps in the voting machines and force our government into providing us with verifiable paper trails in all of our elections. There are over 4 ½ million kids that would be added to the voting roles. I think the vast majority of them want peace over war."

"Line two, you're on the air."

"Hi, my name is Lance and I spent two years in Iraq. I enlisted when I was eighteen. The recruiters did a great job selling me on the benefits and I took the bait hook, line and sinker and jumped in before my parents knew what was happening. I've been out for three years now and I can't get medical coverage to compensate me for the wounds I sustained. They keep classifying the degree of injury at a much lower rate than it's supposed to be at and I don't have the money to take them to court and fight for my rights."

"Lance, I read about what you're talking about and Time Magazine did an article about it. It seems to me that with the money we are spending on war that the very least we could do is to make sure our veterans are cared for properly when they come back home. If we can't do that then we have no right asking our citizens to fight. I'm sorry for your situation sir and I hope that we as a nation will get our collective act together and redirect the funds that are necessary to support our vets."

"Thank you Jim, I couldn't have said it better myself. I think I'm just going to take the rest of the night off and let you handle it... you seem to have it under control." (Laughing)

"PLEASE don't do that Mr. McManus... I'll be good I promise!"

"Okay, I'll give you a breather. This Country spends 400 Billion dollars a year, that's BILLION with a "B" **every single year** on war. That's the amount that is budgeted. What most people don't know is that we spend an additional $100 BILLION dollars on black ops... through unidentified channels. Go ahead and tell the IRS you don't know what happened to a fifth of your income and see what happens.

Before I forget I want our audience to know that Jim's letter and petition can be found at our website at **w w w dot W I Q R dot com**.

Cynthia, you're on the air."

"Hi gentlemen I just wanted to say that I am very impressed with this young man. I have two kids in college and I wish they were this aware of the situation. Is there anything we can do to help?"

"Tim?"

"It's okay sport... go ahead."

"Hi Cynthia, Thank you for the kind words. I wanted to point out that it wasn't just me doing this. A lot of my friends were there and we debated and talked these issues through for half the night and all

I did was take the point and write a letter and start sending it off to anyone who would listen. We're talking about putting up a website and starting blogs and petitions but we are all students and we just finished with our Finals. The summer is coming and hopefully we'll be able to make some more progress soon. I'll leave my contact information at the station for anyone who would like to help us."

"Okay, last call. Brent from Philadelphia, you're on the air."

"What does a dumb ass 18 year old pussy know about the world? Now he wants to let children rule things? How stupid can you get! What a bunch of liberal bull(beep) pussies you all are!" (Click!)

"Sorry to end on such a sour note Jim, our engineer normally does a better job screening out the mentally infirm from our show. Do you wish to address his, um, statement?"

"I don't mind Tim. Without the freedom of speech we have nothing. We're taught in debating class to walk in the other guys' shoes so we can truly understand his position and his pain and thereby become more able to deal with it in a rational manner. Some may think I'm just a dumb 18-year old... but I care about what's happening both here in this country and in the rest of the world. I've taken the time to understand the issues so I can start dealing with them throughout my life and not just for this moment in time. If the label "liberal" means that I believe in peace over war then I wear that classification with pride. I know we could do better with our $500 billion every year. I think we need to force our government to be honest and elect leaders that will trust the true values of our population. I see love and joy in most children and hate and bigotry in many so-called "adults". I'd rather trust the children with our future and do my best to educate the rest of the population so they become more inclined to do the right thing and not just follow the leader and feather their own beds."

"Mr. James Thoreau, it has been my pleasure to have such a thoughtful young man on our show tonight. I look forward to watching you continue to grow and know that with leaders like you on our horizon that we will be in good hands. That wraps up another night here on the *"Door to Door"* show at **WIQR, 103.5 FM, Baltimore**, every **Sunday night at 10pm**. As always we look forward to hearing from you either by the phone, or e-mail at: tim@wiqr.com. Thanks for listening, dream well and goodnight."

*"Jesus kid, I'm impressed!"*

"Thanks Tim and thanks for making this painless. I was pretty scared out there at first."

(Jack) "Nice job Jim, you should be proud of yourself."

"Thanks Jack. Thanks for everything you've done for us."

(Chrissie) "Mr. Thoreau, may I have your autograph?"

"No Chrissie you **may not**, but I could sure use a back rub!"

"Later Mr. President, how about a hug for now?"

"Sure!" (Laughing)

(Squeezes and chuckles) "You're so tense; we're going to have to do something about that tonight." (Chuckles again)

## *"Patriots or Terrorists?"*

Two men in business suits arrive separately at a small roadside diner in Gaithersburg, Maryland and meet for dinner.

"Did you get the name of the shooter I was looking for?"

"Not yet Mr. C. but I have one of my best men on it and he expects to have it no later than 18:00 hours tomorrow."

"Good, I need to arrange a meeting with him as soon as possible. No phone calls about this Skip, no electronic communications or paper trails of any kind… just mouth to mouth on a need to know basis within your squad unless I tell you otherwise. Do you understand?"

"Yes sir. It's just me and one other man right now… just the three of us until we bring the shooter in."

"Good, keep it that way and come see me as soon as you've been able to confirm his availability for this target. I want to set up a meeting with him within 72 hours. Which of your men is on it?"

"McClellan sir, we've been together for four years and I know he's rock solid. I watched him take down an informant with his bare hands and the other guy was formidable. I got him out of Charlie's squad when it was disbanded, that was a year before you took us over. He's as cold as ice sir. Do we have an approved target yet?"

"We're down to three. Rico's squads are in-place running surveillance and gathering data. I trust Ric like my own brother. If you ever need help you can trust your squad in his hands. Just tell him *Sparrow's Free*… then follow his orders."

"Okay. Do you want me to contact the shooter and set up the meeting?"

"No, just confirm his availability. I'll want to see McClellan and brief him myself. Then he can contact the shooter again when we're ready. We need to keep our elements as isolated as possible Skip or the FBI and NSA are going to tear us all new asses before we get anywhere."

# *"Final Arrangements"*

Thirty-six hours later two men in casual attire meet in the same roadside diner in Gaithersburg, Maryland and order lunch.

"Skip speaks very highly of you Steve."

"Thank you sir."

"What was your impression of the, uh, gentleman you met?"

"A bit strange to say the least. I think he's taken down more than his fair share."

"What was his name?"

"Messer sir."

"Ah, they got us Bob Messer, now that's one cold son of a bitch."

"Yes sir. He sure as Hell seems the type. I mean this guy even spooked me. They say I'm cold... but this friggin' guy made me seem like a warm summer day. He's not even big... that's what's weird... just something about his demeanor that makes you back off."

"Well, don't worry. Our commanders have used him before and he's one of the best. We were lucky to have drawn him for this project."

"Yes sir. Skip tells me you want me to meet with him again."

"Yes, tonight. You know where he's staying?"

"Yes sir. He's not moving until he hears from us."

"Okay good. Now listen hard. No paper trails, no phone calls, no e-mails... mouth to ear communication only. Do you understand?"

"Yes sir, loud and clear."

"When this one is over there's going to be Hell to pay and we don't want to be anywhere near the shit storm that's coming. Got it?"

"I understand sir. It stops at me."

"No son, it stops at me but we're not letting it get that far now are we?"

"No sir."

"Okay. Memorize this address. 2145 Blackbird Lane, Charlotte, North Carolina."

"Got it. Who's that sir?

"It's the head of the nuclear weapons division at Lockheed Martin. He's 59 years old, gray, pot bellied and about 5'10. There's no one else in the home that vaguely resembles him."

"Got it sir."

"That's one of the divisions that are making them rich using our tax dollars while the government ignores the non-proliferation treaties that are in-place. Now you understand. We've got to stop those weapons before we lose an entire city somewhere. This guy has an armored car but the forty foot walk to his front door is wide open… that's where Messer can take him out without API rounds. There *are* surveillance cameras on the roof but no guards in the house and no dogs so tell Messer to make sure his face is covered. We expect our target after work between 9 and 10 pm so he'll need a night scope."

"Any bodyguards?"

"Just one, his driver in their black Mercedes S600. It's Messer's call whether or not he needs to put him down too. The distance looks to be about 500 yards depending on where he makes his nest. We need this done in the next 72 hours or he'll be at a stockholder's meeting in Chicago. He's got about 36 to 48 hours to work out the fine details."

"Got it sir. I'll have him totally briefed by 16:00 hours."

# *"The Assassin"*

McClellan climbed the motel stairs and knocked on Bob Messer's door.

"It's open…" Came the reply from inside.

"I brought you some sandwiches and sodas. I wasn't sure if you had eaten anything since we met earlier."

"Yeah, I ate but thanks anyway. How did you make out?"

"You're on for sometime within the next 72-hours. We figure you'll have 36 hours to work out the fine details, maybe a little more but I should have most of what you need to know right now."

"Okay, but if I can't work out those *details* then I'm gone. Got it?"

"Well, that's not my call but I heard the plan and it seems pretty straight-forward. I think I could do it if I were a little better shot."

"How long is it?"

"It depends on where you set up but no more than 450 to 550 yards."

"That's do-able… what time?"

"He gets home between 9 and 10 pm."

"Night scope, we're still okay."

"He arrives home with a bodyguard who doubles as his driver in an armored Black Mercedes S600. There are video cameras on the roof but no guards in the house so they won't be of any use. Just keep your face black. You've got about forty feet of walkway and stairs to take him out before he reaches the front door."

"He doesn't use a garage? How stupid. That armored car won't do him any good walking to his front door. Does he wear Kevlar?"

"Jeeze, I didn't think to ask but I seriously doubt it."

"No problem, that's what armored piercing bullets are for… or maybe a head shot just to be sure. What about the driver?"

"He's your call. Put him down if you need to. Those two should be alone but don't shoot any women or children who may wind up at the door. We're not looking for any more enemies than we already have."

"Just so you know, I'll be taking down the driver so he's not chasing me in that tank. What other problems need to be *worked out*?"

"There's a ten foot brick wall that surrounds his mansion and the gate can't be penetrated. Then there's your escape. You may not be able to park very close. There are a lot of very expensive houses without any convenience stores or gas stations nearby. Other than that how good a shot are you?"

"Good enough that you never want to be in my sights son. What about trees? What's the visibility from the top of the wall?"

"Sorry sir, I don't know. You're probably better off inside anyway. You'll definitely have one surprise shot but the driver won't be very far away from the car so you may need to take him out first or he'll just duck behind the armor."

"I was thinking the same thing. Payment as usual?"

"No one talked to me about money so I'd have to say yes. They hold you in high esteem and I'm sure we're going to want to use you again."

"What's the address?"

"2145 Blackbird Lane, Charlotte, North Carolina."

"Okay, were done here… I've got some driving to do."

"Don't you even want to know who it is?"

"No… I'll read about it in the papers."

# *"Preparations"*

Steve McClellan left the second floor motel room, went down the stairs, entered his car and drove away. Fifteen minutes later Bob Messer dropped the motel keys into the night depository and the sandwiches into the trash bin outside the office. No sense taking any chances to save a lousy $10 bucks. He took a second look at the sodas and then threw them in as well. He hadn't survived this long by taking unnecessary chances and he wasn't going to start now. "If you know it and you don't use it *then you don't know it*." he thought to himself."

He got into his white Grand Am rental and drove twenty minutes through heavy traffic to the Ronald Reagan Washington National Airport. Then Messer dropped the car off to the outside Hertz attendant, picked up his luggage from the trunk and walked inside to Avis, where he, or rather Bob Blackman, rented a black Lexus LS430 where the desk agent courteously printed out driving direction for him. As good as National Security was it couldn't compete with the almighty dollar and nearly perfect credentials were only a phone call away.

He then drove out of the airport and began his 380 mile journey to Charlotte. On the way he stopped at the first Wal-Mart that he saw and bought a can of flat black spray paint, work gloves, masking tape, an eight foot aluminum ladder and a hunting mask. It took twenty minutes and he was back on his way with a fresh cup of coffee from the Dunkin Donuts inside Wal-Mart. *Now that was handy...*

Let's see... I-66 West to US 29 South to US 29 West to... *Perfect...*he thought to himself... *miles, exits and everything*. Six hours should do it... a little longer than usual but with a nice relaxing ride ahead and time to survey the situation tonight...everything was going smoothly. He set the cruise control to 68 MPH and settled in to the fine leather seat. *Nice quiet ride, feels like a magic carpet.* Five hours and forty-five minutes later he was stopping at a gas station in Charlotte and getting another cup of coffee.

2145 Blackbird Lane was on the perfect street. Lined in old Maple trees and not a shack around for a dozen miles. The cheap seats in that neighborhood would cost a couple million dollars. 2145 was among the nicest homes and it appeared to be a fortress to the novice eye. A ten foot brick wall wasn't even as hard to overcome as a good German Shepard. Hmmm, he didn't ask about dogs.

Messer rolled down the front windows and took two passes in every direction. No cops, no security guards and best of all no dogs barking. The best place to hop the fence was from his neighbors' yard on the east wall. They had let their privet hedge become overgrown and he could enter without any problems at all camouflaged by their lazy landscaping. Damn, I could drop the ladder off right now and not even paint it! What a joke! Slow down and think... Okay, where do I park?

The lights were on in most of the houses until midnight when they started to flicker off one by one. Only a few blocks away they went out quite a bit earlier and there was parking on the street. Not too bad... no streetlights here and maybe a three minute walk to the wall. Hmmm, are there any shortcuts?

If I cut through this yard I can save a block and at least a minute. I can use that on the way out as long as there's no dog then that'll be perfect. If there is then tough luck for the dog, I'll just have to shoot it. Okay, bring the pistol and silencer. I've got two passes at this... so dress dark but not suspicious night one. Only go covert on the second night, if I even need a second night.

What about trees inside the compound? Forget it, it doesn't matter since entry is going to be easy I can pick my spot inside and not have to straddle the wall for my shot. That's less exposure and more mobility. Good enough, time to eat and get some rest.

A half hour later Bob Blackman was ordering dinner at drive-through in Charlotte and checking into the Holiday Inn next door. In bed before 2:00 am he thought. *Perfect.*

## *"Preparations II"*

8:00 am and Messer was up and completely refreshed. He showered, shaved and got dressed into jeans, T-shirt, Converse sneakers and a baseball cap. His sunglasses were in the car along with the folding ladder, which was in the trunk with the rest of the preparations. He packed his small bag and headed out to breakfast at the same drive through he had eaten at seven hours earlier.

He drove out of town until he hit the woods and found a dirt parking lot meant for hikers. No one was there as he popped the trunk, took out the plastic bag and emptied everything but the paint and gloves. He wouldn't need the masking tape after all. He grabbed the ladder and walked a short way down the trail. Then he checked the wind direction and walked into the woods leaving the trail 40 yards behind. If anyone did walk by they wouldn't see him and better still, they wouldn't smell the paint. Finding a nice secluded spot he set up the ladder, put on the gloves, tested the wind again and gave it a light first coating of paint. Ten minutes later he gave it a second coat so there was no shine left on it at all.

Impatiently he waited the 30 minutes for the paint to dry and then packed up the can and plastic bag. No hikers were on the trail this early on a weekday morning and he carried the ladder first back to the trail and then out to his car where the remote control allowed him to pop the trunk before he got there. Quietly he put everything back into the trunk, put the gloves in the plastic bag and drove back to Charlotte.

He drove down Blackbird lane at 11:00 am and then again at 11:15 and it was quiet both times. No one was out walking their dogs, no one was parked on the street and many of the houses were hid behind their own assorted walls of brick or hedge. On the second pass Messer stopped at the East corner of the brick wall and popped the trunk. Taking one last look around he pulled the ladder out of the trunk and slid it behind the overgrown privet hedge and then pushed it in five feet so it wouldn't be visible from the street. He drove away without passing another car or person for three blocks.

## *"9 Holes?"*

"Hey Ric, this is Joe how're you doing?"

"Good bud, what's up?"

"Up for some golf?"

"Always, when?"

"I was hoping today, my schedule is pretty packed for the rest of the week."

"Ouch, today is tough... can we do it late this afternoon."

"Yeah, that would be fine. Just need to get out and stretch my legs."

"Everything okay with the family?"

"Yeah, everything's good... We'll talk later, I know you're busy."

"Okay bro, see you at the club, say 4:00?"

"Yeah, 4:00 is good. Later Rico."

Tony Rico knew that call meant more than 9 holes of golf and that something was on his friends mind, but what? Everything on his end had gone well. The highest priority target had been successfully isolated during his team's surveillance. Maybe something had happened with the shooter. Or maybe the target was pulled out of his routine unexpectedly. It could be almost anything but there was no sense worrying about it now. He'd just have to wait until later to find out.

# *"Disparate Systems"*

"Hey McNulty, what's got your panties all up in a bunch so early in the morning?"

"Nothing different Chief, just the same old shit. One step forward, two steps back."

"Come into my office and talk to me. Close the door."

"You've given me this task force Walt and I feel like a computer geek without any training and not an FBI investigator."

"Synching up the systems is tougher than we imagined?"

"You have no idea and for the life of me I don't know why. My counterparts are all trying as hard as I am but the damn programmers and system analysts keep coming up with more and more problems and less and less solutions. None of these systems were intended to work together and we may have to scrap the whole damn thing."

"Alright, here's what I want you to do. I want you to get us two bids. One from EDS and one from Ross Perot's new company, I don't know what he's calling it but it shouldn't be hard to find. They're systems integrators and if we need to scrap these seven systems and put in one that will work for all of us then let's find that out before we waste anymore time and spend another fortune. I know everyone loves their hardware but what good is it if it doesn't get the job done?"

"Sounds like a plan Sir. Your name carries quite a bit more weight than mine so is it okay if I use it to get the ball moving quicker?"

"Absolutely Mark. Just keep me posted and let me know if you need me to kick anyone in the ass."

"Will do Chief, but knowing you're behind it should be enough for the other children to play nice together. (Laughing) Anything else Sir?"

"Yes. I'm meeting with the Attorney General next Friday and I want to be able to talk to him about funding this. It's going to take the consulting companies at least a few months to help us figure this thing out. Meanwhile, let's get our facts as accurate as possible. I want you to help me figure out how much we've been spending, how much we'll be spending if we stay on our current path and how much we could save if we shut all seven regions down right now and invest in something new. That'll give me a good idea of what we have to work with before I go begging for more with my hat in my hand."

"Do you have any suggestions on how to start Walt?"

"I'm not a programmer Mark but those folks are pretty damn smart. Pick your top analysts and lock them in a room and don't let them out until they've hashed out how we're going to do this. Have the other six regions conduct the same exercise and then coordinate the findings and summarize the consensus opinion for me. At least that way I'll have some foundation to compare the consultants' advice against."

"Will do sir."

"I want four things in your report: 1) Should we stay with our current systems or revamp the network entirely? 2) How much... ballpark the project low to high? 3) How long? And, 4) A wish list of the functionality needed broken down into two parts; a) **must have** functionality and, b) would sure as Hell like to have functionality but we can wait a little while longer."

"I'll set the conference call up with my counterparts immediately."

"Good, make sure they're all there, no exceptions! If anyone is out on vacation they'll need to be found and made available. I'm not going to have anybody crying in my ear that they weren't in the loop on this. Do it under my authority Mark and light a fire under it. I'll need a written summary on my desk no later than next Wednesday by 4:00 pm so I can be ready for the meeting with the Attorney General. Let's get the consulting people in the week after next to help figure out our options. Talk to the Presidents of those companies, we're going to

44

need their best people and we have to make sure they have the proper security clearances."

"Thanks Chief I'm feeling better already. Maybe sometime this decade I can get back out in the field and catch some bad guys."

"That's were I need you son. No one is better at putting the pieces of a puzzle together than you are. I'm sorry to have to saddle you with this internal stuff but we're all doing more than our job right now and I trust this most in your hands. There just aren't enough of us to fill all the sand bags that are needed and the water isn't slowing down one drop."

"Ain't that the truth!"

"Get on it Mark." Walter Dobson ordered…

"You got it Chief."

## *"Counterparts"*

"Sally, do you have the contact list for my six counterparts in the other command centers?"

"Yes Mark, what do you need?"

"A 45-minute conference call sometime tomorrow before 8:00 pm eastern time. Everyone needs to be on it… vacation or not."

"Okay, let me check their availability and see if everybody can make it."

"Sally, Chief Dobson said everyone will make themselves available *no matter <u>where</u> they are*. Is that perfectly clear?"

"Yes Mark. What should I tell them?"

"The time, dial in number and access directions to the conference call. I expect them all to be there five minutes before whatever time you establish. You can move my appointments around as needed. Tell them this is a *priority one* call and Walter Dobson may be joining us."

"I'll get right on it and keep you posted."

"Thanks Sally, I know I'm going to be working for you one of these days."

"Sooner than you think slugger…"

McNulty laughed… nodding affirmatively.

"I don't doubt it Mrs. Martin."

## *"Tee Time"*

The two squad leaders met at one of their favorite golf courses in Elkton, Maryland just in time for their 4:00 o'clock tee-off. They both took pride in their game even though they rarely had enough time to play or focus on it properly.

"Hi Joe, you're looking a bit tense there fella. Don't worry I'll take it easy on you today." Rico teased light-heartedly.

"Hardy har har har, like I'm quaking in my boots over here. What was it six strokes that I beat you by last time?"

"That's right… God DAMN water trap… lost two balls there and then couldn't play for shit for the rest of the game!"

"I brought you plastic balls for that hole Ric… just in case."

(Both laugh.)

"Looks like two foursomes in front of us."

"Damn, they're running late again. I hate waiting!"

"Now, now Mr. C… patience, patience."

"Patience my ass! If I wanted more patients I'd been a doctor."

"Sounds like something your kid would say Joe."

"He did say it… I thought it was pretty funny."

(Laughing)

"Yeah, yeah…coming from a ten year old. What's on your mind?"

"It can wait until we're out on the course. Just try and stay on the fairway this time Rico so we can talk. Think you can handle it?"

"$50 bucks says your ass is mine today wise guy."

"Make it a hundred and you have a bet."

"You're on… 9 holes… *no mercy!*"

(From behind them...)
"You two want to double up? We're a twosome too."

"Thanks but we've got a private little war going on and we don't need any distractions. Maybe next time…"

"Sure, maybe next time."

(In a muffled voice..)

"That was cute Ric."

"I thought so."

# *"Conference"*

"So how are you making out Sally?"

"We're almost all set. Everyone is good for 2:00 pm Eastern except for Cooper who's fishing for salmon somewhere in Canada."

"No beeper?"

"They tried but it's such a remote area they may not have coverage."

"Alright, lock-in the conference call for 2:00 pm EASTERN TIME tomorrow and then get the access information to Dick in his hotel."

"Or his tent you mean…"

"Damn it Sally, *he needs to be there*… Just **WOW** me OKAY?"

"Don't I always?"

"Yeah, pretty much... Also, I need a meeting with Cassandra Jones, Ashim Roy, and that new guy… you know… the super geek?"

"Roger, *Mr. McNulty*… his name is Roger Harris. Don't ever let him hear you say that or he'll probably lay you out flat… and I'll be right there laughing at you when he does saying *I told you so*."

"I'm sure you would. Probably make your whole day."

"Well, maybe not the WHOLE day… (Laughing) When do you want it Mark?"

"The sooner the better but my schedule is a disaster right now so just let them know I'm going to need all three of them for an hour as soon as I can fit them in."

"Will do…"

# *"The Game"*

Ric and Joe had reached the green on the par 5 first hole in three strokes each. Ric with two solid drives and a nice 7 iron to within 8 feet of the cup and Joe with a terrible first shot, nice second drive and a killer two iron than rolled up to the fringe of the green about 30 feet away from the flag.

"Okay Joe, what's going on?"

"The commanders met with the committee when you were out on surveillance and they're stepping up pressure on all of us. They're looking for some serious impact quick."

"Did they say why?"

"Politics… it's always politics Ric, one way or the other. They're looking to sweep the entire upper echelon of our government out of office during the next election and we've got eighteen months to make them and their cronies look like Laurel and Hardy."

"They're doing a pretty good job of that all by themselves."

"No argument there. But they are better liars than politicians and most Americans are too damn lazy to go after the truth on their own. They need to have it spoon fed to them and we know who owns the media, the propaganda machines and the PR firms and it's not us."

"So what about Charlotte?"

"It looks good and this guy's one of the best. We'll know for sure by Friday but my money is on our team."

"Nice shot" (As Joe's 30 foot putt lands two feet from the hole.)

"You too!" (As Rico sinks his 8 footer for a birdie.)

"Shit!" (As Joe's 5<sup>th</sup> shot slips by the hole and settles six inches away.)

"I'm looking forward to spending your hundred bucks Mr. C."

"Yeah, I better get my mind into this game."

Walking to the second hole they see the twosome behind them has landed another pair of players.

"That'll slow them down and give us more time to talk."

"So how do they define stepping up the pressure Joe?"

"They've been tracking our results since the last election and our three regional commands have only averaged one significant kill a month. That's nowhere near enough to produce the market upheaval they're after. They think we should be taking down one target a month *PER SQUAD*, which is totally ludicrous. We pretty much convinced them that one hit per platoon made a lot more sense and that's what we're building towards… quickly, ten quality hits a month."

"That's a huge increase Joe! It takes at least three weeks to set up a target and we only have three on our approved list now."

"That's why we've been moving towards specialization within each squad. You have five now, at least two *have to focus on surveillance*, one on sniping, one on munitions and acquisition and one for up close and personal attacks. Each platoon leader will be authorized to add a sixth *"death squad"* that will specialize on counter-intelligence and assassination of would-be infiltrators. Pick your five best men for that unit right now and make sure they're tight. I'm going to use your team to work out the tactics we've initiated. Make this your top priority Ric so you can protect your platoon from the security agencies that'll come after us once they realize how badly our shit is hitting their fan."

"Damn it Joe. I don't mind taking out these murdering bastards when I have a say in the matter but I'll be God DAMNED if I'm taking down any Tom, Dick or Harry just because they say so. I'm not a fucking rabid dog and I have my own scruples to listen to."

"Cool down Rico. They know our mission as well as we do… but it's their money and without it we have no mission."

"I won't be part of an unscrupulous death squad."

"Don't worry about that now. Run any objections you have by me and I'll listen to your argument and between the two of us we'll figure it out. You have to admit that for a war our current rate *is* pretty pathetic."

"But you told me we needed to start slow."

"We did, in order to get organized and minimize our exposure until we were ready. Well we're ready now and we're just beginning to make a dent. Once we crop up on the FEDs radar we're all going to have agents crawling under our beds. We better damn well be prepared or we're going to take some serious hits. Keep your squads isolated Ric and only pass information downward on a need to know basis."
"I trust your judgment Joe but make damn sure that when this is all over that our families will know that we were the good guys and not just killing machines in the service of tyrants of a different color."

"I agree and so do the other commanders… we're all on the same page. We'll have choices as long as we do our jobs and make an impact that produces the results the committee needs. What I'm worried about is their simplistic understanding of how we need to operate in order to remain invisible. They want us traveling too much. That problem is in Aaron's capable hands and I'll let you know the solution when I hear it. Meanwhile, start thinking about moving targets between regions where we may have very little advance notice but a great opportunity if we're prepared."

"That makes more sense to me. It's far less dangerous being on home ground and much harder for our enemies to track our movements."

*(Crack!)*

"Nice drive Joe… looks like 220 maybe 230."

"Just venting… need to channel this adrenalin. *Shit*, that one looks like 240… *you fucking bastard Rico!*"

"You talk too much…" Rico taunted. "Just play."

"So far we've been lucky... the FBI has had their heads so far up their asses that we should be able to stay on top of any infiltrators at least until the Presidential election. Your team's successful screening of our tactics is going to be critical to our mission."

"Nice second shot Joe, you're on the green about 20 feet from the pin."

"Go ahead bro… I'll shut up and let you take your shot."

Rico's 3-wood shot lands in the sand trap on the left side of the green.

*"Damn it!"*

"Looks like an easy wedge for you. You're not too bad off if you ever took the time to practice that club like I told you." (Laughing)

*"Fuck you, you slimy bastard!"* (Laughing) "What about the money Joe? This one job is expensive. Do they have any clue as to what we had to pay to get Messer for this hit? And he may not even score!"

"He'll score okay and ·*"yes"* these folks know money, inside and out. Plus they're expecting us to pick up the slack with the teams we have in place. So our snipers need to be sharp, practiced and ready and they have to do that out of the public eye… no more firing ranges Ric."

"Who are these guys? How are they funding us… from their own pockets?"

"Not likely… or at least very begrudgingly. These guys may be empty suits when it comes to warfare but they are marketwise politicians and industrialists who know how to turn a dollar. They know industrial espionage and how to manipulate the stock market and *I'm damn sure* they know how to use the likes of Messer when necessary… probably from long before we were born. If we do our jobs right I think money will be the least of our worries."

"And what do you estimate our worst worries are?"

"That question is like a moving target Ric. It's never going to be the same from week to week and year to year. Our complacency and over-confidence with each success is going to be a major problem. We can't afford to get sloppy but our successes will make the squads feel invincible when in reality we are as fragile as egg shells. We have to be concerned that the National Security Agency and FBI will finally get their systems up and running and fully coordinated. Once they do who do you think the targets are going to be? This one is going to get real bloody before it's over my friend and I just hope to see it through to the other side and that we can make this world a better place in the process. Meanwhile, our money machine could wind up being as corrupt as our current leaders are. If they learn who we all are then we could be dead in one fell swoop. Right now they only know the three primary commanders and the General… God forbid they ever infiltrate us… we'd be at their mercy unless we took them out first. Remember that. Your teams needs to be totally invisible and I would give my life to protect that."

"I know you would Joe… you're closer to me than any of my real brothers. Hey, do you think those guys have been waiting long?"

(Laughing)

"Fuck em… take your time with that sand wedge. (scoop) Not bad Ric, only a 14-footer to make par."

Joe took a long read and stepped up to his putt and gave it a firm even stroke."

*"You son of a bitch!* You just sank a twenty-footer! *SHIT!"*

"I must say… *That's <u>was</u> a pretty birdie.*"

*"Shit!* And mine was an ugly-ass bogey."

"I think that makes us even Bro."

"Yep, we're even. Just one more thought Joe…"

"What's that?"

"What *IF* these guys start running scared and decide to pull the plug on us?"

"We talked about that after our meeting was over. There were a lot of pissed off ex-commandos in that room. We decided upon a contingency plan just in case any of our suits think they can corrupt the mission and make a power play for themselves and squash us in the process. Each of our commanders has his primary targets already assigned and you'll be getting instructions on what to do with two of mine in case a double cross becomes apparent. Within a month you will need to have the solution planned for those two kills… your counterparts will have their own targets assigned but nothing is to be done without a direct order from me or General Andersen. If any of them turn on us then they'll be dead within 72-hours and that should wake the rest of them up and get them thinking straight again."

"Sounds like I better get cracking on our surveillance if we're going to keep pace with you."

"Yeah, like yesterday… we've got plenty of work waiting for us. Third hole Ric… me or you?"

# *"Preparations III"*

Messer returned to his motel room a little after noon carrying a sub sandwich and quart of milk. He was going to relax, eat and make final preparations for this evenings' mission. *No reason why I can't be through with this tonight...* he thought to himself, *as long as our man is punctual.*

He ate half his sub and downed two small glasses of milk before putting the cardboard container into the bathroom sink filled with cold water. He visualized the exact activities he would perform leading up to and through the event and then went over more options in case a police car stopped him on approach, or exit, or if a dog was set loose, or a jogger somehow wound up in the wrong place at the wrong time. *Not likely...* he thought... *but there aren't going to be any serious-threat witnesses left standing.*

*No problem going in...* he thought... *but coming out is going to be another matter.* As long as there aren't any random patrol cars on the road for those crucial three to four minutes then this should be a cake walk. He would make a slow disciplined approach looking like a local with his briefcase in tow... hop the fence easily, courtesy of the neighbor with the sloppy privet hedge and then locate the best place to set up his nest inside the wall. He remembered the cameras on the roof and made a strong mental note: ***DON'T FORGET THE HUNTER'S MASK....*** Up until that instant it had totally escaped his mind.

Once the Mercedes arrived he would wait for the driver to open the CEO's door and allow the primary target to get half way to his front door before taking down the driver with a single chest shot with an armor piercing bullet, just in case he was the Boy Scout type and was wearing a Kevlar vest. With any luck he'd have a second or two of stun time before the primary target would be able to react. If he's not on the ground within three-quarters of a second then he was going down with a head shot. If not, two rapid chest shots were all he could risk without waking up the entire neighborhood. The ladder would be left in-place followed by a careful, controlled decent back down the wall.

by a careful, controlled decent back down the wall. The hedges would cover his exit beautifully and give him precious seconds if needed. ***NOTE: Don't rush the exit from hedges!***

## *"The Intern"*

Chrissie Edwards and James Patrick Thoreau had enjoyed the rest of their Baltimore trip together. The radio show was over and he hadn't made a fool of himself. In fact, he was complimented profusely for... for doing what... for being an adult and communicating an idea well? Big deal... *I am an adult...* So what if I communicated the idea well, okay... good job but no biggie right? *I'm just glad it's over.*

Chrissie had been the one who had made the biggest fuss over me and our night together was Heaven on Earth... at least for me. But what was it? We're just friends... at least we were just friends... now what? I like her a lot, a heck of a lot... but we're not in love. Damn, why does this have to be so confusing? In a few more weeks she'll be going home to Indiana for the summer and I'll be looking for a job. If I hadn't wasted so much time on this paper and radio interview I could have had one by now. Now there's so little time and I still have no clue where to go... other than these menial jobs they keep posting on the bulletin board. I need something challenging... but what?

"Hello, this is Jim Thoreau calling for Jack Bennett. Yes, I'll hold."

"Hi Jim, how are you doing?"

"Pretty well, finals are over and we're winding down now. I wanted to ask you and Tim for some advice, if that's okay?"

"Sure, what's up?"

"I'll be graduating in a few weeks and I was wondering if you folks had any kind of summer intern program that could use my skills."

"For a bright young man like you Jim... we should have something. It won't pay very much and it's not going to be rocket science but it should be interesting enough. I'll need to check with Tim and the Station Director but it could be a nice fit. They loved the job you did on the air...you know?"

"Thanks, that's nice to hear."

"Can I reach you at the same number as last time?"

"Yes, for a few more weeks anyway… then I'll need to get a cell phone or give you my mom's number. Our house is only twenty minutes from campus."

"We won't need a few weeks to make this happen so don't worry about wasting money on a cell phone. Do you have a place to stay?"

"Not yet but maybe I can stay with my Dad. I think he still lives down there."

"You don't know?"

"No, he and my mom got divorced when I was twelve and I was real angry with him for a long time. We just lost touch with each other."

"I'm sorry Jim, that's a tough deal. We may have someone at the station that wouldn't mind a room mate for a few months if that's okay with you."

"Yeah, that would probably be better since I have no idea about my Dad right now and it would be so weird after all these years anyway."

"I understand. Give me a few days and I'll get back to you, okay?"

"Thanks a lot Jack, I really appreciate this."

"You're welcome Jim. See you later…"

"Thanks again, goodbye."

# *"Assassination"*

Messer looked out the window and took note of the sun and how much daylight he had left. He then finished the milk and threw the half-eaten second half of his sandwich into the trash can. He took a quick shower and shave, no cologne and then dressed into his dark business suit and leather shoes. He packed his bags and cleaned up the room, wiping it down for any careless fingerprints left behind.

At 7:00pm he exited the motel popped the trunk to his Lexus, took the hunters mask and placed it into his small leather bag, which he then took out along with the leather briefcase and entered the car.

Driving to Blackbird lane he removed the ten ounce Glock G17 9mm pistol from his bag and holstered it under his left arm. He then removed the spare 17-round clip and placed it in his right suit jacket pocket. The silencer went into his left jacket pocket a few seconds later. Then he took out the hunters' hood and stuffed it halfway down his pants.

*Still too light* – he thought to himself… so he did a quick 15-minute reconnaissance of the area before settling into his pre-planned parking space on the street three blocks away. He left his empty leather bag on the floor in front of the passengers' seat and then grabbed his leather briefcase before locking the doors behind him with the remote control.

The walk to the east end of the wall was almost relaxing. No one was on the street and the beautiful homes made for a good view. One jogger passed a block in front of him heading in the opposite direction of the right turn he'd be making in another minute. The night air was a bit cooler this evening and the humidity was low.

He made the right turn onto Blackbird Lane and estimated the distance to the corner of the wall to be 120 yards. He picked up the pace gently but not so much that any one would think twice about it. Ninety seconds later he was taking his last look around and ducking behind the privet hedge. The ladder was exactly where he had left it.

He took a full minute to compose himself by taking some long, deep and slow breaths. Then he put on the full-face hunters mask and unfolded the flat black ladder. He climbed halfway up and placed his briefcase on the top of the two foot wide wall and then pushed it a few more feet out of his way. Still invisible he took a good look around and no one was near. Two more steps and he was straddling the wall and pulling the ladder from one side to the other. Fifteen seconds of exposure now but there wasn't anything he could do about it. Ten seconds more and he was inside the complex with suitcase in hand… invisible now, even to the rooftop cameras thanks to the giant Oak trees between them.

A quick check of the time… 8:15 pm… *perfect…* he thought. Then he perused the entire expanse before him. It was impressive to say the least. It was speckled with old Oak and Maple trees with a fair amount of landscaping closer to the front. It was well manicured and the brick wall all around it made it feel like a castle. *A castle without a mote…* Messer thought to himself.

From his point of entry he could survey the entire kill zone and quickly noted that there were plenty of good spots. Two snipers could be done in a half second flat and out in thirty more. Being alone meant taking out the driver first without the primary target getting behind the vehicle, or worse still back into that armored car. A side shot would be best over there… that way there would be no cover.

He waited until it was dark enough that the cameras would have difficulty picking up any movement. Slowly he traveled down the east wall until he was able to see the front steps plainly from the side. He then moved 40 yards closer to the steps and nestled behind a hundred year old oak tree. From this position that tree would block out the camera's view completely.

He then opened the case to his custom made Winchester 30-06 and assembled it in less than two minutes. He put on his thin leather gloves, mounted the scope and inserted the 6-bullet clip, which gave him instantaneous access to the next round… without the archaic bolt action to slow him down. Looking through the scope to the kill zone he estimated his range to be 70 to 75 yards… child's play for him. Funny how the surveillance team took the worst possible estimate… *they must have thought I'd be shooting from near the front gate.*

It was now 8:45 pm and the wait was on. He took note of how few cars passed the front gate, which was nearly five hundred yards diagonally to his front and right. That's good… he'd have the car in view for at least a minute before they would pull up to the steps. *Come on now Mr. Big Shot don't be late.* It was dark now but the doorway was illuminated and night vision wouldn't be necessary. He made the final adjustment to his scope and waited patiently.

It was now 9:10 pm and the adrenalin was pumping… he knew it could be any second now. Then 9:20… 9:30… 9:40 and Messer began getting a little too antsy. *Deep breaths…* he said to himself… *long, slow deep breaths.*

He was two minutes into his deep breathing when the gates opened electronically and the black Mercedes crawled up the winding driveway past the magnificent Oaks that guarded the road. *Not today.* He thought… *you're not going to be able to guard him today.*

9:44 pm and the bullet proof car eased to a halt exactly where Messer expected it to. He made a final site adjustment on the bodyguard as he exited the driver's door and then followed him as he walked past the front of the car and around to the passenger's side where he stood with his back to the assassin as he opened the door for his employer. The pudgy CEO stepped out and muttered something to the driver before proceeding slowly up the stairs.

Messer counted to five slowly and then put the first shot into the right temple of the driver as he passed in front of the car. As expected the executive turned fully around and stood there gawking at his fallen bodyguard trying to fathom what had just happened. *Too slow Charlie…*he thought to himself. Then taking the extra second he needed for perfect precision Messer put a bullet in his forehead and another one in his chest a half second later.

With surgeon like precision he disassembled the gun and put it into its case. The front door was still closed as he hurried along the inner east wall and up the ladder. He took one look back and the front door was just opening up. A few seconds later he was lying prone on the top of the wall and dropping his briefcase down. *Now just don't land on that and you'll be fine...* he thought before lowering himself somewhat cautiously to the ground as the screams and yells followed.

His heart pumped dangerous levels of adrenaline through his body as he fought to regain his composure. He removed the mask and tucked it down his pants. Then he reminded himself to take a good look around before exiting the temporary sanctuary and for what seemed like an eternity he took long, slow, deep-breaths before stepping out onto the broad sidewalk.

He headed toward the first corner and then the short cut as the lights began to appear on porches and windows around him. Every fiber in his body told him to run but his discipline allowed him to maintain a steady unhurried pace that seemed like ultra-slow-motion but already had him well out of the primary area that the neighbors were interested in.

He reached the house with the shortcut and took a few extra seconds to make sure this was still a good idea. No stirring in there at all... no lights coming on... so he cautiously walked up the driveway and unlatched the safety strap to his 9mm holster. He elected not to remove the weapon or screw in the silencer and quickly cut through the shadows of the back yard and into the adjoining yard that led to the street where he was parked.

Distant sirens could be heard as he reentered the street and then walked the remaining thirty yards to his car. He used the key instead of the remote entry to avoid the sound that it emitted and opened the trunk to stash his briefcase. Then he used the key to open the drivers' door and got in. He took a good ten seconds to look around while continuing to breathe deep and slow to calm himself. Then he started the car and drove slowly away from where the sirens were approaching. Fifteen minutes later he was heading to Atlanta where another job was already waiting.

# *"Connecting The Dots"*

Mark McNulty entered his FBI office in Washington DC at 7:15am. He grabbed a cup of coffee and went to his office to read the morning paper. The headlines in the Washington Times read;

### *"Top Lockheed-Martin Exec Murdered"*

John Richards, an executive of the Lockheed-Martin nuclear weapons division, was gunned down last night along with his driver Martin Wolfe at approximately 10:00 pm. They were in inside Mr. Richards' estate in Charlotte, North Carolina and both men were pronounced dead on the scene. Mr. Richards had only been with Lockheed Martin for eighteen months when he was hired to replace Sr. Vice President Adam Cohen after he died in what was called *"a freak skiing accident"*. Anyone with information concerning these horrific murders should contact their local law enforcement agency immediately. Our sincerest condolences go out to both families.

*Jesus...* Mark thought... *Why take this guy down? How many Fortune 500 executives does that make this year... and why them?*

"Good morning Mark how are you today?" His secretary asked.

"Good Sally, at least until I saw this..." McNulty turned the paper to show her the headlines.

"My God, why would someone want to kill him?"

"That *is* the question... hmmm... **strategic nuclear bombs Sally**. I'm pretty sure they're the ones working on the next generation of those weapons. They merged with Martin Marietta who picked up that division from General Electric in the 90's sometime. Call the Bureau responsible in Charlotte and ask them to fax up their report on this."

"Sure Mark and just a reminder that your system analysts will be waiting for you in the conference room at 8:00 am."

"Thanks Sally… but we're going to need to push that back to 4:00."

# *"Knowing and Proving"*

Merrill Ruth Schneider was appointed Commissioner to the Securities and Exchange Commission by President Clinton in 1998. As one of five such SEC appointees she wielded more influence than most CEOs of major corporations. When sworn into office she had promised to **protect investors, maintain fair, orderly, efficient markets and to facilitate capital formation.**

Unlike the banking industry, where deposits are guaranteed by the government, tools of the Investment Industry, namely stocks bond and securities can lose value and are susceptible to market manipulation and fraud. Protecting the integrity of these markets is essential to the growth of our nation and to the security of the jobs of our citizens. Without the effective governance of these marketplaces we could not hope to improve, or even to maintain our current standard of living.

When Mrs. Schneider read the headlines about the murdered executive alarm bells began to go off in her head. Within four hours she was able to ascertain that a significant amount of insider trading had taken place… a clear indicator that quite a few people knew about the assassination before hand. Unfortunately, knowing that a crime had been committed was infinitely easier than proving it. She reached for the phone and called her Executive Assistant.

"Cheryl, get me Walter Dobson at the FBI…ASAP!"

"Yes Commissioner."

## *"The Sniper"*

"Major, Stanton's back in camp Sir."

"Alive? I thought we'd lost him."

"Me too sir, he was MIA five days ago. His spotter didn't make it."

"What about his target?"

"Confirmed kill sir… from other sources."

"How many does that make for him Captain?"

"Thirteen sir."

"I guess it wasn't his unlucky number after all."

"No, just his spotters and they were close… together from the start."

"You taking care of that letter?"

"With your permission sir, David asked if he could write it."

"No problem, just make sure he runs it past you before it goes out."

"Yes sir."

"Where's the Sergeant now?"

"Chowing down sir..."

"Send him right over, he can bring his food."

"Right away sir."

"Sergeant Stanton Sir, the Captain said you wanted to see me?"

"Yes Sergeant, have a seat and keep eating. I understand you had a tough one this time?"

"Yes sir, we did."

"Care to talk about it?"

"Not really sir."

"I understand that your partner was killed."

"Yes sir, Sergeant Ramos. He was a good friend."

"You have my permission to write to his family. Captain Cooper told me that you had asked."

"Yes sir, thank you sir."

"Congratulations on the kill. That was an important one for us. How many was that for you son, ten?"

"Thirteen sir."

"That makes you one of our best men Sergeant. We're proud of you."

(Silence)

"We'll make sure Sergeant Ramos's family is well taken care of."

"Thank you… anything else sir?"

"Just one more thing… how did you get out… it must have been forty miles over some of the toughest enemy terrain we've seen."

"I don't know how I made it sir. We were leaving the nest after our attack and heading down the mountain to the LZ when he was hit. I tried to carry him to the chopper but it was too far and under heavy attack. When I put him down he was already gone. I ran for the treeline and worked my way out of the area. I don't know why I made it."

# *"Alliances"*

"Chief Dobson, this is Commissioner Schneider over at the SEC. I presume you read the article about the Lockheed exec this morning?"

"Yes Commissioner, I was thinking you might call."

"Your alarm bells went off too?"

"After six of these murders in the last five months… *absolutely!* The problem is turning them off." Dobson replied.

"They're not wrong sir… we have a linkage here just like the others."

"Damn, how did you do that so fast?"

"From what I've been told our systems are a little more up to date than yours are sir and we don't have to worry about all of the other homeland security agencies like you do."

"We should have your system analysts talk to ours real soon. We are looking into what it's going to take to drag these things into the 21st Century."

"I doubt you can do that sir. We had to rewrite most of our software from the bottom up and put them on open architecture systems."

"Can you elaborate on that Commissioner?"

"The problem we had, and I wouldn't be a bit surprised if it's the same one you're going to discover, is that all of our so-called "State of The Art" computers *haven't been* since the 1980s. They were built upon proprietary software...now that's all well and good as long as *everyone* is running under the *SAME* umbrella. Try to communicate transparently between competing proprietary systems and it's like trying to negotiate at the UN without any interpreters. It's a real mess sir. The world has moved away from that paradigm in favor of *open architectures*, which will communicate with one another seamlessly. It was a big pill to swallow but it was the only way for us to go."

"Hmmm… that makes a lot of sense. It explains why we haven't gotten very far. I'll be sure to pass that information along to our people that are on the project."

"There's one more thing that may help."

"What's that?"

"Some of your people may be experts in the old IBM mainframe world but they're probably neophytes in the new world. Expect some turf battles and misinformation because no one likes to be put out to pasture… at least not too early. We hired a consulting team from EDS who turned out to be superstars for us. I won't say it was smooth sailing all the way but it was the correct decision and at least now we know with absolute certainty that we can get new functionality when we need it."

"Thanks Commissioner, on both fronts. Can you e-mail me your preliminary findings on the insider trading figures that you're uncovering?"

"I'd be happy to Chief and I'll have one of my best people ready for you when you need some of the data explained."

"Thanks Commissioner. Please, call me Walter. I think we're going to be working a lot closer with each other from here on in."

"Yes sir, I mean, yes Walter. Feel free to call me Merrill."

"I will Merrill, thanks again."

"Goodbye."

## *"A Job Well Done"*

"You did good, real good Steve."

"Thanks Skip, we all did."

"Mr. C. was very pleased with the operation. Nice and clean... no one hurt that didn't need to be."

"Except the driver."

"Nah, he wasn't a civilian. He was a bodyguard, probably from Blackwell. You live by the sword you die by the sword."

"That goes for us too you know."

"Yeah, but at least we're fighting for a better future for our kids. What the Hell was he fighting for? A paycheck! They're fucking mercenaries and sell out to the highest bidder. Fuck em all I say."

"I think we may have used them ourselves."

"If we did then we're just plain stupid. Write them a big enough check and they'll blow our entire operation. They don't want peace... their whole fucking company is based on war and the world's need for men willing to kill and die for a God damn paycheck."

"What are you willing to die for Skip?"

"My wife, my kids, my Country... or at least the Country our founding fathers envisioned. Not for the assholes that are running it now. What about you?"

"I just want to die an old man with my legs wrapped around some luscious twenty year old."

(Laughing)

"Okay, you win. Put me down for two."

## *"School, Statistics & Slaughter"*

"Good evening listeners and welcome back to **Door to Door**. Tonight I'd like to focus our attention on the slaughter that's been occurring in our schools across the country. I ran a Google search this morning in preparation for the show and typed in two simple words. What do you think those words were? (Short silence) **School shootings**… That's all… nothing fancy. I expected to see the ones we all know about, you know, The University of Texas, Columbine, Virginia Tech. but I wasn't prepared for what I found. It was a six page table of murder rampages in our schools from February of 1996 to April, 2007. **Six pages!** Each page contained an average of nine entries, any one of which could have been the three I mentioned a moment ago. Each entry identified the location, the assassin, the number of murdered students and teachers as well as the number wounded. It also included the ages of the murderers. Just for **shits and giggles** I plotted the ages of the hit men… **all of whom** by the way were **men**, except for one 14 year old girl named Bush, go figure. How old do you think the youngest assassin was? (Short silence) Write it down, this is a quiz. He was 6. Okay, maybe that one was an accident but what the Hell is a 6-year old doing with a gun? Next youngest… write it down…11! There was one 12 twelve year old, three 13 year olds, **nine** 14 year olds, **gotta love that good old testosterone**, nine 15 year olds, but only three 16 year olds… I figured most of them were getting laid by then and that explains the big drop off. Six 17 year olds, five 18 year olds, three 19 year olds and then nothing until age 23. I figured the armed forces had the killers by then and that's why we don't see anything again until age 23, which is the guy who shot the students and faculty at Virginia's Polytechnic Institute in 2007. Then there's one at age twenty-five… that was the ex-marine who slaughtered people from a 28 story tower at the University of Texas, **see the military did have them**, one at age 27 and one at age 32. The two Columbine murderers were 17 and 18. So that's a total of 45 murderers, most of whom were children. I didn't have my calculator with me or I'd have given you the total number of dead students and faculty, plus wounded… but suffice it to say it is an incredible number especially when you realize that this is for a period of only a little over 11 years! Alright, enough of listening to me… what do *you* think about these statistics? Good evening caller you're on the air."

"Hi Tim, this is Meredith in Herndon, Virginia. My daughter was in class when that young Korean boy went on his rampage. We spent a long time talking about it."

"Was your daughter injured in anyway Meredith?"

"No *thank God* but she did witness some of the murders."

"I'm sorry, that must have been very difficult for her."

"Yes it was, it was traumatic for all of us but we jut prayed and tried to do what we could for the poor families who lost their children."

"Were you able to gain any understanding of why Cho Seung-Hui might have done this?"

"My daughter told me that he was teased mercilessly. She told me he was very shy. He was a Korean boy and he had an accent that was very difficult to understand. She said the students were very mean."

"And what did the teachers do when the students harangued Cho?"

"I don't think very much… they'd tell the kids to stop it but Mary said that there were so many of them doing it that if they were all thrown out there wouldn't be any class left to teach."

"I see, so the teacher did basically nothing?"

"I guess, but what should he have done."

"… to stop the murder of 32 people? *Everything!* He should have sent *all of the class* to the Principal's Office if necessary if they couldn't control their childish taunts. Do you think this murderer just woke up one day and said; *Hmmm… nice day out… I think I'll go out and shoot five or six dozen people.* He's probably been teased since the day he came to this Country and that day he finally snapped. I'm not a shrink but that would be my guess."

"You may be right Mr. McManus. My daughter feels the same way you do."

"Thank you for your call Meredith."

"You're on the air… talk to me."

"Hi, this is George from Gaithersburg. What I want to know is where the Hell are these kids getting the guns from?"

"Now that is a good question George. Where do you think?"

"I guess they are getting them off the street or from home?"

"I imagine some of them buy illegally but I'd be willing to bet that most of them stole the weapons from their Dad, who was too damn stupid to secure the weapon properly. Adults can buy guns legally but children can't and most kids wouldn't have a clue or the cash to buy them illegally."

"Yeah and if they did they probably wouldn't have enough money."

"Okay callers… assume for the moment that the weapons did come from the parent, Dad or Mom, I don't care. What should be done to them if their child shoots someone?"

"Hi Tim, I'm June from Washington DC and my son was shot and killed in a gang incident two years ago."

"I'm very sorry to hear that June. How old was he?"

"He was only sixteen."

"Was he a gang member?

"Yes, he was."

"… and did he carry a gun?"

"Yes sir, he did… a lot of the kids do and they don't feel safe without one of their own."

"It sounds like they've learned real well from our militarized society."

"Yes it does."

"So what do you think we should do about it?"

"We need more activities for the kids after school. A lot of us are single moms and we don't get home from work for at least two or three hours after them. That's when a lot of the trouble happens."

"So you're saying more Police Athletic Leagues and sponsored activities and things along those lines?"

"Yes, perhaps even arts and crafts, tennis, basketball…. Anything that gives them a positive place to go that's safe. Parents would definitely be supportive of that."

"Thank you June, those are good insights and we'll do what we can from here to help."

"Thank you so much."

"You're very welcome. Good bye. Caller, you're on the air."

"I want to address your earlier question."

"Sure, and who are we speaking with?"

"This is Tom from here in Baltimore."

"Okay Tom, go ahead."

"If a kid shoots anyone with a parents' gun then we should throw the parents in jail."

"Both parents?"

"Well, at least the one who the gun is registered to."

"Okay, I think that's more reasonable."

"What sentence do you propose?"

"I guess that depends on what the kid does with the gun."

"Okay, let's just give three instances and I'd like you to put a sentence to each."

"Okay, shoot, uh, I mean go ahead."

"That's okay Tom, we know what you mean. Number one: The child is found with a gun in his possession and reported to the authorities. Two, the child fires the gun and accidentally hurts another person but no one is killed. Three: The child goes on a rampage and intentionally tries to kill someone, successful or not."

"Hmmm…. That's a tough one."

"What sentence should the parent who owns the gun receive? We'll worry about the child's sentence later."

"Okay, it seems to me that some jail time is needed for all three offenses."

"No probation?"

"No sir, the situation calls for more."

"I agree with you… Please, go on…"

"The first offense, where no one is harmed should carry the lightest sentence, the second should be more severe and the third the longest."

"Why? Aren't all three offenses by the parent the exact same?"

"No sir, they aren't. People died in the third situation and no one was even hurt in the first."

"This is where you and I disagree. The parent did the *exact same thing* in all three instances. He left a licensed gun in a place where his child could get to it. Your three sentences should be different for the child but not for the adult… At least not the way I see it."

"I can see your point. Then what sentences should the parent get?"

"I think the only way we're ever going to make a dent in this problem is to make the penalty for first offenders as harsh as possible. I would propose that the guilty parent would get a felony sentence of **Voluntary Manslaughter**… injury or not."

"Ouch, but what if the child just took it out to show his friends and never intended on hurting a soul… why not a lesser sentence, a misdemeanor?"

"Okay, and what if that child accidentally shot his best friend and that little 6 year old girl was your daughter?"

"Dear God, I don't know."

"In my way of thinking the parent did the exact same thing whether there's an accident, a mass killing or no harm done at all. They've allowed *their weapon* to be accessed and taken control of by a child. Your sentence is a misdemeanor, whereas Voluntary Manslaughter is a 1st degree felony and will carry a harsher sentence."

"So you think 1st time offenders should go to jail?"

"Yes sir, I absolutely do. The first time offender could be the reason twenty students are murdered. If people can afford to buy a gun then they can afford a combination safe-box to keep it in."

"Thank you for your call, next caller."

"Hi Tim, I'm Christine from Rutgers University."

"Hi Chrissie, how's Jim?"

"I was wondering if you'd recognize my voice. (Laughing) He's fine."

"Yeah, that's what they pay me the big bucks for. So what's on your mind?"

"I think what's going on in our society is horrible. It's almost as if we want our kids to grow up to be warriors."

"Can you expound on that a bit for us?"

"Sure, the toys we give our kids, the video games, the movies… they're all so violent and most of the boys love them. They learn that killing is fun and exciting and they all dream of becoming big heroes. It's embedded into our culture."

"I think you have a very valid point there. So what are we going to do about it?"

"That's the problem… everything I mentioned is legal. The movies are rated according to their content, the games are sold with warning labels and Parental Advisories, the video arcades are set up with all of the weaponry our military has… and it's all legal."

"Good ole America… land of the free and home of the brave. So what do we do about it?"

"Well, the first step is what we're doing now, like you've said before; *at least we're talking about it*. We need to find ways to motivate our people to stop buying these games for their kids or to put age restrictions on them at the store, like with cigarettes. I think we need to find a lot of money so we can start advertising on TV to help raise public awareness."

"I think those are all good points and I'd like to focus our calls for a few minutes on this topic. Thanks for you call Chrissie."

"Hello, this is Marty from Philadelphia… very good show today!"

"Thanks Marty, what's on you mind?"

"I think I know where we can get the money we need."

"Are you a billionaire Marty?"

(Laughing) *"In my dreams!* No, but our Department of Defense is."

"Hmmm… I think I know where you're going with this… go on."

"**$400 BILLION** a year for our military from *OUR* taxes… another **$100 BILLION** from unknown public sources for black ops… I think, with a little help from our friends we could use those funds."

"I agree, we have more money in our annual war budget than what… the next six or eight largest industrialized countries combined? That's absolutely ridiculous! I think you're right Marty; it's time for our government to start spending *our money* more intelligently. Caller you're on the air…"

"We need income tax revisions that would allow us to say what portion of our taxes can be used for what."

"Interesting point… and who am I speaking with?"

"Oh I'm sorry… this is Payton from Atlantic City."

"… and what if NOBODY directs their money to war?"

(Laughing) "Wouldn't that be wonderful… but it would never happen. All the profiteers would direct 100% of their money there… a lot of soldiers and veterans would, I'm sure a good portion of the population would make a reasonable contribution based on their own common sense."

"I'm sure you're correct… but what if the war budget went from $400 billion down to $150 billion overnight?"

"That's a good point. We'd probably be in a Hell of a jam."

"Here's a thought… Let's put a committee together to…."

(Interrupting) "Now *you* sound like a politician."

(Laughing)

"No, no… hear me out… We put the finest minds into a room and lock the door until they come up with a plan. Military types, Peaceniks, Nobel Peace Prize and Economy experts… tax and law experts… balanced politically so that no single contingent can dominate."

"Okay… and what do we want them to come up with Tim?"

"A *phased in* approach to the issue you raised. They could determine a safe way to allow Americans to direct a portion of their income taxes into something other than war. They could direct a portion of the war tax to care for the veterans instead of bombing some poor third world country into the Stone Age. That would allow for the scaling down of our aggressive nature while providing more funding for civilization to thrive. Maybe even have our own ***Department of Peace*** that would help to heal the needy and helpless people and not rob them of their natural resources like some schoolyard bully."

"Wouldn't that be wonderful?"

"It sure would… Thanks Payton. Next caller…"

"This is Madeline from Fredericksburg and I want to thank you for this show tonight. We need more discussions like this."

"Thank you. What would you like to add?"

"You mentioned sentencing for children but I didn't hear any one discuss it yet."

"Did you hear the three samples I gave before? No injury… just found with the gun, accidental wounding by child to anyone and malicious attack with intent to kill?"

"Yes Tim I did."

"How would you dish out justice if you had the power?"

"It's a complicated question, especially when you're dealing with a child."

"Yes it is Madeline. Do you mind if I ask what you do for a living?"

"Why no, not at all. I teach 10th grade English."

"Wonderful, then you bring quite a bit of insight into this question."

"I believe I do... although we've been lucky and have never had this kind of horror in our school. I know we're not immune to it. As far as sentencing the very young child who innocently brought a weapon to school I think the punishment should be very mild and mostly educational as to the danger they put themselves and their friends into."

"Okay, I'm with you on that. What about the child who accidentally wounds someone?"

"It's more serious indeed but we'd have to try and determine his *intent* to see if there was any maliciousness in the act and then we could decide the level of punishment from there."

"I'm still with you… but what of the last one… the vicious killer?"

"I guess there are two ways to go with that. Was he insane or was he just a bad seed? If he was just a cold blooded murderer who acted sanely prior to the outburst then I have no qualms at all about putting him to death… painlessly of course, but quickly… no more of these ten year appeals and million dollars defenses courtesy of our tax dollars. That's total garbage when there are credible eye witnesses, perhaps even video, that can settle the question easily."

"So you'd be in favor of killing a child?"

"If he intentionally murdered someone? Yes, I think that's harsh but it's better than the alternatives. Why should we pay to keep this child locked up in prison for 50 or 60 years? And why should we let this murderer back out on parole someday… that would be negligence on our part."

"You make a good argument but at least half the population of this country disagrees with you. What if we could find an alternative that would let him live while removing all chances that he could ever hurt someone again and then put him to work for the benefit of society?"

"How, with a lobotomy?"

"I'm sure someone's toyed with that idea… but it's not likely. I'm really not sure… but there must be a humane answer to this question and not one that defines humans as murderers. We need to discover how to channel that person into something productive and yes, protect society from him (or her) in the process."

"I think we'd just be making them our slaves Tim. We'd be exchanging one devil for another… yours or mine?"

"These *are* tough questions but we need more debate and expert opinions on the matter before I'm going to dance with either devil."

"I'm sorry Madeline, but we're out of time. Thank you for your valuable insights and to all our callers and audience this evening. This is Tim McManus at **WIQR, 103.5 FM - Baltimore.** Thanks for listening, dream well, goodnight."

## *"Self Defense"*

Maxwell Dreyden read the news of the assassination while being chauffeured to his brand new office building in downtown Atlanta. The Dreyden Center was a marvel in modern engineering and his executive offices consumed the entire 33$^{rd}$ top floor. It wasn't the tallest building only because he didn't want the extra attention directed at his company. It was however, at the pinnacle of modern engineering ingenuity and no expenses were spared to assure that it stayed that way for decades to come.

"Lou, did you hear about the Lockheed executive in Charlotte?"

"Yes sir… I heard it on the news last night and read more about it this morning."

"What do you think happened?"

"I think he got sloppy Sir. They said he was there only a short time; less than two years and he got shot on the front steps of his house after stepping out of a quarter million dollar armored Mercedes limo. The car was probably one of the perks of his position and he wasn't trained on what to do in case of an attack. That's what I think. Based on the hits to the head of both men plus the chest of the primary target it looks like he froze like a deer in the headlights after his driver was shot."

"Why take down the driver? Even if he was a bodyguard once his boss is dead why bother?"

"He had to be inside the compound to get that angle from the side. They didn't say much but he was probably well out of range of the driver's handgun. He most likely figured that he'd be taking a lot of return fire during his escape and just didn't want the extra noise."

"I see your point…. But why shoot the driver in the head? Was that some sort of statement."

"I guess that's possible but unlikely. The shooter was a pro and he wasn't taking any chances. He probably assumed the worst case scenario and that the driver was wearing Kevlar. If I have to go before my time then the head is where I want it. The driver never knew what hit him… he was dead before the sound of the shot got there."

"Jesus Christ! That means his boss had almost no warning. We'll be using the garage from now on Lou for me and the entire family… no exceptions! Is that clear?"

"Yes sir, I was about to suggest it."

"Also, double check the entrance to our home and figure out how we can make it more secure. I want the garage armor doubled. Then get your boss to look over your suggestions before we implement them. Money is no issue, if it makes sense then just go ahead and do it."

"Yes sir... and what about here sir?"

"Same thing… figure it out *now* Lou and have your boss come see me when your preliminary report is ready."

"Will do."

They arrived at the Dreyden Center and were waved past the security guard at the underground parking lot before proceeding to the Max Dreyden's private elevator. The bodyguard got out, walked to the elevator and pressed the five digit security code that gave him instant access. The door flew open three times faster than a normal elevator as Lou walked the eight feet back to the car, looked around thoroughly and then opened the door for his boss. Dreyden got out and made it a point to thank him before walking briskly to the elevator and pressing one of the two large "door close" buttons. The door slammed shut equally fast and he was quickly whisked up to the 33rd floor where his private fiefdom awaited him.

*Another day, another million dollars…* he thought to himself and smiled.

# *"Targets, Strategies & Communication"*

The commanders had met amongst themselves only a month earlier after hearing the wishes of their *"financiers"*, for lack of a better term. The ante had been raised significantly and they were trying to escalate the mission too fast. It had already been agreed that the eighteen month time-line was critical to the success of the political results that were being sought but the methods known to be most effective were now being manipulated unprofessionally by amateurs who were only business executives and not soldiers. The bones of contention that remained had to do with the number of targets, who those targets were going to be, how and when they were going to be taken down and most importantly, by which commander's squad.

Before the top four commanders had left the meeting with the industrialists each of them had been given a flash card with their portion of the two hundred and sixteen qualified targets encrypted onto it. None of the names would be shared between areas unless a distant squad was needed to participate in a hit. The recommendation to have squads move more freely throughout the territories had been met with harsh rebuttals from the commanders, all of whom were ex-military men of significant combat talent and rank. Their leader was a retired Three Star General who was recruited into the movement after his civilian politics became known. All in all the meeting had been a success and the significant increase in cash that was needed had been agreed upon without argument… the stakes were simply much too high to cut corners now.

At the commanders private meeting afterwards they discussed tactics, controlled escalation, squad specialization, anti-infiltration tactics, dissolving infiltrated squads, reformation and recruitment, counter surveillance, the critical nature of isolating squads, the coordination of squads against moving targets and how to optimize communications while simultaneously safeguarding it. The last item was exceedingly difficult but was essential to their success. Without secure communications they were lambs being led to the slaughter… and every man in the room knew it without it ever being said.

*"I know how to solve the communications issue gentlemen."*
Commander Joe Clark offered…

# *"Necessary Evil"*

(Telephone intercom squawks)

"Mr. Dreyden, Blackwell Security is here for your 2 o'clock meeting."

"Thank you Gladys, please tell him I'll be just a few more minutes."

"Yes, Mr. Dreyden."

Max Dreyden finished the paragraph he was writing to his friend in Congress and cleared his desk for the meeting. He pulled out the notepad with ideas from his driver on how to improve security and gave them a quick review.

"Gladys, please show Mr. Thompson in."

"Uh, yes sir."

"Mr. Dreyden, this is Emily Thompson."

(Laughing with obvious embarrassment)

"*Ms.* Thompson, please forgive me."

"It's not the first time Sir... you should see some of the looks I get when I walk in. Yours wasn't *too* bad... I actually enjoy it, which is why Mrs. Chicorella didn't warn you."

(Laughing) "Sorry Max... I owed you one."

"You did warn me... okay Gladys we're even now right?"

"I'll have to double check my notes but I believe so."

"*Close the door behind you Gladys.* Welcome *Ms.* Thompson… Thank you for coming on such short notice. How was your flight?"

"It was very pleasant Sir. Thank you."

"I've got a list of security improvements that your man recommended. I've been very concerned about my family's safety after the events of the last few months."

"You mean the past **SIX** months Sir."

"Excuse me?"

"There have been *seven* top executive deaths in the past six months."

"I didn't realize that."

"All of the deaths were Fortune 500 company senior executives Sir."

"Dear God, you're not serious."

"The first executive was shot, this week's murder in North Carolina makes two by gunfire, one died in a car crash, another slipped on the ice and broke his neck, another committed suicide by overdose, there was one heart attack and one boating accident. That's just too many to be coincidences Sir. Maybe one or two of the five *apparent* accidents but figure in the assassinations and it looks like someone is really trying to shake things lose."

"It sure looks that way but why? Does your company have a take on any of this yet?"

"No Sir, I mean we have varying opinions from our top people but these things are happening all over the country and until now seemed to be primarily accidents. Two of the *accidents* are still under investigation. It's not until you factor in the two sniper killings that they all begin looking suspicious. We think the two assassinations were done by the same shooter."

"REALLY… and what leads you to that presumption?"

"MO was similar Sir and the ammo was *identical* in both cases."

"Method of Operation?"

"Yes Sir, both subjects were taken down in a sniper attack with a high powered rifle using 30 caliber *armor piercing* rounds."

"Armor piercing? I thought the victims were hit outside of the car?"

"That's correct Sir, they got sloppy and made it easy for the killer."

"Who was the other shooting victim?"

"He was president of the voting machine company that was convicted of tampering with our elections. You know… the machines that had no paper trails and could be tampered with remotely?"

"Yes, I read all about that. Can you provide me with a list of the others and any pertinent information you have on them? I'd like to take a closer look at what's going on here."

"I don't see why not sir but let me run it past legal."

"Is Lou as good as I've been told?"

"Mr. Farentino is the best there is sir… in anyone's army, up close or with a gun. He'll take a bullet for your family and still tear the guy a new ass hole before he dies. He's also very, very smart Sir."

"Thank you Ms. Thompson. You've done a fine job today… now please stop calling me Sir… Mr. Dreyden or even Max will be fine but you don't need to salute anyone around here… got it."

"Thank you Mr. Dreyden. Please feel free to call me Emily. Are you ready to talk about the enhanced security measures we have in mind?"

"Yes Ma'am."

"Is anyone in your family allergic to dogs? ..."

### *"Paradise Hotel"*

Messer got into Atlanta early the next day and checked into the prearranged hotel using the Robert Blackman alias that the rental car was still under. His meeting with the local squad leader wasn't scheduled for another two days so he ordered room service and took a long hot shower before collapsing into a deep sleep.

Six hours later he was wide awake and ordering a hearty steak dinner from room service. As he waited he opened the phone book to the yellow pages and turned to the escort section. Atlanta had quite a few exceptional services to choose from and he immediately found what looked to be the most opulent of the bunch. He picked up the phone and dialed the local number.

"Hello, this is Stairway to Paradise, may I help you?"

"This is Mr. Blackman in room 1705 of the Westin Peachtree Hotel. I'm looking for the best young lady you have and money is no issue."

"Yes, of course sir, that's our specialty. Will this be cash or credit?"

"Cash"

"And what's your price range for this evening sir?"

"At least two grand if she's as good as I'm looking for."

"And how long will you be needing her services?"

"Four hours."

"What time would you like her to arrive?"

"8:00 pm is fine. Just don't let me down and I'll call again."

"Yes sir, I'm sure you won't be disappointed. She'll be expecting full payment upon arrival. Enjoy your evening Sir and thanks for calling Paradise."

# *"Anonymity"*

Matt Creagor headed up the twenty-one man squad in the Atlanta region. His was one of the largest single units within the new militia, which had both its' advantages and disadvantages. The size of his unit was too small to provide him with his own Command status and too big to be the finely tuned self-sufficient squad that had proven so difficult to penetrate. Within this small platoon he had three seven-member squads each sharing four specialties; sniping, demolitions, hand to hand combat and surveillance. Every mission he received was eagerly accepted and carried out with maximum precision.

Having read of Messer's early success he knew his team would be under pressure to finish their surveillance a few days sooner than expected. That wasn't going to make this easy *or* safe. This was a fairly sizeable problem since the target was not only an important one but had proven to be fairly elusive and difficult to pin down.

He signed onto the Internet and entered his Yahoo Messenger name of *"Silly Rabbit"*. From there he sent an instant message to the three surveillance team members, each of whom had no less than six seemingly harmless identities on the chat service. The rotation of these identities and the actual content of their communications would make it exceedingly difficult for any intelligence agency to discover or track. Even *"if"* they had transcripts of the actual e-mails and chat records they would appear to be benign.

(He typed...)

"Reminder - 18-holes tomorrow, 7:00 am at the clubhouse."

The next time his three surveillance men turned on their computers and logged onto the internet the little icon would pop up and flash the notification of the instant message awaiting them. A message they all knew was a direct order to meet Creagor at the Friendly's restaurant at 07:00 sharp. No replies were needed.

That form of communication had been Commander Joe Clark's idea, which he had gotten from his teenage daughter by overseeing her activities in cyberspace. His fatherly warning to be careful... *"you never know what kind of freak you may be talking to..."* set off not only parental warning bells but put a sly smile across his face when he realized the potential of that medium. Two parts of him watched over his little girl... the loving father and the astute Commander.

## *"Disjointed & Uninformed"*

Mark McNulty had spent most of the day gathering as much information as possible on the recent Fortune 500 victims. What he was astonished to find out was that there hadn't been just six or seven fatalities among this select group in the last six months but over **twenty in the last two years!** Now there's no way that many fatal accidents make sense. *I'd sure like to know the statistics on this.*

Okay, who were they? Two from Lockheed, a tobacco exec, the voting machine guys, PR professionals, oil executives, weapons manufacturers, accounting execs, plus the heads of all four SUV divisions of GM, Ford, Chrysler and Toyota… at least we've been working on that one. *Dear God… we're under a systematic attack and we're just figuring it out!*

(The intercom squawks alive…)

"Mark, the analysts are here for your four o'clock meeting."

"Thanks Sally, tell them to go back to work and I'll call them when I'm ready."

"Got it."

(Dialing)

"Dobson here."

"Chief, you're not going to believe the preliminary results of the investigation on the Fortune 500 execs."

"Look like a conspiracy?"

"Why yes Sir, how did you know?"

"Commissioner Merrill Schneider at the SEC gave me the heads up earlier… she found what appears to be insider trading linkages."

"At the very least Sir... it looks more like a war."

"What did you find out?"

"Over twenty top executives plus some of their company's best engineers have died in the last twenty-two months and that's just what we've been able to put together so far. That's got to be off the map statistically Walt… and that's not the half of it. Most of them were producers of high-tech weaponry, including WMD and SDI or were primary contributors to the pollution problem and destruction of our natural habitats, like that pipeline guy up in Alaska we spoke about a few months ago. That's still unsolved. Two of the deaths were execs of the accounting firm that screwed its employee's out of their pension plan before jumping out with multi-million dollar golden parachutes. Another two were about to be indicted for voting machine fraud. I think we have a revolution underway and nobody ever stopped to tell us about it."

"And do you know why we didn't see it earlier Mark?"

"I think I do Sir… because our damn systems don't like to play together. We've just been hit by a twenty-two month long Pearl Harbor and we didn't even notice."

"Yes that, and the probability that they didn't want us to see it coming too soon. Don't blame yourself… they most likely wanted to keep their activities quiet for as long as possible while they grouped their forces. Now we've got to root them out before they escalate. Get us moving on our systems integration project Mark… that's your number two priority right behind this investigation."

"Yes Sir. I'll light a bonfire under it."

"Last thing Mark… make sure the analysts and your counterparts understand that they are going to be team players or they are going to be looking for a new job... no matter how important they think they are they're totally worthless to us unless they're all pulling in the same direction. You have my total backing on this... understand?"

"Yes Sir, completely."

## *"Taking The Lead"*

(Intercom squawks to life at Sally Martin's desk...)

"Sally, have Cassandra, Ashim and **Mr. Harris** meet me in the conference room in five-minutes."

"Yes Mark. I'm glad to see you were listening to me earlier."

"Sally, I always listen to you... you know that."

(Chuckling) "Yes, I can see you've been working on it."

"Five-minutes, okay?" (click)

Mark gathered up his notes to the investigation and put them into his briefcase. A few minutes later he was heading to the conference room where Ashim and Roger were already waiting.

"Good morning Ashim, Roger... where's Cassandra?"

"She's finishing up a call and will be right in." Ashim offered.

"Sorry I'm late... did I miss anything?" Cassie said as she entered.

"No, we just got started." said McNulty.

"I want to brief you on what's been going on under our noses for the past two years and we're just getting a whiff of it now. Then we're going to figure out how to tie our computer systems together once and for all so this won't happen again."

"Is it about the recent murder?" Cassandra asked.

"Make that question plural and the answer is affirmative. Over twenty to be more accurate... we're still not even sure of how many."

(Looks are exchanged as demeanor changes became serious.)

"It seems as if we've been under attack and our systems haven't been coordinated well enough to connect the dots for us. We finally had enough to figure this out manually but it's *too little too late*. I need each of you to give me a quick overview of your depth of knowledge in the computer industry so I can understand what our internal skill set looks like. We have a major problem and it's up to us and the other regions to figure this out quickly. They'll all be going through similar exercises and my counterparts and I are going to put an internal task force in-place to fix it. Our combined recommendations are going to be analyzed against those provided by two top consulting firms before we implement the solution."

"How long do we have Mark?" .. asked Roger.

"Figure two months to have our final recommendation… sooner if possible but it will probably take at least that long for the consultants to be in-place and finished. I'll let you know if that target moves either way. Okay, Mr. Harris, you're the newest amongst us so why don't you go first."

"Yes Sir. I've been with the team for a little less than three years. Before that I was finishing up my Master's Degree from MIT in Computer Science. My primary expertise is writing software programs in C, C++ and encompasses all Open Architecture Distributed Systems developed on either UNIX Operating Systems or competing platforms."

"Do those competing platforms work together?"

"Yes sir, that's what *Open Architecture* is all about."

"Thank you Roger… Ashim?"

"Thank you Sir. I studied and received my Masters degree in Computer Science at India's Jadavpur University. I came to this Country fifteen years ago to help write code for the telecommunications industry. My studies were similar to Mr. Harris's but they were directed primarily backwards to the IBM Mainframe world, which was preeminent in the 1960's, 70's and 80's and still make up the foundation of many very large companies around the world."

"So you write software code as well?"

"Yes sir, but I'm more of an expert in the older languages of the IBM world such as COBOL, FORTRAN and things of that nature. I also know C and C++, which, as Roger mentioned are Open Architecture languages vs. the proprietary ones that I've spent most of my career on."

"Thank you Ashim."

"You are very welcome Mr. McNulty."

"Cassandra, last but not least… tell me about your background."

"I'm actually pretty close to right in-between Roger and Ashim. You may not know this but I actually recruited Roger from my old Alma Mater directly onto our team."

"Ask her how she did it sir." Roger chimed in.

"Cassandra… care to enlighten us?"

"We had a position that needed filling when an executive recruiter put his resume in front of me. Roger's a very bright young man and he had the exact skills we were looking for. Then I noticed that he ran track and was a pretty good miler… he actually ran just under four minutes for his personal best." (Smiling coyly but stopping cold…)

*"AND?"* Mark said egging her on…

(Roger grabs the story…)

"So there I am all decked out in my fancy track suit running warm-ups and intervals and along comes Ms. Jones jogging harmlessly in the opposite direction."

"What was it you said to me Roger… do you remember?"

"Yes I do (laughing)… I said you were running in the wrong direction. You were you know… (still chuckling) Then she asked me if I was fast."

"No, no… what I actually said is; *are you any good at this?*"

"Okay, that's what she said… and I tried to be cool and nonchalant and she asked if she could jog with me a bit and maybe pick up a few pointers. *No problem*, I told her and we just starting chatting… I remember trying to be extra careful to keep the pace easy for her."

"*Painfully slow*… although that was nice of you Roger. Then I began asking him questions that I already knew the answers to and told him that I worked for the FBI and he seemed genuinely impressed. I knew he had the skill set we needed and his background check was clean so, having already set the bait I asked if he'd be interested in working for us."

"Yeah, I remember how excited I got *before* I realized how lousy you guys paid and there I was one of the top students at MIT and able to write my own ticket and that excitement dwindled pretty fast."

"So I playfully egged him on until I saw for sure that he wasn't going to accept my offer. So I made a bet with him instead." She said with a wide grin.

"Oh?" McNulty asked with an inquisitive smile in his voice.

"I told him I used to be pretty fast as a kid and if I could beat him in a 200 meter dash would he come and work for us."

"You forgot the part about *was I an honorable man?*"

"Oh yeah, I asked him that first." (Trying to hold back her laugher)

"And of course you told her that you were, right Roger?"

"Of course Mark, how else can anyone answer that question? So we waited for the track to clear in front of us and I offered to let her do the count down. You know… *on your mark, get set, go!*"

"I should have known something was wrong when she said I should do it and mentioned something about being a woman's libber. That was the last time I saw her face."

"So how much did you beat her by?"

"I didn't know you were such a chauvinist Mark." She said playfully.

"What do you mean Cassandra?"

"Who said *HE* won?" (Laughing out loud now)

"I thought you were a sub four minute miler Roger?"

"Yes sir I am… or rather *I was*. That's a middle distance race and not a sprint. As it turns out *Ms. Jones over there* was once a world class sprinter and she quite easily *smoked my ass!*"

(Everyone in the room was having a good laugh now…)

"So how much did she beat you by?"

"I'd rather not say sir." (Truly embarrassed.)

*"Cassandra?"*

"Let's just say that we would have needed *car lengths* to answer that question Sir."

"In my defense Sir she was only three quarters of a second off the World Record in her prime and only one second slower than that back then."

"Is that record still standing?" Their amused boss inquired.

"Yes Sir, Flo-Jo set it at 21.34 seconds in 1988."

"Flo-Jo?" asked McNulty.

"Yes Sir, that's how everybody in the sport knows Florence Griffith-Joyner. I never did beat her although my PR came running against her that year. She was the most amazing athlete I ever knew… pure poetry in motion."

"People are capable of some pretty amazing things… we should all keep that in mind. McNulty said. Okay, that's enough entertainment for this morning, let's finish this up."

"You never did give me that rematch Cassandra."

"Anytime… anyplace youngster and I'll still spot you 20 yards."

"Okay folks… serious now. I want each of you to work together to understand the strength and weaknesses of our internal systems. What can be saved, what needs to be trashed and a wish list that includes ***must have*** functionality and would like to have capabilities but that you'd be willing to wait for. Identify what is standing in our way and what problems are insurmountable and must be overcome and how. We need your best ***guestimates*** on cost. You know a hundred times more about this stuff than I do so educate me at the strategic level and work together to come up with a reasonable ***long-term*** solution for us. Assume for the moment that money is no issue and that we'll find it."

"And the rest of the teams?" Asked Cassandra.

"Our counterparts will be doing the same thing at their ends and we'll be comparing notes shortly and coming up with an overall strategy. I need a preliminary report on my desk no later than Tuesday 4:00pm so get on this now people."

"Mark?"

"Yes Cassandra?"

"I just wanted to mention one more thing. You probably never heard of Jadavpur University but that's one of the top computer science colleges in the entire world. I know Ashim would never mention that to anyone. Do you know where their students go when they've been turned down by Jadavpur? … MIT sir. "

"Thank you Cassandra." Ashim offered modestly as they exited the room.

### *"Friends & Lovers"*

Jim Thoreau couldn't get Chrissie Edwards out of his head since their intimate night down in Baltimore. It was so much more than he had expected... all of it was... and now, as he planned for summer work he became more and more aware of how much he was going to miss her. Without another moments hesitation he picked up the phone and called her dorm room.

"Hello?" a sweet young voice answered.

"Hi Chrissie, this is Jim."

"Hi Jim, I was wondering when you were going to call me."

"I'm sorry Chrissie... it all happened so quickly and with summer vacations almost here I've been torn between wanting to see you and needing to find a job and it's been very confusing for me."

"I've been trying to figure out what I did that might have upset you."

"Nothing at all... I mean, our time together was really special to me... I just didn't expect what happened and now I'm caught between wanting to see you and not wanting you to go away for the summer and needing to find work. I don't know where we're going or even if there is a "we". Does that make any sense at all?"

"It makes perfect sense Mr. President... and I want to see you too... as much as I can. When are you free?"

"I'm getting ready for another trip down to Baltimore soon."

"Oh yeah, what for?"

"I'm going to meet with Tim again and the Station Director to talk about their summer intern program. It looks pretty good. I'm just not sure where I'll be living yet. It doesn't pay very much but it's the kind of experience I want so that part doesn't matter too much."

"Sounds like a nice opportunity. How long will you be gone?"

"Just a few days this time... probably next weekend into Monday, I'm not sure yet. Would you like to come along?"

"That sounds great... I'd love too. My aunt lives down there and we're very close. She'd love to have me come and stay for a while and I'm sure you'd be welcome too."

"That would be great and it saves me from worrying about a cheap motel. I just wish we didn't have to go our separate ways this summer. It's going to be a long couple of months."

"It doesn't need to be..."

"What do you mean?"

"I'm sure I could find something temporary down there even if it's just waitressing. I don't mind at all Jim, I'd much rather be near you. I can still visit my parents for a week before heading down and that would give you a chance to settle in to your new job."

"That's if I get it... that would be so wonderful. You'd do that for me?"

"No... but I'd do that for *us*. You're very special to me and I don't want to lose that."

"You've been a great friend to me Chrissie but this is all happening so fast... I don't want to do anything to screw up our friendship."

"You're the smartest, sweetest boy I've ever known and I doubt there is anything you could do that would ever hurt me. We'll just take it easy and see where this goes. You know I love you don't you Jim?"

"Yes, I do… you're the best friend I've ever had. I love you too… I've loved you since we first met."

"Maybe we could stay with Aunt Norma this summer."

"That would be unbelievable." He said stunned at the way this was all coming together.

# "Work Hard, Play Hard"

Ignoring the **do not disturb** sign hanging from the doorknob Mathew Creagor knocked at room 1705 of the Westin Peachtree Hotel at exactly 11:00 am Saturday morning. A few moments later Messer opened the door. He was a slender man of relatively small stature. Creagor noted that he was perhaps five feet nine inches tall and no more than a hundred and sixty-five pounds. He had piercing blue eyes, light brown hair and was perhaps in his late forties or early fifties. **He looked harmless enough...** Creagor thought before reminding himself that the opposite was true.

"Good morning, I'm Matthew."

"Come in." Messer said blandly.

In his bed was a beautiful young woman with strawberry blonde hair and green eyes. She was obviously surprised by the unexpected interruption and covered herself with sheets in feigned modesty.

"I'm sorry sweetie but I have business to get to. You need to go."

The night had been a very profitable one for her and there was no need to act insulted now. Instead she stood up naked in full view of both men and then hesitated just long enough for Matt to drink in the full magnitude of her beauty. A few minutes later she was dressed in her slinky evening gown and heels and was heading for the door.

"Thank you for a wonderful evening Bob." She said before kissing him on the cheek and then giving Matt a seductive look as she closed the door behind her.

"Well you sure have good taste anyway." Creagor quipped.

"Yes, she was a pleasant distraction. So how did your team do?"

"Not as well as we had hoped. We thought we would have a few more days but I seriously doubt if that would have mattered much. This guy has been a lot tougher than the others."

"So are you telling me that you have nothing planned yet?" Messer said with obvious annoyance.

"Nothing I feel that good about Sir. We do have two scenarios I wouldn't want to do by myself."

"Let's have them." He said brusquely. "Best one first..."

"That one is a sniper shot that you may or may not be able to make... you'll have to tell me. You'd be on the roof of an adjacent twenty-three story building and shooting nearly straight down to street level at his armored car, which slows to about three miles an hour to negotiate the tight entrance into the underground garage. You'd have three to five seconds at most to shoot."

"That scenario will do fine. I'll need a Barrett M82A1 .50-caliber rifle and scope. I never travel with mine unless *I know* I'm going to need it ahead of time. I already have the armor piercing rounds with me and no car I've ever seen can stand up to them, armor or not."

"Where the Hell did you get those? We were told they were illegal to buy by civilians. We've been keeping a low profile around here so we just didn't question it any further and went for standard munitions."

"Well, you've been misinformed. Our Department of Defense needed an outlet for their huge excess of .50 caliber ammo so they created a *Conventional Demilitarization Program* to pay a US company to take possession of their surplus. That company in turn refurbishes the ammo and sells it back into the civilian marketplace to the tune of hundreds of thousands of rounds *every year*... and half of those are armor piercing. Your sources on this end are full of shit. Check with your bosses... I'm sure they know about it and I'd bet they have a significant stash of their own already. Where will he be sitting?"

"Uh, who… the target?"

"No… *MICKEY FUCKING MOUSE*… who else do you think I'd be talking about?"

"Sorry, my mind was still trying to get around what you just told me about the ammo. He'll be in the right rear passenger seat of the car."

"Alright, then just get me the Barrett… I need that penetration power on this one or it's no go."

"I'm sure our sniper team has at least one of those… that model number is still in my head along with the $8,000 price tag. We're definitely going to need that rifle back when you're done."

"I'm leaving it on the roof… the rest is your problem."

"Fair enough, we'll be there working with you on this."

"I work alone… or didn't they tell you that?"

"Our guys are top notch… they've been trained by the best. Two will be on the ground to alert you of the targets approach and they'll never even see you. The other can act as an extra set of eyes and will take care of the weapon afterwards. That way you'll be free to focus on the target with at least thirty seconds of lead time before it gets there."

"Okay, as long as you're the guy on the roof. What type of car is it?"

"No problem, I'll be there. He'll be in a Forest Green Rolls Royce Phantom with the custom armor plating upgrade."

"What an asshole."

"What do you mean?"

"You'd think someone smart enough to run a company would have half a brain in his head. He goes out and spends close to a half million dollars on a car that can withstand AK47 fire from 10 feet away and we're going to take him out with less than a hundred bucks worth of ammo. This is one dumb-ass bastard. What time does he arrive at the garage?"

"Typically between 7:00 and 7:30 am."

"Good, nice and early before most people get in to work."

"We'll have surveillance at his house too, just to let us know what time they leave. That'll give us thirty minutes to get to the roof and set up. We've got the keys already so that's no problem."

"Good. I'll need you to get me to a safe shooting area where I can test the weapon and make the final adjustments."

"Sure, that's easy enough… how about tomorrow morning?"

"That's fine... but early… same time as the hit. I want to be taking my first shots at 7:15 am."

"Done… I'll pick you up Sunday morning at 6:30. How long do you think you'll need at the range?"

"Two hours should be plenty. Let's get this done with… I hate hanging around places that I don't know."

"Yeah, I could see that when I walked in this morning." Creagor said with a smirk.

"She's right in the phone book anytime you want her."

"Thanks, but not likely… I don't think my wife would appreciate it very much."

"That's where you know I'm smarter than you are Matt."

"Single?"

"Yes sir and Matt, one more thing…"

"Yes?"

"You did real good on this… I mean it. You didn't know my capabilities but you still gave me everything I needed."

Matt nodded his appreciation before offering his handshake and then leaving the room. *Now that's a good man…* Messer thought before heading for a hot shower and another round of room service.

## *"Shut Up and Listen!"*

Emily Thompson joined the Dreyden family at their estate on Sunday morning at ten o'clock as planned. The servant that opened the expansive front door was a tall and distinguished looking Negro. From his thick and powerful build she immediately presumed that he was more than he appeared.

"Good morning." He said first.

"Good morning." She replied politely. "Would you let Mr. Dreyden know that Emily Thompson is here."

"Yes Ma'am... please come in."

He left her in the foyer and proceeded to the den. He knocked quietly before entering uninvited. A minute later Maxwell Dreyden appeared from the door and waived her in.

"Good morning Emily." He offered with enthusiasm. "It's good to see you."

"Thank you Mr. Dreyden. You seem chipper this morning."

"Beautiful day and everything seems to be going well... and now you're here to help make sure it keeps on going that way."

"Yes sir, I mean Max. We've come up with a number of recommendations for you and your family."

"Great! Come into my study and let's get comfortable. Would you care for some coffee or tea?"

"No thanks, I'm fine."

Closing the door behind them he guided her to a luxurious leather chair next to the unlit fireplace. He took the seat across from her, sat down and waited silently.

"First off…" Emily began. "Much of what we're going to discuss today were ideas generated by Lou Farentino. Being with you so much of the time has allowed him to see patterns in your movements that are extremely dangerous."

"How so Emily?"

"If the enemy knows where you're going to be and most importantly, *when you're going to be there,* then it's a simple tactical exercise to plan and carry out their mission, whatever it may be…"

"You mean assassination and kidnapping, things along those lines?"

"Yes sir. Your status makes you a high-profile target for both. A third area also concerns us. Your company's products make you a target to anyone with a rifle and a scope who has lost a loved one to cancer. It's not easy to prepare for a madman who is willing to die for a lost loved one."

"I see, but that's what your good at right? Keeping my family safe?"

"Yes, we can improve your chances of survival and help protect your family."

"You're talking as if we were already under attack."

"There are strong indicators across the country that we are Mr. Dreyden, even if no one has made an attempt on your life just yet. We feel it may be imminent or at least we're working under that assumption in order to prepare for the worst case scenarios. We need to be ready for them as early as possible in order to do our jobs properly."

"That makes sense. You had mentioned something about dogs?"

"Yes, that's a good first step for the home. We have access to trained German shepherd's that will give your family more security… and yes… they are perfectly safe unless you command them otherwise. They will never turn on the family. You will need to attend a training session to take advantage of their skills but that's easy and it should be fun. Anyone in your family over the age of thirteen can attend."

"Okay, my kids will get a big kick out of that… they're fourteen and fifteen. My wife said she was okay with it as long as they were safe around the family."

"Yes Mr. Dreyden, they will die to protect your family if necessary. These are very special pairs of animals that are precisely matched and mated for life. That makes them committed to each other as well."

"We don't need any pregnant watchdogs Emily."

"Of course not… that's already been taken care of. The reason we use dogs that are **bonded**, which might be a better term, is because they act differently than putting two males or two females together. They seem to compliment each other more effectively this way. They're both more loving and devoted while being more dangerous to anyone trying to harm **their family**. It'll take a little time for you all to adjust to one another but this is one of the most effective things that you can do around the home at any price."

"Just out of curiosity… how much are they?"

"Twenty-thousand a pair Max, trained and ready to move in. They're worth every penny… so **please** trust me on this one."

"Done… what else do you suggest?"

"Take the black and brown pair over the white… they'll be harder to see at night in case you have an intruder in your yard. It is probable that this step alone would have saved the Lockheed executive's life."

**"Sold!** What else?"

"You need to vary your movements. Lou says you're as predictable as a watch."

"Why didn't he say something to me?"

"He did sir, a few times but it stopped there and nothing ever changed. He doesn't have the authority to do it without you taking the lead."

"Ouch, I'll have to apologize to him but I do a lot of my reading in the car and tend to zone out on everything else."

"That's another mistake Mr. Dreyden. I don't want you to walk around paranoid or anything but I do want you to take ownership in your own safety and pay more attention to your surroundings. You may wind up saving your own life."

"That's a solid point. Do you have any training programs that could help?"

"Yes we do. Forget basic self defense in your position... by the time they got close enough for you to use it you'd be long dead. What we do offer our clients is a more practical common sense approach. We teach you how to break out of your predictable routines and what to do in various crisis situations so you don't freeze. You won't need defensive driving unless you accept my next recommendation."

"What's that?"

"Alternate your route to work and even more importantly, don't rest so much faith on that armored Rolls of yours. Remember, John Richard's had one too and it didn't do him a bit of good."

"His was a Mercedes."

"Do you think a .50 caliber armor piecing bullet gives a shit sir?"

"I see your point Emily... sorry."

"No apologies needed but this is **THE most important thing** you have to think about right now. It's more serious than your company's stock portfolio, where you're going to on vacation, or even your wife's birthday. If you make a mistake here then you're just another dead target that was taken down by some angry Tom, Dick or Harriet with a sniper rifle. Have I made myself perfectly clear sir?"

"Yes, Emily you have and I do appreciate it. Thanks for suggesting that my wife and family **NOT** attend this meeting. How do we start?"

"We start **right now** Mr. Dreyden… let's call in Lou to talk about travel security issues and measures we can implement to negate them."

"That sounds good to me."

"One quick question about your, um, doorman? Navy Seal?"

(Laughing) "Something like that… without the water."

"Good, I'm glad I passed on the coffee."

"Me too."

# *"C minus, Not Good Enough"*

Joe Clark opened his portable computer, plugged the compact flashcard reader/writer into the USB port, inserted the rectangular card into the correct slot and then turned on the PC. He listened as the powerful HP whirred to life and watched as his Windows Operating Systems materialized before his eyes on the plasma screen, he clicked the question mark icon to access the bullet proof security program they had purchased and then pointed its' high powered algorithmic code at the single file contained on the remote flash card. When the password prompt appeared he carefully entered the random sixteen digit alpha-numeric code that he had laboriously memorized.

A few seconds later the list of 90 names, addresses and short company bio's appeared before him in their order of importance determined by the committee. ***Dear God...*** he thought to himself... ***They can't be serious...*** He looked past the first two names and saw that the next five targets were all ones that he could concur with. He then scanned the rest of the list and counted a total of thirty-three names that he definitely had a problem with. All of the targets were within his region and he had plenty to get started on. The others were going to need some serious discussion with General Andersen before he or any of his men were going to get involved.

He memorized the first ten targets for his five platoon leaders and then closed the file, removed the card and brought it to the attic. Once there he tied a string through the heavy metal washer and around the plastic case that protected the card before dropping the bundle behind the drywall where it fell eight feet inside the enclosed wall.

Returning to his office he erased his previous keystrokes from the computers memory with a special software designed for that purpose. Nothing was left to point to the reader/writer or the program that was read from that external drive. Then he signed onto the Internet and entered his Yahoo Messenger name of ***"Dopey"*** and his password. From there he sent an instant message to ***Deputy Dog***, which simply read: ***57 out of 90 on test... Need help on the ones I missed. Thanks.***

## *"Forgiveness"*

Three Star General Aaron William Andersen tuned on his computer and another instant message popped up on his screen. He entered his password and clicked on the message from Dopey. This was the second one he had received from his commanders since the flash cards were distributed and both contained similar inferences to the identical objection.

So far, including his take on the overall list they had 105 targets that were agreeable to two of his commanders. The third, Sergeant Major Wallace would probably contact him in the next few days or he would take it upon himself to initiate that communication.

Meanwhile he logged out of Yahoo messenger as Deputy Dog and logged back in as *Snow White III*. Then, rather than send one message to both of his "little dwarves" he made sure to send them each their own to minimize any attention that his communication might otherwise draw from prying eyes. He simply wrote; *"I agree… we'll talk about it later so I can clear it up for you."*

Within 24-hours the third commander had contacted him with the same complaint. Of the 216 total targets on their *financier's hit list* there were now a total of 72 targets that were off-limits and those names would never be known by any of their platoon leaders.

This was serious enough to require some delicate planning before the money men recognized what had been done behind their backs and began to question them about it. Each of the commanders had received permission to continue down the list of agreeable targets and they were on course to escalate their actions to the next level without further guidance.

Now it was up to Andersen to work out their differences with the industrialists who still thought they pulled all the strings. For now no action was necessary... he'd simply wait until they raised the red flag on the issue and continue the mission as he saw fit. ***Forgiveness is easier to obtain than prior approval...*** he reminded himself.

## *"Hunting Grounds"*

Matt Creagor called up to Messer's room from the hotel lobby phone at precisely 6:30 the next morning. They had a brief exchange and then met downstairs before proceeding to Matt's two year old Chevy Impala. They were on their way before Messer asked;

"How did you make out?"

"We had a choice of two Barrett M82A1s… looks like you guys are in agreement as to which gun is the best. We have the one with the superior scope."

"It's not the best anymore but it's pretty damn close and only the military can get the enhanced version. They're mostly minor things anyway, light and noise suppression systems… mainly so the enemy doesn't know where the shooting is coming from. That won't help them if they need tracers to pinpoint their fire. There are times when I actually prefer the noise and use it to my advantage… it scares civilians half to death and their panic makes it easier for me to withdraw."

"That's interesting… I'll remember that. You didn't mention it but I brought three dozen standard .50-caliber rounds in case you didn't have enough with you."

"Good, I was thinking we were going to have to wait until a gun store opened up."

"Not on Sunday… we'd be off until tomorrow to try again."

"That's right… I lost track of my days there. Thanks for picking up the dropped ball on that one Matt."

"My pleasure Bob... I understand how taxing a little R&R can be."

"You have no idea… that pretty little lady damn near killed me."

(Both men laughing at the thought of dying that way…)

"Hell of a way to go though… with a great big shit eating grin on your face."

"Try explaining that one to the missus."

"No thanks… if I wasn't dead yet she sure would finish me off. What if it's overcast like this tomorrow? What does that do to our plans?"

"This? This is nothing… as long as I can see the car clearly from the roof we'll have a good target. Okay?"

"Sounds good… the weather report says it's going to get a little worse before clearing up later tonight so I think we'll have a clear morning."

"How much farther is it to your range?"

"Right up there… we all hunt deer on this guy's property and he doesn't mind us practicing from time to time. He loves venison and my wife is a great cook and always freezes a lot for him after a kill."

"What about the noise Matt? These aren't exactly 30-06s we'll be shooting."

"No highways nearby… this a rural road with only farms speckled a few miles apart, plus this guy is about 80 and pretty hard of hearing. He'll probably think he's having a good day because he can hear the rounds."

"Alright Matt… just remember to help me clean up any trace of our presence here. We don't want any shell casings on the ground. We'll set our target at the distance we'll be shooting tomorrow and take as few shots as needed to sight-in the scope. If your sniper is any good it should take a half dozen rounds… otherwise it might be a dozen or two."

The two men pulled down the dirt road heading onto the farmers land and found a spot that would provide the distance and elevation needed. The angle would be less than optimal but that could be compensated for. It took Messer only eight shots to feel confident that they were completely ready.

# *"Molon Lobe"*

"Good evening ladies and gentlemen and welcome to another episode of ***Door To Door***. Last week you may recall that I got a little agitated by the senseless deaths in our schools. This past week, following the slaying of John Richards and his driver in Charlotte, I did a little investigating on my own. No, I'm not a P.I., gumshoe or even an avid fan of Nancy Drew mystery novels... but I am able to type, *with two fingers mind you*, ask reasonably intelligent questions and wait while vast amounts of public domain knowledge come flooding across my computer screen from around the world. ***Jack, turn off the phones...*** because tonight I have something to say to all of you... something I learned this week and it's something we all need to know about but ***nobody*** *and I mean* ***NOBODY*** is talking to us about it. So tonight for the first time in my career I'm telling my audience; ***You're NOT on the air... I am!*** Then, ***IF*** I'm still alive next week... and that's a ***BIG "IF"*** we will take your questions and go back to thinking that we're all safe and in ***the very best of hands*** with our current leadership.

Does anyone know what weapon killed Mr. Richards? It was a 30-06 sniper rifle. You know, the kind of gun we like to hunt Bambi with. It's a very nice weapon and with a good scope it's accurate for maybe a thousand yards or so. You can even buy armor piercing bullets for it in case your deer has a metal plate in its head. Okay, I can live with that... hunter's have rights too, just as we do, the average law abiding citizen and ***I DO*** happen to *believe in our constitution* even though many of our elected leaders think it's time to dismantle it piecemeal.

Alright, so there I am typing away and asking questions about sniper rifles and lo and behold up pops more information than I could ever want to know about the .50-caliber versions of that lesser 30-06 rifle. Do you happen to know how old you have to be to buy a hand gun? Come on... write it down... tick, tick, tick... ***twenty one!*** Now isn't that strange when we send our adult children, or are they just children-children... we never did figure that out last week... anyway, we send them off to fight our wars when they're only 18 and they can't even buy a lousy handgun ***legally*** until they're 21. ***Assault & sniper rifles,***

**grenades, bazookas, bombs,** all at the age of 18… *as long as they're in the military,* but **no handguns** for you kiddies here at home.

Okay, they've got it half right… Or rather, half-correct… I don't want any flaming idiots out there thinking I'm standing up for the right wing extremists of this country because I think you're all a bunch of greedy lunatic war mongers. They got the part correct about having to be *twenty-one* to be old enough to get a handgun and that should be true of *any weapon, any where!* There's the proof that the military has been stealing our children out from under our noses and we *"the loving parents"* have been letting them. I'm not looking for a rerun of last weeks show so let's get on with the new materials, shall we class?

Okay, an 18 year old walks into a legitimate gun store and puts his Photo ID license on the counter and asks to buy a handgun. *Nope, sorry kid, come back when you're 21 and as long as you haven't committed a felony by then I'll be happy to sell you one or two, HECK… as many as you want!* Okay, so this same kid walks out the door, makes an about-face and walks right back in. *"F" the 9mm…* he says; *Give me the .50-caliber sniper rifle, matching scope and 1,000 rounds of ammo. Make half of those rounds armor piercing and half of THOSE incendiary rounds.* Now here's another question for you… got your pencil ready? What does the owner of the legitimate gun store say? Tick, tick, tick… times almost up… *ready?*

He says *"OKAY"!* Takes the kids' 10 thousand dollars, *he probably charged it on his brand new credit cards* and everybody is happy. No laws were broken; the store owner just made a killing, oh excuse me, must have been a Freudian slip, I mean he just made a nice big profit and the kid, who was 17 years old only *yesterday* just walked out of the store with a state of the art killing machine. Now is it just me or is this scenario just a little bit out of *whack*? Damn, there I go again… I mean; *a little bit out of the bounds of logic and reason?*

The flood of information kept drowning my computer and then all of a sudden there it was; *the maximum range of the 50 caliber round is between 7,000 and 8,000 yards, depending on the specific type of ammunition.* Okay, that's interesting but what does it mean? So I scratched my head for a second and remembered that there are 5,280 feet in a mile and three feet in a yard, times 8,000 yards equals 24,000 feet, divide that by 5,280 feet and that equals 4.5454545454545454... you know, one of those *repetend* numbers that goes on forever? After I got over the absolute beauty of that hypnotizing pattern I woke up and realized it meant that this highly accurate *armor piercing weapon* could shoot for *four and a half miles!*

The kid could take down a plane at *four and a half miles!* He could blow up an oil refinery at *four and a half miles!* He could incinerate any propane tanker on a truck or on a train or just plain sitting there **stationary** at that *giant* depot in YOUR back yard at *four and a half miles!* He could take out a chemical factory... like at Bhopal India for example. If he was so inclined he could kill thousands and thousands of people with any *single* API round. Oh, excuse me, that's military jargon for ARMOR PIERCING INCENDIARY munition. That's the one that blows up AFTER it cuts through your quarter million dollar armor-plated passenger car like it was made of butter. Sorry for all you millionaires that may be listening but you will no longer be able to feel safe in your armored cars because any lunatic, that hasn't been convicted of a felony, can buy one of these guns and shoot you like a fish in a barrel anytime they damn well please and it's all compliments of our ever popular *Military-Industrial Complex*.

I have a fairly morbid sense of humor and that's probably why half our listeners are out there... because you're all as sick as I am. I just figure if you can't laugh at the situation then what do you have left? Fear or rage, I personally prefer laughter. Anyway, I'm getting away from the point I was trying to make. I was trying to prove that the escalation of war doesn't work and is a *total waste of our time, intelligence and short tenure on this planet as the dominant species.* Example number one; our astronauts complained that their pens didn't write upside down in outer space... okay, we can fix that NASA says and out comes the, *what was it... the rollerball*? Now I happen to like that pen... *I'm drawing mushroom clouds with it right now.* I heard it cost a *million dollars* of R&D to develop it. Do you know what the Russian's did with the exact same problem? Come on, here's you chance to get your score back up to even... tick, tick, tick... *ready?* *They used pencils...* at a nickel a piece. Gotta love the *kiss* principle. Okay, so you're all reasonably smart listeners, what do you think example number two is? (Pause) *RIGHT!* It's the kid with the ten dollar bullet against the executive with the quarter million dollar armored car! *That's* why Star Wars will never work... *our "SDI" - Strategic Defense Initiative* is just our latest and greatest game show where we can all watch our children's educations get poured down the drain of some trillionaire's bidet. But that's okay... the executives need better armor plated cars because the ones they're using right now really *aren't* safe anymore. So let's talk about star wars for a minute. You're all aware of what it is, aren't you?

It's that *STRATEGIC UMBRELLA* that's going to protect us *AND OUR* ALLIES from nuclear attack. Forget the fact that we're *spitting in the face* of those we signed arms treaties with... and why, so we could build a whole new generation of *TACTICAL NUKES.* You see, the ones we already have are only going to last another fifty years or so, which mean that we *must have* a more appropriate deterrent... you know, the kind of nuclear device that can fit into a suitcase or dive through the ground as easily as a .50-caliber bullet can cut through bullet-proof glass. We need to be able detonate our multi-megaton weapons on anyone, anywhere and in any way that we see fit... to HELL with international laws... we've got the biggest stick the world has ever seen and we're not afraid to use it. Thanks Teddy.

It doesn't matter that *no one* is attacking us. What matters to *our leaders* is that they *might*. You know they're right, there's that damn word again but it fits this time, they're right that the populations of entire countries might go into suicidal mass hysteria... just look at Palestine, hmmm, or even IRAQ. It matters little that grossly negligent policies inflicted upon those populations by US-backed Israel against Palestine or the United States, all by ourselves, were responsible for these pockets of insanity. What matters is that we keep the world on the brink of destruction so we can profit more.

So we decide we need these bombs because the tens of thousands of nukes we have already aren't enough and so we *break the treaties.*

Now what would you do if you were an industrialized Nation other than America? Tick, tick, tick - bzzzz. **_Defend yourself!_** Wouldn't you? Or would you just let some future Hitleresque-type march into your country and kill who ever he pleases? So, thanks to our all but brilliant leaders and tacticians the arms race is now on again full tilt.

Think about this for a moment; our species has never done anything but *escalate war*. It has never gone to less lethal methods and let's all share a little secret that we already know, *it never will!* Let's see; stones to bones, to clubs, to spears, to bows and arrows, to swords and shields, to crossbows, to guns... Okay, you get my point. What we have *never tried* as a species is *PEACE*... pure and simple peace. You almost have to whisper that word in this country or the right-wing will try to convince everyone that you're some kind of *red-bellied, liberal-pussy, anti-American, chicken livered communist!*

Doing this research there was about an hour there where I had to lie down until the desire to vomit subsided and then I had the realization. *What the Hell was I getting all worked up about?* And I had to laugh at myself again... you should too. What I had forgotten was that this potentially dumb psycho kid I've been talking about *couldn't even buy a hand gun*. All of a sudden I started feeling safe again.

It's really *not as bad* as I was making it out to be. Even if he, or any one else bought one of these cool .50 caliber weapons they could only hit *large targets* at that four and a half mile range. Small targets, like our heads... are only sure shots at much shorter distances... say a half mile. That's not so bad for an amateur now is it? And our theoretical kid isn't even trained yet... you know like the kind of training our military is going to give him. When he comes back home that kid will be able to hit a grapefruit at a mile or more! I sure am glad that I'm not a grapefruit! Or he could practice on his own at some neat targets like planes, helicopters, natural gas storage tanks... jeeze, the list just goes on and on... oil pipelines, electrical transformers, fiber optic cable installations, heads of state, kids with bad complexions and maybe even Bambi... just to keep it looking nice and reasonable.

Now what would you think if our own ***Department of Defense*** was responsible for this? By selling ***hundreds of thousands of... get this now... "EXCESS".50-caliber munitions EVERY SINGLE YEAR*** to a company that's just across the river from the Pentagon... for ***a buck a truck load*** mind you. They refurbish it and sell some of it back to the military and some to the general population. Don't worry though, that same company also makes explosives with the gunpowder that's recovered from the ammo that they can't reuse and it's used for road construction. So you see it's really quite alright... they're beating swords into plowshares... and that's a good thing... right? And that's exactly how these Public Relation firms work... brag about the good and hide away the evil and everything else is just fine... at least at the bottom line of this ally to our Pentagon.

So now you too can be the first kid on your block to be able to take down a 767 in mid-air... just like in the war games they've been feeding us since before we could walk. Half of those munitions sold to the public by this friend of the Pentagon's are ***armor piercing munitions*** and a good portion of those are *incendiary rounds*... You remember, the kind that go **BOOM** and start fires, big ones after they penetrate armor. Were you aware of these facts? I sure as Hell wasn't.

Before tonight's show raised your consciousness did you know that there were literally many ***hundreds of thousands*** of these .50-caliber munitions in the hands of our law-abiding citizens? Only God knows how many are in the hands of criminals, drug dealers and terrorists.

But I'm okay now so don't you worry about me. My new friend Jim made me feel better when he called me today. I don't know if you heard the show a few weeks back but he was the one talking about lowering the voting age to at least sixteen. He made a good case for it. Anyway, I was spewing out a lot of what was bothering me about tonight's topic and he shared some very interesting insights with me.

First he told me that I was blowing the sniper rifle thing way out of proportion and what I should be worrying and talking about are the tens of thousands of ICBMs Russia and America still have pointing at each other and those (23) Trident submarines that we have patrolling the world. Here I am worrying about a few thousand .50-calbier sniper rifles with a *one-shot one kill capacity* and then all of a sudden he had me thinking that only one Trident nuclear submarine out of our first-strike arsenal could launch *twenty-four* intercontinental ballistic missiles *simultaneously* mind you. Okay, I thought… guestimating that to be a nuclear yield of perhaps twenty-four Nagasaki and Hiroshima attacks, which is what I told him before he corrected not only my math but my understanding of our current capabilities.

He said; *Tim, Tim, Tim… you've got it all wrong. EACH of those twenty-four missiles is capable of deploying seventeen SEPARATE warheads that will hit within 300 feet of their target which can be up to 7,000 MILES away.* Then he walked me through the math with a simple drawing. He told me to take blank paper and put a single dot in the middle; *that's ONE of those subs…* Then he told me to draw random lines in all directions and distances reaching the far edges of the paper. *Those are the (410) TEN-megaton ICBMs that one ship can launch simultaneously and this paper represents HALF THE WORLD!* Please remember that the horrific bombs that leveled two of Japan's cities had only a *one*-megaton yield each. A single sub has *Four-Thousand-One-Hundred-Megatons* of killing capacity… and we have *twenty-three* of these on patrol and our government wants us to believe that our nuclear arsenal is out of date and that we should give them more of our tax dollars! I'm game… how about you?

So it seems that I owe you all an apology for wasting your time tonight talking about such trivial matters as hand guns versus sniper rifles. I've been talking about pea-shooters when Dirty Harry is out there with a Magnum at our head, which was a .44-caliber weapon by the way… with a bullet that isn't even half an inch wide. Pfffft.

(Softer, slower now… more retrospective)

So there I was absorbing all of this lunacy and trying to figure out a way to end violence before humanity destroys itself once and for all… and now here I am… mad as Hell at the World's leaders for letting it get this far out of control. Then I thought back to the Pentagon Officials who seemingly let the Jeanie out of the bottle with this stupid dissemination of awesome firepower… and then I settled upon the wisdom of our Founding Fathers and the foresight to write the 2nd Amendment into our Constitution, *"the right to bear arms"*… *so* we can defend ourselves against our enemies *both foreign and domestic.*

Then I recalled a bit of research that came up this morning that was interesting but I had laid it aside…it was little Latin phrase; *"Molon Lobe".* It was shouted at the Persians by the ancient Greeks of Sparta when they *were TOLD to surrender their weapons.* They were yelling back to the incredible mass of humanity that threatened them; *"Molon Lobe" "Molon Lobe" "Molon Lobe" Come and get them!*

I now see a day when our law-abiding citizens will all have tens of thousands of semi-automatic weapons and .50-caliber guns with API rounds and our government will cry in outrage that they should be banned, that they are a threat to our national security and have no obvious use *except for terrorism.* Yesterday I would have agreed with that argument but today, in light of all we've learned, I feel differently. We *DO* have an obvious use for them that our founding father's warned us about over two-hundred and thirty years ago.

There will come a day when our corrupted government will come knocking at *OUR* doors with their aircraft carriers and their ICBMs, their F-14 Tomcats, F-16s and F-18s, with their stealth fighters and stealth bombers, with their armored helicopters and tanks, with their privatized prisons and their stupid gas guzzling tax rebates for SUVs and let's *NOT* forget *the* 23 Trident Nuclear submarines…and they're going to yell; *surrender your weapons* or we will take them from you and we're going to shout back from the roof tops' *COME AND GET THEM! COME AND GET THEM! … Bullets first!*

I know there's a lot more to say about all of this and hopefully we'll be able to exchange a civilized conversation in the months ahead and maybe, just maybe our leaders will start listening to us for a change… but that's all the time we have tonight. This is Tim McManus at **WIQR, 103.5 FM – Baltimore**. Thanks for listening, dream well, goodnight."

## (1978 - 1982)

### *"Coming Home"*

David Stanton had returned home from Viet Nam three years earlier while serving his third voluntary tour of duty "in country". He was two months shy of completing it when the "Huskie" HH43B helicopter he was being transported in was shot down by an enemy rocket grenade near Saigon.

In the crash he herniated a disk in his lower back and fractured his right hip but somehow still managed to pull the pilot and one of the injured soldiers out of the burning chopper before it exploded, killing the three men still trapped inside. The blast threw him another twenty feet into a ditch where he fractured his collarbone and broke the femur of his left leg. When the medics arrived he ordered them to take care of the other men before collapsing into unconsciousness. It was two days before he awoke in excruciating pain in a nearby mobile army surgical unit.

For his valor he was awarded the Distinguished Service Cross while recuperating from his injuries in a Veteran's Hospital back in the States. His injuries were serious enough to keep him bed-ridden for the next six months, which was followed by another two years of painful physical therapy before he would be able to walk without a cane.

His high school sweetheart had filed for divorce during his second tour of duty and it was granted while he was still fighting for his country. She would never understand how he could choose to fight and risk death over coming back home to her and starting the family they had dreamt about. What he would never allow her to see was the horror written into his soul or how the inhumanity he witnessed could crawl under your skin and eat away at you until you didn't even recognize your own reflection.

They never discussed why he had been so adamant about getting married before he left but she suspected his motives and they frightened her. David was always carefully planning for their future and was now planning for hers in case he didn't make it. A widow's ransom was significantly more than a girlfriend's. What David never knew was that divorcing him was her way of saying; *I don't want the money my love, just come home to me.*

By the time he tried to reestablish himself as a civilian his wife was remarried and he was enduring the full brunt of the anti-war activists, many of whom treated him like a criminal because of the *My Lai Massacre* of 1968, which had happened when he was in eighth grade. Devastated by his losses and bitter over the treatment he had received from so many of the American people he found himself afloat in a sea of hostility, self-pity and rage.

It was while in this state of mind that he was recruited into a covert paramilitary organization within the US Government that specialized in political assassinations throughout the world. As soon as he was physically able they had him back in South East Asia sniping high-ranking South Vietnamese officials and military men who had traded their lives for those of thousands of American boys, most of whom were under the age of twenty one. Before he came home again, in September of 1981, his personal body count was up to twenty-seven souls... souls that would be burning in Hell for the rest of eternity... along with his own.

The next year Maya Lin's Viet Nam Memorial was built and dedicated in Constitution Gardens in Washington, DC. Major David Michel Stanton was only one of the millions of visitors that made the pilgrimage to *The Wall* that year. In full military dress he knelt before the memorial and wept uncontrollably like a child who had lost his mother. Onlookers were so overwhelmed at the sight of him that they couldn't help but cry themselves. A small boy, perhaps six years old, was the first to go to him and gently touch his bowed head. The mother and father of the child quietly joined him as did other families and soldiers who then knelt around him in a lifeboat of humanity. More than 58,000 souls were watching from the wall at that moment and every one of them was crying. Two and a half million more watched and asked why... why our country?

# *"The Hardest Part"*

At 6:00am Messer checked out of his hotel and retrieved the Lexus LS 430 rental car from the underground parking lot. Turning right onto the street he picked up Creagor who was waiting for him two blocks away wearing a dark blue business suit and carrying a Samsonite leather briefcase. The two men drove quietly to the twenty-three story building adjacent to the Dreyden tower and parked in the underground garage next to the service elevator that Creagor's team had secured access to.

Messer was also dressed in his dark blue suit and the two men exchanged final instructions before checking the time and popping the trunk to remove the rather large bag that contained the Barrett rifle. Meanwhile, Creagor had walked over to the elevator and pressed the button... by the time the door opened Messer was joining him. The time was 6:30 Monday morning.

They traveled the twenty-three floors in silence and when the elevator came to a stop Matt took out the keys he had obtained and locked the elevator in-place so no one else could access it. Matt then pressed the "door open" button and stepped out checking the top floor for any activity before directing Messer to the adjacent door that led to the last flights of stairs and onto the roof. Both men carried their primary handguns in a shoulder holster and a smaller pistol in their jacket pockets in case anyone was unlucky enough to get in their way during their escape.

On Matt's signal Messer stepped out of the elevator and pushed open the door to the stairwell. Matt followed closely behind as both men climbed the final two flights of stairs before reaching the locked door in front of them. The time was 6:34 and they only needed five minutes to set up from the roof itself so they made their final preparations inside the stairwell and awaited the phone call that would let them know their target was thirty minutes away.

"I'd feel a lot better Matt if you unlocked this door for me."

"Getting a little claustrophobic are we?"

"No… not hardly… I just want to make sure you have the God damn key!"

Messer laughed lightly to himself as Creagor unlocked the door.

"Feeling better?"

"Absolutely."

"Do you want to take a quick look?"

"We've got time Matt… it'll still be there in half an hour. There's no sense giving up our advantage too early… there're lot of windows in those skyscrapers out there. Did you bring your mask?"

"Yeah, it's right here."

"Be sure to put it on *before* you step outside that door… we don't want any surveillance cameras getting a look at our faces."

"Roger that."

"Did you check to make sure the phone had reception up here?"

*"Oh shit! No, I didn't!* A few harried moments later Matt was breathing a sigh of relief. "It works… good signal strength."

Messer laughed quietly again as Creagor fumbled with the phone…

"You should have seen your face Matt." He said still chuckling.

*"Fuck you!"* Matt offered back obviously unnerved.

(Ring…. Ring….)

Matt didn't answer the call, which rang only twice… he waited to get the caller ID number off the disposable phone and identified the number as his man on the Dreyden's house surveillance.

"Why didn't you answer that?"

"I saw his phone number so we know they're on the way."

"What if something's gone wrong? How would we know?"

"He's got five minutes to call back if necessary."

"That's pretty slick… no phone records?"

"Right, none… and these are unregistered disposable phones. The next call means they're thirty seconds away. Time check"

"6:52… that means ETA of between 7:20 to 7:30… we need to set up at 7:15. Until then we just wait right here. Hold on to you mask."

"I hate this part."

"It could be a lot worse… someone could be shooting back."

"How fast does that gun shoot Bob?"

"How fast can you aim and pull a trigger?"

"How many rounds in that clip?"

"It takes ten but I've got eight in there so it won't jam."

"What's the kick like?"

"Ever fire a 12-gauge shotgun?"

"Yeah… plenty of times."

"It feels about the same… only quite a bit faster."

"6:55."

# *"Reflections"*

By 6:49 am Lou Farentino had finished cleaning the windshield of the Rolls and was opening the armored garage door with the remote control built into the luxurious rosewood paneled dashboard. He watched as the doors closed behind him and then drove down the long driveway before pressing another button that activated the motors on the custom made Adamantite alloy armored gates. *"Those babies must have cost the boss a fortune…"* He thought to himself as they slid effortlessly in opposite directions.

Exiting the driveway he turned right down the broad residential street that pointed gently downward like an express runway directly at the city of Atlanta. If not for these old trees his boss could fly from here… he mused as he enjoyed the distant view and the way the sun's rays bounced playfully off the modern skyline.

The morning air was crisp and clean and the white billowy clouds foretold of a beautiful day. Then the red fuel warning light flashed on the dashboard and he had to grimace at the thought of having to fill the beast up one more time. If there was a car out there with worse gas mileage he couldn't think of it… oh yes he could… those rocket cars had to get worse mileage than this pig… *but not much worse.* He chuckled to himself. *I'll stop at the first gas station….*

## *"Easy, Smooth, Relaxed, Gooood"*

At 7:14 am Messer and Creagor pulled their masks over their faces and adjusted the eyes and mouth holes. Messer then picked up the blanket that contained the weapon and motioned Creagor to the door. *"Slowly..."* He cautioned as Matt opened the unlocked door and paused for a few moments to allow them time to adjust their eyes to the bright sunlight.

*"So much for being overcast..."* said Messer softly as he looked around at the windows looking down at them from adjacent buildings. *"Next time take the longer shot and get me as high as possible... Okay, let's go..."*

Creagor led Messer slowly to the spot along the east wall that had been identified by his surveillance team. The strength of the sun's reflections was a concern but nothing that a good pair of sunglasses couldn't overcome. Creagor then pointed to the Dreyden tower across from them and to the executive offices ten stories above. He then pinpointed the underground parking garage that was twenty-three stories below.

"That's a Hell of a shot from here..." Matt offered.

"Not with this setup it isn't..." Messer replied matter-of-factly. What's the time?"

"7:20..." Creagor replied with a hint of anxiety in his voice.

"Relax son, the eye catches motion so just stay still and low behind this wall and we'll be fine."

"7:25..." Creagor offered.

"Deep, slow breaths Matt... Easy... smooth... relaxed... good."

"What's that you're saying?"

"It's just a little mantra I taught myself during long hard races and mountain workouts when I was on the high school track team."

"What does it mean?"

"Nothing much, it's a reminder to keep running smooth, easy and relaxed. That little mantra helped me to focus my attention inside to my body's mechanics instead of being outside where the pain was."

(Ring… ring)

"Game time…" Messer said as he took a long deep breath and then gently exhaled, positioning his gun over the ledge and focusing the scope on the garage wall.

"I see it!" Creagor said excitedly.

"Got it…" Messer replied.

They both watched as the beautiful Rolls slowed and began the tight turn. Messer focused down to the gas tank for his first shot… it would be heavily armored but still no contest for the incoming API round. He exhaled, held his breath and squeezed the first shot off gently.

The explosive sound of the gunshots startled him more than the explosion of the car below. Creagor watched in silence as Messer squeezed off all eight rounds in rapid succession into the gas tank and right rear passenger area. The car buffeted from the explosions as it tried to get through the garage entrance but it stopped abruptly like an animal taken down with a head shot a short moment later. The car was clearly visible through the flames and Matt could swear he saw a nine inch hole carved into the vehicle where their target had just died.

Moving fast and low the two men left without policing the .50-caliber casings that had been ejected. They entered the doorway and locked it behind them. The gun was quickly packed away and the masks followed a few seconds later. The two men moved efficiently down the two flights of stairs and then took twenty seconds to breath together and compose themselves.

*"Easy, smooth, relaxed... good..."* Messer coached the young squad leader quietly.

Those seconds seemed like an eternity to Creagor as every fiber of his being was screaming to get away... ***what are you insane?*** His inner voice was echoing through the pounding in his temples and into the useless mass that was once his brain. Watching Messer he began to take long, slow, deep breaths until he had some of his composure back. It had taken thirty critical seconds before they were exiting the stairwell and making their way back into the frozen elevator. Matt reached for the keys clumsily and chastised himself for not having them ready. He then unlocked the elevator and pressed the lowest floor of the parking garage. When the door opened he could see the results of their surveillance had paid off as they exited into a nearly empty level of the garage. Then Messer set the pace to the car, which was thirty feet away and grabbed Creagor's wrist to make sure that he matched it. He popped the trunk and door locks simultaneously with the remote control and then placed the oversized bag inside. Twenty seconds later both men were heading for the exit that was furthest away from their attack. Messer pulled up to the parking attendant and handed him a dollar along with the ticket and drove away. A few seconds later they were turning onto the crowed street and heading away from the scene of their attack. Messer took off his thin leather gloves and put them into his jacket pocket next to his Beretta .32 caliber pistol.

"For a moment I thought you were going to kill that guy Bob."

"Is that what you would have done?" Messer replied.

"I don't know... I hadn't thought it through."

"We're supposed to be the ***good guys*** Matt. We don't kill indiscriminately... or there's no difference between us and them.

You're in line to be a commander and you need to start thinking more about what it is we're doing out here."

"How did you know that? I thought you were a hired hit man."

"That's what our soldier's think Matt... for my safety. Andersen asked me to give him my personal appraisal of you. I just did son."

Matt Creagor sat there in silence absorbing what he had just heard. Only the commander's knew Andersen by name so Messer couldn't just be a run of the mill assassin.

"May I ask where you know Andersen from Sir?"

"Cut the *sir* crap Matt... it's gonna get you busted. I shot a few bad guys for Aaron when were overseas."

"You two go back a long way?"

"Yeah Matt, we've been through a couple of lifetimes together."

## *"No Survivors"*

Emily Thompson was driving to her office when she heard the initial reports come over the radio. ***"Commuters heading into the downtown area of Atlanta avoid the blocks surrounding the Dreyden complex between…"***

Before waiting to hear anymore she immediately pressed the speed dial number for Lou Farentino's mobile phone. The phone rang through to his voice mail which she knew he rarely used. She left a brief message to call before dialing Maxwell Dreyden's personal line at the office… when his voice mail picked up she left another message and then selected the option that passed her call to his Executive Assistant… the phone rang seven times before an anxious woman's voice picked it up.

"Hello?" Was all that the distraught employee said...

"Is this Gladys… Mr. Dreyden's secretary?"

"No Ma'am… my name is Barbara Evans and we have an emergency here. Is your call of a critical nature?"

"My name is Emily Thompson and I'm with Mr. Dreyden's security team. Is Mr. Dreyden in Mrs. Evans?"

"No… Miss. Thompson… not yet."

"Would you please tell me what's going on over there?"

"Yes Ma'am… there's been an explosion outside of our parking garage. A few of our people are headed down there to find out what happened. We heard gunshots and an explosion coming from below."

"Do you know how many shots were fired?"

"No, we don't... everyone seems to have heard something different. The only thing we agree upon is that there were a lot of shots and then they just stopped."

"What did *you* hear Barbara?"

"At least five or six shots and an explosion… it was all over very quickly… they were all very close together. There's smoke coming from a burning car in front of our parking garage… that's all I know right now."

"Thank you Barbara, you've been very helpful."

"I'll let Mr. Dreyden know you called."

Emily hung up her portable phone expecting the worst and then drove the remaining five minutes to the scene. She was forced to park four blocks away and took the first space she could before ignoring the meter and running to the Dreyden complex. *"Damn, I should have asked which side of the building."* She thought to herself as she covered the distance as fast as she could. Close enough now to smell the burning rubber as she envisioned the horror she was expecting to see. As she turned the first corner to the Dreyden complex she was immediately hit with the full magnitude of the scene.

Less than fifty yards in front of her was a dark luxury sedan still burning out of control. She recognized the car immediately and pushed back a wave of nausea as her pace slowed to a bent-over walk. The black smoke had filled the air between the towers and the smell of burning flesh was now as obvious as the smell of the tires. When she reached the police barricade line she waived over the first policeman that looked in her direction. As he approached she pulled out her security credentials while noticing how the car was butted up half against the wall and half into the opening under the building. It was obvious to her that Lou had tried to get them underground but that the explosion had blown them too far off track. When the officer got to her she showed him her Dreyden Security Clearance and then joined him inside the barricade.

"Officer, were there any survivors?"

"No Ma'am… the driver was burned to death when the car exploded."

"What about Mr. Dreyden?"

"I don't know Ma'am… there was no one else in the car."

# *"Mr. Dreyden?"*

Upon hearing the officer's report Emily Thompson immediately pressed the speed dial code for the Dreyden residence. A rich, deep Negro voice answered the call.

"Hello, may I speak with Mr. Dreyden please? This is Emily Thompson."

"Yes Miss Thompson, one moment please."

(Twenty long seconds later…)

"Emily, good morning… and to what do I owe this pleasure?" He said in an uncharacteristically light mood.

"Sir, listen to me carefully. There has been an assassination attempt on your life."

"That's absurd… I just finished a lovely breakfast with my wife for a change."

"Sir, Lou's dead… He burned to death outside of the Dreyden building in your Rolls less than fifteen minutes ago."

"Dear Lord Emily… what happened?"

"In a second sir… please put your bodyguard on the phone first."

"Jason, I need you to speak with Emily Thompson…"

"Yes Miss Thompson, how can I help you?"

"There was an attempt on Mr. Dreyden's life this morning. They took out the Rolls Royce and Lou burned to death trying to get it into the underground lot. I think the killers are under the impression that they succeeded but I still need you to get Mr. Dreyden and his family into safe mode and keep them there until we can take the necessary next steps."

"I understand… we have a contingency plan for this."

"Thank you Jason… keep this line open and I'll get back to you as soon as I know more about what's gone on over here at the scene."

"Would you like to speak with Mr. Dreyden now?"

"No, tell him I'll be there within an hour and explain to him what you need to do **RIGHT NOW**… *you're the one in charge over there!*"

"Yes, I understand." (click)

*"Jason, what the Hell's going on?* Why did you hang up?

"The assassin's think they got you sir so we need to get you out of sight, *right now!* Then we need to get your family back together and wait for Emily to call with an update so we can decide where to go from here."

"Okay, my wife's here but we need to get the kid's out of school."

"I'll call the police sir and have them bring your children home."

"Thank you Jason. What else do you need me to do?"

"Just stay out of sight and try to relax and care for your family."

Emily Thompson hung up the phone and found the ranking officer on the scene.

"Are you in charge?"

"For the moment Ma'am. Why did that officer let you in?"

"I'm on Mr. Dreyden's security team and that's my man Lou Farentino in the driver's seat."

"I'm sorry Ma'am… It looks like he never had a chance."

"Can you walk me through the scene Officer?"

"Detective, Detective Ron Morrison... and you are?"

"I'm Emily Thompson." She said while showing him her ID.

"Well Miss Thompson we won't know a whole lot more until the fire is out."

"Why haven't they put it out already?"

"They wanted to but there's no one left to save and nothing left to burn… so I stopped them before they washed away our evidence."

"That was quick thinking Detective… So what *do* we know?"

"Look over here…" He said as he guided her to the driveway immediately in front of the entranceway. "What do you see?"

"Holes… Looks like one here, here… and here… and then one big one over there. They look like bullet holes… but they're awfully big if they are… and what the Hell is that big one… some sort of explosive?"

"I'm pretty sure they're *all* going to turn out to be bullet holes Miss Thompson… most probably .50-caliber API rounds."

"Armor piercing, right? But what's the "i" mean?"

"*Incendiary*… that's what ignited the gas tank."

"Then why that one big hole over there?"

"I figure he shot the fuel tank first and then riddled the passenger area with semi-automatic fire. The three small holes were shots taken as the car was moving. I'm guessing the big one is from a tight group fired when the car was stationary."

"I could fit my basketball in that hole and your telling me it came from I tight grouping of **bullets**?"

"Yes Ma'am, that's exactly what I'm telling you. We'll know for sure when this thing cools down and we can get a good hard look at the evidence."

"If you're correct Detective then why isn't that big group still out of view underneath the car?"

"As I see it, the first motion that caused the scattered pattern was caused by your driver trying to escape. There were probably two shots already in the car before he even heard anything. He would have felt it before he heard it. The first shot probably hit the gas tank and that began the explosion sequence that threw the car to where it is now. The third and fourth shots probably happened while the car was moving away from your driver's efforts and the explosion moved it sideways preventing him from getting it underground. I'd be willing to bet that there's a nice tight group of bullet holes in the roof that were made after the car stopped."

"How could you possibly put all of this together so fast Detective?"

"I'm and Ex-Marine sniper Miss Thompson… trained at Quantico. I've shot groups this tight at over a mile away. This was a cakewalk for our shooter... the distance looks to be well under 150 yards."

"What's the maximum range of this weapon?"

"Big target, four miles easy… little target, perhaps a third of that."

"Do you think this was the same shooter as last week in Charlotte?"

"I seriously doubt it... that guy used a 30-06."

"I'm going to meet with Mr. Dreyden now... and Detective, please do whatever you can to keep the newshounds at bay, at least until the morning so we can secure the family."

"And how do you suggest I accomplish that?"

"I don't know... this is your town. Tell them Mr. Dreyden would be very thankful for anyone helping to protect his family and very angry at anyone who wishes to *fuck* with it."

"I'll do my best Miss Thompson... I'm very sorry about your man."

## *"Why Shouldn't You Be a Target?"*

Thirty-five minutes later Emily was calling the Dreyden residence to gain entrance at the front gate. The moment she arrived the gates were opened by the bodyguard stationed in the home. She drove her Ford Crown Victoria up the drive glancing in the mirror just long enough to see that the gates had closed behind her.

She pulled up to the front stairs ignoring the spaces reserved for parking and left the car immediately in front of the house. A few seconds later she was being greeted by Jason at the door.

"Is everything secure Jason?"

"Yes Miss Thompson it is."

"Please forgive me but we were never properly introduced. I'm Emily Thompson."

"Nothing to forgive Miss Thompson... I'm Jason Roberts. I'm very sorry about Lou... he'll be missed."

"Yes... thank you. Where's the family?"

"Mr. and Mrs. Dreyden are in the study. The children have been picked up at school and are on their way home in an unmarked police cruiser. Go ahead in, they're expecting you."

Emily showed herself to the door, knocked lightly as she had seen Jason do it and walked in, closing the door behind her.

"Mr. and Mrs. Dreyden... Jason tells me the children are safe and are on their way home right now under police protection."

Max Dreyden stood and gestured Emily to the chair directly across from him and his wife. She immediately noticed the vacant look in Mrs. Dreyden's eyes and the empty tumblers on the table.

"May I offer you a drink Emily?"

"No thank you Mr. Dreyden. Mrs. Dreyden, how are you holding up?"

"I've been better Emily. I'm scared half to death."

"Honey, we're all okay thanks to Lou." Her husband offered.

"How is it that you **weren't** in the Rolls this morning Sir?"

"It was Lou, Emily. He saved my life today. I was getting ready for work when he reminded me of our deal to start changing our routines so we wouldn't make such easy targets. He convinced me to have a nice breakfast with my wife and drive myself into work in an hour or two in my wife's Audi. The last thing we talked about was a defensive driving course for me so I could use my sports cars more effectively."

They all sat in silence and considered how narrow his escape had been and at the sacrifice that had been made on his behalf.

"Thank God you listened to Lou. I'll make it a priority to get you trained behind the wheel but we have other concerns first and I want to go over them with you... okay?"

"Yes, thank you."

"Mrs. Dreyden, you can stay or leave if you're not feeling well and I can brief you later on this if you'd like."

"Thank you Emily but I want to wait until my children come home."

"Yes Ma'am. Right now Mr. Dreyden the people that did this think you're dead. From what I can ascertain at the scene... and this is very rough sir since the car was still aflame when I left... is that the shooter was on the roof of the building next to yours. He used .50-caliber armor piercing rounds with an incendiary material to explode the gas tank."

"Jesus…" Julia Dreyden moaned in torment.

"Dear, please… go and lay down, I'll send the children right up."

"Yes, maybe that's best for now. I'm sorry Emily."

"Please don't be Mrs. Dreyden… you may be suffering from shock and should take it easy for a while. Max, you should probably get your family doctor over here right away to take care of her."

"That's a good idea... I will."

Max offered his wife his hand, gently helped her up and walked her to the study door. He opened it to find Jason standing just outside.

"Jason… please help my wife to our bedroom and then call Doctor Shavers and have him come right over. I'd like him to make sure that Julia is comfortable. When the children get in have them see their mother right away and then come and see me when they're done."

"Yes sir." Max eased Julia's arm to Jason who then led her upstairs.

"Thank you Jason…" Both of them said at almost the same time.

"and Jason…" Emily chimed in from the study doorway… "For now we don't know where Mr. Dreyden is… is that clear?"

"Perfectly, Miss Thompson."

"And after you've called the doctor please get me the local FBI and the Chief of Police… in that order. We need to tighten things up quickly and see if we can't use this break to our best advantage."

Jason Roberts led Mrs. Dreyden up the lavish stairway as her husband closed the door to the study behind him. He and Emily then returned to their chairs and he poured another drink before speaking.

"Are you sure you wouldn't like one Emily?"

"No sir, *especially* not now. That should be your last one too Max and I suggest you let the doctor take a look at you when he's finished with you wife."

"Wouldn't that be the kicker; I can see it in the tabloids now… *Executive Narrowly Misses Death by Assassination Only To Die of a Heart Attack Hours Later…*"

"Don't think it hasn't happened. Shock can be as fatal as a bullet."

"I'm not in shock Emily… I'm just ticked off."

"Your wife appears to be … did you notice her eyes?"

*"She'll be fine and so will I."* He said a little too authoritatively.

"Yes you will… because you turned out to be a better listener than I expected you to be. So you have another day to keep on learning and I get to keep my job." She said with equal aplomb.

"Yes, I'm sorry but this really pisses me off. I mean I'm sad about Lou and all but why is it that these idiots think they can shoot any goddamn person they wish?"

"We've touched upon this Max. You're *not* just anyone… and trust me when I tell you that these people don't have a stupid bone in their bodies… You've got to learn to see things from their perspective."

"Oh… and how's that?"

"Are you ready to listen to me real hard?

"Yes Emily."

"Your family has been selling *cancer* for generations with complete foreknowledge of that danger… so let me turn your question around. Why is it that you think you can go on enticing innocent people to smoke your product when you know *full well* that millions of them are going to die *every single year* as a direct result? Look me straight in the eye and tell me why you *shouldn't be a target?*"

# "Operative Words"

"Chief, this is Mark… did you hear the news from Atlanta?"

"I just caught it on CNN… looks like the bad guys took out another CEO."

"The operative words there boss are; *"looks like"*. I've already called down to the Atlanta PD and they put me in touch with a detective that was near the scene when it happened. Dreyden's not dead sir."

"But CNN just confirmed it on the air five minutes ago."

"They blew up his armored Rolls Royce, which killed his bodyguard but as luck would have it the boss wasn't in the vehicle."

"That's one lucky son-of-a-bitch."

"You know it Walter."

"From what I learned from Detective Morrison it was probably a semi-automatic .50 caliber API round that caused the car to explode. They hit it turning into the underground garage from the rooftop next door. Twenty-three floors up and the shooter hits the gas tank, puts three bullets into the kill zone *while the driver's trying to get away* and then another tight group of perhaps four to six more rounds right through what would have been Dreyden's body if he were in there."

"Jesus… that guy was one Hell of a shot."

"That's the kicker boss… he may have been… but according to Detective Morrison, who just happens to be an ex-marine sniper, almost anyone that was qualified on the .50 cal could have done this. That weapon is accurate from much farther away. What's amazing to me is how the API rounds went straight through both layers of armor before they punched holes in the cement under the car."

"Still, the shooter stayed calm throughout the attack… *and the explosion*… Don't assume he's an average marksman Mark."

"Duly noted sir."

"Another shooter, that's just what we need. Do you think it's the same guy as Charlotte?"

"The Detective doesn't think so but my gut tells me otherwise Chief. These two shootings were just too close together in both time and geography and too proficient in execution to be a coincidence even if the rifles were different. Snipers are professionals just like anyone else and they can change weapons as easily as Jack Nicklaus could change golf clubs."

"Now that's where we should be Mark… hitting the greens with the Golden Bear."

"I wish… but not anytime soon. With your permission I'd like to head down to Atlanta and see if we can't snare a couple of bear of our own. Dreyden's got enough pull to keep himself dead for awhile and he doesn't even care about the stock hit his company is taking. He wants these bastards as much as we do."

"He's probably buying it as fast as it falls. That reminds me to check with Merrill Schneider over at the SEC and see what kind of activity is going on around this. That should help us connect some more of these dots."

"Excellent, we're going to need all the help we can get. This may be the best break we've had and it's thanks to Ron Morrison who was cool headed enough to keep the firefighters out and preserve our scene. So we have the element of surprise on our side for a change."

"Good job Mark."

"I haven't done much yet sir…"

"What about that bodyguard's boss... what do we know about her?"

"Not much except that she's with Blackwell and assigned to providing the Dreyden's family with security. Whether or not they saved his life is still an open question..."

"Get to Atlanta today Mark and co-ordinate our field officers with local law enforcement and try to keep our advantages intact for as long as possible."

"I'll be on a flight in a few hours... just need to pack a few things first. Why do you think they tried to take this guy out Chief?"

"Is this a real question or are you just testing me?"

"Just checking your perspective before I give you mine."

"I think it's obvious based upon your recent findings. His family sells death... so he's a legitimate target to these home grown militia men of ours. The questions that concern me now though are; what are their numbers, how well armed and coordinated are their forces and how well are they led? In short, *what the Hell are we up against?*"

"I don't think we're going to like the answers to any of those questions Chief... and they're smart enough not to brag about their successes and tip their hands. It wouldn't surprise me one iota if the SEC linkages turn out to be our best shot at getting at them en masse."

"Let's tie this up fast Mark or it's going to get bloodier real fast."

"Will do... by the way, Cassandra was telling me about a radio show that was broadcast from Baltimore on Sunday night that had some interesting insights. She's getting me a copy of the program so we can hear an outsider's perspective on what's been going on."

"Do you think it's really worth our time?"

"She heard the show live and thinks so… and she's a very sharp lady. In fact we have a Hell of a computer team right here and with your permission I'd like them to take the lead coordinating the rest of the analysts' data and be our lead-interface with the consultants."

"Consider it done Mark… now just make sure it happens. Don't forget your report for my meeting with the Attorney General."

"I won't…. thank you Chief."

"Have a safe trip son."

# "Gathering Evidence"

As FBI Agent Mark McNulty was making final preparations for his trip to Atlanta Detective Ron Morrison's team along with local FBI agents were gathering evidence at the scene. The heavy bullet fragments were carefully recovered from the pavement and sent to the ballistics lab... none were intact. There was little hope that they would be able to identify the weapon using the striation marks left on the bullets that had accelerated out at their target at 59,000 pounds psi of force before tearing through the layers of armor like it was made of cloth. With any luck the bullet that ignited the fuel might still be intact and embedded in the lower layer of shielding that protected the underbelly of the gas tank.

Few people were aware of the incredible penetrating power that these tungsten-carbide API rounds possessed. The incendiary aspect of the projectile added a pyrophoric capability that would ignite any flammable substance it came in contact with. Upon impact a very short pyrotechnic fuse would delay the explosion of the main charge before scattering the flammable zirconium payload into the fuel.

Meanwhile, eight .50 caliber casings were found on the rooftop of the adjacent building and the logical escape route was quickly ascertained and traced to the basement garage where the attendant had witnessed two men leaving at an unusually early hour. His labored description of the men in blue suits left much to be desired but he did notice the out of state license plate on the late model LS 430 as it drove away. He didn't catch the number but was certain that the plate was from Virginia.

The car had cooled enough to allow Morrison a close look at the top and trunk. One lone penetration hole was centered over the gas tank in the armored trunk. Three shots were scattered in the right rear passenger seat in a 24-inch radius. The final four seemed to confirm his theory and were lodged over what would have been the head and shoulder area of the right rear passenger in a radius not more than 12-inches across. *This guy was definitely a pro...* He noted.

## *"Scattered Pieces"*

Less than twelve hours from the attack on Max Dreyden's limousine Mark McNulty was being met at the Hartsfield-Jackson International Airport in Atlanta by Detective Morrison. They shook hands and exchanged a few pleasantries before taking the nearest exit to where the unmarked car was waiting at the curb. Mark took the parking ticket in stride and placed it into his inside jacket pocket as both men got in and drove away.

"So what new information do you have for me?" The FBI agent inquired.

"My theory about the shooter seems to be accurate since the bullet holes in the roof were where I expected them to be. Eight shots, not ten as I has guessed originally, we have those casings. That means this guy KNEW that the .50 caliber semi-automatic has a nasty habit of jamming when you load all ten rounds into the magazine."

"When did you first become aware of that problem Detective?"

"During Marine sniper training school… our instructor pointed it out to us and said it didn't happen too often but if your mission was critical then we better be sure by removing two rounds."

"Is this common knowledge?"

"No, unless you're a Marine sniper or a professional assassin who may have learned about this on his own."

"So where are we headed?"

"I thought it would be a good idea for us to meet with this guy Dreyden and his security team and start formulating a plan before the world finds out that he's not dead."

"Good. Any chance we're going to be able to read striation marks on any of those rounds?"

"Not likely on the seven rounds that went through the passenger seat… they all fragmented as they passed through the layers or armor and flattened out pretty bad. We may have a chance on the one that went through the armor around the gas tank since it didn't punch all the way through the underbelly layer of armor below where the gas tank used to be."

"What about the driver?"

"He's another Blackwell hired gun whose primary role was to protect Mr. Dreyden. He barely knew what hit him."

"Barely?"

"He would have felt the hit of the first round… a .50 caliber packs quite a jolt. By the time it registered in his brain the next three shots were ripping holes behind him and to the right… which may have caused permanent deafness had he survived. Those gunshot noises didn't even reach his ears until the shots were already through the car and the gas tank was in the process of exploding. He barely had time for an escape before the car was lifted halfway off the driveway. When he hit the accelerator it was already too late and he hit the wall before the explosion killed him. He was so badly roasted that calling off the firefighters when they arrived wasn't that much of a decision. As we already discussed, the last four rounds were center mass over the head and shoulder area where Dreyden was supposed to be and they were in a very tight group. "

"Jesus… Do we have any eye witnesses or video from nearby surveillance cameras?"

"We're still checking the camera's in the area. I'm pretty certain that we'll get something on the roof. The garage attendant said he saw two men in blue suits leaving shortly after the shooting occurred but he couldn't give us much of a description. They were white, the driver was older… forty's or fifty's and the passenger was perhaps thirty or so. He said they didn't seem in a hurry but he did notice that they were driving a late model Lexus LS430 with out of state plates. He didn't get a number but was pretty sure they were from Virginia."

"I thought this was the same shooter we had in Charlotte Detective and that car makes me fairly certain of it now. That's the third piece of circumstantial evidence we have… timing, MO and now this car passing right past both victims."

"I didn't think so at first Mark, but I'm definitely leaning your way now."

"Do you have any more on the car yet?"

"No, but we've expanded the search to see if we can get it leaving the scene and hopefully we'll get lucky and pick up their faces as well as the license plate number."

"No one saw them besides the garage attendant?"

"No, it looks like they got access to the service elevator keys and had it locked and waiting for them when they made their escape. They were only on the twenty-third floor for the few seconds it took them to circle off the stairs and into the hall and into the waiting elevator. It was a well planned hit and definitely required local support to get those keys."

"Who normally has access to them?"

"At least three or four of the maintenance men but we're just beginning the interrogations now."

"Okay, good. That's a hot lead that we need to turn the pressure up on. All in all we've got a good chance here thanks to your fast work Ron… how much longer until we reach the Dreyden estate?"

"It's a half mile straight ahead on the right."

# *"Buying Time"*

Detective Ron Morrison pulled up to the outside gate of the Dreyden estate and leaned out of his dark blue Caprice to speak into the intercom.

"This is Detective Morrison and Agent McNulty ... we have an appointment with Mrs. Dreyden."

"Yes sir." A rich Negro voice answered. "Please pull your car around back into the garage... I'll open it for you from here."

They drove a half mile down the long winding drive through the opulent estate. The entire property was nestled among hundred year old Georgia oaks, willow and maple trees. Both men were silenced by the splendor of the land and the decades of landscaping that must have gone into these grounds. The smaller flowering pear, peach and dogwood trees were complimented by giant rhododendron shrubs, tri-color viburnums, forsythia and azaleas, which further softened this Garden of Eden.

They approached the magnificent three story house with its upper and lower sets of white columns that were smaller and doubled to form a regal guard to the outdoor entertainment areas of both floors. The columns were decorated in the ornate fashion of the Eighteenth Century by true craftsman and they led into matching white railings on both floors. The front entranceway led broadly up to a gently narrowing staircase paved in matching stone. Approaching the home from the front must have humbled most guests. The front, although quite large on its own, was expanded even further as it was softened by sides that gracefully extended the architecture back and outward at a forty-five degree angle. Matching columns graced the first floor on both sides with comparatively modest second floor terraces along with hand carved handrails. The overall height and scope of the mansion was deceptively large and capped by not only a third smaller floor but by a domed widows' watch atop the structure. Each floor was twelve feet tall and each roof, except for the domed watchtower itself was flat. The third floor was half the size of the main home, which left a huge rooftop from which one could view the grounds of the estate.

Unfortunately they were directed to the rear of the home where the double deep five car garage stood behind bullet proof doors. At least they were thought to be impervious to bullets until earlier that day. The third door was open and they pulled in and sat in the car as the door closed quickly behind them and a tall dark figure approached painted in fluorescent light.

"Hello gentlemen, I'm Jason Roberts." Both Detective Morrison and FBI Agent McNulty heard as they stepped out of the car.

"Good evening Mr. Roberts… I'm Mark McNulty with the FBI and this is Detective Ron Morrison with the Atlanta PD."

The men exchanged nods but didn't take the time to share handshakes before Roberts turned and led them toward the rear entrance to the home. As they walked both cops took the time to notice the Mercedes limo and assorted sports cars and classics along the way. A Porsche 911 and 944, an Audi A8 turbo, a Jaguar XJ12, a Triumph Spitfire convertible, two 60's muscle cars; a Chevelle SS 396, and a Pontiac GTO 454 "Goat" and of course the obligatory red Ferrari. The space once reserved for the armored Rolls Royce would no longer be needed.

They entered into an expansive kitchen where four people were already engaged in conversation around a large oak dining table. They stopped talking as the three men entered and Jason Roberts introduced the new guests.

"Mr. & Mrs. Dreyden this is Mark McNulty from the FBI and Detective Ron Morrison with the Atlanta Police Department."

"Good evening." Morrison and McNulty offered.

"I'm Maxwell Dreyden and this is my wife Julia, this is our security expert Emily Thompson and this is Paul Hobson with the FBI here in Atlanta."

They shook hands as Mrs. Dreyden offered them something to drink and they all took a seat around the table. McNulty asked the first question.

"Mr. Dreyden… how long can you keep undercover for us and pretend that they succeeded?"

He thought hard on that question as Julia Dreyden poured ice tea and coffee for her guests. There was fresh fruit and pastries already on the table.

"At least a week Mr. McNulty… after that it could get prohibitively expensive."

"Exactly how many people know you're still alive as of this moment, not including your immediate family?" The FBI man continued.

"Besides all of us…" He hesitated.

"My boss does..." Morrison chimed in.

"Mine too." Said McNulty.

"And ours as well." Said Thompson for herself and the FBI man beside her.

"No one else?" Asked Mark.

"No one else Mr. McNulty." Confirmed Emily Thompson. "Except Sarah, who cooks for us and lives on the third floor. The other servants were sent home as a security measure still believing Max was gone."

"And who's idea was that?" McNulty asked.

"Mine Sir." Emily Thompson replied. "I have tried from the beginning to keep this knowledge from getting out so the servants were sent home on paid leave until further notice."

"That was quick thinking." McNulty offered.

"They saved my life today." Said Dreyden respectfully.

"It was mainly Lou Farentino who saved your life today Max." Emily corrected.

"How so?" Asked McNulty.

"Lou contacted me about beefing up security around here… especially in the light of last week's murder. That's why I was out here in the first place… He felt Mr. Dreyden would be more open to the changes we were recommending if they came from an executive of our firm and not a bodyguard. It was Lou who strongly urged Max to alter his daily routine so he wouldn't be an easy target. Today was the first day Lou drove the route alone." Emily said with obvious sadness creeping into her otherwise strong yet graceful voice.

"I'm sorry for the loss of Mr. Farentino… he was a hero today." Morrison offered. "And I'm sad that I had to let him burn."

"He would have wanted you to Detective." Emily comforted. "He was already gone protecting Mr. Dreyden and would want you to catch those involved. If burning longer meant that he was still helping us then he would have given that order himself… so don't blame yourself for giving us the opportunity we have right now."

"Then the main focus of tonight's meeting is how to take advantage of this window of opportunity. We need to formulate a plan that will help us find the people involved in the assassination attempt." Said McNulty. "For now let's just speak our minds and offer whatever ideas you might have."

"What else can you tell us about this?" Emily asked while glancing from Morrison to McNulty.

"Not a heck of a lot more than I already told you during the day Emily." Morrison answered.

"We are checking leads now, as we speak and expect to turn up more info in very short order. We definitely know how this was done, where the attack came from and we're pretty sure how they got away and maybe even what they were driving." Spoke McNulty matter-of-factly.

"They?" asked Max Dreyden.

McNulty continued… "This was a team effort sir… It was too clean from top to bottom to be a lone gunman. We're working under the assumption that we have an out of town shooter and a local team of support either in or around the Atlanta area."

"Why my husband?" Julia asked

"We're not sure yet Mrs. Dreyden." McNulty offered. "We have a few working theories but for now let's try to focus on how we might be able to flush out these murderers. Has anyone taken responsibility for this? I was traveling half the afternoon."

"No Mark." Morrison confirmed.

"We've gotten a lot of calls but they were mainly from friends and family seeing if they could be of any help." Offered Roberts.

"What about the newspapers?" McNulty asked.

"What about them?" Max replied.

"What influence do you have over them should they get wind of our situation? They're going to get curious when there's no wake and no funeral." Said McNulty.

"We were talking about that when you came in." Said Agent Paul Hobson. "My boss has authorized us to fake the coroner's records and start the ball rolling on both the wake and funeral."

"Excellent." McNulty said. "The more convincing we are the more time we'll have to gather evidence and smoke these guys out."

"What about my company? I'm going to have an awful lot of ticked off investors when they find out that their portfolios went through the floor unnecessarily." Said Dreyden.

"Do you have any suggestions Mr. Dreyden?" Inquired McNulty.

"Yes… as a matter of fact I do. I'm buying up my own stock as fast as it falls. When all of this is over I don't want the SEC breathing down my neck as if I were the scoundrel here."

"We have connections at the SEC Mr. Dreyden but they're not going to let you take unfair advantage of this situation. Now if you were willing to use these purchases for the sole purpose of *protecting your investors* and redistributing that wealth to cover their losses well then the SEC should see that more favorably for you. I can't speak for them but I will have my boss check it out."

"Thank you Mr. McNulty… that would be fine by me." Said Max.

"Okay, so we've got at least a week or two before anyone else knows Mr. Dreyden isn't dead. You'll need to keep totally out of site and that means NO PHONE CALLS OR E-MAIL MESSAGES TO ANYONE… is that clear sir?" Asked McNulty.

"Yes… perfectly." Dreyden responded dryly.

"Ms. Thompson… what are you doing to beef up security here?"

"Not too much more then we were already planning. For the time being I'm staying with the Dreyden's to assume Lou Farentino's duties." Said Emily. We have a pair of trained German Shepherds coming on Friday. I was thinking about having the trainer stay with us a few days to train the Dreyden's."

"I would suggest holding back on that until Mr. Dreyden is reborn." Agent Hobson offered. "No sense letting any more people in on this than is absolutely necessary."

"What about our servants?" Julia Dreyden asked.

"Keep them on paid leave with the belief that Mr. Dreyden is gone. Let them know you plan on bringing them back in a few weeks. What about Sarah? Has she been with you long?" McNulty asked.

"She's like family and has been with us since our first child was born. You don't have to worry about her." Julia concluded.

"What about the children?" Morrison asked looking around the table.

"Keep them home until Mr. Dreyden is back." Ordered Emily Thompson matter-of-factly.

# *"a.k.a."*

Earlier that day Bob Messer drove to the Hartsfield-Jackson International Airport in Atlanta and dropped the LS-400 off to the outdoor check-in agent at Avis using his Bob Blackman alias for the last time. He had been careful to wipe down the car for any telltale fingerprints as per their escape plan. He then grabbed a single tourist suitcase and a taxi back to town, which dropped him off at the motel he and Matt had decided upon. From there he called Creagor's cell phone and told him to meet at the diner across the street. Fifteen minutes later Matt pulled up and was met outside by Messer carrying two cups of coffee.

The two men then headed north on Interstate 85 and then exited on Virginia Avenue East, which led them to the Hilton Atlanta Airport. The news in the car confirmed their successful mission and Creagor complimented his mentor on a *job well done* and shook his hand enthusiastically as he dropped him off at the Hertz rental facility. He helped Messer with the 30-06 sniper luggage that was left in his care and then drove away. The .50-caliber had already been returned to Creagor's squad member after the morning's attack.

Messer then rented a Blue Ford Taurus under the alias *Roger Thurmond* and began his long drive home to DC where he unloaded his luggage into Bob Blackman's throw-away car that was waiting for him in long term parking at the Ronald Reagan Washington National Airport. He then dropped off the rental car to the outside agent, grabbed his suitcase from the trunk and took an airport bus to his, or rather, Bob Blackman's car. He repeated this exercise one more time to his own car before leaving the throw away on the appropriate street where it would be stripped down to a chassis by morning... just one more broken down vehicle. From that moment on Bob Blackman no longer existed and Messer, who caught a cab to his car, retreated into oblivion as yet another alias. He was home free half an hour later... home to his Maryland condo and to his thirsty plants.

He checked the yellow pages, picked up the bedside phone and then dialed his favorite escort service before collapsing asleep just as the call was being answered…

## *"Follow the Money"*

McNulty called his boss after the meeting at the Dreyden residence and briefed him on the new evidence and their preliminary plans. He also recruited Chief Dobson's support to work closely with the SEC to protect Dreyden as he helped them with the investigation.

"When will you be coming home Mark?" Dobson asked.

"I'm not sure Walter… I think our best chance is **right here right now** so don't expect me for at least a week or two. Meanwhile, any assurances you can get from the SEC for Mr. Dryden could only help us by extending his death for us."

"I understand Mark and will do what I can. I'm still waiting for that report you promised me. Don't leave me hanging with the AG."

"Don't worry… I have most of it written up now and will e-mail it to you on-time as promised. Meanwhile, if you can come up with any ideas for flushing these guys out we sure would appreciate it. We're working with as few people as possible so no leaks get out and that's limiting our resources Chief."

"I understand and will give you my thoughts on this the next time we speak. Now let me go so I can call Merrill Schneider and get that piece working for us."

"Thanks Chief." (click)

Chief Dobson immediately dialed Schneider's number, which was now on his speed dial list. He received her voice mail and left an urgent message to call him without leaving any details. Fifteen minutes later his office phone was ringing.

"Walter, this is Merrill Schneider… what has you working at the office at this hour? Does it have to do with the Dreyden murder?"

"Yes Merrill it does… but guess what?"

"What Walter?"

"They didn't get him… and you're only one of a handful of people who know that so please don't say anything. We're trying to get the upper hand on these assassins and this is a rare opportunity that I need your help on."

"Wow… that's amazing. I've been watching the news coverage all day and I can't believe anyone survived that attack… the car was fully engulfed in fire. They said it had to be a full tank to move that heavy car like that."

"He wasn't in the car this morning or he *would have* been dead. His driver convinced him to alter his routines and then died a few minutes later."

"Jesus Walter… what can I do?"

"I need your department to work with us to protect Dreyden and his company as he plays dead for us."

"I'm not sure I understand…"

"As you can see from the market news his company is taking a beating right now… big time… and the longer her stays dead the bigger the negative impact will be in the near term. What he's proposing… and he's already started without the SEC's approval, is that he has his brokers buy the stock back as fast as it falls and then use that windfall to redistribute the wealth to his investors when this all shakes out and he comes back to life."

"That's not something I can do on my own Walt."

"I know that… but I'm trying to see if this is a reasonable enough idea to put before the Attorney General. I'm meeting him on another matter later this week."

"As long as Dreyden is willing to give us full access to his trading activities from today until this is resolved then I don't see why we can't help him through this without him taking any sort of personal hit… excuse me, financial loss."

"Good, that's all we need to know at the moment so he'll play ball and stay dead a while."

"Alright… I'm pretty sure I can get it moving with that contingency in mind. We'll need to get this all in writing."

"Our man already told him that… just get me the paperwork and I'll get it notarized for you."

"Use an FBI notary Walter…"

(Chuckling) "Yes Ma'am… we will. Meanwhile any insider trader evidence that becomes apparent is extremely important to us now. It'll be interesting to see who's buying up his competitors stock. It may be the only way we can get a handle on any of this. Our teams are still working on what they perceived as separate cases until just a few days ago. We're rethinking all that and are trying to understand how this is all structured and where the money is coming from. We need your help big time on this or a lot of people are going to die before we can crack the code."

"I understand and will only let my boss know about Mr. Dreyden. I'll do everything I can Walter… count on it."

"Thank you Merrill, goodnight."

"Get some rest Walter."

# *"Escalation"*

Within the next ninety-six hours another dozen reports had come in from around the country of high-level assassinations that had taken place. It was by far the bloodiest week in American history for Fortune 500 executives.

Two top airline executives that had stolen millions from their employee's pension fund were found dead in the company's underground parking garage. Both had been shot once in the head and once in the heart by a .38-caliber pistol yet no one had heard a sound.

A Halliburton executive that was found guilty of scamming the American tax payers out of millions of dollars was found in a dumpster with his hands cut off. Ironically, he was overcharging the US military in Iraq for gasoline after his company had been awarded a multi-billion dollar *"no bid contract"*. His hands were found in a mail depository at HQs in a FedEx box marked; *"Return to sender."*

Another executive from an iniquitous accounting company was found garroted in his car… that made three dead from this firm alone.

The first political assassinations took place within three hours of one another and appeared to be connected. All of the Senators were hawks who continued to press for ever increasing funding for the war effort even as their constituencies voted against it. The first man was killed on a golf course with a shot that came from so far away that his head had exploded a full two seconds before the secret service team even heard the gunshot. The second Senator was taken out in a similar manner while walking through her luxurious home. The third Senator was gunned down ferociously by multiple snipers who fired semi-automatic armor piercing rounds through his limousine and the secret service cruiser behind him. The AP rounds had cut through the bullet proof glass and armor as if it they weren't even there. The last rounds exploded the gas tanks killing all seven passengers including the Senator, two members of his staff, both drivers and the two secret service agents assigned to his detail.

In what was *by far* the most dramatic event of the week the entire board of directors of Bechtel was killed by an explosive device that was brought into their conference room in a coffee service cart. An environmentally active newspaper was first to write: "**Bechtel had long been the target of many environmental and human rights groups for its continual abuses against mankind and nature and for the way they circumvented the laws of our land.**" The article continued with a quote that provided just one example of that ongoing abuse. It was from Andre Buffa, the PEACE Campaign Coordinator at the Global Exchange, she wrote;

*"Bechtel has demonstrated brazen moral corruption by first contributing to the development of Iraq's weapons, then pushing for a war against Iraq, and finally (by) profiting from the tragedy and destruction wrought by that war… it is a textbook example of what war profiteering looks like."*

Within twenty-four hours the story of Bechtel and the other murdered executives had hit newspapers all over the world. The American papers carried headlines such as;

- *THE WAR ON TERROR HAS COME HOME!*

- *CORPORATE AMERICA UNDER ATTACK!*

- *TERROR IN THE CORPORATE BOARDROOM!*

- *THE INVISIBLE ENEMY… TERROR!*

These were just some of the sensational headlines that worked American's into a frenzy. Many of whom immediately began selling their entire stock portfolios, which caused a near crash in the market until the FEDs stepped in and closed down the exchange hoping that the imposed pause in trading would allow cooler heads to prevail.

It was then, after the wave of terror had been sensationalized that a lone reporter at **Democracy Now** received an article from what was identified as *"an anonymous source"* … it carried the headline:

*THIS IS NOT A WAR ON AMERICA... BUT <u>FOR</u> AMERICA!*

## *"Fast Mover"*

Joe Clark was watching the news and feeling good about the successes their teams had had in the last ten days. He reminded himself not to become overconfident and that success against an unsuspecting target wasn't that big a deal in military terms. From this point forward things were going to get more difficult with every passing day.

He turned off the news and went to his study to check his e-mail when the icon appeared telling him he had an instant message waiting. He logged in as **Dopey** and received an e-mail from his Central Region counterpart in Minnesota. It simply read: **Fast mover from C2... call ASAP... Doc**. Without hesitation he picked up his disposable phone and called his mid-west counterpart Richard Cooper.

"Dick this is Joe... what's going on?"

"Ever hear of Alliant Techsystems?"

"Of course, they're a large military contractor. They make ammo and guided weaponry right?"

"That's some of it Joe. They also make cluster bombs and depleted uranium shells."

"Got it... so who's your fast mover?"

"Their CEO... he's meeting with the Pentagon tomorrow morning so we only have a short window on this guy... it may not be possible."

"What makes you think it is?"

"We have a secretary on the inside that let one of my people know where he'd be staying tonight. We have his room number and a copy of his itinerary. He's already in the air so you won't have much time. He's meeting with General Richards at 8:00 am and then flying home out of Dulles at 2:00."

"Where's he staying?"

"He'll be in room 454 at the Park Hyatt Hotel on 24th and M streets. Do you know it?"

"Yes, it's a nice place… one of the best in the city. Who's he traveling with?"

"That's the best part… his bodyguard doesn't have security clearance so he left him home."

"That is nice isn't it? What time is he due in?"

"His flight arrives at Dulles at 18:30 hours."

"That's two hours from now… plus a half hour to get to the hotel… looks like this one is mine my friend. Where is he on your list?"

"Number five… the first two were too politically sensitive… and we took out number three and four this week…so he's my top guy right now."

"I've got it… that's going to cost you a round of golf *and a dinner* the next time we're together Coop."

"That's a date Sergeant Major."

"Take care Dick."

Clark grabbed a yogurt and half a banana to calm his stomach and then took a shower before dressing in his best dark blue suit and black wingtip shoes that had been polished to a spit shine. At 5:30 he strapped on his Barretta Cheetah .38 caliber pistol ankle holster and adjusted his pants to conceal its presence entirely. He then took a FedEx envelope and applied a typed white label that simply read; Mr. Bradford Cummings, Alliant Techsystems, Park Hyatt Hotel - Room 454. **CONFIDENTIAL**

Clark then drove to the Metro Park station that was just outside of DC and took the train to the next stop. He then caught a cab to the Park Hyatt. He paid the driver and got out in front of the hotel. The time was 6:45pm.

He proceeded through the lobby carrying the FedEx envelope concealed behind a daily newspaper under his arm. He walked calmly to the bank of elevators and took the first available one to the fourth floor. From there he turned right and moved silently to room 454 and knocked three times. Ten seconds later he knocked again.

"Yes, yes, yes… I'm here… give me a moment. Who is it?"

"Major Searl Sir, from General Richard's office… he has a dispatch for you Mr. Cummings."

Cummings opened the door with the chain still linked across it. *(As if that would help…* Clark thought to himself.) He took a hard look at the plainclothes officer outside his room.

"Okay, just hand it over Major." He said matter-of-factly.

"Sorry sir, I need your signature. This is a confidential document."

"Alright, come in. I just got off the plane and was in the bathroom so let's make this quick Major."

"Yes sir." Clark said handing the envelope to Cummings.

As Cummings opened the empty FedEx package Clark stepped up behind him.

***"What the Hell is going on? It's empt…"*** was all he said as Clark enclosed his thick arms around the CEO's head and broke his neck as easily as if he were popping open a beer. The shocked CEO collapsed to the floor and listened to his last breath as it escaped from the body he could no longer feel. *What a strange way to die…* he thought to himself as he waited for unconsciousness and death to overtake him.

185

Clark retrieved the envelope and tore it into pieces before placing it into his side pocket. He then called the front desk and requested that he not be disturbed until 8:30am when they could provide him with a wake up call. He wiped down the phone, put the "Do Not Disturb" sign on the door, picked up the newspaper that he had left on the floor in the hall and retraced his route home.

## *"Deep-Six"*

"Juan, read this and tell me what you think." Amy Goodman asked of her co-anchor of the **Democracy Now** program.

Juan Gonzalez read the title to the article; **THIS IS NOT A WAR ON AMERICA... BUT FOR AMERICA!** And asked...

"Is this what I think it is Amy?"

"If you're thinking it's the manifesto of the people pulling off the assassinations you're right. It looks like we have the only copy at the moment."

He sat down and focused on the statement before him and began to read;

*For over fifty years the Corporate-Military-Industrial-Complex has been imposing their will over that of the American people. Many of our precious rights, which the Constitution guarantees to all of us, have been stripped away under the guise of national security. We as citizens and as Patriots have the solemn duty to protect our Country as our forefathers intended when they gave us the Second Amendment, the right to bear arms. This right was not intended for some of us but for **all of us** so we would be able to stave off not only external enemies but those from within who would dare to impose their tyrannical reins upon us and steal away our freedom.*

*Our beloved Constitution has been under siege and our freedoms are being plucked away one by one. We as individual citizens are having our votes tossed away by unscrupulous leaders who manipulate our voting systems for their own gain. International Corporations are being granted immunity to grievous acts of environmental destruction and human rights abuses. Their rights in many instances are now greater than those of our citizenry as new laws are designed to protect these behemoths from legal action and financial harm even when legal action **is** warranted. Our leaders not only turn a blind eye to* *these activities but provide the political impetus to assist them with new and immoral laws.*

*Our nation is not made up of war mongers who wish to steal the wealth of the world at any cost. "We the People" do not believe that we have the right to harm innocent populations throughout the world and destroy their fledgling democracies. "We the People" do not believe that the environment is our own personal garbage dump or that we can disrespect it or the creatures that inhabit it.*

*Our leaders would have you believe that we need $500 billion dollars every year to fund our military blood lust and that it is a necessary expenditure to protect us. They would have you believe that creating thousands of tons of nuclear waste is in our best interest and that the sale of weapons and other deadly products throughout the world is justified because it keeps our nation strong... both militarily and financially... even as the morality of our people is questioned by peace-loving nations who seek nothing more than equal rights and justice for all members of the human race.*

*Our leaders would have you think that believing in peace is paramount to treason... or cowardice. They believe we are too stupid to see another road. To envision an America that is a moral leader to the rest of the world and not just another schoolyard bully that is destined to be beaten down when the rest of the boys and girls jump on his back... our backs.*

*Most Americans are good and decent people who are frustrated by the way our country is acting against our will. Most Americans feel too isolated and too small to attempt to fight such a giant on their own. They forget the lesson of Gulliver and of the Lilliputians who united against his invincible threat.*

*We are now engaged in our second war of independence and are encouraged by our own constitution to throw away corrupt leadership in favor of a government that is guided by truth, justice and moral decency. The people we are killing are not innocents as their public relation spin doctors and media whores would have you believe. They*

188

*are responsible for killing millions of people indiscriminately around the world with their products, their actions and their silence. Let it be known **from this day forward** that if you contribute to the downfall and suffering of mankind then you are our target. If you disrespect the environment and its inhabitants with egregious negligence then you are our target. If you lie, steal and cheat the American people or others around the world, then you are our target.*

Let every member of our society know that you are not alone in your search for decency and justice. And let every villain know that you are not invincible… that your half-million dollar armored cars and bullet proof glass can not protect you… that if you are on our list then it is only a matter of time before we add your name to the wall of cowards, war profiteers and indecent beings that DO NOT represent our species as a whole and therefore have been exterminated. There is no hole deep enough for you to hide in and your only hope at survival is to end your personal and corporate atrocities immediately and turn your wealth into peaceful endeavors through reciprocal acts of humaneness. Do this now or beg not for your miserable lives when our professionals come to exterminate you.

*For those of you who would call us terrorists consider the following. We believe in **"one shot one kill"** and not the indiscriminate killing of innocents. **We do not** bomb buildings; **We do not** fire depleted uranium weapons and kill civilians with unexploded cluster bomb munitions, **We do not** leave behind decades of hellacious cancers and birth defects from nuclear waste, **We do not** send out suicide bombers or level cities, **We do not** kill families, innocent women and children, **We do not** target journalists, cover up the truth or spread lies. If you do any of these things then you are on our lists of LEGITIMATE TARGETS and will be dealt with in the same fashion as any other war criminal… swiftly and without mercy. Let no person feel immune; no office – no matter how high will protect you from your crimes against humanity.*

*Your only hope at survival is to reverse your ways with equal vigor and acts of kindness. Turn your weapons into ploughshares for peace or die by our swords. If your weapons left a population cancer ridden then cease and desist all further production of those materials and build and staff hospitals to aide those victimized people. If your manufacturing processes polluted the land then cease and desist all harmful acts and clean up the areas that you destroyed. If your laws rendered harmless those criminal organizations seeking profit over the well-being of the environment then reverse those laws immediately and enact new ones that would force the clean up of toxic spills and other environmental disasters and make those companies responsible, pay their own reparations and not force our citizens to shoulder that burden any longer.*

***We the People*** *from this day forward will protect ourselves without the corruption of our legislators and our courts. You have made a mockery out of justice and we will rebuild those institutions so that no man, rich or poor, will be able to bend the law beyond its moral intent.* ***We the people*** *will not settle for any more half-measures. Either you do as we command or expect a visit from one of our supremely skilled patriots. Read your newspapers and see the people who were on the list ahead of you and learn how every one of their measures at self-preservation failed. Then decide which side you are on... either you stand for truth and justice **or you are the terrorist**... there will be no middle ground that will protect you.*

*We are placing a 72-hour cease-fire starting at 12:00 pm today to allow the criminals we've identified enough time to post their initial plans in the Wall Street Journal to identify what measures they'll be taking to reverse their harmful activities. We will hold you to those promises and return your name to the top of our list should you renege on any of them. Let your large stockholders know that if you are identified as a target that they too will have their names listed right there next to yours. This is not about money or power... this is about **human decency and peace**... it's about ending mass extinctions and man's self-appointed role as God over the animals, it's about the preservation of our natural habitats and ultimately... it's about our own self-preservation as we stand atop this fragile balance of life.*

*Signed,*

190

### Deep-Six ALL Traitors!

### *"One-Shot, One-Kill"*

Juan Gonzalez put the printed copy down, took a deep breath and then let it out slowly before saying:

"***Dear Jesus Amy***, where did this come from?"

"I don't know… it was in my e-mail this morning."

"What are you going to do with it?"

"It's a message to the people Juan… its news, it sounds credible and I believe it's from the people that have been killing those executives. It's our right ***and our duty*** to get it on the air before our government tries to squelch their message. I'm reading it on the show at eleven o'clock and I want it posted on our website by then and sent to every NPR station in our network during the broadcast. Make sure David gets it in time for his show on the West Coast. Get a copy out to Gregg at the BBC now and let them run with it. We're not letting anyone cover this up."

"All Hell is going to break loose on this one."

"Pandora's Box is already open Juan… we're just reporting the story. Anyway, what was it that Jim Hightower said about Hell?"

You mean the quote: ***"Some of these CEOs are becoming so rich they could afford to air condition Hell."*** Juan offered.

"Yes, that one… well, we're going to give them the opportunity to try."

"That sign-off of theirs is going to make some t-shirt company rich." Juan said too late for Amy to hear as she turned and walked away with only fifteen minutes to go before show time.

"Hi Chief, it's Mark. Did you get my report on Cassandra team's suggestions?

"Yes, it looks good but in light of recent events it also seems trivial in comparison to the problems we're up against."

"I agree… but it remains a critical step to coordinate our unrelated systems so we can get some of this information quicker and get ahead of the curve once in a while."

"I agree, so keep on it. Did you hear the latest news?"

"Which *"latest news"* Walter… it's coming in buckets now."

"Someone killed Alliant Techsystems' CEO right here in DC sometime last night."

"Jesus Christ, how did they get him?"

"Up close and personal… they broke his neck in his hotel room. He had a meeting scheduled this morning with a General over at the Pentagon."

"This is getting more frightening every day… they're organized."

"Any luck on your investigation down there?"

"Some, but not a whole lot… we traced the car the attendant saw to the Hartsfield-Jackson International Airport in Atlanta… it was rented by a Robert Blackman last week in DC. We got the tags off of a local security camera as they left the area. More than likely he rented another car and drove that one back here. We're checking it out now but I'm not holding my breath… he was too professional… no prints on the rental and probably at least one false ID, especially, when you can get creditable forgeries for under $2,000 nowadays. The photo of the two men isn't going to be much use unless the lab can cut through the glare... there was a lot of mirrored glass reflecting the sunlight."

"Hmmm, IDs... that sounds like one area we should be focusing more on with this case. Do we have any informer's doing that for us now?"

"I'm sure we must but not how many...I'll check it out."

"We need to find more of these guys and convince them to play on our team... or put them away and open up our own drive through."

"That's a good suggestion Walt... I'll get all of the regions working on that in their areas right away."

"What about the ballistics Mark?"

"We're sure that the weapon used was a .50-caliber semi-automatic but the fragments are useless. The one bullet that was trapped under the gas tank is compressed so badly in the armor that it may be useless as well. The FBI lab down here is applying its magic to it and they give us a one in three chance that enough rifling marks will be left to identify the gun... and that's *IF* we ever have a chance to examine the exact gun to compare it to. It may already be back with the shooter."

"Looks like you were right about the same gunman killing both CEOs."

"Yeah... but that's of little comfort considering I pretty much knew that before I came down here. The shell casings were all clean of any fingerprints and the roof top cameras only showed us the two men dressed in dark suits with masks. Their faces weren't visible and there was nothing unusual about their builds or the way they moved. If it were my hit I'd have two spotters on the ground to let me know when the car left and when it was approaching the garage so I could stay hidden until the last moment. We do know that no calls went into the police until after the shooting. We also know this guy was smart enough about the .50-caliber to pull two bullets out of the magazine to make sure it didn't jam. That took expert knowledge Walt."

"What about the elevator?"

"Three employees and their supervisor currently have access to those keys but we've confirmed that the lock to that elevator has never been changed."

"How old is the building?"

"About twenty years old, which means there could be dozens of keys floating around out there. Unless somebody cracks under questioning it's going to be another long, time consuming dead end."

"How about the play to use Dreyden's death to our advantage?"

"Oh, that reminds me. He said to thank you and Commissioner Schneider for allowing him to protect his company and investors."

"No problem, it was only fair and as long as he plays it straight with us he'll be fine."

"Anyway, without an ID on the local guy or striation marks to compare to a weapon we're pretty much dead in the water. If we can get those marks we have a chance but finding the gun is going to be tough. If we're very lucky the gun will already be identified in one of our databases and we can do a sting on the owner… if not then we're stuck trying to locate and catalog every .50-caliber between DC and Miami so we can test it."

"That's *IF* the gun is still even registered Mark. I've been checking up on that weapon and the laws surrounding it are really screwed up. If I buy the gun I have to register it… no problem. If I sell it to you there's no further registration required by law. Depending on how many times this weapon has changed hands we may never have a chance of recovering it… so even perfect ballistics would be useless."

*"That's fucking great Walter...* We have better gun control for pistols then we do for a sniper's dream rifle."

"That's about the size of it son... and that topic will definitely be in my conversation with the Attorney General this afternoon. Alright, get done whatever you need to down there and come back home... Hobson's agents will have to work it with Morrison's team without you. We've got too many holes in this dam of ours as it is."

"Okay Chief... I'll be back by around noon on Sunday."

"When you get back have your teams locate and interrogate every ID counterfeiter in a two-hundred mile radius of DC. Let's just see if we can't find something else out on this Mr. Blackman of ours. I'll get a letter from the AG so we can get the pentagon's full cooperation identifying our military sharpshooters. I want ALL of them... black ops and the ones they want us to believe are dead. I'll get all the clearances we'll need. I'd bet a months wages that we trained the SOB that did these last two shootings of ours."

"Alright, at least it's a plan Walt. The team down here is still trying to get more out of the garage attendant. He was pretty adamant at first about not getting any details on the two guys in the Lexus but he's willing to work with our sketch artist to give us a rough look at the driver. He didn't see the passenger enough to give us any help and we don't know for sure who was driving... the local guy or the shooter. My money is on the shooter since he rented the car."

"That's good and it could help a lot... especially if we have military ID photos to compare the drawing to. I'm also bringing in a profiler and military intelligence to try to get our arms around this invisible bear of ours. See you on Sunday Mark."

"Take care Chief."

# *"Old Friends and…"*

"General Anderson please, this is Karl Schmidt from Blackwell Securities calling."

"I'll check to see if he's available for your call Mr. Schmidt, please hold. General Andersen, Mr. Schmidt from Blackwell is on line two."

"Thank you Margaret."

"You're welcome sir."

"Good morning Karl, to what do I owe this pleasure?"

"Good morning General. How's the windy city treating you?"

"Well enough, what's on your mind Colonel?"

"What's your take on what's been going on around the Country Sir?"

"What's yours?"

"Looks like a pretty well planned rebellion to me Sir… small but well trained and coordinated."

"I'd have to agree with you although I don't know how large or small it is… that's hard to say yet."

"We can't handle the amount of calls we're getting from frightened executives looking for bodyguards. Most of our force is still tied up in Eurasia and I was hoping you might be able to help us out."

"You know we're not in that business Karl… we focus on anti-terrorism search and destroy work… not bodyguards."

"I was hoping you might be able to figure out how to do both and take some of the pressure off of us. We just can't recruit the quality of people we need and still get them cleared fast enough."

"It's tough being a mercenary now isn't it Karl?"

"Now sir, you know my position on this. We try to fight for the right side and it's not all about the money."

"Maybe not for you, but you have a lot of soldiers who *are in it just for the money*."

"Sir, I didn't call to get into this debate again. I know you're correct on some counts but so am I. I'm doing the best I can to provide a legitimate service so that kids that don't want to fight don't have to."

"Save the propaganda for somebody else. Keeping the moral high ground is the hard part Karl. You're responsible for your soldiers even AFTER they've left your employ and have sold out to the highest bidder. That's the reason I can't do business with you son. You were a great soldier and a fine patriot but I don't believe we can bring peace to our nation by privatizing war."

"What do you believe in Sir?"

"I believe in our Constitution, our liberties and in the universal prayer for enduring peace for all nations. We've both seen the horrors of war and that's not the road to survival. That's what our fight is all about."

"We're not too different from one another in that regard Sir."

"Except we only recover our expenses Colonel while you, your executives and your shareholders get filthy rich off of yours."

"And what's wrong with making money Sir?"

"Nothing, in good hands... everything, in the wrong ones. Thanks for calling Karl, best of luck to you."

"Thank you General."

"One last thing Karl, if your executives wish to consult with us we can help them… but it won't be through bodyguards."

"Thank you Sir, I'll pass that along."

## *"Domestic Black Ops"*

"Joe, this is Aaron. I need you to come on up in the next few days. I just got off the phone with Karl Schmidt and it seems he can't get enough good help these days. This is a secure line so speak freely."

"I imagine their phones haven't stopped ringing over there."

"Exactly Sergeant Major, he tried to recruit my help but I told him we weren't interested."

"But we really are Sir?"

"You have a devious mind Mr. Clark… I like that in a soldier."

(Laughing) "So what can I do for you General?"

"I need each of our Commanders to give up three of their best black ops guys to go help out our old friend. They need to be as secure as you and I Joe."

"What would you like me to tell them about their mission?"

"For now just have them put in their applications and not mention their connection to our anti-terrorist activities. Have them keep their existing aliases intact and make sure they understand that this mission is domestic… none of the overseas mercenary crap Joe. I want them on bodyguard duty back in their own regions pulling double duty for us and these frightened executives. Make sure each region sends in one applicant a week for the next three weeks and then I want them checking back to you on their postings. No one beyond commander needs to know any more details."

"The best of our men hold top security clearances."

"Exactly, which is what's going to make them so damn valuable to Blackwell, excuse me… *Xe*. Bodies are easy Joe… but security clearances aren't. I expect that only the most frightened execs will pay what they're worth. Make sure they know that they're in the driver's seat during salary negotiations and have them estimate the high range of what they think they're worth and then ***triple it*** and <u>stand firm</u>. Blackwell will have no problem meeting their demands with the market the way it is and these fat cats won't have any choice but to cough up some more of their blood money for a little peace of mind. If they can spend a quarter million or more on a useless armored car then they can surely afford our guys."

"Once they're in place sir what would you like me to do?"

"Make your command decisions Joe… I'm not going to be around for ever and you're ready to fill my shoes right now. Just keep it black so they don't lose their cover without good cause. If they do get spooked then make a decision, it's your call. They're the best at what they do and should know when it's time to get out. If you have to bring any of them in then make them safe, cool them down and we'll redeploy."

"I understand General. This will take priority over their current duties but they may still be able to fill some gaps for us on occasion and will definitely help isolate target ops."

"That's it exactly… this is your baby now Joe. I don't need to hear anymore unless you have very good cause. Was that you in DC?"

"Yes Sir."

"Nice work… but don't take too many of those kind of chances, we can't afford to lose you."

"I won't sir… it was a fast mover and I was the only one available in such a short time frame."

"***I understand…*** but if it comes down to losing you for one target then we'll be the big losers… so be smart. You have my permission to say no."

## *"Little Pieces, Big Puzzle"*

"Detective Morrison please, this is agent Hobson at the FBI."

"Hey Paul, how are you making out?"

"We finally have some good news… our lab was able to get the glare out of one frame just enough to give us a decent ID on the passenger."

"Outstanding! That's good work! McNulty is convinced that's he's the local guy since the shooter rented the car in DC and probably was the driver all of the time in that vehicle."

"Alright Ron… we need to play this close to the vest… and find him fast while Dreyden is still playing possum for us. Then we need to put his nuts in a vice."

"Ouch, that hurts just thinking about it. You're not serious right?"

"Of course not Detective… but I need all the help you can muster on this. We're running the picture now through our facial recognition program against the Motor Vehicle database for the State. I'm hopeful but the picture is only decent… it's far from perfect."

"What about your sketch artist Paul?"

"She's working on it too and that should produce a better visual for the human eye to match but it won't be any good for the computer."

"Okay, get me a copy as soon as it's ready and I'll get on it. Is there any other news?"

"Just that we're pretty sure that both the Charlotte and Atlanta shooters are the same guy and that he probably lives in the DC region… we've got a rough sketch on him now."

"Okay, that's something anyway. Thanks Paul"

# *"Profiles of Elephants and Ants"*

"Good morning Chief, Miss Annachiarico is here for your meeting."

"Thank you Sally, send her right in."

"Miss Anna-chi...." Dobson tried to say but fumbled with her name.

"Anna-key-air-ee-coe" She said slowly with a smile on her lovely face. But please feel free to call me Sandra."

"That's a lovely name Sandra... just a little tough the first time."

"Just think musically and it will roll right off your tongue."

"Yours perhaps... mine isn't that talented." He said before he realized the unintended sexual overtone and blushed before clumsily adding; "Agent Mark McNulty will be joining us in just a moment."

Sandra Annachiarico was nothing less than breathtaking. Early to mid thirties, petite, with dark hair and eyes that were so sensual and exotic that it was easy to get lost in them. Without realizing it Chief Dobson's mouth had opened like some kind of stupid fish looking for flies. Fortunately the embarrassment that followed was interrupted as McNulty knocked and entered uninvited.

"Hi Chief... and hello again Miss Annachiarico."

"Hi Mark, how have you been?"

"Busy but well thank you. How's the world treating my favorite profiler?"

"Amusingly." She said with a giggle and a sideways glance at the Chief who had lost the blush and regained his composure.

"Glad to see you two know each other." Said Chief Walter Dobson.

"Yes, we met a few years ago on another case."

"Did she crack that one for you Mark?"

"No, as a matter of fact. We never found him."

"Maybe it was a woman." Sandra offered only half jokingly.

"Yep, maybe." McNulty nodded in agreement.

"So what have you put together for us young lady?" Dobson asked.

"Mark and I began by looking back over the last thirty-six months at cases that were similar to the killings we've been experiencing recently. In my opinion we're dealing with a lot of loosely knit cells working independently from one another but with a command structure in place that is centered in a military paradigm."

"This is a military operation?" Asked an astonished Chief Dobson.

"No sir, not exactly." She continued. "Their leaders are definitely military strategists and I'm confident that most, if not all, of their cells are ex-military people as well with highly honed skills. Like your sniper and the black ops killing in the hotel room and the dozens of other highly organized hits that we've seen. These aren't the random acts of terrorists and their manifesto only substantiates my hypothesis. This is a revolution, nothing less. I traced what appear to be the initial hits to almost four and a half years ago. That's when I believe they began organizing… recruiting, quietly, in secret without any fanfare for the tactics they were laying in place. The fact that they've come out in the open now tells me that they're completely armed, organized and are ready to do exactly what they said they're going to do. They killed over a dozen hard targets in a little over a week and we still don't know who we're fighting. That takes skill at all levels. They're Special Forces people and highly trained marksmen and they probably have their own surveillance expertise and the ability to take their victims out quietly, like a seal or a marine might have to do. Most of all sir… these are hard core patriots who believe that tearing down this society from the top down is the only way to save it. Frankly, their manifesto makes a Hell of a lot more sense than our domestic and foreign policies do... and they're counting on that to garner popular support. They're fighting on home ground for *their* country."

"*Jesus...*" Chief Dobson moaned. "I suspected a lot of what you've told us but this is far more serious than I imagined."

"That's only half of it Walter." Sandra continued. "If these modern day minutemen are half as organized as I think they are then our economy can be destroyed without that much bloodshed. These are strategic strikes that they're making... they've been nuking us from within while we're still learning to share information. What good is a half trillion dollar annual military budget against them? We can't nuke ourselves... forget our subs, forget our navy, forget our jets and our armies and all the crap that goes along. They can do as much damage with a $5 bullet as our military can with a hundred million dollar offensive strike. Plus they have the same advantages that the Vietnamese had against the Chinese, the French and us. We've got a bunch of elephants trying to ward off an under-ground attack of army ants... ants that can never be eradicated... *never!*"

"What do you suggest Sandra?" Mark asked.

"As I see it we have two options, as usual... war or peace."

"Please elaborate Miss Annachiarico." Dobson asked.

"You're a quick learner Chief." Sandra said with a smile at the musical way he played with her name. "If we choose war then expect much of the same... at least five to ten killings of key people *every single week*. Think of what that's going to do to the stock exchange. We're going to continue to have massive sell-offs like the one we already saw and huge swings in the stock market that's going to reverberate world-wide and destabilize our economy. There's likely to be widespread panic and riots among portions of our population. Besides the rioting I'd expect to see major increases in crime as would-be patriots act out randomly with too much violence and too little reason. We're heading into a maelstrom that this Country has seen only twice in our entire history."

"1776 and 1861..." Mark said from deep within his thoughts.

"That's a pretty bleak picture young lady." Dobson rebuked. "How could this upstart militia possibly fight the resources we can bring to bear on them?"

Mark answered without giving Sandra a chance.

"I read a story about a man named Hathcock, he was our best sniper in Vietnam... had something like ninety confirmed kills. The military was testing a new multi-million dollar infra-red sniper detection system and this guy Hathcock slipped away during the demonstration and snuck up to within twenty feet of the observers and said bang bang, you're all dead. He defeated their technology with a ten dollar plastic umbrella. That's how sir." Mark concluded.

"Hmmm, just like the armored car against the API munitions..." The Chief said agreeing with McNulty's point.

"They can hurt us a Hell of a lot more than we can hurt them... even if we get every last one of them." McNulty said.

"So what about the alternative? How do we get there from here?" The Chief asked.

"Peace? That's easy... all we have to do is turn off greed and selfishness in the world." Sandra said matter-of-factly. "It sure would be a prettier picture to paint. All weapons of mass destruction are halted and disassembled, environmental hazards eliminated and the environment cleaned up, our war economy is restructured to become a high-technology energy efficient one, peace movements and civil rights around the world would replace victimization and privatization. Other than the growing pains to get there from here there isn't anything I don't like about their scenario... and that's how the population is going to feel and why it might even work… it doesn't take that much relative force to get a boulder rolling downhill Walt."

"I know what our government is going to do…" The Chief began… "They're going to throw every branch of the service into weeding out these people… they're going to hunt them down like dogs and a lot of innocent people are going to die in the process. They're going to take out that God DAMNED BIG STICK and start beating at anything that moves. We'll be lucky if we don't wind up under Marshall Law."

"Hey Chief… you said *"they're* going to…" Mark corrected.

"I did, didn't I..." Dobson replied introspectively.

# *"WIQR's New Intern"*

"Hi, I'm James Thoreau and I'm here to meet with Tim McManus and Irv Evans."

"Yes. Mr. Thoreau, please have a seat and I'll let Tim know you're here." Said WIQR's pretty receptionist.

A few minutes later Tim was greeting the young man in the reception area and walking him back to the Station Manager's office. Knocking lightly on the already opened door Tim said:

"Hi Irv, do you have a few minutes? I'd like to introduce you to James Thoreau."

"Yes, of course… come on in. Tim and Jack have spoken very highly of you Jim, or do you prefer James?" Evans asked as he offered his hand.

"Either way is fine Sir." He said shyly as he accepted Evans' firm handshake.

"Please Jim, call me Irv… have a seat. Would you care for some coffee or juice?"

"No sir thanks, I'm fine."

"What do you know about our intern position?" Evans continued.

"Not a whole lot sir, I'm sorry, Irv… I know that your station is looking for someone good at doing research and doesn't mind odd jobs as they come up."

"What kind of hours can you put in Jim?"

"Whatever it takes… once classes are over I'm here to work and learn so I'll do whatever needs to get done. I'm a fast learner."

"That's fine because your hours may be all over the clock. I presume you've been keeping up on what's been going on around the country?"

"Yes sir, it's horrible."

"Not for our business it isn't. We're busier than ever and need to stay on top of this… thing… whatever it is. We need you to help our people with whatever research needs to get done. I also understand that you're a pretty good writer."

"Thank you… that's very kind."

"You'll be writing up a lot of what you find to make it more efficient for our people to cut through to the information they'll need. Is that clear?"

"Absolutely… I do it now every time I write a term paper."

"Good. You're going to report to Tim McManus and concentrate mainly on his program, which I know you're already familiar with."

"Yes, very much so… a lot of kids on campus tune in but the show doesn't always reach us up in New Jersey."

"We're working on that and should double our range through affiliate stations within a few months. There will be others that will ask you to do their jobs for them but don't take on any tasks without clearing them with Tim first."

"I understand."

"Do you have a place to stay yet?"

"My girlfriend's Aunt is letting us stay with her. She's about twenty-five minutes from here."

"What about transportation Jim?"

"My girlfriend has a car but I'd hate to borrow it and leave her stranded. I was planning on taking mass transit Mr. Evans."

"That won't do… I need you to be mobile. Don't worry; we'll get you set up with a decent car. You do have a license and a clean driving record right?"

(Laughing lightly) "Yes Irv, no points or accidents."

"Okay, that's good. Tim, get him in contact with Barry down at Lee's Chevrolet and tell him he's got $3,500 to put Mr. Thoreau into a safe vehicle. Have Claire put him onto our insurance policy so he'll be covered as soon as he starts."

"Will do Irv." McManus confirmed.

"Thank you very much Irv… that's very kind of you."

"Wait until you see your paycheck before you get all excited. Did Tim tell you what this job pays?"

"Not exactly, but he did warn me that it wouldn't be that much."

"It's good that you have someone to stay with or it wouldn't be worth your time. But I promise you it will be a learning experience that you'll never forget."

"That's primarily what I'm after… that and enough money to buy books and have a little spending money back at school so my mom won't have to worry about it."

"You'll have plenty for that Jim. Tim, make sure he gets one of our credit cards and explain to him what we cover."

"I'll take good care of him."

"Do you have any questions for us Jim?"

"Yes, when can I start?"

"How soon does school let out?" Evans said with a big smile.

"Class is out in a few more weeks and then one more day to move some of our things down to Chrissie's Aunt's house."

"The sooner the better…" Evans said. "I just wish you were here the last few weeks… it's been a madhouse."

"I'll get down as soon as I can sir… and thank you very much for the wheels. I wasn't expecting that."

"You'll be earning them every day Jim. Just don't wrap it around a tree." Evans said only half kidding.

"I won't. I'm a pretty good driver and I don't drink."

"That's good to know…" Tim interrupted. "I can use a dedicated driver once in a while!"

"If he ever calls you up drunk Jim… do us all a favor and call him a cab." Evans said with a little annoyance in his voice.

"No problem sir."

"Alright… we've got a busy day ahead and Tim needs to prepare for his show tonight. It's been a pleasure meeting you Jim… see you in a few weeks." Evans concluded, stood and once again offered his hand.

"Thank you Irv… I'm really looking forward to working here." Jim said as he shook his Station Manager's hand and followed McManus out the door.

"Irv really like you James… that cheap SOB never gave anyone a car… except maybe his daughter." McManus confided.

"***That was unreal!*** I've been so nervous about this interview and it was actually fun!"

"That's because he knew you had the right stuff before you got here... Jack and I made sure of that. We need you a Hell of a lot more then you need this gig. You could be earning twice as much somewhere else."

"Maybe, but I'd be lucky to be learning half as much. Thanks for everything you've done Tim."

"It's my pleasure James. I'm looking forward to having your help around here. I can't even answer all of my e-mails anymore. Hey, you can help with that too. Answer the ones that seem easy to you and compose an answer for those that aren't and run them past me for approval. Are you up to that?"

"That's a piece of cake Tim. ***Challenge me*** this summer and I won't let you down."

"You're on! Can you hang for the show?"

"Not really, I don't know Chrissie's Aunt yet and they'll be anxious to hear how things went today. I should get back over there. We'll all be listening for sure though."

"I've gotta run too... Why don't you say hello and goodbye to Jack on your way out. I'm sure he'd like to see you."

"Thanks Tim I was planning to so I could thank him. Thanks again Tim... see you in a few weeks."

"Keep me posted by phone, ***not e-mail***, so I'll know when to expect you."

"Will do."

Jim met briefly with Jack Bennett to thank him for helping secure his intern position and then he thanked the receptionist while leaving the station. If there was an elevator man he probably would have thanked him too. He was so excited he couldn't feel his feet on the ground for the two blocks it took to get to the bus stop that headed out of Baltimore toward Chrissie and her Aunt Norma.

# *"Silent Blessings"*

When Jim Thoreau arrived at Aunt Norma's house Chrissie was sitting on the front porch waiting for him. She could tell from half a block away that he had gotten the job just by the spring in his step. She left the broad porch and ran to greet him.

"Hey there!" She called to him from forty yards away.

"I got it!" He called back to her as he too began to run and close the distance that was left.

They hugged tight and he spun her around twice before gently letting her back down. He wanted to tell her what had happened but not nearly as much as he wanted to look into her beautiful eyes and kiss her. The two young lovers embraced on that sidewalk outside of Baltimore and felt the world disappear... leaving just the two of them.

"Jim, I'm so proud of you!" She said with genuine enthusiasm. "When do you start?"

"As soon as school is over and I can get down here. They're even getting me a car for the summer!"

"Really? That's fantastic! I was going to offer you mine."

"I couldn't leave you stranded Chrissie... that wouldn't be fair... but now we don't have to worry about it."

"Let's get back to Aunt Norma's house... she's been excited about having us come and stay a while."

The young lovers walked hand in hand back up to the house and up the porch stairs where Aunt Norma was standing. She had a big smile on her face and it was obvious that she had just witnessed their joyous reunion.

"It's good to finally meet you Jim." Norma said still smiling.

"Thank you so much for letting me stay this weekend. I'm sorry I couldn't come here first but my interview was waiting downtown."

"Don't be silly… you're right on time. Dinner's just about ready. He's even more handsome than you said." Aunt Norma ribbed Chrissie just loud enough to elicit a blush out of Jim.

"He got the job Norma!" Chrissie nearly shrieked in excitement.

"I could tell sweetheart just by watching you two. I hope you like roast beef and mashed potatoes… it's one of Chrissie's favorite meals."

"I love it! It's been a long time since I've had a home cooked meal. *It smells so good!*" He said as they walked into the house.

"You two just relax and I'll get dinner on the table."

"Can I help Aunt Norma?"

"No honey, everything is under control… just sit and relax… dinner will be ready in fifteen minutes."

"I am soooo hungry Chrissie I hope I don't embarrass myself."

"Here… have a hot roll" She said and then buttered it for him. "Now you won't have to shovel it in with both hands."

Jim devoured the roll in two bites and then took a long drink of water that was already poured and waiting on the dinner table.

"Okay, that helped." He said only mildly relieved. ***"It smells so good!"*** He repeated himself.

"Norma's a great cook… ***much better*** than my mom." She said laughing.

214

"Chrissie, could you come and give me a hand for a minute?" Her aunt called from the kitchen.

A few moments later the two women entered the dining room carrying the roast beef, mashed potatoes and gravy. Then Norma went back in to the kitchen and returned with string beans garnished with almonds and a plate of fresh corn on the cob.

"Does your family say grace Jim?"

"No Ma'am…" He said awkwardly.

"Neither do we… I just didn't want to insult our guest. And Jim, please call me Norma… I'm not even sure if I know what a Ma'am is."

"Thank you Norma." He said relaxing more from her natural warmth and graciousness.

"Dig in… I know you must be starving." Norma urged as she handed him the plate of roast beef and waited for her guest to get started.

Chrissie already had her mashed potatoes scooped out and was filling the huge pile with gravy. She looked up just long enough to see Jim smiling at her and her un-dainty portion.

"I see you're a little hungry too Chrissie." He said.

"Wait until you taste these potatoes… Aunt Norma's gravy makes them the best thing you'll ever eat. That's why I'm taking mine before you figure that out for yourself."

"There's plenty of food *children*…" Norma said amused. "Just don't make yourselves sick eating too fast. Don't they feed you up there at Rutgers?"

"Not like this!" Jim said. "The food's okay and all but it's not home cooking." He said as he slopped a greedy portion of potatoes on his plate and then copied the way Chrissie had made a crater and then

215

poured in the gravy. He was eating as slowly as he could but couldn't wait for the corn or the string beans before shoveling down half of his mashed potatoes. ***"This is fantastic!"*** He said between bites.

"Please pass the string beans Jim." Chrissie asked trying not to point out his poor table manners.

"Oh, I'm sorry…" He said and hurried to pass everything closer to them.

Norma giggled as she watched her guests enjoy themselves. "It's been too long Chrissie… I've really missed you."

"You too Norma. This feels so wonderful doesn't it?"

"Yes sweetheart, it's good to have family in my home again."

They settled into their feast with the joy of having loved ones all around. Talking less but passing grateful glances to each other throughout the meal. Chrissie knew they would be welcomed to stay but didn't want to interrupt their Norman Rockwell moment by asking for that favor now. There would be plenty of time for that later. Each of them counted their blessings that evening and although no prayer had been said at the beginning of the meal each of them gave silent thanks for the blessings that were being bestowed upon them so generously this evening.

## *"Venting"*

"Good evening. I'm Tim McManus and you're listening to ***Door to Door*** here at ***WIQR – 103.5 FM*** in Baltimore. Last week I monopolized the airwaves with a tirade that has generated more e-mail, faxes and phone calls than ever before in the history of this radio station. I'm glad you were listening and took the time to send in your thoughts, most of which were thoughtful and interesting perspectives. I would however like to read a few from the other pile. So in keeping with one of my main objectives… keeping the show entertaining… here are a few for you're enjoyment.

- McManus, you are the stupidest mother ***bleep*** that I've ever heard. Why don't you just shove one of those .50-caliber pistols right up your ***bleep!***

- Love it or leave it jackass!

- You're nothing but a communist faggot who probably never did one day's honest work.

- People like you should be hunted with dogs and hanging from trees. You're nothing but a liar and a ***bleep***'g traitor.

We had about two-hundred and fifty of these types of messages and I want to say just one thing to all of those sensitive and creative people, it was something that Voltaire said; ***"I may not agree with what you have to say but I shall defend to the death your right to say it."*** As good fortune would have it we also received some of the other kind of correspondence… the constructive kind from people who actually use their brains and love their children ***and*** their country. All of the phone calls, e-mails and faxes in support of doing something positive about our problems totaled two-thousand seven-hundred and fifty-three. So it looks like the total idiots listening are outnumbered by more than eleven to one. So that means I get to keep my job for another week.

Anyway, that's enough of me for a while… what do you want to talk about? Jeremy from Towson, what's on your mind?"

"I was over in Iraq and those people never wanted us there. Now we've got mercenaries running around murdering people and they aren't held up to the same standards that our military personnel are."

"You know this to be a fact Jeremy?"

"Yes sir, absolutely! If anyone in the army does something wrong there are formal procedures that are followed. People get court-martialed and imprisoned if necessary. These guys work for companies like Blackwell, Triple Canopy and DynCorp and thanks to Order 17 are immune to prosecution."

"Order 17? What's that?"

"It was issued by Paul Bremer in June of 2004. It grants immunity to civilian contractors and makes them immune to legal action."

"Bremer was our man in Iraq. So these civilian mercenaries can do anything they please and get away with it?"

"Yes Mr. McManus, he was the Coalition Provisional Authority. They're getting away with murder, rapes… you name it."

"And what are we doing about it?"

"Not a God Damn thing sir. That's why you never heard about it. But we see these guys all the time. Half our soldiers hate their guts because they're making us all targets and the other half wants to sign up and get the bigger paychecks they're pulling down."

"Privatization…what a lovely concept… thanks for your insights Jeremy."

"Pauline from Philadelphia, what's on your mind?"

"Hi Tim... Thank you for taking my call. I just wanted to say that your show last week really touched my husband and I. We appreciate your truthfulness."

"Thank you Pauline. What's on your mind tonight?"

"This last week has been so crazy with all of those executives and Senators getting killed. It's all very frightening."

"Yes, and that was only about twelve or fifteen people... imagine what it's like for those poor families in Iraq."

"It's horrible."

"Did you hear or read the letter from the organization calling itself Deep-Six?"

"No I didn't Tim."

"It's only a few days old but you can check the Democracy Now website or give us another day or two and we'll post it as well. Once you understand what's happening it will be less frightening to you."

"Thank you Tim, I'll look for it. God bless you."

"Thank you... next caller please Jack."

"I saw pictures of that tobacco executive's armored car and I think your program is responsible for his murder."

"You do? And may I know who I'm speaking with?"

"Bill."

"Okay *Bill*... why do you think we're responsible?"

"Your show gets a lot of people riled up and the next thing you know this guy gets blown away just like you said on your show."

"Oh, I see your point. But let me ask you something?

"Do you think the shooter heard my show and then drove down to Atlanta to blow Mr. Dreyden away?"

"Well, yes… it's possible. Maybe his wife died of cancer or something."

"Okay, I'll give you that one as a possibility… but you know our station doesn't broadcast that far south right?"

"I don't know how far your station broadcasts!"

"Well, out of the three-hundred million people in this country let's just say that we can only reach a very small fraction of them. So how would you explain all of the other murders that are taking place around this country?"

"I don't know about them."

"Thanks Bill. It's obvious you don't know about a lot of things."

"Mary Anne from Fredericksburg… you're on the air."

"Good evening Tim. I heard that manifesto and at first I thought it was a terror group. I had to go back to the website and read it again to fully understand what they were saying."

"And what did that message mean to you Mary Anne?"

"Once you get over the shock of it and try to understand what they're saying it's really pretty simple. Either stop waging illegal wars, stop polluting our environment and stop stealing from us or we're going to kill you."

"And what do you think about that? Isn't it a bit barbaric?"

"Compared to what Tim? Compared to slaughtering women and children with cluster bombs that don't explode until long after they've been dropped? No, I don't think it is too barbaric at all. I think they're just saying the system is broken so badly that we can't fix it from the inside. So they're going after a more expedient solution."

"So you are buying in to their logic to tear down our institutions in order that we may rebuild them?"

"It's hard to say for sure but their words make sense. They're not trying to tear down everything... just those who profit by waging war."

"And polluters, and politicians and anyone ***THEY DEFINE*** as targets."

"Well look who they've killed so far... people that are in the business of death... one way or another. That CEO Dreyden deserved to die... how many millions of people have died of cancer or heart attacks or strokes because of his families cigarettes? How many millions of dollars does one family need? Yes, I think the targets they've been choosing are intelligent ones."

"But who died and made these assassins Judge, jury and chief executioners?"

"I guess our Founding Fathers did Tim... you understand *that* don't you?"

"Yes Mary Anne I do. I just wanted to hear your opinion and not my own. Thank you very much for your call."

"Mitch from Gaithersburg, you're on the air."

"I wanted to say something about the depleted uranium weapons our military is using."

"You're talking about the DU238 munitions that can cut through armor right?"

"Yes Sir, that's right. What most people don't know is that these weapons are illegal. Using them makes our leaders war criminals."

"Why is that Mitch?"

"Because the radioactivity doesn't diminish for thousands of years and harms innocent people long after the battle is over. The Iraqi population is suffering from cancer at ten times the normal rate since we started using these weapons. Their birth rate mortalities are occurring at five times the normal level and many of these stillborns are just grotesque masses of pulp. How would you react if that was your child and you knew that horror had come from the United States?"

"It helps us to understand the extremes people will go to in order to fight back." McManus affirmed.

"Here's the exact information Tim. Weapons ***must meet*** four criteria under existing international humanitarian and human rights law in armed conflict:

1. Weapons must be able to be limited in effect to the field of battle… that's known as the territorial limitation.
2. Weapons must be limited in effect to the time period of the armed conflict… that's known as the temporal limitation.
3. Weapons must not be unduly inhumane… that's known as the humanity limitation.
4. Weapons must not unduly damage the environment… that's known as the environmental limitation.

Depleted Uranium usage in weapons is illegal under these criteria."

"Thank you Mitch that was very useful information to hear."

"This is Katie from the Baltimore VA Medical Center."

"Hi Katie, what do you do at the Hospital?"

"I'm the Head Nurse here at the VA."

"What's on you mind?"

"Your last caller hit the nail on the head with his warning about depleted uranium in our weapons. Thousands of our soldiers have been complaining about illnesses we didn't recognize since the first Gulf war. I'm sure you've heard the term *Gulf War Syndrome*?"

"Yes, I'm sure we all have Katie."

"What causes it is exposure to the DU238 that's in these illegal weapons your caller was talking about. It harms not only the Iraqi population but our soldiers as well who found themselves camping out on the ruins of their enemy who were annihilated by our radioactive munitions. They're suffering from radiation poisoning and not stress disorders as our government would like you to believe."

"Why would they lie to us about their illnesses Katie?"

"So they can reduce the compensation our veterans are entitled to… it's that simple."

"That's a pretty strong accusation… can it be substantiated?"

"It's well documented now Tim. A few years ago they would have fired me for making this call. Now anyone can simply type in: *radiation poisoning and gulf war syndrome* into their search engine and learn as much about it as they want to know. You don't have to take it from me… its common knowledge now."

"So what's being done about it?"

"Not nearly enough. There are class action suits and organizations taking this on but we're up against the entire Corporate-Military

Industrial Complex and our political leaders are nothing more than puppets in their hands."

"So what do you think about this manifesto that just came out?"

"Where do I sign up... *that's what I think!* And anyone that thinks I'm wrong can spend a few hours with me at the VA hospital and I promise I'll change their minds. Just imagine that one of these poor kids was your child and then face the facts. The least we can do is take care of our Veterans. If we can't afford to do that then we have no right to wage war."

"Thank you Katie... our Vets are lucky to have you fighting for them. We're all behind you."

"Thank you to Tim... you show is a beacon for democracy."

"Doug from Atlantic City... what pulls you away from the tables tonight?"

"I'm a guard down here... I don't gamble."

"Alright, what's on your mind?"

"The Second Amendment..."

"Yes, that seems to be everyone's favorite recently. What about it?"

"I just want these corrupt leaders of ours to know that there's a whole lot of us that are just watching and waiting for them to try and take any more of our rights away. If they think the last week was bad wait until John Q. Citizen picks up his gun against them."

"And who's *"them"* Doug?"

"The liars and cheats... and crooks who steal our pension plans and then spend a fortune on propaganda telling us all how great they are.

We all know who they are Tim... We're not as dumb as they'd like to believe."

"So do you have a specific question or point or just this vague threat?"

"I just want everyone to know that we have the right to build a better country, one that isn't corrupt and that it's okay to fight back and not run away. There are nine-hundred and ninety-nine of us to every one of them... and like you said before... their big weapons don't mean *bleep* against us. This is *our home*, this is *our country* and the only way I'll ever give up my weapons is *bullets first*!"

"I understand and am sure a lot of people out there agree with you."

"Well folks, that about wraps up another night here at *Door to Door*. We encourage you all to write and tell us how we can bring peace to the world or to address any other issue that confronts humanity. Please just don't send letters complaining about the issues... ask yourself what you would do if you had the power to make positive changes and remember what the great Albert Einstein once said;

*"The world is a dangerous place, not because of those who do evil, but because of those who look on and do nothing."*

I'd like to end tonight's show with a short poem, entitled, *"Snowfall"*.

*"We are all but snowflakes floating for a brief time through gentle winds, sometimes not... but all together in our separateness... we are unique, yet so alike that from a distance we are the same... until we reach the ground and look up at all our brothers and sisters gently joining us... surrounding us with their caresses and their lives... pressing us together into one beautiful landscape... one entity... and we are no longer alone. For it is not in our aloneness that we are great and wonderful... but in our togetherness."*

This is Tim McManus at **WIQR, 103.5 FM - Baltimore.** Thanks for listening, dream well… goodnight."

# *"Some Distances Are Just Too Great"*

"Hi sweetheart... how's school been this semester?"

"Good dad, are you okay? You sound a little down."

"No baby... I'm just tired and I miss you. How's Dean doing?"

"We're doing good Dad, don't worry about us. I just wish I could see you more. Can you come visit soon?"

"I'll try hon but work has me traveling quite a bit lately. How are you two set on money?"

"We're doing okay… Dean got a new job at an insurance agency but he's frustrated because he really wants to go to school but his mother can't afford to send him."

"What does he want to study?"

"He's still not sure… first he thinks he wants to be an architect and then the next time I ask he says something else. It's hard for him because he knows he can't go."

"Tell him if he can figure it out then I will help with his tuition. You two going to Temple University together will make your lives more enjoyable. Have him go talk to their admissions people and then give me a call when he has a plan put together. Tell him not to worry about the money."

"Really Daddy? You can do that for us?"

"Business has been good Gen so just have him take a serious look. He'll need to earn it… I'm not paying for him to get lousy grades."

"That's more than fair Dad… I can't wait to tell him when he gets home. He's been depressed about having to sell insurance… it hasn't been easy for him and it doesn't even pay that much getting started."

"Is your mailing address still the same?"

"Yes it is, why?"

"Don't worry about it… I just want to send a little something to take the pressure off … that's all."

"You don't need to Dad… just bring yourself."

"I will baby, as soon as I can. I have to run now… another plane is waiting."

"I love you Dad."

"I love you too sweetheart." David Stanton said as he hung up the phone.

A few minutes later he went to the bathroom and washed his face and blew his nose. When he looked into the mirror he barely recognized his own face. His eyes were not only red and swollen but dark with an age he had never been before. He'd seen it before in soldiers who had seen too much death and were convinced they didn't deserve to live any longer. He hadn't been thinking that way until now… as his own ghostly apparition stared back at him.

He finished dressing and went downtown where he had the bank draw up ten one thousand dollar money orders. A little further down the street he deposited it into a Federal Express envelope bound for Philadelphia. His two children didn't know it but they were only a heartbeat away from being financially secure for the rest of their lives.

Stanton went back home and finished packing. Then he took a cab to the Baltimore Washington International Airport. From there he took a United Airlines flight to San Francisco traveling coach under the name of Richard Jones.

228

## *"Foxes and Chickens"*

"Come in Miss. Thompson, Mr. Dreyden's in his den." Jason Roberts said showing her in.

"Good morning Max, how's life on the other side?" She said trying to keep the situation light.

"I don't know how much more of this I can take Emily. I feel like I'm in fucking prison... ***shit...*** My kids and wife are going stir crazy and then that mock funeral... damn it... how am I supposed to feel?"

"Damn lucky sir to be able to sit here and bitch about this prison palace of yours. Your kids will get the last few weeks off of school and finish at home with a private tutor and your wife will have to forego her normal life for a little while longer, as will you. Considering the alternative that's not too bad now is it?"

"No, it's just damn frustrating... I'm not used to sitting still like this."

"I think it's time to bring those dogs in for you Max... they'll be fun and you can get your family's training out of the way while you're all together."

"That's sound good. What's the news on your end? Any luck using my death to find these bastards?"

"We've made quite a bit of progress but not enough to raise you from the dead yet. We've got drawings of both men that were involved in the shooting. One we believe is local and the other one we think was brought down from the DC area for John Richards in Charlotte and for you. It may have been Richard's killing that prompted Lou to warn you about being too predictable. His instincts were excellent. Max, these killers are professionals... as soon as they find out that you're alive they're coming back."

"Can't we use that to our advantage? I mean if playing dead doesn't work then why not try something else?"

"I don't think you want to be a target Sir. It's not all that much fun... and if you think you feel enclosed here think about guards around you twenty-four/seven. There may be an alternative that is far less risky."

"Really, what is it?"

"Karl Schmidt runs our company and he told me that there's a security agency that specializes on anti-terrorist activities for the government that may be of some help to us."

"I'm not sure I understand."

"They aren't offering bodyguards... that's more our line of work. What their company provides in this situation is consulting. They would come in and help you determine the best course of action."

"I thought that's what you were doing Miss Thompson."

"We focus on protecting you... these guys are more proactive in getting to the terrorists that are after you and eliminating them Max. We don't do that on American soil."

"I see... so they're going to become my own private swat team."

"I honestly don't know the scope of their work but that seems like a reasonable assumption. They can definitely add a valuable perspective and perhaps even other options. I'd do it if I were in your shoes."

"And what about their security, how sure are you about these guys?"

"Their company is headed by a three star General, his name is Aaron Andersen and he's one of the most respected military leaders we've ever had. Karl Schmidt was in his chain of command during Dessert Storm and they knew each other fairly well. His people are hand-picked and they all carry at least top secret security clearances."

"Does he know I'm alive?"

"No sir. We wouldn't let anyone know unless you authorized us."

"Hmmm… let me sleep on it for a day or two and I'll let you know."

# *"Primal Forests and Old Friends"*

In the forty-eight hours since the manifesto had been read on the air not one person had come forward to identify a plan that would reverse their current direction. The Wall Street journal had been contacted by numerous executives and government staffers asking if any articles of this nature were going to be published and each one had to be advised that; *no articles of that type had been authorized for print as of this time*. No one wanted to be the first "coward", as they saw it, to step forward with their personalized mea culpa.

Meanwhile every newspaper, radio station and television show around the world was picking up on all sides of the new media debate. Despite the spin doctors and damage control experts that the neo-cons brought to bear with all the ferocity of a nuclear war the moral media was more than able to hold it's own against the vastly superior force. Together they were able to get the manifesto out in its entirety and stage a number of solid debates that embarrassed the war mongers who were torn apart one after another with undeniable logic and moral argument. Even a number of Nobel Peace Price recipients had stood up and applauded the so-called "terrorists" and "thugs" that the Bill Duke's of the world had tried to discredit. The louder the extreme right-wingers screamed the more ridiculous they sounded like wild animals howling in the woods. The logic posed by the progressive left was indisputable and most Americans were not fooled by the mega-media's best propagandists who repeated the same transparent rhetoric over and over again without answering any of the valid questions that had been directed at them.

Commander Marshall Wallace met Messer at the United Airlines baggage claim at San Francisco's International Airport. The two men shared a familiar handshake before picking up Messer's luggage and heading out to Wallace's car in the short-term parking area. They drove sixty-five miles north of the city to a primal Redwood forest. Messer grabbed boots out of his luggage and changed into his hunting clothes. Then Wallace picked up his new XM107 .50-caliber rifle and escorted Messer to the target area that he had laid out about a half mile from the remote spot where they were parked.

"What a beautiful place Marsh..." Messer said to his old friend. How old do you think these trees are?"

"At least a thousand years... some may be two thousand or more. I never get tired of visiting them. Anyone who can't appreciate the splendor of nature is dead from the neck up."

"From the heart up Marsh, it starts at the heart. Where's my target?"

"You'll need the scope Bob. Look down between those four giant trees to the bottom of the slope. About ten yards up the hill are three targets... can you see them?"

"Not yet... okay, yes... you left our lunch down there." He said with a grin. "That watermelon shouldn't go to waste Marsh... how about I go for the cantaloupe instead?"

"Sure..." He said laughing. "Can you see the third?"

"No..."

"I'll give you a hint... its yellow."

"You put a fucking lemon a mile and a half away?"

"It's closer to 8,175 feet and I have a fifty dollar bet with Andersen that says you can do it with less than a magazine."

"You're a sucker my friend... one in twenty maybe... but distance is tricky in the woods even with that new range finder of yours. Who sighted this baby in?" Messer asked.

"I did... it's the best .50-caliber the army has right now... it should be more accurate than that Barrett you like so much, especially with the new ammo we're using. It has an extremely high ballistic coefficient and should give you a few hundred extra yards in accuracy."

"Alright, let's see how close you've got her…"

Taking a prone position and carefully adjusting the spiked feet of the bipod Messer slowly and deliberately focused in on the Watermelon. Aiming dead center he gently squeezed and let one round fly. Both men were watching as the watermelon exploded. Messer watched through the rifle scope and Wallace through his Swarovski ATS 80 HD spotting scope.

"You were about three inches off-center to the right and low by about an inch…" Wallace informed his friend.

"No Sir, you were off by that amount. I was dead centered on my target." He laughed as he adjusted the M3A scope for the wind that was now blowing gently from left to right at about five miles an hour.

"Okay, where are you going with the next round Bob?"

"Look at the larger half of the watermelon… I'll show you dead center."

Messer took his time aiming, exhaled and squeezed off another round. Three point four seconds later Wallace watched as that section of watermelon exploded into tiny fragments.

"Nice shot but I can't see where you hit it."

"Just watch the cantaloupe Marsh…" he said to his friend before exploding the melon as if an M80 had been planted inside it.

"That leaves you seven rounds to make me fifty bucks."

"A hundred bucks says I can do it in two…" He said with a very serious look at his friend.

"You're on!" Marsh said with typical military bravado.

Messer took a few deep breaths and released them slowly while thinking to himself; *easy… smooth… relaxed… good. easy… smooth… relaxed… good… easy… smooth… relaxed… good.*

Then he held his expired breath squeezing gently until the first trigger position clicked, which moved the second trigger position to within a hairs pull before it would fire. Messer squeezed the remaining few pounds of pressure more with his mind than with his finger and felt the jolt and explosive release of the M107.

*"Shit!"* Wallace groaned as the lemon disappeared into a yellow mist. "I should know by now not to bet against you."

"Don't worry Marsh… Andersen is picking up half your tab." He said jokingly.

"You ever try collecting a bet from the General?"

"I never had to." Messer said with a wide grin on his face. "Besides, look at all the money I just saved you on ammo."

"*You're a wiseass!* Now let's see if you can do that to our target and I won't be so upset about the money you just sharked me out of."

"Who is it?" Messer asked with an obvious change in mood.

"That bastard Jensen the one who outted Ambassador Winston's wife. Bill tries to tell the truth and stop an illegal war before it gets going so what do our leaders do? They ruin his wife's career by blowing her CIA cover. This one is personal Bob."

"Is this the actual distance and angle?"

"As close as we can figure it… maybe fifty yards more... the angle is correct. He's giving a commencement address at a local college."

"I hate doing this in front of the kids Marsh… don't we have any options?"

"Not without significant collateral damage. Besides, at least half of those "kids" as you call them will applaud his death. They've been protesting his visit trying to prevent him from even coming. It's seems he's a last minute replacement for a Congressman who backed out after being booed off the stage for singing that stupid war song. What a fucking moron. What gets into these clowns?"

"Who knows… amnesia, fame… or they can't handle the power rush. It's too bad really… I used to like that guy. Now I can visualize him in my sights at night."

"He's was on my list Bob but I pulled him off."

"Keep an eye on his candidacy… if he gets too hot you'll never get near him, especially in the last one-hundred and twenty days."

"After that stunt of his he's already dead politically. He just saved us a bullet."

"How safe are we on this one Marsh?"

"My men will have the gun in-place for you and you can just leave it."

"Is your team picking it up? It's a Hell of a weapon to waste."

"No, we want that weapon traced back to the team we stole it from. They're a bunch of punks who think it's alright to kill surrendering soldiers for fun. Their unit has been back from Iraq and they're getting ready to redeploy. They haven't even reported the gun missing. We have a sergeant on the inside who would like to shoot the whole damn bunch of them. He'll be joining one of my squads as soon as he gets his discharge... that's if they don't frag him first."

"What's going to happen to him when this thing blows up?"

"Not a thing, he reported the missing weapon to his LT and the Lieutenant buried his report along with the other atrocities. He kept a copy of course so he'll be fine."

"Good. What about anti-sniper tactics?"

"We're shooting at close to world record distance on this one… so the protection they'll have in-place will be much closer in… we figure a mile or so. You'll be long gone before they can figure this out. I'll tell you the details on the ride back. Let's get packed up and get something to eat I'm starving."

"What time does he give his speech?"

"About two hours after our cease-fire ends."

"Good… too bad it wasn't one minute after it ended. Any chance we can move it up a few hours?" Messer said half-wishing that his joke could come true.

"Let's just hope he doesn't chicken out like the last guy did."

"The President's man thinks the President's men can protect him… let's teach them all a lesson with this one David." Marsh slipped.

"Be careful ole friend… the name's **Bob**… Bob Messer."

# *"Counter Measures"*

Like his counterparts Commander Joe Clark had taken his seventy-two hour cease-fire to plan multiple attacks with the platoon leaders under his command. First came the retrieval of the small flash card from behind his attic wall. This had been easily accomplished with a child's magnet tied to a nine foot string, which he had lowered to the inner floor capturing the metal washer that was tied around the plastic case protecting the high-density digital card.

From there Clark had accessed the encrypted information and selected twenty-five new targets for his five platoon leaders before re-securing the compact flash card. Each platoon leader was responsible for prioritizing his list and managing the resources of his four to six squads, which would be brought to bear on the upcoming missions. Each platoon leader commanded an autonomous militia of between forty to fifty-five highly skilled warriors who had been working together for no less than three years. Their expert skills ranged from surveillance and munitions to sniping and hand to hand combat to other essential personnel who were responsible for the acquisition of needed materials, including those from the black market. All squads were led by battle hardened Sergeants who had been personally recruited by Sergeant Major Clark or their own Staff Sergeant leader.

During those silent seventy-two hours prioritized targets were isolated and tracked all across the country. Every available asset was brought to bear on obtaining inside information on itinerary's and other vital data that would allow the lists to be refined, finalized and executed. When the cease-fire ended all teams would be free to carry out their missions as they saw fit; expeditiously, professionally and with as many risks as possible identified and compensated for.

Meanwhile Bob Messer and Marshall Wallace were preparing for their mission, which was now only four hours away. The nest was armed, the weather was cool and the wind was blowing at a gentle eight miles an hour at a direct right angle to the line of fire. Eight-hundred chairs faced the five foot tall oak lectern, which stood atop the stage guarded on either side by two rows of faculty chairs slightly behind the speaker.

The secret service was busy surveying the campus area and checking credentials of everyone moving in and out of the University. Two hours before the event they began placing two man sniper-spotter teams atop campus buildings that had a bird's eye view of the area. The local and State Police departments were also on high alert and had plain clothed detectives as well as uniformed officers inter-mingling with the secret service agents on the ground. They had a SWAT team standing by and a helicopter ready with its own sniper team able to take off at a moments notice.

Ninety minutes before the commencement address was to begin guests began their arduous journey through security checkpoints and metal detectors to take their assigned seats. The guest of honor was relaxing in the teacher's lounge with the Dean, a few celebrity guests and his personal entourage of secret service agents. Cordoned off outside of the event area were thousands of protesters hoping to interfere with the President's political expert who had acted so treasonously against his country without so much as a minor reprimand.

News coverage from all major stations were covering the event but only the select few were allowed an insiders perspective of the upcoming ceremony.

# *"I'm Not a Snake!"*

Four the past two hours Bob Messer had been crawling on his stomach across a gentle slope covered in tall grass. His objective was a rock formation two hundred and fifty yards away where the nest had been waiting since the previous evening. When he arrived he was winded from the exertion and laughed at himself for being so tired over such a short distance. *"It's tough getting old…"* he thought to himself with mock humor.

He made sure his matching ghillie camouflage hat and mask were on perfectly before peaking around the corner with the spotter's scope to check the distance and campus flags for the wind direction and speed. Twenty-five hundred and sixty-three yards he determined. *"If this isn't a world record kill-attempt then it sure has to be close…"* He thought. *"At least the wind is down to three miles an hour… now if only it stays that way."* It was too early to take a chance of exposing himself any further so he just stayed low and checked his watch from time to time. *"Forty-five minutes to show-time…"*

In preparation for this attack Wallace's team had made arrangements to start a number of commotions both inside the commencement area and outside where the crowd of protesters were gathering. That would provide Messer with valuable time to make his stealthy retreat to a small rest stop two hundred and fifty horizontal yards away.

Thirty minutes to go and the Dean was speaking to the crowd that for the most part was now seated. The echoes from the amplifiers could not be understood at the sniper's nest and the garbled effect of that cacophony of sound made Messer wonder if his actions would be.

Then the protesters began to chant and those two conflicting echoes climbed up the hill and mixed into a surrealistic moan of humanity, as if reason and insanity were involved in a death struggle. Ten minutes to go and time to make the final adjustments to the XM107 .50-caliber rifle's scope. Messer removed the plastic cover and lens caps from the weapon and scope and slowly moved it into position planting the spiked bipod firmly into the ground.

From there he focused in on the lectern and made the minor scope modifications that were needed for this distance and wind velocity. Marshall had done his homework well and the elevation angel was nearly identical to the practice range they had prepared at, which allowed the bullet to drop over two hundred feet as gravity took its toll during the long trajectory. There would be time for three shots, no more and then an excruciatingly slow extraction.

Messer was awakened from his thoughts by the mixture of cheers and boos from the audience and protesters. It was obvious that the majority of people in the vicinity weren't going to miss this man. Still, vaporizing a human being was an awful thing for anyone to see.

During the opening the guest speaker was highly animated and moved about nervously. Messer waited patiently for him to calm down and stand more consistently in one place while he spoke. *Easy, smooth, relaxed, good...* (click) the trigger indicated as it reached the hair-pull firing position. Messer repeated silently; *easy, smooth, relaxed, good...* Then, almost unconsciously the first round was lobbed down onto the speakers head. He took his time and fired the second shot two point four seconds later aiming six inches lower. Both rounds hit their target **BEFORE** the sound of the first gunshot got there. Messer knew that a third shot wasn't necessary as his target exploded in his scope. Loud shouts from frenzied agents rose above the chants of protesters.

Almost immediately after the shots were heard machine-gun-like firecrackers began going off in different areas of the protesting crowd. The sound of the crowd began to erupt as if with one voice and screams could be heard breaking over the clamor. The crowd turned into a mob as the panic spread and they surged through the barriers in all directions to get away. The police did their best to contain them and arrested those who resisted but for the most part people fled and left the area unchecked.

When the gunshots were heard the SWAT team immediately left their vehicle and proceeded to their assigned positions protecting the guests and faculty who were sprawling all over the stage. When they arrived they could only see pieces of Bruce Jensen as if he had swallowed a bomb. Larger fragments from the oak lectern were intermixed with the bloody remains.

Messer hid the gun in behind the rocks and began his stealthy crawl horizontally through the tall grass retracing the path his body had already tamped down on the way in. He crawled as if he were twenty again until his body screamed out in agony.

As his senses took hold he was able to slow down to a stealthier pace... less than one minute into the retreat he could hear the helicopter lift off and begin circling the crowd of protesters where the commotion had been ignited. For twenty-five painful minutes Messer crawled as fast as he could while remaining as stealthy as his old body would allow. He never stopped to look around and instead let his ears become his eyes as he entrusted his survival to decades of training and over the will of his own mind, which never stopped screaming; *GET UP AND RUN! What the HELL are you doing? RUN, RUN, RUN!*

Finally, after what seemed an eternity he was in the small patch of woods that separated him from the rest area off of the highway. He stripped off the camouflage jumpsuit and placed it, his mask, hat and gloves into a small duffle bag that was waiting at the exit point where he had left it hours earlier. This gave him ample time to regain his composure and get his breathing under control. He took a good look around before stepping into the clearing where the only car waiting was a dark blue Crown Victoria that looked exactly like the unmarked State Trooper cars that were used in that area. Walking calmly Messer took the shortest route to the car and as he approached he heard the trunk pop open and placed the small bag inside before getting into the passenger's seat.

"It took you long enough old man…" Wallace said with the best humor he could muster.

*"Just drive Marshall…"* Messer wanted to yell at him. "Next time you need a crawler get a fucking kid! *I'm Not a Snake!*"

"Duly noted Sir. How's our target doing?"

"I figure nobody is going to be using his organs for transplants." Messer replied coldly.

"You're assuming of course that anyone would want to." Wallace replied without missing a beat.

The two men drove away slowly and maintained an even clip until they were well out of the area. They then settled back en route to the Stanford Court in downtown San Francisco where one of Wallace's men had already gotten the room and picked up the keys.

"Nobb Hill, nice digs Marsh." Messer quipped as they pulled up to the luxury Marriot.

"Thought you'd appreciate it… Here's your key, you're staying under the name of Chris Johnson, so just enjoy yourself get a good meal and sleep in as late as you'd like. I'd ask you to dinner but all of my teams are getting ready for the next push and I'm still on-duty."

"Don't worry about me Marsh, just take care of yourself. I figure if that crawl didn't kill me then nothing will. Next time though would you take a moment and remember our age… *would you please?*"

Wallace nodded with a smile and a warm handshake before popping the trunk so Messer could remove his luggage. He left the bag behind for Wallace to dispose of. The two trusted friends parted company one more time with another successful mission under their belts.

# *"Guerilla Tactics"*

Not a single person had stepped up and responded to the challenge laid down by the **Deep-Six revolutionaries** as they were now being called. As predicted by Juan Gonzalez three days earlier t-shirts and sweatshirts were already popping up all over the country with the slogan; **DEEP-SIX All Traitors!** printed on them. Other versions added the already familiar; *"one shot – one kill"* slogan under the new one. Many of the new clothes carried pictures of the victims enclosed in a circle with a red line running through their faces. Particularly offensive to most people were the clothes with faces on them that hadn't been "offed" yet. The president, vice-president and many of the well-known hawks were among them.

In the minutes following the end of the cease fire five targets were killed at golf courses around the country. They were trying to get in one-last round before going into their respective hiding places. Expert snipers using a variety of weapons were pleased to give them *their last round*. One industrialist was taken out as he searched for his ball in the woods. His throat had been cut from ear to ear.

Within the next fours hours three more high-profile targets were taken down on airline tarmacs by snipers as they tried to board their commercial jets. Only the weapon that was used to kill Bruce Jenson was ever recovered and the media machine went into overdrive as it articulated the sentiments of the government and the moguls who controlled it. Simultaneously, national public radio and free-speech TV stations across the world were exposing the other side of the myth propagated by the Corporate-Military Industrial Complex. The so-called *"victims"* were in fact **war profiteers** who benefited directly from death and destruction. Once both sides of the story were told very few of America's citizens mourned the losses of these people and none reacted in the riotous way that was predicted by the FBI profiler.

Task forces across the country were mobilized to search and destroy this invisible army but their standard tactics simply didn't work. Without inside knowledge there was nothing to attack except the hundreds of thousands of good citizens who held legitimate gun licenses and the fringe paramilitary groups who were harassed.

On the day following the end of the cease-fire the President addressed the country and placed a $10,000 award for any citizen that had information that led to the arrest and conviction of any person working with the Deep-Six revolutionaries. Deep-Six responded by guaranteeing the death of anyone who accepted this "blood money" condemning all such people as government accomplices and traitors.

The government went after every known paramilitary organization in the country and illegally confiscated weapons and ordinance. These disconnected militia groups' simply regrouped and rearmed and lodged legal cases against the government for violating their constitutional rights.

For every expensive attack, there was a relatively inexpensive counter measure. For every bomb that couldn't be used there were tens of thousands of bullets that could be. The giant that thought it could rule the world was finding it nearly impossible to rule its own population, which was becoming bolder with every successful kill.

Within two days of the end of the cease-fire most profiteers were hiding as deeply as they could while still trying to operate their businesses. The assassinations continued a layer or two below those leaders who refused to reverse their courses as demanded by the revolutionaries. Meanwhile, the stock market was in total upheaval and company fortunes amassed over many years began to evaporate at an alarming rate. As quickly as these stocks fell to record lows huge blocks were being purchased by the contrarians and elite who could afford to speculate. Hundreds of billions of dollars were changing hands. The dollar was falling in value every day as foreign investors were all too happy to take advantage of America's financial woes.

In effect there were now three fronts to this new war... the physical battle, which pitted the Military and their Industrialists against the revolutionaries, the media battle for the minds and souls of the people and the economic battle, which threatened to bankrupt America.

The new American revolutionaries cause outside of America was almost universally supported by the youth and condemned by the elite. Gatherings around the world with hundreds of thousands of young people demonstrated in favor of the promising new vision of the over-thrown bully who would be replaced by a vital and morally responsible neighbor.

Across the world signs and t-shirts could be seen with the battle cry;

### *"One-Shot, One-Kill"*

The financiers of the Deep-Six revolution were among those who were poised and ready to take full advantage when the right moments came. Together these forces drove companies that were once thought to be invincible into total chaos and in some cases to the edge of a financial abyss. To make matters worse a broad wave of resignations had begun by upper tier managers afraid that they would be the next to take a bullet for bosses who were diving ever deeper underground to avoid assassination.

It was then that Maxwell Dreyden picked up the phone and personally called the number Emily Thompson had given him.

## *"What a Strange Way to Find Lazarus"*

"General Andersen, I have a call for you sir."

"Who is it Margaret?"

"He wouldn't say. He said he couldn't for security reasons. He's on line four if you'd like to take his call."

"Alright... I've got it. This is General Andersen can I help you?"

"Sir, this is Maxwell Dreyden. Karl Schmidt gave me your name as a person who could be of help to my family."

"Sir, I don't know who you are but Mr. Dreyden was killed last week."

"They killed my driver sir. I was home with my family at the request of my security team trying to alternate my routines."

"That was very good advice Mr. Dreyden but you realize I will have to confirm this before we can have the conversation you're looking for."

"I understand General. Mr. Schmidt said you were a cautious man and that you could confirm this with him. He's in his office waiting for your call."

"Does my secretary have your phone number?"

"Not yet Sir."

"Alright, give me ten minutes to call Schmidt and I'll call you back. You can leave your number with Margaret."

"I'm trying to keep this quiet General."

"Don't worry Mr. Dreyden, all of my people carry at least Top Secret security clearances. I'll transfer you to her now."

A minute later General Aaron Andersen was calling Schmidt's private line.

"Good morning this is Schmidt." He answered.

"Morning Karl, this is Aaron."

"Morning General… I guess he decided to call you."

"And who's that Karl?"

"Why Max Dreyden of course. We lost one of our best men saving his life last week."

"I'm sorry for your man, did he have a family?"

"Yes sir, a wife and two children. It's been rough on them all. We're making sure they'll be cared for properly."

"I understand. He was a hero Karl and that's how he should be remembered to them. I just wanted to make sure who I was talking to. I promised to call back when you and I were done. Is there anything else I should know?"

"Just that Dreyden's willing to do just about anything to protect his family and his empire. He's already lost a fortune and he's ready to spend another one to get back at the bastards that are targeting him."

"Alright, I'll see what we can do. Any further communication between us on this will have to be approved by Dreyden himself."

"I understand General. Thanks for helping out."

"Don't thank me yet Karl. We'll be taking this one step at a time and we'll just have to wait and see what his priorities are."

"Fair enough Aaron… thanks just the same for whatever assistance you might be able to offer. Take care sir."

"You too." (click)

A moment later Andersen had Margaret dial Dreyden's number as he waited on the line. The moment the phone was answered she hung up.

"This is General Aaron Andersen calling for Mr. Dreyden."

"Yes Sir." Jason Roberts acknowledged. "He's expecting your call. One moment please."

"Hello General." Dreyden said as he picked up the line.

"Welcome back to the land of the living Mr. Dreyden that was quite a funeral they gave you." Andersen said.

"It was actually a pauper who was interned there. He was supposedly a good man that was just down on his luck so we thought it was fitting to give him a decent burial. We'll change the headstone when this is all over."

"It's good that it didn't go to waste. Now that I've confirmed your identity tell me what you have on your mind Mr. Dreyden."

"My security people said that your company might be able to provide me with options that we haven't considered… that you may be willing to consult with us."

"I told Mr. Schmidt that we don't do bodyguard work Mr. Dreyden, what other types of scenarios do you have in mind?"

"My personal bodyguard said you might be able to form a special team that could go after our attackers."

"Do you have any idea of what that entails sir?"

"Not really General… just that it's going to be expensive. No matter how much it costs it has to be a small fraction of what my company earns every year. We just can't retool our business and do something else as the terrorists would have the world believe. We've been doing our business legally for over two hundred years."

"I understand. How long are you prepared to stay underground?"

"Not a whole lot longer sir without very good cause."

"Stay put until we can meet and I'll work out some options for you. I presume you're living at home?"

"Yes sir, my whole family is here. Our children are being tutored and their instructor is under the assumption that I'm dead."

"How many people know that you're alive?"

"Too many General… That's one of my problems. I've pulled all the strings I have to stay dead this long but it's only a matter of time before this gets out."

"I agree. Let's start with the assumption that it's in your best interest to hold a press conference to announce this before anyone else does. I'd like you to be prepared to read your statement to me when I arrive. That will give me a better understanding of what your objectives are so I can build on them."

"I can do that. When can you make it down General?"

"I'm not sure… but definitely before the end of the week. I'll have to check my schedule and see if anything can be moved. Aren't you going to ask me how much this is going to cost?"

"I thought you'd tell me that when you got here and gave me the options."

"Sir, my time bills out at $100,000 a day… plus expenses. I'll need at least a half day to prepare for our meeting and a day in travel and our meeting together. You're looking at a buck fifty before we take the second step together. Are you sure you're up to this?"

"Yes General. Bring a full projection of our costs for these options and I'll see to it that an account is prepared for the work."

"Figure $5,000,000 will get you someplace safer Mr. Dreyden. Half of that will only get you dead."

"I understand General... thank you."

"I'll have Margaret Fischer call to finalize our meeting. Who would you like her to speak with?"

"Jason Roberts would be fine. He normally answers our phone. If he's not in then please have her ask for me or my wife Julia."

"Alright, then I'll see you in a few days Mr. Dreyden."

"Thank you General. I'm looking forward to meeting you."

General Andersen hung up and pulled out his throw away phone.

"Joe, this is Aaron… I've got some interesting news for you."

"What's that sir?" Commander Clark answered a little surprised by the call.

"It seems as if those terrorists in Atlanta didn't succeed."

"You mean the tobacco guy?"

"That's right. He's been hiding ever since his narrow escape."

"It seems that Schmidt's team altered his routine just in time to save his life."

"That's unbelievable!"

"Believe it Joe… he just hired us to add another layer of protection. I'll be heading down to Atlanta to meet with him in a few days."

"What do you need me to do sir?"

"Put the team on alert."

"Understood."

## *"Just One Small Break"*

Detective Ron Morrison and FBI Agent Paul Hobson had their teams scouring Atlanta with the two sketch-artist drawings and the single poor photograph of the suspects in the white Lexus. After hundreds of hours of monotonous legwork they still didn't have a fix on either suspect. The facial recognition software wasn't able to match any of the photos in the databases from motor vehicles or from known convicts. Time was running out on Dreyden's secret and they were becoming increasingly frustrated at the endless dead ends and false leads. Then, in a supermarket eight miles outside of Atlanta one of the cashiers identified the picture as a regular customer. She didn't know his name but she was certain that he was in the store at least every week or two.

Both teams immediately moved all available assets to the five mile area surrounding the grocery store and continued their relentless search. For sixteen hours a day these teams scoured every business and residence with the complete expectation that the murderer must live within this grid and that he would be found. Meanwhile, two teams of plain clothes FBI agents rotated the stake-out at the grocery store.

Hobson picked up the phone to keep McNulty in DC in the loop.

"Mark, this is Paul Hobson. We caught a break down here!"

"That's great! What happened Paul?" McNulty replied.

"One of our agents found a cashier at a grocery store outside of town that says she recognizes the picture. When we showed her the sketch she said that it was a little off but that she definitely could tell who it was from the photo. We have her working with the sketch artist now to revise our drawing. I'll get a copy up to you as soon as it's ready."

"Outstanding! Who's taking surveillance duties at the grocery?"

"Our team is Mark. We can't take any chances on this one."

"I agree. Just make sure they're loaded with non-lethal weapons, we need this guy alive."

"We're already there with a team inside the store and another one rotating with them on twelve hour shifts."

"Double it Paul. I want another two teams rotating on the outside for continuous backup. Is that understood?"

"As long as the Chief is picking up the tab I don't care."

"Do whatever you need to do… we've got carte blanche on this Paul. This is exactly what we needed… just one small break."

"Thanks Mark. Any luck up there with our shooter?"

"Not yet but I'm sure our people will be encouraged by your progress."

"Alright… let's keep each other posted and see if we can't capitalize on this."

"Good work Paul… talk to you soon."

# *"FUMBLE!"*

Commander Clark picked up his disposable phone and called Matt Creagor on his throw-away.

"Matt, this is Joe… where are you right now?"

"I'm in my car running chores why?"

"*FUMBLE!* You need to come in now. Max wasn't in the car."

"What? Sure he was… I saw his funeral on TV."

"Listen to me son… the man is playing possum. Do you understand?"

"Yes, but how can you be sure?"

"Stop wasting time Matt, I need you to get out of the area immediately as per our plans. Is that understood?"

"Yes sir… I'm coming in now."

"Where's your portable?

"In the trunk… why?

"Good… just follow the plan and you'll be alright. (Click)

As per the escape plan rule number one was to destroy the throw-away phone but he headed back towards the store first to pick up the groceries he had promised his wife. Every fiber in his body was on edge as he fought the urge to run but instead forced himself to be calm. As he pulled into the familiar parking lot he noticed a dark green Chevy Impala with two people sitting in the front seat but not getting out. His instincts took over and he slowly exited the lot. A few blocks later he turned into a side street, tossed the phone out of the window and ran over it twice. He drove to the Atlanta airport where he left his car in long-term parking.

While still in his car he destroyed his identification and credit cards and placed them in his jacket pocket. He then removed his emergency suitcase from the trunk, opened it and took out his false ID and new credit cards placed them into his wallet. He then caught a courtesy bus to the airport and rented a Pontiac Grand Am under the alias of William Allen. He discarded the shredded ID and credit cards at various trash receptacles along his route before beginning his long drive to Indianapolis.

Back in Maryland Clark made two more calls before destroying his throw-away phone and picking up a new one. The first one was to Anthony Rico who would now be responsible for getting the number two man in Atlanta up to speed on the situation and in charge of his new command, which was now reduced to twenty men in three different squads. Creagor's number two officer was Brent Foster and it would be up to him to keep his team off of the investigators radar. Missions already scheduled could be carried out at Sergeant Foster's discretion but any new surveillance planned for the next few weeks was to be postponed until further notice from Mr. C. Clark then made his second call to Commander Dick Cooper in Central and advised him that William Allen would be at the safe motel within 24-hours. That's all he needed to know to carry out his end of the mission.

## *"Close Call"*

"Did you see that?" Agent Hobson asked his partner Linda Parks.

"No Paul, what was it?"

"A white impala drove into our lot and then just drove out again."

"Did he seem to be in a hurry?" She asked.

"No... not really, I'm not even sure it was a he."

"It's probably nothing but we can check it out if you'd like."

"Yeah, just to be safe... call our team inside and let them know we'll be gone for a few minutes." Hobson said.

Agent Parker keyed her two-way radio and waited for one of the officers inside to respond. She then told him that they were checking out a suspicious white impala and would call in when they returned. Hobson was already on the busy street heading in the same direction as the Chevy had been thirty seconds earlier. He drove a few blocks but the car was already gone.

"That's strange." He said. "I can't find the car."

"It was probably a local who forgot their wallet and they already turned off to get it. Want to check the side streets Paul?"

"Nah, it was probably nothing and we should be watching the other team's backs." Hobson replied.

"Alright with me... mind if we grab a cup of coffee first?"

"Sure thing, I can use one too." And they pulled into a Dunkin Donuts only a few hundred yards down the street before heading back to their stakeout.

## *"The Money Trail"*

"Mrs. Schneider, I have Walter Dobson on the line three for you."

"Thank you Cheryl, please let him know I'll be with him in just a few moments."

"Yes, Ma'am."

"Good morning Chief, your timing is good."

"Oh, how so Merrill?"

"We just finished our first comprehensive pass of suspected insider trading and I was going over the findings."

"So what did you find... anything interesting?"

"Oh yes, plenty. First off this thing is global. We've got evidence of questionable trading going back at least a year. We haven't looked farther yet but I suspect it's been going on before then too."

"We think this has been building up for at least four or five years Merrill so if you can check that far back it I would appreciate it."

"We were planning on looking back until the irregularities stop. The other thing that is of interest is that there seems to be a core group of heavy duty traders that knew these events were coming and took full advantage of them by spreading their investments around the world through as many brokerage firms as they could. There's also a new wave of investor who seems to be betting on these activities but they seem to be more speculative and don't appear to be illegal."

"Hmmm... betting on what exactly?"

"From where I'm sitting it appears that they've grouped their bets against the corporate-military companies in favor of the green ones."

"So they're betting on the revolutionaries doing a lot of damage to those giants?"

"It appears so Walter. These aren't the typical large trades but the millions of smaller ones adding up to a pretty significant impact on the market overall."

"That's interesting. What about the insider trading? What else can you say for certain?"

"At this moment, only that it *is* happening but they are doing a pretty good job of spreading it around to minimize any exposure. That part is going to take more time to prove as we try to connect all the dots."

"What's the make-up of those traders Merrill?" Can you tell?

"It's mostly wealthy, powerful people from right here in the United States with other trades taking place all around the world. We've found quite a few ties back to our own government, Senators and multi-millionaires mostly who are either incredibly intuitive or involved in this in some way."

"Do you think they could be the funding source for this Deep-Six paramilitary group?"

"I don't know Walter, I suppose it's possible but I don't have access to that kind of information... you do though."

"Yes, Ma'am... we do. I just need to pull a few strings to get it all started. Can you send me a report summing up your findings and the suspects on your list? I want the Attorney General to know about this as soon as possible so we can get our offense off the bench."

"I'll have it sent over via messenger as soon as I've finished my report."

"Thanks Merrill, you've been a big help!"

"You're welcome Walter… let me know if there's anything else you need."

# *"Suspect One on the Run"*

"Mrs. Creagor, I'm Detective Morrison and this is Detective Monetti, may we speak to your husband please?"

"Oh, thank God. I thought you were here to tell me something had happened to him."

"Why is that Ma'am?"

"He left to run errands yesterday and we haven't seen him since."

"May we come inside please?"

"Yes, of course... I'm sorry."

"What type of car does he drive Mrs. Creagor?"

"A Chevy Impala... please, what's this all about? Is he okay?"

"We don't know where he is Mrs. Creagor but he's probably fine. Does this photograph look familiar?" Detective Paula Monetti asked.

"Yes, that's Matt... where did you get it?"

"It's from a camera outside of a downtown garage." Monetti offered.

"We don't know where he is but we're investigating the murder of Maxwell Dreyden and his driver and we wanted to ask your husband a few questions since it appears he was in the area when it happened."

"Matt could never be involved in such a thing. He doesn't even own a gun. No, no... There has to be some explanation he could never do such a thing. You don't know him like I do." She reaffirmed as much to herself as to the detectives.

"What color is his Impala Mrs. Creagor?" Morrison asked.

"It's white… why?"

"Nothing Ma'am, we're just trying to put all the pieces in place."

"He's not even driving his car in the picture you showed me. Maybe it's just someone who looks like him."

"That's possible Ma'am but you did identify him without hesitation. That's why we need to speak with him as soon as possible so we can clear him and get on with our search." Said Monetti… trying to keep her from becoming hysterical. "He may have nothing to do with this but maybe he saw something that can help us."

"Oh dear God… I wish I knew where he was but I don't. I'm afraid he did see something and now he's lying dead somewhere."

"Mrs. Creagor, please don't worry. We'll do everything we can to help. Has he ever gone off like this before?" Morrison continued.

"No, never… well once when we had a big fight but that was a long time ago and we haven't been fighting."

"Okay, try to relax and do your best not to worry. Take my card and please call if you hear anything at all. Tell him we want to help and all we want to do is talk to him… alright?" Morrison said reassuringly…

"Alright…" Cindy Creagor replied through her tears.

The detectives left the Creagor home knowing they had one of their two suspects in their sights and on the run. The surveillance, wire taps and records search could now get underway full tilt and should produce information on the Deep-Six team operating in this region. With any luck it might bring the entire thing down Morrison thought but he also knew he was being childishly optimistic. It was never that easy… especially against calculating professionals like these. If only he could figure out how Matt Creagor got word in time to flee… perhaps we already interviewed one of his associates he presumed.

## *"Common Sense"*

As General Andersen approached the Dreyden home in his Audi A8 rental car he dialed their residence as previously instructed. As soon as he drew near the gates they retracted into the wall and he drove to the rear of the home where the garage door was opening for him. He pulled inside and watched as the door closed behind him quicker than expected. The garage was fully illuminated and he took a moment to look around at all the cars before getting out and greeting Jason Roberts who was watching from a few feet away.

"Good afternoon General." Roberts said as he offered his hand. "I'm Jason Roberts."

"Good morning Mr. Roberts." The General said as he took the strong hand being offered and returned an equally firm handshake.

"Nice car." Roberts said with a smile as he nodded towards the identical model only a few feet away.

"Not a bad collection." The General said as he followed Roberts into the house.

Roberts led General Andersen into the kitchen where Max Dreyden, his wife and Emily Thompson were sitting around the large oak table. They all rose when the General appeared.

"Good morning, I'm Aaron Andersen." He said with genuine warmth. "Please, sit... I'm retired." He added with a smile.

"Thank you for coming on such short notice General Andersen." Max Dreyden said sincerely as he offered his hand. "This is my wife Julia and this is Emily Thompson who heads up our security team."

The General greeted everyone in turn and then took the seat he was offered.

"Would you care for some coffee General?" Julia offered.

"Yes I would, thank you Mrs. Dreyden."

Julia Dreyden poured the coffee that was already in a carafe on the table; "Please help yourself to anything you'd like." She said as she served the coffee to the General and pointed to the Danish and fruit on the table. "… and please call me Julia."

"Thank you Julia. This will be fine. Well I must say Mr. Dreyden that you look remarkably well for a man who has been in the grave for over a week."

"Thanks to Emily and Lou." He replied.

"I presume Lou was your driver?" Andersen asked.

"Yes, he was primarily a bodyguard." Emily chimed in. "It was actually Lou Farentino who suggested that Mr. Dreyden alter his routines, including his drive into work that day."

"He did his job well and Karl Schmidt tells me his family is being taken care of." Andersen confided.

"Yes, Julia and I have established a trust fund for his children and his wife will receive substantial benefits from Blackwell so they'll be alright financially." Max replied.

"That's good. Tell me what you folks have on your minds relative to what's been going on." General Andersen asked.

"The FBI and local Atlanta PD have asked us to stay underground for as long as possible so they could try to use that to our advantage and hopefully flush out the assassins." Emily Thompson summed up.

"How has that worked out so far?" The General inquired.

"We have sketches of the two men who probably did the shooting and we're pretty sure we have the name of the guy who was providing local support." Emily advised.

"That's a good start. Do they have him in custody?" Asked Andersen.

"No, he's on the run, but his wife ID'd the photograph taken outside the garage that was used to access the building in the shooting." Emily continued. "The FBI is distributing his photo to all law enforcement agencies across the country. It's only a matter of time before we get him. His picture will be on TV as soon as we decide the best way to put it out. Meanwhile, they're checking all of his records and looking for the team down here that supported him. We think the shooter was from Maryland and the FBI is trying to hone in on him now."

"Do you have those pictures with you?" Andersen asked.

"Yes Sir." Emily responded and then pulled the sketches and photograph on the table for the General.

Andersen saw that both the picture and sketch of Matt Creagor was good enough to nail him with and was relieved when he saw the sketch of his old friend Bob Messer was off target by quite a bit.

"This photo is the local guy and this sketch is the one you think did the shooting?" Andersen asked.

"Yes." Emily replied. "He was driving the same car that came through North Carolina, where John Richards was murdered only a few days earlier. The FBI thinks it's the same shooter."

"Looks like you have a good start. How long can you keep undercover Mr. Dreyden? Andersen asked.

"Not much longer. I'm prepared to go public sometime this week. The sooner the better as far as I'm concerned." Dreyden replied.

"Did you prepare a statement as I asked?" Andersen asked.

"Yes I did but it's still pretty rough. I haven't thought out the way to release this information so it's hard to know exactly what to say when I don't know who my audience is yet."

"That's okay…" Andersen said. "I just need an idea of what's going on in your head to see if the options I have for you are going to mesh with your goals and reasoning. If not, then we both have our work cut out for us. I'd prefer to do this one on one Mr. Dreyden, if that's okay with you."

"Sure, I'd actually prefer it that way myself." Dreyden said bluntly. "Julia, Emily, Jason, would you please excuse us."

They all nodded and it was obvious that Emily Thompson was disappointed and wanted to be in that meeting but she nodded and left with Jason Roberts. Julia stayed and offered them sandwiches, which were declined and then Max Dreyden led Aaron Andersen into his study.

"Would you care for a drink General?" Dreyden asked.

"No thank you."

"Emily seems to think I've been targeted because my family produces a product that can cause cancer."

"Can cause cancer Mr. Dreyden? It does cause cancer and you know it." The General responded sternly.

"Well, it is a contributing factor to be certain… but it's not illegal."

"Sir, if anyone killed someone you loved with a product that they knew could cause their death how would you feel?"

"Angry and bitter I suppose."

266

"The legality is besides the point Mr. Dreyden. The point is that your product does kill millions of people every year. That's a fact and you and the rest of your friends in the tobacco industry know it. That's the reason you're being targeted right now. It's really as simple as that. Does your statement have anything to do with moving your company away from that product and into areas that don't cause harm?"

"No, not really." Dreyden responded.

"Then you're going to remain a target Sir and there's not very much I can do to help you." The General replied.

"So your suggestion is to change my family business, reverse everything we've done for over two hundred years and just go do something else?"

"Yes Sir it is. Your company is worth billions of dollars. You are in a far more significant position to do that now than at any other time in your family's history. You're holding on to a product that will kill more people than all the wars mankind has ever fought put together. How can you stand there and justify that... because it's legal?"

"Well, yes." Dreyden said trying not to buy into the obvious solution.

"You don't have to do it all at once. Come up with a plan that phases out tobacco over time. Just don't make the period too long or they might continue to see you as a target. You could be the first and lead this country in the proper direction. That would give you a strong position to build whatever you'd like for your children while slowing the distribution of such a harmful product."

"Distribution won't slow down one bit General. My competitors will joyfully pick up the slack."

"Yes, and they will remain the targets while you and your family will get on with your lives with a better business. Your top stockholders will support you because they've been named as targets as well. So there's really very little holding you back except tradition and your desire not to make any changes."

"You make a good argument General but what time frame would be acceptable to these murderers and how do I know they'll live up to their end of the bargain and call off their snipers?"

"They've tried to take the moral high-ground on everything they've said, written and done and if they reneged by killing you then they would lose that position. All you need is a reasonable plan that you're willing to print in the Wall Street Journal and then stick to those commitments and you should be perfectly safe from them."

"What about others who would kill me just to make it look like the Deep-Six group did it."

"That's a valid concern but I doubt any other organization, short of the government itself, would have the resources to do that very easily. You're going to remain a target either way… the only question left is which side of this debate do you want to risk your family's lives on? As far as a time-line is concerned I would think five years should give you plenty of time to phase out the tobacco products and move into something more productive for society. Why not develop clean solutions to our energy needs? We sure as hell could use some genuine leadership in that area."

"We do have a strong position in the market that could make something like that possible. It wouldn't be easy but I'm sure it's within our capabilities." Dreyden said mulling over the sensible approach. "Do you have an alternate plan for me should I wish to keep my business running *as is*?"

"Build underground Max… build everything you'll ever need for the rest of your life underground… then stay there with your family. It's the only way you're ever going to be truly safe."

"What about going after these guys ourselves?"

268

"They've killed dozens of high-profile people in just the last few weeks and you have a couple of bodyguards. To consider growing your capabilities to attack them is one of the dumbest things I've ever heard. You'd most likely be dead before you could even identify any of them. Retool your company Max; it's the best future you can give to your family... that's my **strongest recommendation**."

"Thank you for your insight and for your candidness General. I will seriously consider it. You know, I could have saved myself a hundred and fifty thousand dollars...."

"How's that Max?"

"Emily Thompson kicked my ass about this very topic the day after the attack."

"Smart gal..." the general said before collecting his check and leaving.

# *"Lazarus is coming..."*

After the General left Max went to his wife Julia who was in the den reading and sat in the matching leather chair across from her.

"Where were the children, I thought they'd like to meet General Andersen."

"I thought so too but they wanted to visit friends since they've been cooped up for so long. They nearly *ran out of the house* when I told them they could go."

"It's just as well... let them get some time out on their own. What do you think the General's final suggestion was?"

"I imagine he said something along the lines of what Emily did dear."

"You're right, he did. I wanted to fight them but he said that would be the stupidest thing I could do. Still, I hate just giving in."

"How could you possibly fight them? Look what they've been doing and no one has laid a hand on them yet."

"So how do you think I should go about this Julia?"

"Well, you don't have to do it all at once... you just have to come up with a reasonable plan and stick to it. That's what they said in their manifesto didn't they?"

"Yes... but my family has been in the tobacco business for almost two-hundred and fifty years."

"Do you think they would have entered into that business knowing what we do today... about how smoking contributes to cancer, heart attacks and stroke? Would you have started a business knowing that your product would do that?"

270

"Why of course not… but…"

"***But nothing dear***… we do know that and I think it's time we did something else. I'm all for it and it's not all that bad now is it? It's not like we're starting from scratch."

"That's pretty much what Andersen's point was. We're in a very good position to do something… constructive. He even suggested that we tackle some of this country's energy problems by investing in products and services that could reduce pollution."

"I think that's a wonderful idea and one that these assassins would have to respect. I don't want you to be a target anymore. I just want our family to be safe and able to enjoy our lives."

"Alright, we'll do it then. I just need a few of the major stock holders to go along with me. Even with the shares we've been buying back I'm still just a minority stock holder."

"I think you can sell them on a future that's safe for them just as General Andersen did for you. They believed in you… just look what happened to their shares when they thought you were gone."

"Alright… I'm going to need a plan that I can articulate to the board that they can sign off on and then we need to put that in the Wall Street Journal as per their demands. I think I should do a press conference as well to announce this all at once… that could have a positive effect on our stock."

"How many of the top share-holders do you need to sway the vote?"

"Two or three, that's all. The timing is going to be an issue but this could work out fine. I just need to get them in one room and then spring Lazarus on them."

"That should be fun… watching their expressions I mean."

"Yes, a lot more fun than playing dead. I need to get back to work now before I go totally stir crazy."

"The children and I are looking forward to that too dear." Julia said with her sweetest smile.

"Honey, I need you to call Jim Robinson, Collin Farrell and Patricia Jensen. Tell them there's something in my will that pertains to them and let's get them all here at the same time. I don't want to have to sell them on this new direction of ours one at a time… Then call Lance and have him buy another ten million of our stock back. I'll do some research on where we could be taking our company. We don't have much time I want surprise to be on our side."

"Okay dear, just give me their numbers and I'll get them here as soon as possible."

"Hmmm… this is interesting and much more promising than going to war."

"One that you couldn't win Max…"

"I suppose you're right, but I'm not totally giving up on that idea yet."

"Leave revenge to the Lord or you'll just be risking our family's safety. Please don't put our children in harms way."

"You're right; I need to focus on the positive now."

Julia took her husbands hand and watched him as he drifted into his thoughts. *This could actually be a blessing…* she thought to herself trying to remain optimistic but fully understanding the risks that still lay ahead.

## *"Demotions and Second Chances"*

Dick Cooper would have one of his platoon leaders handle the new man from Atlanta. He would have to prove himself just as any new member would for the safety of the entire command. Coming in from *"out of the cold"* was not going to be easy for Matt Creagor, a.k.a. William Allen. Especially when his face was being plastered on news networks across the nation. Making use of this man was now Cooper's problem and one he didn't cherish owning. He put his best man on it, Staff Sergeant Charles Pippen with instructions to keep him isolated from his men to the extent possible. Pippen called the Super 8 Motel on Emerson Avenue and asked to speak with their guest William Allen.

"Hello." A tentative voice answered from room 14.

"William Allen?"

"Yes, this is he."

"My name is Charlie Pippen and I've been asked to lend you a hand."

"Thanks Charlie, I can use it."

"What room are you in?"

"Fourteen."

"Stay inside and I'll be there in an hour. Have you eaten?"

"No, just drove until I got here."

"Okay, I'll pick something up. Stay inside until we can work this through... is that understood?"

"Yes Charlie, I understand."

An hour and a half later two men were outside of room 14 knocking.

"Coming..." Creagor said instinctively and then opened the door surprised to see two rather large men outside. "Yes, may I help you?"

"I'm Charlie Pippen and this is Joe... are you going to invite us in?"

"Yes, yes I'm sorry. I was just a bit startled seeing two of you."

"Are all of your belongings out of the car?" Pippen asked.

"Yes, why"

"Then give your keys and rental paperwork to Joe... we don't want anyone tracing your steps into our region. I'll explain it all to you after Joe's gone."

Matt Creagor handed Joe the keys and paperwork and watched as he looked it all over.

"Atlanta..." Joe said a bit bummed out at the journey that lay ahead.

"That's right." Creagor confirmed.

"See you two gentlemen later..." Joe said before heading out to the Grand Am.

"He's taking the car all the way back to Atlanta?" Creagor asked in amazement.

"Yes. Otherwise it would be a one-way drop that could point the Feds in our direction. He'll have to catch a bus back and I know Joe hates busses so you're going to owe him a dinner or something when you two get to know each other."

"That's a relief... when I saw the two of you I thought I was dead." Matt shared sheepishly.

"Why waste a good man? Play it straight with us and we'll take care of you. Fuck with us and I'll cut your throat myself... understood?" Pippen said with the assuredness of a hand to hand combat expert.

"I understand completely Charlie."

"Now give me your portable PC." Pippen ordered.

"Why, I need that!" Creagor argued as he watched Pippen pull out another one from his bag and hand it to him.

"There's nothing on that machine but trouble. We'll reformat the hard drive and use it again but everything you know from Atlanta has to be erased and forgotten until this thing is back under control. Do you understand?"

"Well, yes and no. What about my wife and kids?"

"For the time being they're on their own. You know your phones will be tapped and the Feds will be using all of their resources to track you down and expose your squads. Cooper told me you headed up that region but for now you're just a grunt in hiding trying to save his ass. Am I making myself clear?" Pippen said forcefully.

"Yes Sir..." Matt said subordinately.

"Alright... let's get started. This PC is yours and your new Yahoo messenger name is "Willie_136". For now the only contact you are allowed within our command is with me. In an emergency you can call me on my cell phone, which is 317-338-1276. The messenger name you can reach me at *sparingly* is PiperCub4242."

"Do you fly?" Creagor asked.

"Yes... helicopters and small planes." Pippen replied. "It's important that you don't contact anyone back home or in your old command. I can not stress that point enough. Now give me your phone."

"I destroyed it before I left and didn't have time to pick up another one yet." Creagor said.

"Good enough. Here's a throw-away I brought for you. Use it carefully… I prefer the net." Pippen reinforced.

"I understand… I ran three squads back home." Creagor said trying to get his rank across to this platoon leader.

"Like I said before… this is a new life for you and you'll need to earn our respect for security reasons. You know the drill." Pippen said.

"Yes, I do… what's next?"

"Getting you to a point where you can be useful to us and not just a drain on our resources. Tell me about your combat skills."

"I was a Staff Sergeant with two tours of duty in the Gulf. I'm fully trained in hand-to-hand and a pretty decent shot with either a pistol or an M16… I'm not a sniper… but pretty good from under 500 yards."

"Do you have any surveillance experience?" Pippen asked.

"Sure, we all took our turns doing surveillance work for this new mission of ours."

"Do you have any special physical skills?"

"I'm no black belt but I'm pretty good up close and personal when I have to be." Creagor replied.

"Does this place have a refrigerator?" Pippen said looking around.

"No, I was hoping to find a bar and snacks when I got in but no such luck."

"Oh, that reminds me. I picked you up a couple of subs and iced teas… they're in the bag on the table."

"Thanks Charlie, I'm starved... mind if I chow down while we talk?"

"No, go right ahead."

Creagor grabbed the first sub and eagerly unwrapped and devoured it as if it were a small sandwich. Then he washed it down with the iced tea as Pippen watched giving his new man a chance to revitalize himself. Creagor thought about the second sandwich for a moment and then decided to let his body digest this one first.

"Your picture is already appearing on TV as a person wanted for questioning in the Dreyden assassination."

"*Really*... that was quicker than I expected. Do you know he's not even dead?"

"No, I hadn't heard that yet. Is that fact?" Pippen asked obviously astonished.

"According to my commander he wasn't in the car that morning and has been playing possum trying to get to us."

"That's a kick in the ass. We're going to have to change your look significantly before you can get out in public. One of my team members is pretty good with cosmetic disguises. Ever wear a beard?" Pippen asked.

"Not for a long time... my wife says it made me look too old."

"Right now, old is good... maybe ten or twenty years older would do you some good and let you get out a little."

"Alright, let's get going... I've got anther room closer to my home for you. Here're the keys to your new room. Leave yours there on the table for the maid to collect." Pippen said. "Put on this cap for now." Pippen said handing him a Colts cap. "Get your bags and let's go."

The two men left the motel and headed over to Pippen's Black Camaro. Thirty minutes later Charlie was dropping William Allen and his bags off at the Red Roof Inn with the promise that he'd be back in touch shortly.

# *"Cover Up and Linkages"*

"So what's happening in Atlanta Mark?" Chief Dobson asked.

"They almost got the local suspect but somehow he got wind of our approach and is on the run." McNulty replied. "Looks like he saw Hobson and Parks in the supermarket just sitting there in the car and that was enough to spook him."

"That doesn't add up Mark unless he was already spooked and on the lookout for trouble." Dobson responded.

"They said a white Chevy Impala drove into the lot and then drove out again without stopping. It didn't seem like much at the time but they followed anyway and by the time they turned onto the street he was already gone. They thought he lived on one of the side streets but when they found his home later it wasn't that close to the grocery store. His wife ID'd the photo and she also told Morrison that he drove a white Impala. His car showed up in the long-term parking lot at the airport."

"***Damn***... we almost had him!"

"Exactly Chief, now he can be almost anywhere. His name is Matt Creagor but no one by that name flew out of any of the regional airports or rented a car. He's probably already assumed an alias like the other guy did."

"Crap... this group is serious Mark. They even have escape plans ready to go on a moments notice! I wish I could figure out how he got wind of our closing in on him." The Chief said reflecting on his own question.

"I have no idea but we're expanding our search to other airports in the region and looking into all one-way drops on rentals to see if we can figure out where he went. Meanwhile, we've got a tap on his phone and a search warrant was issued for the home. His wife seems to be in total shock over this and it doesn't look like she's involved unless she's a great actress... at least according to Morrison." Mark added.

"Dig up his life Mark... I want to know **everything** about this guy. Then get taps on his friends phones and see me if you run into any trouble getting whatever you need."

"They're on it Chief and I've already told Morrison and Hobson to call me if they get stuck on anything."

"What did this guy do for a living?"

"He was a plumber... self employed. Don't say it Chief."

"What... so he's used to being knee deep in shit? Not like the kind I want to put him through. Get the news out that he is now a suspect and not just wanted for questioning. I want the heat so high that he'll be afraid to show his face. Then get our graphic artists some of his family photos and have them do different looks on them so we'll have an idea what he is going to look like... what he probably already looks like if these guys are as half as sharp as I think." Dobson added.

"I'm on it Chief."

"What about our guy up here?"

"Nadda... if he is up here he's a ghost. We've got a thousand man hours in already but not a single legitimate lead. He may live here but he also may be on the road most of the time." McNulty said.

"Then make sure we keep our best drawings at all the airports in the area and see if we can find him coming or going." Dobson said.

"That's already done Chief but no hits yet. What's the latest on this Bruce Jensen murder?"

"Besides the fact that only a few men in the entire world could have made that kill?" Dobson said. "That may wind up being a major break for us… I have the Attorney Generals' authority to get the pentagons full cooperation on this. They're going to prepare a short list of master-sharpshooters that could have made that kill. It was so far away that it was beyond the maximum barriers set up by the CIA. He belly crawled out for at least twenty to thirty minutes and no one knew he was there… until they found the weapon a few hours later."

"We've got the sniper rifle Chief?" McNulty asked pleasantly surprised.

"Yes, it was a .50-caliber stolen from a squad in between tours of duty in the gulf but their Lieutenant squashed the report that it was missing. He's being investigated and brought up on charges now."

"Could the shooter be one of them Chief?"

"Not very likely… their best rifleman could have done it from half that distance but not one of them would have had a snowballs chance in Hell of doing it from that far away. They're investigating the cover up and linkages but it's not as promising as the short list itself. They may have gotten too cute with this one. Two shots, both hits that literally tore him apart. He was dead before anyone heard the first shot."

"Jesus… this guy is better than our sniper." McNulty said astonished at the skill levels being executed so proficiently. "Looks like Sandra Annachiarico's military profile is accurate."

"These are not just soldiers Mark… they're elite and that's where we need to be investing most of our time. We need linkages son… find me every soldier Matt Creagor ever commanded or worked under. I'll bet my bottom dollar that this boy has one heck of a military record and that his line of command is rich with suspects. Find out which of them live near him and get the surveillance teams going NOW!"

# *"I Have a Plan"*

When Jim Robinson, Collin Farrell and Patricia Jensen saw Max Dreyden they were seated in his study waiting for something entirely different and not knowing why the others would be there at the same time. Their immediate shock was palpable and Julia had her wish granted as she sat with them watching their individual reactions as her husband walked through the door. *"I wish we had set up a camera..."* were the first words spoken by Max Dreyden as he smiled at his old friends and welcomed them all with warm handshakes and a hug for Patty Jensen who was in tears.

"My God Max how did you escape that horrible attack?" Patty Jensen asked with a mix of emotions ranging from pure joy to absolute amazement.

"I got lucky Patty... I was having breakfast with Julia when that happened." Max replied knowing he truly had been lucky. "My people had suggested that I start altering my daily routines and after the murder of John Richards I figured I had better start listening to them. If it hadn't been for his assassination only a few days earlier I probably would have been in that car.

"It's good to see you old friend." Jim Robinson said hugging Max now.

"You too Jim, sorry to have to put you all through this but we were trying to use my death as an opportunity to flush these bastards out."

"How's that been going?" Collin Farrell asked.

"We think we have one of them identified but he's on the run. That should give the FBI a good starting point to root around and find more connections." Max said. "They think the shooter was a pro from the Maryland area and they're working off sketches to find him."

"So I presume you are coming out soon." Farrell said matter of factly. "And that maybe now I can start getting some of my money back."

"Yes, yes… you're all going to be fine financially." Max said. "I have been working with the FBI and they went to the SEC to get me permission to protect our company in order to allow me to play possum for them. I've been buying back our stock to protect us with their foreknowledge and approval. It will be redistributed at very favorable rates to all of you when this thing settles out. Meanwhile we have some important business to discuss… starting with the fact that you're all targets too."

"Yes, I heard that during the reading of the terrorists manifesto." Patty Jensen confirmed.

"I heard that too but I think its pure bullshit Max." Farrell said still angry over the loss of tens of millions of dollars from his stock portfolio.

"You should do more reading Collin… no less than eight investors have been murdered already in other targeted companies identified by that Deep-Six Group. We're on that list and that means you're all on that list too… believe it or not." Max said forcefully.

"My wife and I have been thinking about selling all of our stock Max to get off of the list." Robinson offered.

"That may still not be enough Jim. They want us to make positive steps to reverse our actions and stop injuring people with our products. Anything less may not be acceptable to them." Max said.

"How the HELL are we supposed to do that Max?" Farrell asked in his typically obnoxious manner.

"That's why you're all here… I have a plan. I've had weeks to think it through and I've even hired a number of very smart people to help me with it. Now would you like to hear it and help me shape our company's future or would you prefer to leave and continue your lives with bull's-eyes painted on your foreheads?" Dreyden said pointedly.

## *"Lazarus Speaks"*

"This is Linda Thompson and welcome to WSB-TV *Action 2 News in Atlanta*. We're interrupting our normal broadcast with an exclusive report live from the Maxwell Dreyden Estate." The attractive anchor woman announced.

The view from the TV anchor news desk changed to the den in the Dreyden home where a camera is focused on an empty leather chair behind an ornate two-hundred year old oak desk in front of an expansive library of books. A moment later a handsome man in his late forties with dirty blonde hair and blue eyes took his seat dressed in an expensive business suit. He looked at the camera and stared into it for a full ten seconds until a broad smile appeared on his face.

"Ladies and gentleman and to all of my friends and fellow Atlantians I am Maxwell Dreyden and I'm very pleased to be here with you today. Only through the advice and heroic sacrifice of Mr. Louis Farentino am I still alive. His years of loyal service and his last heroic deeds will never be forgotten by me or our family. I wish to take this opportunity to extend my sincerest condolences to his wife Marie and to his children Louise and Paula. I am sorry that I could not have done this sooner but we have used this opportunity to find his killers and I am happy to report that our law enforcement agencies have generated strong leads that are being pursued aggressively.

It is painfully apparent that my company and I were targeted by the revolutionaries known only as *"Deep-Six."* Their recent actions against our American institutions are almost unprecedented. We'd have to go back to the Civil War to find an American nation that was in greater turmoil than we are in today. They claim to be patriots yet they use murder as their tool.

Still, during the hundreds of hours I've spent in reflection since their attack I have grown in understanding of their methods and although I do not agree with them I do respect the direction they are trying to lead us.

When my Great-Great Grandfather started our tobacco company nearly two-hundred and fifty years ago we were but a fledgling nation whose patriots had barely cast off the shackles of our English rulers. The guerilla tactics of the day were not that dissimilar from those being used now against *our* institutions. Before we all rush off to condemn them as terrorists consider for a moment our Founding Father's warning against *tyrants from within* and of their desire for us to be able to protect ourselves by granting us the right to bear arms. These were the revolutionaries of my Great-Great Grandfathers time and I'm sure England would have referred to them as terrorists. Yet who were these men? Do any of us think that George Washington was a terrorist?

When my family started growing tobacco in the late seventeen-hundreds it was a meaningful and legitimate business and it remained that way for many generations. It wasn't until science caught up with the facts and my Father and his competing CEOs lied to Congress about the harmful effects of our products and the way we manipulated them to make them even more addictive did we turn from a whole-some and respected company into a criminal enterprise. I inherited this empire from my forefathers; most of whom had no desire to do any harm and in fact weren't even aware of the negative effects that their product caused as has been amply demonstrated by science over the last few decades

I have sat and discussed this matter in detail with my wife Julia, our family, some of our top shareholders and even with a Three Star General and we are all of the same mind. It's time for us to change our direction and reduce as quickly as possible the harm we have been bringing to humanity with our products. The government may choose not to intervene and let endless lawsuits tear our company into shreds as I'm sure many would like to see happen... but what I am hoping for instead is an opportunity to help reverse the negative effects we have caused by implementing positive ones that will be demonstrable in the immediate future and will be carried on for many generations to come - the goal being to **contribute at least as much good** to our society as we have bad with the negligence of our last generation of leadership, including myself. I know that this is asking a lot for anyone to trust us but I intend to invest my family's entire financial well-being on the positive outcome that I am promising to you today.

It's too early to give you an exact road map of where we will be going but let me take a moment to tell you where the next five years will be taking us. *One;* and this is a promise that I make to all of you today... *WE WILL reduce our production of tobacco by one-fifth of our current level for each of the next five years*. This means that by the sixth year we will no longer be in the tobacco business in any way. *Two;* we will be investigating technologies where we can direct our vast resources to the benefit of mankind. Some of the areas we will be researching over the coming months will be in green technologies such as emission free cars and alternate modes of transportation, solar, wind and water power so that more destructive methods of producing energy may be reduced or perhaps even eliminated and last but not least, *three;* we will be investing in healthcare and to the ongoing research for cures and prevention to cancer, heart disease and stroke, which our products have unfortunately contributed to so significantly.

Finally, to my former competitors who are listening and licking their chops at the prospect of picking up our market share... I encourage you all to join me in this new direction, but be forewarned that we fully intend to turn over all evidence, all of our research and develop-information concerning the addictive nature of our products, the way that knowledge was manipulated to our advantage and the extensive measures that our industry has undertaken to cover up those facts through lobbyists, political contributions and through our multi-billion dollar PR machine. This *business as usual* approach will no longer be acceptable to my company and in fact we will become the expert witnesses against those companies seeking to remain on their current courses so I urge you instead to join us voluntarily and as quickly as you can so that *together* we may rid the world of this addiction once and for all and end the unnecessary death and heartache that our companies have brought to all of humanity with our products.

On a personal note I would like to thank my family and friends for helping me come to this decision. It was not my first choice but your patience and logic could not be denied and it is in this spirit that I commit all of my resources to first slow down and then turn this great company of ours onto a more appropriate course. Thank you for your time today and for the many kindnesses that were shared with my family over the last few weeks. God bless us all so we may preserve and advance the ideals of the American people."

"Ladies and gentlemen this concludes our special report from WSB-TV *Action 2 News* in Atlanta... Join us tonight at six for expert commentary... now back to our regularly scheduled programming, which is already in progress."

"Jesus Max, you weren't kidding we you?" Jason Morgan said as he shook his old friends hand with a firm grip that both men held onto just a moment longer than usual.

"It's just good to be back Jason. It's not all that much fun on the other side." Dreyden said with a smirk.

"Are you really going to pull this off?" Morgan asked still shocked at his friends commitment.

"Either that or I'm going to die trying." They weren't all wrong you know." Dreyden said matter-of-factly.

"Who's that Max?"

"The assassins."

## *"Not Bad for a College Intern"*

Dear Mr. McManus,

American Airlines top executives split close to 200 million dollars in stock bonuses while their workers got nothing. Their greed has put some of America's hardest working families in jeopardy. What can we do about it?

Signed,

Disgruntled.


**Dear Disgruntled,**

**It sounds as if you need to communicate this information to the major newspapers and NPR stations with whatever proof you can submit and see where that leads. Good luck to you and please keep us posted.**

**Tim McManus**

\* \* \* \* \*

Dear Tim,

How do you think Al-Qaeda got many of their munitions? Legally, right here in the USA and then shipped overseas… like the rest of the terrorists we've been arming since day one. That's our good ole *Military-Industrial Complex* doing what it does best… bringing us to the brink of disaster so they can send our children in an pull us back… not *too much* now… just enough to keep this profitable see-saw bouncing around for another hundred years.

Signed,

Mark in Frederick


**Dear Mark,**

**Thank you for pointing out the illegitimacy of our so-called "arms-business." We sell these products to almost anyone with money and then cry when they point them back in our direction. So how do you think we should deal with this problem?**

**Tim McManus**

* * * * *

Hey Mick-Anus,

Who the fuck do you think you are talking down to anyone with an opinion that is different from your own? Why don't you take that opinion of yours and shove it up your ass where it belongs!

Don't fuck with me, Chuck

* * * * *

**Dear Fucked-Up Chuck,**

**Please resubmit your insightful comments with the appropriate sized jar of petroleum jelly. Please do your best not to use any of it before hand.**

**Tim McManus**

* * * * *

"How's it going Jim?" McManus asked looking over his new temps' recent handy work with a grin.

"Good Tim… I was going to bounce this last idiot off of you but this is what I feel like telling him." Thoreau answered.

"I'm okay with most of it Jim… except for the foul language. Be careful not to get too carried away."

"No worries Tim, most of these are good letters and easy to respond to."

"Good, so are you enjoying yourself?"

"Yeah, for the most part. Your work is more interesting than some of the grunt work they have me doing but I figured that was how it was going to be."

"Hang tough Jim, this is an incredible news cycle and you're going to have a chance to check it out from the inside."

"I know… I just wish there was something I could do to help get to the heart of what's going on out there." Thoreau replied.

"Your time will come kid… for now just learn the ropes and keep your brain open. Irv wouldn't have gotten you a car if he didn't have some plans for you. I know there's an anti-war protest going on in DC next weekend; did he say anything to you about it?"

"No, do you think I could go to it?" Jim asked excitedly.

"I don't see why not… it's a good story and a chance for us to let you fly on your own a little. Let me check with him and let you know."

"Thanks Tim that would be great! Would you ask him if I could take Chrissie along?"

"If he says yes to your going then just take her. I do suggest that her meals come out of your pocket though so there won't be any problems when you get back." McManus warned.

"No problem at all… I figured that would be best anyway."

"Alright… so how many of these do you have left?"

"I don't know… a hundred down a few thousand to sift through. Do you mind if I throw some of the garbage on the bottom of the pile?"

"Not at all Jim, you've got good judgment just don't give me a reason to doubt it."

"Fair enough, thanks Tim, have a great show tonight!"

## *"Tom from Baltimore, You're On The Air"*

"Good evening. I'm Tim McManus and you're listening to *Door to Door* here at *WIQR – 103.5 FM* in Baltimore. Before we get to our callers I wanted to take a moment to talk about Lazarus, as some of our more creative reporters have started calling Mr. Maxwell Dreyden in their uniquely amateurish fashion. Okay, he came back from the dead, Lazarus came back from the dead but the way they are ripping in to him for "giving in to terrorism" as they prefer to describe it sounds more to me like the Militarists yapping like Chihuahuas and not the words of wise men.

Let's face it folks, if any of us had a militia after us we too would rethink our position about selling harmful products. I personally give the guy a lot of credit for having the balls, chutzpah, courage… whatever you want to call it to do what he's trying to do. You know this is not a stupid man and I know he's well aware of the fact that there's at least as much chance that our establishment will try to knock him off now that he has switched sides."

So why is he doing it? I think he's doing it for exactly the reason he said he was… because it's the right thing to do. And I bet he didn't need to speak with his PR firms to figure that out either. He made his case directly to the people… his words are in print everywhere we look so if you simply take the time to read them and not the dozens of derogatory articles about them then you'll be in a better position to judge for yourself. As for me… my vote goes to the guy with the balls. Welcome back to the world of the living Mr. Dreyden!"

"Rick from Bowie, you're on the air."

"Hi Tim, it was pretty amazing but the way our TV news covered it they made it sound like something totally different."

"Yes, it's amazing what can be communicated in a twenty-second sound bite. That's why we're going to post his entire comment on our website. It seems the battle over the truth is still a major bone of contention here in America. Jill from Reston, you're on the air."

"Hi Tim and thank you for keeping the truth out in front where it can't be hidden. I for one am routing for Mr. Dreyden."

"Thank you Jill and what exactly would you like to see happen?"

"I would love to see him set the lead for all the executives that don't have the courage to go it alone. I know being first is tough and I'm praying that this will open the gate for more to follow."

"The first one is the hardest... hopefully you'll be correct and we'll see some movement now. Thank you for your call. Kevin from Trenton New Jersey you're on the air."

"This might be a little off target for tonight's show Tim but considering the last month or so I wanted to call in and share something with your audience."

"Sure, be my guest Kevin."

"It's something that I read and thought it was from a raving lunatic but then I got to thinking on it and now I understand what he was saying."

"Go on, read it to us."

"This person wrote:"

> *"If we're not smart enough to totally ban nuclear weapons then Homo sapiens don't deserve to inhabit this planet. Disarm or LET 'EM FLY... so the Earth can begin to heal from our gross stupidity."*

"Hmmm... that's pretty far out there. Do you agree with that sentiment?"

"Well, not at first but after a while I began to agree with him. After all, what right do we have to destroy everything on the planet? I know he's being factitious, if that's the right word, but it makes sense that we need to get ourselves under control or we don't disserve to be here… that the planet would be better off without us."

"We know it would be a cleaner planet Kevin free from the threat of nuclear war but it is nuclear war itself that would lead to our total destruction."

"He knows that… and he also knows the earth will heal itself after we're all gone. I believe that. I do construction work and its amazing how fast nature rejuvenates after we've torn her up. All she needs is our absence."

"Thank you very much for your thoughts Kevin. *All she needs is our absence…* sounds like something my wife would have said to me. But all kidding aside I think you're right and we all need to learn how to live in harmony with our Mother Earth and stop disrespecting her. Tom from Baltimore, you're on the air."

"This whole thing sounds like a plot from one of my novels. I just wish I had written it before they did it."

"Is that you Mr. Clancy?"

"Yes Tim, I've enjoyed your show for years but I must say that for the last month or so you've been taking us on a different kind of ride."

"It's not my ride sir… it's our world as it exists today… *non-fiction*."

"Exactly, but you're playing it like it's some kind of military exercise. What's going on is as serious as a heart attack to all Americans and to our allies around the world. We are under attack by an unknown force from within our own borders."

"So how am I ***playing this***… I don't quite understand your meaning."

"It's like a big game to you… you're probably higher than a kite on ratings and are either unable or unwilling to separate your sense of duty from your desire to gain mass acceptance."

"And what should my sense of duty be telling me to do?"

"It should be telling you that your country is in real trouble and that backing any kind of plot to overthrow our government is traitorous."

"I see… so no matter what our government wants to do it's okay with you."

"***I didn't say that*** and I wish you people wouldn't try to put words in our mouths. What I said was our country is in deep trouble. I simply don't agree that it's time to throw the whole thing out and start from scratch… which is what these so-called patriots of yours are trying to accomplish."

"Alright, I understand your point but answer one question for me if you would be so kind."

"Go ahead."

"We know you're a smart man, perhaps even brilliant… so please tell me what Maxwell Dreyden said that is offensive to you."

(pause)

"He didn't say anything that was offensive to me personally."

"Do you smoke?"

"Yes I do and ***yes it's a very difficult habit to break***."

"If you could go back and never have that first cigarette wouldn't that be a god thing?"

"Why of course it would… but blowing a guys head off to make that point is just a bit extreme don't you think?"

"No, not really… killing five million human beings a year because of that product is a lot extreme. Let's get our priorities straight here Tom. One life versus five million…"

"No argument there but I believe in exercising our legal resolutions until they are exhausted and not depending on violence."

"Alright, I don't disagree with you except for the fact that you have a lot of money and getting legal representation must be relatively easy for you."

"Well yes, yes it is."

"But what of the hundreds of thousands of victims who can't afford to use *"the system"* to get the compensation they're entitled to. What are they supposed to do? Just die and stop complaining because they're too poor for any of us to care about?"

"That's a valid point Tim… but I still think we need to use the system we have in place or this country is going to take an unnecessary hit that we may never recover from."

"It's kind of an all or nothing game here then isn't it Tom."

"Yes, it does appear to be heading in that direction."

"Well, it was an all or nothing proposition back in 1776 as well… and then again in 1861. I think it was Jefferson who told us that our Liberty Tree required the blood of patriots and tyrants from time to time in order to flourish."

"Yes, it was Thomas Jefferson. I just hope all of your listeners know that what's in front of them isn't a gladiator sport… it's a war on their homeland amongst their own children and it's not going to be a pretty thing to see."

"Kinda like watching Viet Nam on the nightly news in the sixties... that wasn't very pretty either. Perhaps sir, you could pick up the plot from here and write us all a better ending."

"If only it were that easy Tim I'd do it in a heartbeat but Pandora is a fickle lady and this thing may not fit back into any of our boxes. Please keep that in mind the next time you have the urge to cheer on a revolution."

"I definitely will Mr. Clancy and thank you for sharing your wisdom with us... it was greatly appreciated. This is a more humble Tim McManus saying thanks to all of our callers and audience from here at **WIQR-103.5 FM – Baltimore** - every **Sunday night at 10pm**. As always we look forward to hearing from you either by the phone, or e-mail at: tim@wiqr.com. Thanks for listening, dream well and goodnight."

## *"Yes, 10:00 Will Be Fine"*

After his job in California Bob Messer had taken a well deserved break and spent a week enjoying San Francisco before heading up the coast to Seattle where his next assignment was waiting.

On the drive north he heard the replay of the Dreyden press conference and was shocked to hear that his prey had gotten away from what felt like a perfect hit. He instinctively knew that the silence over the last few weeks had to mean that the FBI was keeping it quiet in order to flush out the team and he was even more concerned when he caught up with the TV news and saw Matt Creagor's photo and artist's sketch accurately portrayed on the screen. He was relieved to see that his own sketch was off by quite a bit... at least enough not to have to worry about it for the moment. His primary concern was in the knowledge of what they would do to Creagor when they caught him and of the imminent danger that would put those squads in. His own identity was safe through the isolation tactics he had been honing for nearly thirty years. For now he would just wait and do nothing, ignore his curiosity and rest assured in the knowledge that he would be contacted if he was in imminent danger.

When Messer reached downtown Seattle he checked into the Crowne Plaza Hotel under the alias of Roger Thurmond and took a luxurious room on the thirtieth floor. As soon as he tipped the bellboy for bringing up his luggage he took out his portable PC and logged on to the internet. *Good, no messages...* he thought to himself. *No news is good news.* He took a few minutes to look over the room service menu and then placed an order for a rare filet mignon with baked potato and fresh asparagus in hollandaise sauce and a tall glass of skim milk. He then ordered bottles of Riesling Spatlese and Pinot Noir for later in the evening before heading off for a quick shower. Refreshed Messer opened up the yellow pages and found his favorite Escort Service where he placed his second order of the evening for a delightful young brunette who wouldn't mind spending the night...

"Yes, room 3014… ten o'clock will be fine." Anymore business would just have to wait…

# *"The Gloves Are Off!"*

In the weeks following the Dreyden announcement no less than five-dozen companies submitted their plans to the Wall Street Journal to move away from the military endeavors they had been involved in. For the most part these were mid-sized companies that had the vast majority of their success in manufacturing and had only just begun competing for military contracts over the last ten years. They promised to stay away from further military endeavors as soon as their existing contracts expired and many of these companies gave the expiration dates of when their obligations would end.

All of the corporate-military-industrial giants refused to cave-in to the threat and began their own counter-offensives using all of their connections within the pentagon and government to lobby for the resources needed to stop the terrorists dead in their tracks. Most of these giant corporations lost high-level executives and R&D personnel who feared that their own names would reach the top of the assassins list much more quickly now that their illustrious leaders were moving deeper into hiding. The stock market assaulted these companies even further as major share holders bailed out *en masse.* Some of the largest stock-holders even placed ads in the Wall Street Journal to notify the assassins that their family was no longer involved with the company. Board of Directors members of these firms were emptying faster than the waters of a broken levy. The economic war was most definitely being won by the Deep-Six revolutionaries.

The war in the media was a different matter. Although National Public Radio and public television stations had taken up the fight by clearly articulating the cause of the rebels the mega-media moguls soon joined forces to denounce the *"cowards who caved in"* and the *"terrorists who were trying to destroy America"*. This phase of the war was now underway full force and you couldn't turn on the news or pick up a paper without hearing another debate or sound-bite arguing the matter one way or the other. The fight for public opinion was on and would most likely determine the outcome of this new kind of warfare. The younger Internet savvy crowd tended to side with the rebels and the older newspaper readers more with the establishment… it was middle-aged American adults who would swing this debate.

Peace marches became common place throughout the land and the banners to end the war and stop all aggression outnumbered the anti-patriot factions at least ten to one. A number of the peaceful marchers were so seriously injured by excessive Police force that the Deep-Six squads took it upon themselves to retaliate after the first death occurred to an eighteen year-old college freshman girl who was shot through the eye with a "non-lethal" rubber bullet. The local Deep-Six squad isolated and eliminated the Chief of Police and three officers who were responsible for the attacks on the public in Detroit. These assassinations were not *"one-shot one-kill"* attacks but more brutal up close and personal. The biggest offender was in LA and he was disemboweled in a public theater by two masked men as shocked onlookers watched helplessly as the victim died slowly before their eyes. It was time again for Americans to experience the sight of death first hand and not through the gladiatorial white-wash of television.

The gloves were now off… ***"Attack democracy in any way and you are going to die"*** was the message being sent loud and clear by the Deep-Six conspirators as reported by the NPR stations and the free media. Meanwhile, the bounty initially placed on their heads by the President was raised to $25,000 for any information that would lead to the arrest and conviction of any of the terrorists. Matthew Creagor's picture was now on every right-wing news broadcast throughout the country along with the many variations provided by the FBI to demonstrate what cosmetic alterations could do. He had been rushed to the FBI's top ten wanted list as his family and friends were being harassed mercilessly by neo-conservatives.

Meanwhile, Creagor's three squads, who had always kept their tactical distance from one another, were working out of the limelight on their list of active targets. Brent Foster was a capable new platoon leader and this region had barely missed a beat thanks to the escape of their former leader. Of the five active targets they were pursuing when the freeze was ordered by Clark only two of them had disappeared off of their radar with the latest escalation. That left Foster's team with three live targets that were actively being stalked.

"Some people just don't know when it's time to get in out of the rain." Foster said as he spotted for his top sharpshooter who was sighting in another war profiteer... *"670 yards, wind is about 15 miles per hour."*

"We'll teach him right now…" Rodriguez said as he exhaled and held his breath to steady himself.

Just as the target's partner began to swing his one wood a single shot rang out taking the forty-eight year old executive unaware as the .30/06 bullet pierced his skull through his left-front temporal lobe at 2,700 feet per second blowing out the right rear of his head an instant later and taking twenty-five percent of his brain with it.

*"Hell of a drive…"* Foster said as the startled golfer cracked his ball two hundred and forty yards, twenty yards farther than ever before, as the sound of the shot barely preceded his contact with the ball. *"Your shot wasn't too bad either…"* He told Jesus Rodriguez who had just made another perfect kill.

The two assassins watched as the startled man saw his drive soar and then turn to his friend only to find him sprawled out on his back with a pool of blood expanding slowly around his head. A split second later he was on the ground trying to take cover where no cover was to be found.

"Too bad he wasn't a target…" Rodriguez said. "It would have been an easy two-fer."

"Let's get going Jesus." Foster said to his man as he disassembled the rifle in a matter of moments and placed it into its portable case.

The two men then faded slowly back into the woods where their ATV Quad vehicles were waiting a short distance away. They followed the hunting trails for three miles to a prearranged spot one hundred yards from a public hiking entrance and gave the gun case to another one of their squad members, who would stow it in the trunk of his car in just a few minutes. The two men then continued their back country ride to a remote area four miles away where they located their 4x4 Chevy truck and loaded the two quads onto the trailer. They took the dirt road out of the woods and pulled onto a local highway that led to the parking lot where Rodriguez had parked his vehicle. The two men parted silently with only a nod between them before returning home to their families.

### *"Black Like Me"*

Matt Creagor had been sitting tight in his motel room under the alias of William Allen counting on his new squad leader to keep him supplied with the bare essentials, which unfortunately didn't contain the beer or rum he had requested. *"These subs were getting boring..."* he thought to himself and imagined a nice thick steak as he took a bite into the Chicken Teriyaki sandwich. Just then a firm knock came through the door and Creagor almost spat out the mouthful he had taken but composed himself and answered the door.

"Yes, may I help you?" He said to the young slender stranger before him... still chewing the bite he had taken.

"Mr. Allen?" The stranger asked.

"Yes, how can I help you?" Creagor said worried that this stranger might recognize him.

"Charlie sent me... may I come in?"

"Yes, please do." He said standing aside with the door open.

"My name is John Wilson and Charlie asked me to see what I could do to help you change your look." He said as he opened up his bag on the table and extracted the most recent FBI artist renditions that were now on every major news channel across the country. "I suppose you've seen these?"

"Yes, they've got me down cold don't they... no matter what we do I l think I'm still fucked." Creagor said.

"I thought so too..." Wilson said. "But then I remembered a book I read as a kid. Have you ever read *Black Like Me?*"

"No, I haven't... what's it about?" Creagor asked.

"It's about a white man who dyed his skin so he could pose as a Negro and experience first hand the racial prejudice in our country."

"Is it a fiction?"

"No sir, it's about his actual experiences as a black man in the deep south around 1960. Now look at those FBI sketches again…"

"No black men…" Creagor realized.

"Exactly… I think that's your best chance Sir. I hope you're not prejudiced."

"No, not at all John… but this is so far out. What about my hair?"

Corporal Wilson pulled out a few high-quality Negro wigs and handed them to Creagor. "One of these should work fine as long as you get a marine cut first and then die your hair."

"Who was the guy that did this and how did he make out?"

"I had forgotten his name until I started researching this assignment. His name was John Howard Griffin and he started this in 1959. He shaved his head and took a drug called Oxsoralen, which is normally used to treat vitiligo – which causes white splotches on the skin. He then underwent long ultra-violet light sessions to darken himself. He had a doctor monitoring this accelerated treatment and he did fine so you should be safe too. He then spent a few months traveling through the Deep South and was faced with all of the racism of every other black man at that time. No one at all thought he was white."

"Were there any side effects from the procedure?"

"Nausea and lassitude… I had to look that last one up. Lassitude is sluggishness, weariness… but this guy wasn't in good health in the first place and that could have been from the stress of his experiment or from the injuries he sustained in World War II… this guy was a hero sir. Plus the way he was treated throughout his journey must have been very stressful. It won't be like that for you up here."

"Damn... that's one thing that never even crossed my mind... me as a Negro. ***Damn! That might actually work!***" Creagor said encouraged by his new found hope.

"I think it's your best chance sir." Wilson agreed.

"So how do we get started John? I hate being cooped up like this."

"Now that you've agreed we can get our acquisition team to get you the medicine... that shouldn't be very hard. I'm a bachelor and if you don't mind living in my basement we can set you up with the ultra-violet lights right down there. You can use my weights to keep in shape and that should help you relax. Pippen told me you're going to need to remain totally underground until this is finished and then we'll relocate you to a place where you'll blend in better."

"I hate to put you out that much John." Creagor said sincerely.

"Hey, it's no trouble at all. It's just good to know that we support each other like this. Who knows, I could be in your shoes someday."

"Alright... that's fair enough. What do you want me to do now?" Creagor asked.

"For now just stay put and let me get the ball rolling for you and then I'll come get you when we're ready. Here's a couple of grinders and sodas to tide you over... I got some fruit in there for you too."

"How about a nice thick steak next time John?" Creagor said jokingly. "These subs are getting old."

"That'll be our first meal when you come over. Just be patient... at least we have a plan that makes sense."

"Do you have any black men in your squads now?"

"Yes sir, three that I know of… but we keep the teams pretty isolated from one another so there's probably more."

"Good, I didn't want to be the only one."

"You won't be Mr. Allen." Corporal John Wilson said before gathering up his things and leaving.

## *"Tell Me About His Service"*

McNulty had been working hard with his people in Atlanta and the Pentagon to find out everything there was to know about Matt Creagor. With the preliminary information now in hand he met with Chief Dobson to help him with his investigation.

"Tell me what you know Mark." Dobson said as his protégé sat down.

"You were right chief he had an excellent military record. Four tours in the gulf. He was in Afghanistan in 1999 going after Bin Laden before 9/11 even happened... he was awarded the Silver Star for bravery when he took over his squad after his Sergeant was killed. He led them on a counter-attack that destroyed most of the force that had ambushed them. He was promoted to Corporal during his first tour and came back as a Sergeant in his third... he served in Iraq for the first year of the invasion and was discharged honorably in late 2003 after being awarded the Bronze Star for meritorious service. In 2002 he took shrapnel to his right leg but insisted in staying overseas and returning to the fight after he healed six-weeks later." McNulty concluded.

"A good soldier... makes you wonder what the Hell he's up to now." Dobson asked himself more than Mark.

"I guess he really believes in what he's doing Walt."

"We'll be lucky to get this man alive. What else do you know?"

"Before his service he was an above average high-school student but he couldn't afford to go to college. He joined the military on his own when he was twenty-three after drifting between some pretty menial jobs."

"So that makes him about thirty-two." Dobson chimed in. "Keep going Mark..."

"Chief, he started his business after two-years of trade school that was paid for by his military benefits. He's never been in trouble with the law, has shown a small profit every year with his business growing slowly and he's a father and family man. Other than our photograph, this guy is as squeaky clean as they come."

"So if he's so clean why is he running Mark?" Dobson asked seriously.

"Because he's a man with a cause… who's trying to put America back on a better path." Mark replied.

"Don't start drinking too much of the cool-aide son." Dobson warned. "What else do we know about him? What are his skills?"

"Other than his obvious leadership skills he's pretty average. He's an average shot, he's good but not great in hand to hand combat, nothing spectacular about his physical attributes. He does seem to have a very keen strategic mind though. The way he led his troops when he was just twenty-three during that ambush probably saved their entire squad. He also demonstrated strong competence throughout all four of his tours and he was highly commended by his superior officers in every one of his evaluations."

"Sounds like he could have been a career man... any idea why he left the service?" Dobson asked.

"Not really sir. If there was any cause the records don't reflect it. Maybe he just got tired Chief."

"Or maybe he didn't think we should be spending blood for oil. That would be more in tune with the way this guy thinks."

"We're also compiling lists of all of the men he has served with and reported to but so far none of them live in the Atlanta area." McNulty said.

"Get the photographs of those men down to Hobson and Morrison and have them re-canvas the area using the pictures. There's a pretty good chance that some of them may be there living under aliases." Dobson concluded.

"We've been trying to locate all of them but it hasn't been easy Chief. I may need you to kick a few more asses for me to get this thing moving a little faster."

"Just let me know who's blocking you and I will set a fire under their ass… alright, what else?"

"That's about it… the search of his home didn't turn up anything… except a licensed .38 caliber pistol that was properly locked away. His wife didn't know anything about it but we found it on the top shelf of his closet. It hadn't been fired in a long time. The phone records didn't turn up anything but calls to friends and customers… mostly her friends. He pretty much worked and spent time with his family."

"Yes, when he wasn't planning a hit with his undercover squad." Dobson reiterated. "There has to be more than that Mark… go find it!"

"Yes sir." He responded automatically as he rose and left the room already anticipating the Atlanta team's reaction to a second canvassing of the region.

# *"Is This A Private Fight? Or Can Anyone Join In?"*

"The Dreyden residence, may I help you?" Jason Roberts said as he answered the phone.

"Max Dreyden please, this is Senator Bradford calling."

"Yes sir. One moment please and I'll check to see if he's available." Roberts replied.

"Edward, to what do I owe this honor?" Dreyden asked in an uncharacteristically cheerful voice.

"Hello Max, I was very pleased to hear that you hadn't bought the farm."

"It was close but I got very lucky." He said more seriously now. "What's going on Ed?"

"How serious are you about the speech you just gave?"

"As serious as a heart-attack... why do you ask?"

"Good, I just wanted to hear it directly from you. I'm considering a run at the Presidency and I'm looking for a man of substance to be my running mate. Do you think you might be interested?"

"Jesus Ed, I've never even considered it. I'm not a politician and I have no experience running government. How can you even consider me?" Dreyden asked shocked at the strange offer.

"Well, in case you haven't noticed our current government isn't very popular these days. Most of the people are backing the revolutionaries and your speech was exactly where I see this country going. I'd love your help getting her there." Senator Bradford replied.

"My God Ed... I honestly don't know. I'd be happy to help you but I'm not sure I'm the right man for the job. When do you need my answer?" Dreyden asked.

"You're my first and only choice right now Max. There isn't another Senator or Congressman that I would trust as my right hand man. I doubt I'd even run if you don't join me. I'm that serious about what you can bring to our mission."

"This is amazing... and only a week ago I was considering waging my own war against these assassins."

"They're not all wrong Max. Everything they've said makes sense. Even their tactics have been carried out with the precision of a surgeon's scalpel. We need to reel them in before permanent damage is done to our economy."

"And how do you plan on doing that Senator?"

"By running on a peace platform and redirecting our war machinery into useful, positive endeavors along the same lines that you outlined. I've got quite a few good ideas that I'd like to share with you."

"Sure, talking never hurt anyone."

(Laughing) "You've never conducted a filibuster..." Bradford answered.

"No, thank God, I haven't had that pleasure." Dreyden said laughing along with his friend. "You know that this platform of yours is going to make you a target don't you."

"Of course... that's one of the best signs that we're on the right path Max. Anyway I figured you'd know some good bodyguards."

"You'll need more than bodyguards you'll need your own army... look at what they did in the sixties to escalate the Viet Nam war Ed."

"That's why it's time to take our country back before it gets any further out of hand than it already is or these new minutemen tear us down so far that we won't even recognize her."

"I'll give it some serious thought Ed, but I honestly don't know right now. There's a lot for me to do just getting my company launched on the course that I've promised."

"I understand… but look at it this way. From the inside you will be able to influence the laws that can help the entire country onto the course you spoke about. That's why I know you're the perfect person for this job. This is one of the most critical junctures in our nation's history and the status quo simply isn't going to be enough." Bradford said sincerely.

"Why don't you come down and spend the weekend. We'll talk and see if we can't figure this thing out together."

"How does this weekend look Max?"

"It's open… I'm still not out of my hermit mode yet and it'll be nice to have your company. Can you bring Mary along? Julia and I would love to have her company as well."

"I'm sure she'd love to come. I'll let you know what our itinerary is as soon as it's arranged. And thanks Max, we really could make a great team."

"We'll see you on Saturday then… goodbye."

Max Dreyden sat in his den stunned at the conversation that had just taken place. There was no denying the honor that had been bestowed upon him by his former college classmate but the reality of his request was still unfathomable. He needed his wife's perspective and began counting the minutes until she would return from her excursion with the children.

# *"IDIOCRACY"*

"So how did the peace march go in DC Jim?" McManus asked.

"It was great! There must have been fifty thousand people there and for the most part it was peaceful. There was trouble once but it seemed to die down quickly, I'm not sure what happened it was too far away from where Chrissie and I were." Thoreau told his new boss.

"I saw that on the news... they made it seem like the whole rally was filled with trouble makers. The cops took on about fifteen or twenty students who wouldn't get out of the street when they were told to. They just sat there until the cops started pepper spraying them. I was waiting for the dogs to be brought out but that never happened."

"I couldn't believe all the people... I never took part in anything like it. They had signs like; "Get Our Troops Out or We'll Get YOU OUT!" "Try Listening To Us For A Change!" And, "Stop Lying To US!" I was glad to be there Tim, thanks for letting me go."

"You were sent for a purpose... so I could get a better feel for what the people are feeling. What was their mood concerning the Deep-Six group... did they think they were terrorists or patriots?" McManus asked.

"The vast majority of the people were all for them. No way did they think they were terrorists. Just about everyone I spoke with felt they were trying to pull our country back to a more just society and that if we couldn't do it peacefully then maybe they were right to pick up arms. I feel the same way Tim... we're so far off track now with our policies it's hard to see any other way."

"Our audience sure agrees with you Jim. I'm still pretty worried about what will happen when the NSA starts fighting back. So far they've been relatively quiet but it's only a matter of time until our government starts to protect itself... it's going to get ugly and that scares the crap out of me. What if they declare Marshall Law and all of a sudden we're all living with a curfew hiding out in our houses?"

"I hadn't thought about that. Could they really do that to us?"

"It's possible Jim... they'll do whatever they can to stay in power and won't give up without a fight. Their problem is the stealthy attacks the revolutionaries are using... they don't have a hard target to go after... so that leaves the exposed militias and anyone who stands up against them."

"What do you think the people would do under Marshall Law?" Thoreau asked.

"I think they would revolt en masse. I think that would set off riots and we'd see a repeat of the sixties with cities in flames." McManus estimated.

"Dear God, I'd hate to see that happen." Jim said with real concern in his voice.

"I wouldn't be surprised if our government started inflaming the situation to drive public opinion against the revolutionaries."

"How could they do that?"

"Blow up some propane trucks, take out a few gasoline storage tanks, assassinate some innocents, kill a few woman and children in the process and start making it look like the revolutionaries are involved with those attacks. That kind of thing would be easy to fake and then they'd put their media machine into full gear to sway as much of the population as possible with their propaganda." McManus guessed.

"What if you spoke of those possibilities on your show before they pull that tactic on us?" Jim asked hoping his suggestion might help.

"I've been thinking about it Jim. I'd need to get Irv's sign-off on that due to the backlash he'd probably receive."

"You know what they say about *forgiveness* don't you Tim?"

"What's that?"

"That it's easier to obtain than prior approval."

"Hmmm… that's a thought. It's my show right?"

"You've got the audience behind you big-time Tim… why not take advantage of that?"

"I'd need someone to call in and raise the issue… so it doesn't seem like my idea. Yeah, that could work out fine."

"Chrissie and I can take care of that. What was your favorite sign at the rally?"

"I saw one I liked a lot. I couldn't read it all at once but I taped the demonstration and focused in on it later. It said:

### <u>IDIOCRACY</u>:

WHEN A BUREAUCRACY,
WHETHER THROUGH MAL INTENT
OR SHEER INCOMPETENCE,
FAILS TO PERFORM THE
DUTY OF ITS OFFICE"

\* \* \* \* \*

"Is that a real word? I've never heard it before."

"No, I looked it up to be sure… but it sure sounds like a good one to add to our vocabulary."

"That is a good one, too bad I didn't see it and speak to whoever wrote it."

"It was in the group of kids that got beaten up."

"I guess the truth hurts!" Jim said laughing.

"Alright, send me your notes and thoughts on the trip as soon as they're ready. I want to incorporate them into my thoughts for the next show."

"Will do… Chrissie has been writing about her experiences too, would you like a copy of what she's written?"

"Absolutely… her perspective would be helpful. Thanks Jim… it's good to have you on the team."

"It's my pleasure. Thanks for pulling the strings to get me here! By the way I was wondering what you'd think about an interview with that Dreyden guy? That might make an interesting half-hour."

"That's a not a bad idea Jim but I doubt he'd leave his nest to come up here and it can be tough doing one of those over the phone…"

"Who knows… he might want the opportunity to talk about his new direction. His stock took a twenty percent hit with him dead… he might think your show could help get his message out. And with the power being boosted soon that would mean an even larger audience."

"Hmmm… makes perfect sense to me. That could be a fun show, especially if he were in the studio. Why don't you get his number for me and I'll make the call."

"Give me a few minutes and I'll bring it to you." Jim Thoreau said eagerly as he headed for his cubicle and his networked computer.

# *"Social Change and Rocket Fuel"*

Edward & Mary Bradford arrived at the Dreyden residence at ten-thirty Saturday morning after a comfortable first class flight from Logan International Airport in Boston. Jason Roberts met them at their gate in Atlanta and escorted the handsome couple to the Dreyden's Mercedes, which was in the short-term parking lot. When Mrs. Bradford went to hand Roberts her bag he hesitated knowing that they would be safer if his hands were left free but then he realized the threat was low and accepted the task without complaint.

"How was your flight?" Roberts asked as he took Mary Bradford's bag.

"It was fine." She replied and then thanked him for carrying her bag.

"Mr. and Mrs. Dreyden are waiting for you in the residence. We felt it would be safer for you not to be seen with them just yet." Roberts added as if to apologize for their absence.

"No problem at all Mr. Roberts." Senator Bradford said cheerfully. "At least he didn't make us take a cab." He continued jokingly.

"Never sir. he would never treat a guest like that." Roberts responded ignoring the humor that was intended.

A short while later Jason Roberts pulled up to the front of the house, got out and opened the door for Senator Bradford and his wife. He then escorted them up the beautiful stone walkway and stairs that led to the front door. By the time they got to the top of the steps both Julia and Max had opened the door and were greeting their old friends warmly on the front porch.

"It's so nice to see you two again!" Julia said enthusiastically as she gave Mary a hug and Edward a kiss on the cheek.

Max gave his friend a warm handshake and graciously accepted Mary's kiss, which see planted on her host's cheek.

"You're looking good Ed!" Max said sincerely as he eyeballed the handsome Senator approvingly.

"You're looking tired old friend." Bradford said as they were escorted into the home. "I guess being dead isn't much rest after all."

"Not hardly... they were the toughest weeks I've ever spent." Max confirmed.

Julia led them to her lovely dining room where fresh fruit, pastries, coffee, tea and an assortment of juices had been prepared.

"Please, help yourself to anything you'd like." She said as she began pouring coffee into the fine china cups.

The Bradford's accepted the coffee and each picked out a fresh Danish before sitting at the beautiful oriental table that was the centerpiece of the room.

"Perhaps we should have Jason taste it first Senator." Max said jokingly just as Ed took his first bite.

"Now you tell me." Bradford said laughing at his host's poor joke. "So what do you think of my offer to your husband Julia?"

"Quite frankly it scares the Hell out of me Ed. Do you really think he would help you on the ticket?"

"There's no doubt about it. He's exactly the right man at this time. Have you ever heard of Tony Kushner?" Ed Bradford asked his hosts.

"Is he a political expert?" Max Dreyden guessed incorrectly.

"No Dear, he's a playwright." Julia chimed in. "He won a Pulitzer for *Angels in America*. What does he have to do with my husband's candidacy?"

"I read something he wrote quite a long time ago that I've always carried with me." Senator Bradford said.

He said; ***"There are moments in history when the fabric of everyday life unravels, and there is this unstable dynamism that allows for incredible social change in short periods of time. People and the world they're living in can be utterly transformed, either for the good or the bad, or some mixture of the two."*** Ed Bradford quoted from memory.

"And you think this is one of those times Ed?" Max asked his friend already knowing that it was.

"Most certainly… and I know you understand that too Max." Bradford said with conviction. "This opportunity has been circling our Country since September eleventh, 2001. Our illustrious leaders have squandered their opportunity and much of what America stands for in the process. They've taken us in the opposite direction of where we need to go." Bradford said trying not to get too worked up over the way his country was pillaging other nations while being pillaged itself.

"And what about all of these murders Ed. They almost murdered my husband." Julia said not to argue his point as much as the methods that were currently being utilized.

"Please understand me. I'm not in favor of a revolution nor do I support the tactics being used by this military underground. I'm just saying that they've picked a good time to stir the pot and that we now have a great opportunity to control the boil and bring America out the other side as a better nation." Senator Bradford argued gently.

"I don't disagree with you Ed… but why me? I'm still not convinced how putting my name on the ticket helps you." Dreyden said honestly.

"Max, you were the first one with the guts to come out and take your company into a more… a more suitable direction. Your words were genuine and well received by the public and that's exactly what I am trying to accomplish. We need to redirect the power away from the Corporate-Military-Industrial-Congressional-Complex and into more worthwhile endeavors. The citizens of this country are ready for this and it's one of those unique times in history when we could actually pull it off. I need you and your talent and your sincerity to help us get there." Ed Bradford said with all of the conviction he could muster.

"Do you think I want to exchange one set of assassins for another Ed? Just look what they did in the sixties… anyone who tampered with the military-complex was executed. What makes you think you and I would be any safer?" Dreyden argued convincingly.

"I never said it would be easy Max. But I do believe it's a chance worth taking. We're just two lives… but look at all the slaughter that continues on around us everyday. I can't believe that you'd want to walk away when we're in a position to make such a positive change."

"I didn't say I wanted to walk away Ed… but it was my family and not yours that just had one of our friends blown away. It's my wife and children who almost lost a husband and a father. This isn't just about me." Max said trying to weigh-in for his wife.

"Honey…" Julia said gently. "You may always be a target… no matter what you do. The revolutionaries targeted you because of the damage from cigarettes that your family's business caused. You told me yourself that you may wind up being a target by any right-wing group opposed to your *changing sides* and retooling your company. So what's the difference if you're a target in this scenario? At least you'd know who was after you."

"Great… so at least I'd know that our military is after me. Jesus Christ Julia, do you really want to go through all that? They may not stop at just me and might take you and the kids out just to make a fucking point!" Max Dreyden said upset at the thought.

"What about General Andersen dear?" Julia added insightfully.

"Who's General Andersen Max?" Ed Bradford asked.

"He's a three star General that I consulted with before I went on the air. He would definitely be someone that you and I should talk with before we move on this Ed." Dreyden said mulling over the thought that the General may be able to safeguard them. "Alright… here's my bottom line. If the General can convince me that he can protect us then I'm in. Otherwise it's too great a risk for my family and I just can't take that chance."

"That's fair enough… it was on my list of topics to discuss with you anyway." Ed Bradford confirmed. "I'd like to meet this man and see what he can teach us… it should be interesting."

"He's good but he's not cheap my friend… $100,000 a day just to consult with us. That's before we put any of his suggestions into action." Dreyden said.

"That's what we have contributions for Max. Don't worry… we'll find the money we need." Bradford said.

"Well then, that settles it. Who's up for some lunch? We have quite a feast planned…" Julia said trying to cool down the atmosphere.

"I'm famished just smelling it." Mary added lightly.

"Would anyone care for a drink?" Max asked. "I sure as Hell need one."

"Sure. Honey what would you like?" Bradford asked his wife.

"A glass of white wine would be lovely." She answered joyfully.

"Do you remember what I drink Max?" Bradford asked.

"Rocket fuel…" Max replied. "At least twelve-year-old rocket fuel… I have a bottle just for you… it's twenty-five year old rocket fuel though… hope you don't mind. I sure as Hell couldn't taste the difference."

"That'd be great Max, thanks." Bradford said laughing at his friend.

"Honey, what would you like?" Dreyden asked his wife.

"Would you pick a nice bottle of white wine for Mary and me?" Julia asked.

"Two white wines, Meyer's rum and fresh OJ for me and rocket fuel for the next President of the United States." Dreyden said as he headed for the wine cellar.

# *"Communications, WiFi & Virtual Invisibility"*

"Cassandra, would you join me in my office please. Bring your notes on the computer situation." McNulty added as he hung up the phone.

A few minutes later Cassandra Jones was at his open door knocking lightly as she came in and sat down at McNulty's small round conference table. He finished his call and picked up a blank pad and joined her.

"Good morning Cassie, have any luck figuring out what we need to do with these systems of ours? Mark asked.

"We've had the consultants in and they've taken stock of our systems, what they do and how they work for us. We filled them in with our priorities and wish-lists and they're now moving between regions trying to figure out how to link it all together most effectively."

"How long are we talking here?" McNulty asked.

"At least a few months for their recommendations and then at least a year or two to do what is needed. I already know what they're going to tell us Mark."

"How could you… they've only just started." McNulty asked still not grasping the technology from their earlier meeting..

"As we discussed earlier we basically have two types of systems, proprietary and open architecture. Open systems are designed to communicate with one another easily so those won't be a problem. We still have critical data on our mainframes that never migrated to the new technology. That's where our problems are… they are going to determine how many disparate systems we have and which ones can be migrated efficiently to open architecture platforms. The other dinosaurs will still need to share information but they have so much software code to convert that we may have to let them co-exist and simply wither on the vine. Meanwhile, we continue to write new code for applications as needed. That could take years for us to ease them out but it's the only way to go, there's just too much code to rewrite."

"I'm not sure I am following you. You mean we still may wind up with both proprietary and open architecture systems?"

"Yes, that's the probable outcome. You have to realize that some of those systems have been around for decades… they contain millions upon millions of lines of software code and they've been taken as far as they can effectively go. The only solution is to use them up and write the programs we need on current technology platforms in the open environment. It's quite likely that it will be another ten years or more before those old systems are totally antiquated and allowed to die. By then all of our newer applications will have been written around them and render them obsolete without having to rewrite those specific programs at an incredible cost. We're trying to accomplish as much as we can in the shortest time period possible but some tasks are not worth the investment. One way or the other we're going to need to build a secure, and I mean bullet proof system to protect our data. This is a major undertaking Mark and don't expect to see too much very soon. I can tell you with absolute certainty that the longer we wait the harder and more expensive this is evolution is going to be."

"So much for using these systems to catch the bad guys…" McNulty said softly, mostly to himself.

"The bad guys have been light-years ahead of us on this. They don't need to maintain the databases we do… linking to each other is child's play compared to all of the overhead we have to concern ourselves with. It's a *no-contest* situation Mark." Cassandra Jones reiterated.

"What about using the technology to help us catch them… do you have any suggestions?"

"First off, forget using what we have now. They're probably communicating over the internet and via these new throw away phones like the drug dealers do. We need to catch someone on their team…

then we'll be able to trace that user to everyone he's in touch with. It's too bad you didn't get that guys PC in Atlanta."

"We did… but it didn't help us… it was totally clean."

"They have to be using portable PCs then. So that means they're probably using WiFi stations and internet chat services, which allow instantaneous communication and virtual invisibility."

"Virtual invisibility? What the Hell does that mean Cassie? And what's WiFi?"

"It means they think they're invisible but everything is tracked and logged. The problem we have is finding the needle in the millions of haystacks… it's nearly impossible unless you get hold of one of these PCs and start following the bread crumbs from user to user. The WiFi technology is a wireless high-speed internet connection that you can connect your equipped PC from anywhere that service is established. You see them going in a lot now at malls, coffee houses, book stores, places like that."

"So fixing our computers won't help us with this problem?"

"Not directly… it would have helped us pick up on the patterns that were developing for the last five years but it wouldn't have made a bit of difference in finding these guys."

"I wish you had said something about this earlier… I could have gotten something going."

"Mark, first off this is common knowledge and I'm surprised you're so in the dark about it. Second, what are you going to do… have a thousand investigators reading hundreds of millions of chat room conversations trying to find some obscure clue that will probably be incredibly vague at best anyway? That isn't going to work and all you're going to do is ruin a lot of people's eyesight in the process."

"We need one of their machines…" McNulty confirmed.

"That's it. Without the initial break our vastly superior force is turned into a bunch of deaf, dumb and blind mice."

"Alright... just put some more of that beautiful grey matter of yours onto this problem and see if there isn't something else we can do to help deal ourselves a break."

"A nice little EMP would help do the trick... just do it over Atlanta and not DC please." Cassandra said joking as she picked up her notebook.

"Electro magnetic pulse... yeah, I'm sure the City of Atlanta would just love us to do that!" McNulty said sarcastically.

"It sure would get a whole lot of PCs into the shop!" Cassie said only half joking.

"Right ... I can't believe how close we came to that guy Creagor. *DAMN IT!*"

"That would have been a great break Mark." She consoled. "You're good at making your own luck... just keep the faith that another opportunity will come along." Cassandra said as supportively as she could before gathering her things and leaving his office.

# *"The Ticket"*

Max Dreyden and his friend Edward Bradford left the company of their wives and continued their conversation in the Dreyden study. The ladies continued catching up on what had happened to them since their college days together, about their children and how strange it was for fate to have brought them all together again.

"It looks as though Julia will back your decision no matter what you decide Max."

"I imagine she would Ed... I just don't know if I want to put us all through it. Why should I? We're comfortable and this can only bring stress and hardship to my family."

"That's why the American people will believe in you. You have absolutely nothing to gain from this."

"Other than the illusion of power... I can hear the press now."

"Power my ass... you already have more money than God for Christ sake... how would being the number two man add to that?"

"They'll twist it as they always do... it's definitely a prestigious position and they'll play up the egomania attack on me. I'm not exactly the most modest person you know." Dreyden argued.

"No, but you are one of the most sincere and honest people I've ever met and the people will see that in your character. Just look at how your stock rebounded after your speech. You just have to trust in their intelligence and be honest with them, which is what we'll be bringing back to government." Bradford argued convincingly.

"Alright, I'm not sold yet but I am willing to listen to some of your ideas seriously now. What do you have for me Ed? Why should I vote for your sorry ass fourteen months from now?"

"Take a look at these statistics Max." Bradford said as he handed him a list of military expenditures by nation for the past year.

- **Military Budgets Throughout the World**

  o USA $420 BILLION (43%)
  o China $62.5 BILLION (6%)
  o Russia $61.9 BILLION (6%)
  o England $51.1 BILLION (5%)
  o Japan $44.7 BILLION (4%)
  o France $41.6 BILLION (4%)
  o Germany $30.2 BILLION (3%)
  o India $22 BILLION (2%)
  o Saudi Arabia 21.3 BILLION (2%)
  o South Korea $20.7 BILLION (2%)
  o Italy $17.2 BILLION (2%)
  o Australia $13.2 BILLION (1%)
  o Brazil $13.1 BILLION (1%)
  o Canada $10.9 BILLION (1%)
  o Turkey $9.8 BILLION (1%)
  o Israel $9.7 BILLION (1%)
  o Netherlands $9.7 BILLION (1%)
  o Spain $8.8 BILION (1%)
  o Taiwan $8.3 BILION (1%)
  o Indonesia $7.6 BILION (1%)
  o Myanmar $6.9 BILLION (1%)
  o Ukraine $6 BILION (1%)
  o Singapore $5.6 BILION (1%)
  o Sweden $5.6 BILION (1%)
  o North Korea $5.5 BILION (1%)
  o Poland $5.2 BILION (1%)
  o Iran $4.9 BILION (1%)
  o Norway $4.7 BILION (<1%)
  o Greece $4.5 BILION (<1%)
  o Kuwait $4.3 BILION (<1%)
  o Colombia $3.9 BILION (<1%)
  o Switzerland $3.8 BILION (<1%)
  o Pakistan $3.7 BILLION (<1%)

- Viet Nam $3.5 BILION (<1%)
- Belgium $3.4 BILION (<1%)

"Now look for all of the *EVIL EMPIRE* players and add them up." Bradford said as he watched his friend diligently search for North Korea, Iran, Iraq, Syria, Libya, Sudan and Cuba.

"I only found North Korea and Iran for a total of $10.4 billion dollars." Dreyden answered. "That's chump change compared to what we're spending."

"That's right… right now Iraq is on our expense account, not theirs while hundreds of thousands of barrels of oil get lost every single day. Where do you think that oil is going Max?"

"I don't know… but I can venture a pretty good guess."

"All of the countries *combined* don't spend what we do on their military. We're consistently spending over $420 billion dollars every year and that's *before* you figure in the money appropriated from other sources, which kicks us up over $600 billion a year and rising fast." Bradford said pausing long enough for this information to sink in.

"I knew it was bad but this is unbelievable." Dreyden said still engrossed in the numbers.

"I'd like to read you a quote from one of our founding fathers; it was from James Madison in 1795." Bradford continued…

*"Of all the enemies to public liberty war is, perhaps, the most to be dreaded because it comprises and develops the germ of every other. War is the parent of armies; from these proceed debts and taxes … known instruments for bringing the many under the domination of the few. No nation could preserve its freedom in the midst of continual warfare."*

"Our military expenditures have been growing more extravagant under every adminstration since Kennedy was murdered. Just look at this chart which shows our expenditures since 1998."

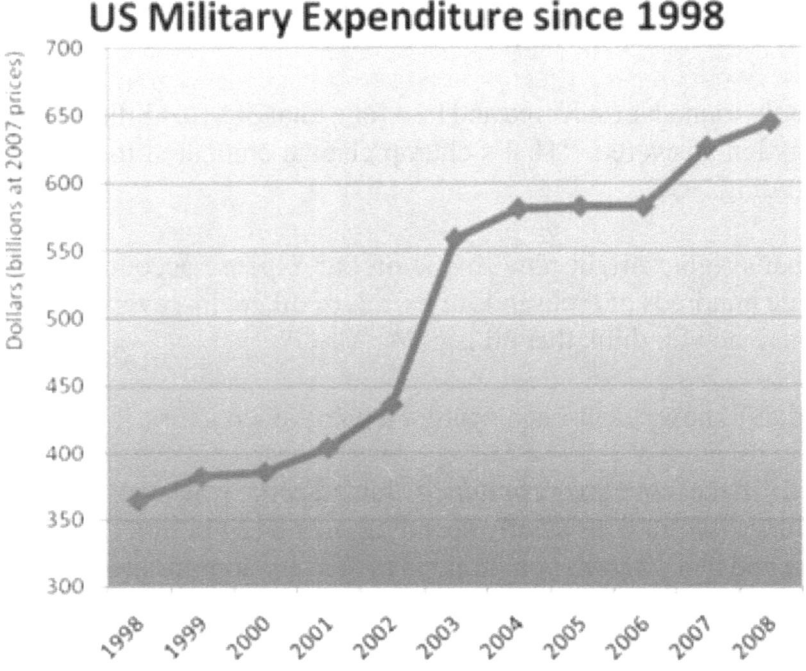

## US Military Expenditure since 1998

Sources: Friends Committee on National Legislation, Center for Arms Control and Non-Proliferation, 2006, 2007.

See important notes about data in accompanying table

"Furthermore, most of this money goes to supporting U.S. military activities throughout the world, including interventions *and not* on protecting American citizens. These are primarily foreign military operations that our tax dollars are funding and not on homeland security as our beloved government would have us believe." Bradford said obviously annoyed at the sham against the American people. "We're making enemies faster all the time with our pre-emptive war strategy... we can't let this thing go unchecked Max... we can't be so afraid that we'd be willing to sit and watch this happen right in front of our eyes."

"I'm still with you... tell me your whole plan." Dreyden said more seriously now than at any other point.

"Good..." Bradford continued. "Now take a look at this slide. It shows where America's tax money went in 2006."

"It's amazing how little of our budget goes to essential services." Dreyden saw immediately.

"Universal Health-Care is something we can achieve if we can rein in the military expenditure." Bradford added.

"How do you propose on doing that?" Dreyden asked dryly.

"I want to introduce a new five year tax-plan that will let Americans decide where their money will be going. It's going to be an anchor within our campaign platform. Similar to what you said you want to do revamping your company over time I want to do with our Country. For each of the next five years our citizenry will have a greater say on where their tax dollars will be spent. We'll need to develop a phased in approach to allow for existing commitments to be fulfilled but we sure as Hell don't need to remain the world's bully cop." Bradford said with conviction.

"Hmmm... I know the people will love the idea but what kind of a fight are we going to have getting it through?" Dreyden asked.

"That's why we need to get the people behind verifiable elections and the paper trail that is needed to make sure our election process is returned to legitimacy. Then we can get the people to vote in whatever changes make sense." Bradford said matter of factly.

"That's easier said than done my friend... we're going to make a lot of enemies with this approach Ed."

"And for every enemy we'll make a thousand friends. We just need to stay alive long enough to see it through. I figure you'd have some ideas on that... with all of your experience coming back from the dead and all." Bradford said as humorously as he could; considering how real the threat was going to be.

"Tell me about the phase-in you'd like to recommend Ed."

"Nothing is written in stone yet but I think 15-20% per year is a reasonable amount to let tax payers direct funds where they'd like. We need to make sure critical programs get what they need but we should be able to do that by controlling only 25 to 35% of the total tax dollars. Even at only a 15% a year redirection they would be able to control 75% of their tax dollars five years out."

"Oh, so now you want me for 8-years…" Dreyden said with a laugh.

"It'll take every one of those years to reverse the course we've been taken down Max… and you know it."

"What about my family's company Ed? I'm the chief executive."

"I'm sure you have someone who could carry on for you and take your company in the direction you've set. We need to look past our own personal interests now."

"No problem Ed… I was just busting your chops… I'm not the guy for the green energy campaign anyway. I was already considering a new president before you called that would be more appropriate."

"I know the vast majority of tax payers are going to love us closing down loopholes for the wealthy and allow them a major say in where their money is going. If we don't cut the military budget in half in our first term I'd be very surprised." Bradford said with conviction.

"Alright... keep talking Ed."

"I want to shut down off shore shell corporations so these giants of industry won't be able to sidestep their fair share of taxes. If they try to block us, which I know they will, then we'll impose duties on their imports that will be more painful to them than our taxes.

We're going to reverse the laws that provide tax shelters to polluters and encourage waste... like that stupid SUV rebate... what a slap in the face that was to all concerned citizens. We're going to hold companies responsible for their mistakes and reverse the laws that have been written that now hold them harmless.

I want to follow Dennis Kucinich's lead and develop a department of peace that will help us reverse the harm our militarists have inflicted upon our society since the end of World War II.

I want to bring us back into the world of international law where the laws are meaningful and have real teeth. That will mean stopping the use of depleted uranium weapons and cluster bombs immediately and supporting the laws so others will stop using them as well.

We're going to provide incentives to develop clean environmental alternatives to our energy needs and become a world leader again in reversing the damage that we've been at the heart of unleashing. You and I are going to become a mean-green-climate machine. Your company can re-tool to take advantage of that but I would strongly suggest that you phase out your shares first to avoid a conflict of interest.

We're going to close down the new nuclear arms race in its tracks and stop all development programs now working along those lines. We're going to restart the treaties aimed at downsizing nuclear arsenals and develop a long-term plan for the storage and safeguarding of nuclear waste with the ultimate goal of disposing of those hazardous materials when new methods can be developed and deployed safely.

We're going to assure an all voluntary military force and make sure that the money is appropriated to guarantee that our veterans get the medical help they deserve and not the pittance that is being given to them by insiders trying to reduce those funds to substandard levels. These vets will be protected by outsiders looking out for their interests and not by a privatized military complex looking for even greater profits. We will defend our wounded soldiers so they will never again have to worry about receiving proper care and the assistance they deserve.

We're going to make government agencies accountable again and take back our elections with corruption-proof, verifiable processes that will motivate *all* citizens to take part in deciding our future path.

No longer are we going to be known as the bully with the big stick but instead we are going to become a moral leader within the free world of nations. We are going to be a sincere and active participant in the United Nations and not its biggest debtor. Do you know that out of over $600 billion in debt owed to the UN's by its membership for peacekeeping missions we owe over $500 billion of that debt?"

"You're kidding there, right Ed?"

"No, I wish I were… I've got that fact sheet back in my office. I'll get you a copy.

Our people deserve universal health care and the savings we'll have by redirecting military expenditures will help get us to that goal relatively quickly. We'll need to stop price gauging at every point and effect laws that will put corporate criminals in jail and not let them off with fines that they'll simply pass along to their customers.
Speaking of military expenditures, explain to me why we need the next generation of fighter planes when our previous generation of aircraft is still the best in the world. We're going to close down that kind of development… the development of weapons as if we're still in the midst of the cold war. The real danger now is us… and we need to reverse that direction and take the targets off of our citizenry."

"Is that all? What'll we do in our second year?" Dreyden said with a smile as he refilled his friend's rocket fuel.

"So much is broken Max… I pray that Tony Kushner was correct and that this is *one of those moments in history* when we can make a difference and that you'll be right there beside me making it happen." Bradford said, obviously drained by the intensity of his emotions.

"You can count on Julia and me Ed. Just don't do or say anything until we've had a chance to consult with General Andersen and learn what we can do to protect ourselves. We'll also need to discuss who else will best fill out our leadership team for the nation."

Just then Julia knocked and let herself in. "Honey, I have a Mr. Tim McManus from **WIQR Radio** in Baltimore on the line for you... can you speak with him?"

"Take his number hon and tell him I'll call him back." Dreyden said.

"What do you suppose he wants Max?" Bradford asked.

"Probably an interview... it's not everyday that someone comes back from the dead." Dreyden said raising his glass.

"Hmmm.... Maybe you and I could give him an exclusive Max. That would be a nice little coming out party for us. You have to figure that DC can hear his show... probably even Philly and part of Jersey. "

"Not bad..." Dreyden said. "But I doubt it even reaches New York and I've got a better idea that would allow us to have our platform out in full public view in only a few days from our announcement."
"It can't all be coincidence Max." Bradford said as he finished off his Scotch.

*"One of those moments in history..."* He repeated to himself softly. "Looks like it's time to call my friend over at Channel 2 News..."

## *"General Andersen please…"*

"General Andersen please… this is Max Dreyden calling."

"Yes, Mr. Dreyden. One moment please and I'll see if he can take your call." Margaret Fischer said as she placed the call on hold and then accessed the intercom. "General Andersen, I have Mr. Dreyden on line four for you."

"Thank you Margaret… I'll be right with him."

"Yes sir, I'll tell him."

"I enjoyed your speech Max… I thought you did an excellent job." Andersen said as he picked up the call.

"Thank you Sir, I have you to thank for the wisdom you shared with me." Dreyden confessed.

"I think you would have come to that decision eventually Max… otherwise you wouldn't have been able to communicate your plan so sincerely. You did real well and I'm glad to see that your television broadcast cracked the damn a bit and helped a lot of companies follow your lead. You should be proud of yourself."

"Is this a secure line General?"

"You've been watching too many movies Max. Nothing is secure anymore… even if my end were clear you're end isn't. Do you really need this communication to be totally private?" Andersen asked, curious about his client's cloak and dagger paranoia.

"Perhaps not yet… but soon, yes, I think that would be prudent General."

"What can you share with me now?"

"I've been asked to run for political office sir... the Vice Presidency."

There was a long pause as Andersen mulled over all of the implications of that simple statement. Perhaps a little paranoia right about now wasn't totally out of order for both of them.

"That's very interesting." Andersen said as casually as he could. "Without naming anyone else... how do you feel about your running mate?"

"I'd say he's the best man I've ever known. He's the only person in the world that could have convinced me to run with him and I believe in his platform entirely." Dreyden said with all sincerity.

"And now you're calling me... I once told you that we don't do bodyguards Max."

"I know that General but I respect your opinion and if we do move forward and announce our candidacy then I'd like to have you in our corner pointing the way so we'll have some chance at surviving this campaign."

"I understand but before I say yes I'd like to read your platform. When can you get me a copy?"

"I'm sure we could e-mail it to you in a few days General."

"Forget e-mail. Have it printed out and sent to me via overnight messenger. You're going to have to keep thinking about who's listening, is that clear?"

"Yes sir, crystal clear. That's why you were my first call after I accepted."

"Alright, I'd suggest telling no one about this until you're ready to make a public announcement during your press conference."

"I agree. What's the next step after we get the platform position paper over to you?"

"If I believe in your position then we'll set another meeting with your partner."

"And if you don't agree with our position sir?"

"Then I'll wish you both good luck and point you to someone else who might be able to help."

"Thank you General, we'll get that together for you right away. Should I use the address on your card?"

"Yes, that's best and don't forget to mark the package confidential. And Max…?"

"Yes General?"

"Better get some fresh air while you still can."

"I understand sir. Thanks again."

Julia had been sitting with her husband as he made the call. She had made her husband promise to keep her in the loop on all of this since it was her family too and without her approval she wouldn't put them at risk. They both knew that his candidacy was her decision as much as it was his.

"How did it go dear?" She asked.

"About as expected. He wants to read our position paper before making any commitments but he sounds supportive."

"Do you even have a position paper yet?" She asked incredulously.

"I doubt it… I just wish I had a tape recorder running during our meeting. It was all right there… all it took was a little rocket fuel to get Ed to unwind and let it flow. He's such a good man Julia... I know the General will want to help us."

"Alright then... you better let him know what needs to be done. You two don't have that much time left until the next election. Better get to work buster!" She said playfully as she got up and gave her husband a gentle kiss allowing him to pull her into the luxurious leather chair with him.

# *"Guess Who May Be Running…"*

"Roger Thurmond please." The tall stranger asked the desk clerk at the Crowne Plaza Hotel.

"We can't give out room numbers sir but if you'll give me your name I'll see if Mr. Thurmond is available. Please wait by the courtesy phone." The young man asked politely pointing to the guest phone before dialing room 3014. "Good morning Mr. Thurmond, there's a gentleman here… his name is Marshall, that would like to speak with you. Would you like me to put him through?"

"Yes, please" Messer answered. "Thurmond here…"

"Are you alone or entertaining old friend?" Marshall Wallace said already suspecting the answer.

"What the Hell are you doing here Marsh?"

"Breakfast with you downstairs in say twenty minutes?" Wallace answered.

"Make it thirty and I'll see you then."

Messer looked over at the young woman who was still half asleep and laying with her bare back to him. He gently kissed her shoulder and neck until she was awake enough to remember where she was.

"You've got time for a quick shower but we're going to have to pass on breakfast this morning." He said gently and then watched her sit up still half asleep.

"Did you have a nice time last night Roger?"

"Very nice Candice… Thank you." He said sincerely.

"Me too…" She said and then walked into the bathroom wearing nothing but her sweet smile.

A few minutes later the shower began to pulsate and Messer found himself responding like he used to before his body stopped growing stronger. A moment later he was enjoying her company under a hot shower and the years melted away as he was transported back into his lover's arms once more. *Marsh would have to wait…* he allowed himself to think momentarily before getting lost in the gentle creature's embrace… wishing he could stay within the self-delusion of making love to his wife as their children waited patiently for them downstairs. He didn't notice her tears when he unknowingly called Candice by the wrong name as he climaxed deep within her. She hid her crying under the shower and let him take her passionately wishing someone felt that strongly about her. A short while later they were saying goodbye knowing they'd probably never see each other again. One with a new lease on life for a few more days; the other a few thousand dollars richer and surprised at herself for entertaining the thought that she would have paid that much just to experience his compassion once more.

"Good morning Marsh." A flushed and vital Messer said as he took a seat across from his friend.

"Excuse me for not waiting old man but I was starving." Wallace said as he watched his friend pour a cup of coffee.

"You see any old men at this table Marsh and I'm going to have to shoot them." Messer said in an uncharacteristically light way.

"I can see you had a very nice evening Mr. Thurmond."

"Yes sir, it was a very nice evening indeed and an even nicer morning. Now what the Hell brings you here to disturb my vacation?"

"The job up here is off. We have some more important business ahead of us in Chicago." Wallace said in an ominous tone.

"Hmmm… and I was just getting to like it up here." Messer continued as if he wasn't getting the point. "I'm starved, *waiter*…"

"Yes sir, may I help you?"

"Yes please… I'll have two of everything this old man just ordered… and make it quick… I'm losing weight over here!"

"I hope I can be that giddy when I reach your age Bob." Wallace said grinning at the untypical behavior of his fellow officer.

"The name is **Roger Thurmond** Marsh and it's very nice to make your acquaintance." Messer said reminding his partner of this weeks' alias.

"Well Mr. Thurmond… if you can come down off of that cloud of yours for a minute we really do need to catch up." Wallace said in a serious tone.

"Come on Marsh, it's me… lighten the Hell up or you're going to give us both a heart attack." Messer said as he stole one of Wallace's slices of toast and wolfed it down. "You can have one of mine when it comes out."

"Are you high?"

"*Absolutely!* If you were in my shoes you'd be high too. And no Marshall I don't do drugs… you should know better than to ask me that."

"Alright… then just enjoy yourself while you can… things are starting to get very interesting."

"Oh… and how's that?" Messer asked still looking for food he could steal.

"Guess who may be running for Vice-President?"

## *"Accelerating Particles"*

As the assassinations began to slow to a half dozen or so a week Joe Clark had been successful at planting nine special operations personnel within Blackwell's paramilitary organization. These eight men and one woman were now the highest paid bodyguards in that company's history. As General Aaron Andersen had predicted the shaken CEOs had no problem meeting the outrageous prices that were being asked. In fact a heated bidding war had quickly ensued over those limited resources and the inflated prices were merely starting points in the real negotiations. The obvious winner was Blackwell itself as they reaped millions of dollars in instantaneous profits from this relatively small contingent of assets.

The highest bidders were from the most powerful military contractors' who had the multi-billions dollars contracts already in-hand and couldn't change their company's direction even if they wanted to. It didn't matter… the costs would eventually be passed back to the military and through government taxation to the American people. As far as they were concerned if the rebels wanted a real fight then they would be more than happy to give it to them. The combined pressure put on the Military-Industrial-Congressional-Complex by the assassins, the stock market upheaval, the international media war and now these corporate behemoths was unrelenting. The reverberations that echoed through the corridors of power grew exponentially as these conditions collided as if thrown into a cyclotron.

Not unexpectedly the government responded by trying to focus its capability inward toward this invisible enemy. Subsequently more and more innocents were harassed, illegally wire-tapped and in many instances brutalized without due cause during legal demonstrations. The predictable result was a backlash of public opinion against the embedded war-mongers in industry, the media and most of all in the government who had taken them down the road of imperialism for far too long. This resulted in more volatile market swings, further devaluation in the dollar and the incessant voices of countries, many of whom were still close allies, clamoring for a reduction in the arms race that we had escalated almost single handedly since the end of the cold war.

Meanwhile, in a downtown Chicago office building on the thirty-sixth floor, Commander Dick Cooper's best surveillance squad was continuing to gather information patiently on their next target. The shell-company they had established allowed them to come and go virtually unnoticed and gave them a birds-eye view of 100 North Riverside Plaza, the new world headquarters for Boeing which was now the second largest military contractor with over $18 billion dollars in contracts in 2005 alone, only slightly behind Lockheed Martin's $19.4 billion and well ahead of Northrop Grumman with $13.5 billion. Besides the obvious reasons for targeting this giant they had also been fined tens of millions of dollars for knowingly selling flawed parts for the Apache helicopter and their supposedly precise but inconsistent joint direct attack munitions known as JDAM, which were intended to make dumb bombs into smart ones were repeatedly missing their targets and killing innocent civilians and US soldiers in both Iraq and Afghanistan. So great was the revolving door between Boeing and the government that even in the face of numerous and enormous scandals they continued to be awarded multi-billion dollar military contracts while being slapped lightly on the wrist with fines.

Simultaneously, in Bethesda Maryland, two of Tony Rico's squads were conducting surveillance on Lockheed Martin employees. In 2000 Lockheed spent nearly $10 million dollars lobbying members of Congress and the Clinton administration, more than twice what had been spent the year before. Among the company's lobbyists was the former Chairman of the Republican National Committee. Lockheed also used its significant influence to press forward the illegal war in Iraq. As far back as 1976 they were known to have paid millions of dollars to the Japanese government and to known gangsters to help sell their planes into that market. Besides their well-know activities creating fighter and surveillance aircraft and missiles they've also been actively engaged in designing the next generation of nuclear weapons. It's been estimated that every US citizen paid $105 in taxes in 2002 to fulfill our governments' contracts with Lockheed. Not bad for a company that only paid an effective tax rate of 7.7% in the same year and that has been known to have made millions from insider trading, falsifying accounts and bribery. Obviously their substantial political contributions on both sides of the isle paid off handsomely for this largest of all arms exporters. Meanwhile orders continue to flow in from the Air Force for the PAC-3 Patriot missile at only $91 million dollars apiece.

# *"Circling The Wagons"*

"Hello General, I'd like to introduce your to Senator Edward Bradford." Maxwell Dreyden said as the General entered his study with another man. "Ed, this is General Aaron Andersen and your guest is?"

"This is Joe Clark, our top security expert." The General said as introductions and handshakes were exchanged all around.

"We received your package Senator and quite frankly sir I was very impressed with your vision." The General said as he took the seat he was offered.

"Thank you General, Max speaks very highly of you and it looks as though we're going to need all of the help you can offer." Bradford said as he studied the two men on the other side of the large coffee table.

"There's absolutely no doubt that you two are going to need to take significant precautions until the Secret Service details are assigned." The General replied.

"And when does that happen?" Dreyden asked.

"Not until one-hundred and twenty days before the election and that's presuming you two will be the Democratic Party's candidates by then and not running as independents." Andersen answered. "Then there will be a period of time when we will need to co-exist with their protection and hopefully be able to stand-down to a large extent after you've been elected, except for specific duties that will be required."

"What type of *specific duties* are you referring to General?" Bradford asked.

"We can provide you with an overview security layer that could have prevented the Dealey Plaza incident in 1963. We'll verify that every security issue is properly addressed. That's why Mr. Clark is here."

"I'm not quite sure I understand General." Dreyden said.

"Assuming you two win the election President Bradford will have the authority to arrange security however he sees fit. Having your lives in your own hands and partially removed from those of the embedded militarists is the best way to assure that no one monkeys around with basic security measures." Andersen said. "You two are going to become extremely high-profile targets the moment your campaign platform is announced. Mr. Clark and I are prepared to discuss some of those considerations with you today. I strongly recommend that you incorporate these strategies into your daily lives or forget the campaign altogether because neither one of you will ever get through it alive. There's just too much to be lost by those who would oppose you"

"Go ahead General… tell us what we need to do to protect our families and our candidacy." Bradford requested.

"Joe, why don't you pick it up from here." Andersen asked.

"Yes Sir. First off you have to recognize that this is not going to be a normal campaign and therefore forget running it as such." Clark began.

"I can't forget what I don't know Mr. Clark." Dreyden said in good humor.

"That's to your advantage sir. It's Senator Bradford that is going to have to let go of everything familiar as we travel down a new path."

"I don't know about everything Mr. Clark but I'm definitely willing to listen and take prudent precautions."

"No sir. That isn't going to be enough. You are going to have to take our directions when we provide them to you. If you don't then we won't be able to protect you and that means we may as well not even begin." Clark countered.

"Just listen to what he has to say Ed. They're only looking out for our best interests." Dreyden injected.

"I know Mr. Dreyden is well aware of the assassins' capabilities and that was just a fringe group and not the entire Military-Industrial-Congressional Complex that you two are about to take on. Multiply what you've witnessed by ten or even a hundred fold and then realize that protecting you is going to be one of the most difficult missions imaginable. There can be no room for error... no countermanding our instructions and preventive measures. It only takes one moment of exposure to end everything you two are trying to accomplish. Am I making myself clear?" Clark said as he looked deep into Senator Bradford's eyes.

"Yes Mr. Clark, perfectly." The Senator answered without hesitation. "Alright then, give us some of the details of what we should expect."

"How were you planning on making your announcement on your candidacy?" Clark asked them both.

"I was going to call a friend here in Atlanta and get some free TV coverage... a press conference... something of that sort." Dreyden said.

"And what security measures were you going to take leaving the television station?" Clark asked.

"Well, we hadn't gotten that far yet. But we do have bodyguards." Dreyden said already realizing how stupid that sounded considering recent events.

"Gentlemen, every one of your movements from the announcement onward will have to be intelligently planned to optimize all available security precautions. For the next sixteen months neither of you or any of your immediate family will be able to move safely without taking the necessary precautions. Assume from this point on that you will be circling the wagons and defending your loved ones and you will have to accept the proper mindset. Think any other way and you

350

two will remain approachable targets." Clark said pausing just long enough for his words to sink in. "The miracle about TV is that it can be taped and played later without missing a beat. You could conduct your entire interview from within the safety of your own home and it can be aired with the same affect as if it were live and in public."

"We can't do that forever Mr. Clark… we have to press the flesh to some degree." Bradford said still clinging on to the tried and true methods of campaigning.

"Sir, with all due respect, you're not hearing me." Clark said as delicately as he could. "This campaign has to be conducted from within a fortress and you are going to have to tell the people why. Give them credit, they'll understand. You can do all of the politicking you need from in front of a TV camera, or a radio station microphone without having to meet hundreds of thousands of people for a quick handshake or a 20-second sound bite. Your issues and your platform will stand on their own and the people will understand the necessary precautions that need to be taken because they're not stupid. When they hear you and can judge the wisdom of your words they will act appropriately on Election Day. You owe it to them to get there alive."

"So you're suggesting that we wage our campaign entirely through the media?" Bradford asked trying to calculate the remote odds that it would be enough.

"Yes Sir, that's exactly what the General and I are saying. The truth stands on its' own and doesn't require an endless plane ticket and a sore right hand to be heard, understood and most importantly, felt by the American people. The very uniqueness of your campaign will have the media debating the wisdom or stupidity of it. Meanwhile, the progressive news outlets will get all of your talking points out to the public *loud and clear*. The internet can help… create a great website and post as many answers to their questions as possible. Let the technology do its' job and let the past go… *become your own campaign reformers!* And remind the people about the harm being done to our country with our present methods of campaign funding." Clark said and then sat back in his chair.

"No, he's not a political analyst Gentleman." Andersen injected.

"He was just one of the best natural leaders and strategists that I've ever worked with. I'd trust his judgment with my life… and I recommend that you Gentlemen do the same."

"We haven't talked about money yet General. Do you have a ballpark of what we should expect for your services?" Dreyden asked.

"Remember that slush fund you were going to put aside to wage your own little war with?" Andersen asked pausing for a moment to allow Dreyden to remember the number. "That should be more than enough to cover it Max."

"Where do we go from here?" Bradford asked still whirling from the seeming insanity of conducting a campaign this way.

"One days wage for me and from here on I'll leave you in Mr. Clark's very capable hands. He'll put teams together for the both of you and maintain overall security over your current assets." General Andersen stated. "Is that going to be a problem with either of you?"

"Not with me General." Dreyden said with barely a moment's hesitation. "I thought you didn't do bodyguards General." Dreyden said as a small barb.

"This isn't about bodyguards Max. It's about the integrity and destiny of our nation and that's dead center in my mission statement. Citizen Aaron Andersen replied.

"I don't have any bodyguards at the moment General, so I guess I'm okay with it too." Bradford said.

"Alright, then the next step is to plan your coming out party. Tell me about this friend of yours in Atlanta." Andersen said as he glanced over at Clark with a nod of approbation.

# *"What's up Doc?"*

"Jason Morgan please."

"May I tell him who's calling sir?"

"Tell him it's the doctor…"

"I'll see if he's available… please hold a moment."

"Morgan here... who am I speaking with please?"

"Memory isn't what it used to be… must be tough getting old."

"Hi Max… I haven't thought of that nickname of yours for a couple of decades."

"You gave it to me bud… better start pumping some Ginkoba."

"So what's up… we've got another busy news day. Did you hear about the Lockheed Martin executive?"

"No, was there another assassination attempt?"

"It wasn't just an attempt Max… they took out an ex-Congressman who used to sit on a military appropriations committee before he went into the private sector."

"Jesus Christ! Which one? They must have dozens of ex-government lobbyists working for them." Dreyden guessed.

"You'll have to catch it on the six-o'clock news doc."

"Drop-dead you bastard…"

"It was Pete McGuire from Colorado."

"You're kidding... I thought he was still in Congress and doing a pretty good job."

"He was, until he got his secretary pregnant and his wife filed for a divorce. His constituents took it real hard since he was always campaigning and showing them how important his family was. I'm surprised you didn't hear about it."

"No I didn't, but then again I don't read the scandal rags... there'd never be enough time to read anything else if I did. How did he get it?"

"It looks as if he was poisoned in his favorite restaurant in Denver while having dinner with a few of his aides. He just keeled over into his prime rib. They said it looked like a heart attack but the guy was in excellent health. We'll have to wait until the autopsy to be sure... They think the meat *was tainted* and everyone else who had it is fine."

"Did they catch anyone?"

"No, as far as everyone could tell nothing happened except for a pretty young woman who stopped by to shake his hand but that happens all the time with these guys. His aides didn't recognize the woman but they said she was *very friendly* if you catch my drift."

"My God... they sure are picking their shots aren't they?"

"They're definitely not fucking around... that's for God damn sure. So what's up with you Max... why the call?" Morgan asked.

"How did the ratings go after my first coming out party?"

"Through the roof... along with more mail and e-mail then we could handle ... and what do you mean by *first?*"

"Are you sitting down Jason?"

# *"It's Almost Showtime"*

"Good evening I'm Linda Thompson and welcome to WSB-TV *Action 2 News in Atlanta*." The young anchor woman began. "As promised over the last few days we are bringing you an exclusive report that you won't want to miss... so get your VHS players or DVD burners ready to record and we'll be back in a moment after a short commercial break." The last irregular line added by Dreyden's close friend Jason Morgan.

Having taken full advantage of the hype over the past seventy-two hours the "short" four minute break that followed had been packed with six very expensive commercials; four thirty-second spots separated by two one-minute ads from some of the stations top advertisers... not a bad week's income for the advertising department.

"Good evening ladies and gentlemen..." A handsome and familiar face addressed his TV audience from a strange venue. "This is Tom Hewlett from WSB-TV *Action 2 News in Atlanta* where we are recording this news conference from the *Great Room* of the Maxwell Dreyden Estate."

The camera panned the huge room that was set up like a grander version of a Presidential news conference with two beautiful black onyx-like podiums sitting atop a small stage facing the forty or so reporters that were there from various television and radio stations as well as local and national newspapers that had accepted their invitations. Behind the two pedestals where the speakers would be addressing their audience was a flat projection screen where images could be summoned to aide in the understanding of their presentation.

The room itself was much grander than the front third being used for the days' event. Rare art from some of the world's most renowned painters in history adorned the room and gave it a museum like appearance. The marble floors were carpeted underneath the five rows of eight comfortable chairs that were well above normal for such an event. Julia Dreyden had suggested that they allow her to decorate the press area with beautiful plants from her own arboretum and the area was significantly enhanced by their presence.

As the guests began to arrive at 11:15 am they were brought through the grand foyer which had been transformed into a security check-point. Press-credentials were identified and checked off the list of pre-approved visitors before they were asked to step through a metal detector, which all but a few did without uttering a word of disapproval. No cameras, microphones or other electronic equipment of any kind was allowed in the conference area and even though they had been forewarned most of them brought it anyway and were asked to turn around and return it to their vehicles. Not even simple recording equipment was allowed into the meeting, which was scheduled to begin promptly at 1:00pm giving them all plenty of time to get their stories onto the evening news.

Once the guests had passed through the entranceway and security check-point they were pleasantly greeted by Jason Roberts who showed them the spread of fresh coffee, teas, juices and assorted pastries and finger-sandwiches that were conveniently laid out in the remaining four fifths of the grand foyer. The few rumblings that were heard passing through security were soon forgotten as a more festive atmosphere took over and the delicacies were eagerly consumed.

At 12:30 pm the guests were shown into the grand hall and allowed to take their seats. Most scurried to the front of the room as quickly as they arrived trying to get the best seat possible while the more astute among them took a single glance at the room and realized that their wasn't a bad seat in the house and took those precious minutes to enjoy the incredible oil paintings by Cézanne, Monet, Rembrandt, Picasso, van Gogh and Rubens, which were magnificently lighted in the darker two thirds of the ballroom from where they had entered.

Up front, the guests took their seats and chatted anxiously amongst themselves with quite a few old friends meeting again for the first time in years. The security entrance was closed at 12:55 sharp and the few stragglers that remained outside were forced to wait but were told that they would receive a complete audio visual DVD of the meeting when it was over if they cared to stay. Begrudgingly they waited and cursed the delay that had cost them this unique opportunity to take part in… in what… they were left to wonder.

At 12:55 pm the two elegant chandeliers that lit the front third of the hall were dimmed inviting the few unseated guests to take their seats. The room grew quiet except for the obnoxious gentleman who had succeeded in capturing one of the third row seats as if it were a child's game.

At exactly 1:00 pm Joe Clark took the stage positioned directly between the two podiums and slightly in front of them. He motioned to the lone camerawoman to begin and the stage lighting rose and the video record began.

"Ladies and gentlemen, thank you for joining us today. Before we begin I would like to explain a few things to you all so these questions will not interfere with today's proceedings. First the most important question anyone will ask today... and that's if you haven't already figured this out yourselves is: *Where are the bathrooms?* Clark said with a smile as the audience chuckled. They are located to the rear of the hall with the ladies room being designated as the one on your left and the gentlemen's room the one on the right.

I would ask that you wait for a few more moments before availing yourselves of those amenities so that I may answer a few of the questions that must be on your minds. Then we will have a fifteen minute break before the speakers address you this afternoon.

The question I know you're all asking is *why no cameras?* Well that's pretty simple. First off, Miss Jensen back there behind the video camera is an award winning videographer and she is recording *all of this* right now. Before you leave today you will have your own *unedited* video record of our press conference on a DVD that you can use in your news broadcasts however you see fit. We have a stack of eight copiers that will allow us to reproduce the master copy very quickly so you will have plenty of time to get this information back to your respective news outlets. Why did we do this? For three reasons, first of all it's a necessary security precaution that we will be enacting from this point forward in all our conferences; second, because it's much more efficient and cost effective for all of your companies versus having to drag an entire film crew along with their equipment just to meet with us, and third; because what you are going to receive here is going to be live, unedited and straight from the heart. If anyone of you tries to manipulate the facts then everyone else will know it.

Okay, that about wraps up my MC duties. It's now 1:15 pm and I invite you to uses our facilities and then be seated prior to 1:30 when our speakers will address you. They will both be presenting material and you may ask your questions at the conclusion of the presentation. No questions will be entertained before then since they will most likely be answered in the course of their talk. Okay… see you all in fifteen minutes." Clark concluded before stepping down from the stage and being bombarded with questions that he was not in a position to answer.

"If you need something to make you comfortable I will be happy to help…" He said loudly so everyone could hear over the commotion. "But if you're looking for a preview then you're wasting your time." He said and then checked with Jason Roberts who was overseeing the two other undercover security personnel he had placed within the hall.

All of the chandeliers were now fully lit while some of the guests nervously hurried off to the bathrooms. Others took this unexpected break to look at the paintings they had missed or ignored on the way in… while some caught up with old friends. Finally there were those diligent few who sat patiently in their chairs wondering what questions to ask when they didn't even know what the subject matter was… most of them guessing incorrectly that it had to do with Dreyden's company.

As before, five minutes before they were to continue the lights were dimmed encouraging the guests to take their seats. All but a few were in their chairs at 1:29 and the other two would have to endure the ribbing of their fellow journalists at a later date. What the audience wasn't aware of was the two video cameras that were tucked neatly among the furnishings on the stage that captured both halves of the audience perfectly… after all this was a public press conference and the inclusion of that portion of the video would come as a delight to some journalists and as an embarrassment to others.

## *"Showtime"*

"Ladies and gentlemen it is my sincere pleasure to present our host Maxwell Dreyden and his guest Senior Senator from Massachusetts Edward Bradford." Joe Clark announced to a surprised audience.

The audience instinctively began to clap when Jason Morgan and other friends began to applaud as if spontaneously as the two smiling men entered the stage from opposite sides and met in the middle first shaking hands and then taking their positions behind the podiums. The applause quickened as the anticipation of something unexpected continued to fill the air. Both men looked out over their audience and smiled and nodded to the many familiar faces staring up at them. The rear chandelier lights were slowly lowered as Max Dreyden put up his hand trying to quiet the boisterous audience. Then the chandelier lights directly in front of the stage were dimmed to half as the lights over the stage were brought up to full intensity. This succeeded in quieting the majority of the guests except for a few that were still too excited to contain themselves until Max Dreyden began to speak.

"Good afternoon..." Dreyden said with a large smile still on his face... "And welcome to *Julienne...* my wife's home." He said with a subdued laugh. "She has graciously allowed me to borrow it so I could introduce you to Senator Edward Bradford... *the next President of the United States!"* He said with genuine sincerity.

The crowd reacted spontaneously with a mixture of excitement and astonishment. Of all the things they had been imagining this had not been one of them and they were all caught off guard and grew silent the moment Senator Bradford began to speak.

"Good afternoon ladies and gentlemen of the press and to those of you viewing this conference or reading about it in our great Nation's papers. I am honored to have this opportunity to speak to my fellow citizens of the dreams that have inspired me to seek the highest office in the land... indeed, perhaps one of the highest offices in any land... at any time.

The people in the audience today represent one of the best aspects of our society… they are among the centerpieces of our Democracy that make it work properly and without them and without their honest opinions and critical minds we could not hope or dream of a better future for our children or for our planet.

Every American watching, whether it be through the eyes of a video camera, the ears of a radio broadcast or the words of a journalist printed in your local newspaper… I invoke you to educate yourselves on the issues of our times and to actively engage in the ongoing effort to guide our country onto a more worthwhile path… a path that our Founding Fathers' would recognize as a continuation of their original vision… *a vision where truth and justice prevails….* Not just some of the time but *all of the time*… a world were equality and freedom is meant for all of mankind and not just for the privileged few who were born to great wealth.

In case you haven't realized it by now I have asked Maxwell Dreyden to be my running mate. I was heartbroken over the news of his loss after that treacherous assassination attempt and overcome with tears of joy when we all discovered that he had somehow miraculously survived the attack. You see we've been good friends all the way back to our days at Harvard… where his wife Julia and my wife Mary were close friends before we even met… a time when our ladies were our sweethearts… that's when Max and I became lifelong friends.

Still, even with our close friendship I had not even considered Maxwell Dreyden as a running mate until he displayed the courage it took to stand up and say that he was going to make sure that his company changed for the benefit of society. I don't think many of you could fully appreciate the courage it took to be first to cower, as some of his antagonists would phrase it… to stand-up and recognize that his family's company had become a pariah… not through some mal intent on his Great-Great Grandfather's part but through science and the knowledge that nicotine, second hand smoke and chemicals used in the filters and in the manufacturing process have been contributing to heart disease and to strokes and to one of mankind's most dreaded enemies… cancer. I lost my father as a young child to cancer and I know from personal experience how hard it is to grow up without a dad. I'm sure many of you do too and that you may even hate Maxwell Dreyden for not making his decision earlier.

All I can say to those of you who would have trouble letting go of your hatred is that his inheritance was not a crime. His father's false testimony to congress was not *his* crime. His failure to reverse the course of nearly two-hundred and fifty years of tradition when he took over the company as a young man … was not a crime. You see, it is still not a crime to sell tobacco… the real crime is that this incredibly hazardous product was never pulled from the shelves the moment its' hazard were well known. How would we all feel if we weren't alerted to some toxic food that accidentally slipped into our grocery stores? What if just one or two hundred of us died from that relatively small oversight in public knowledge? Think of the outrage! Yet the tobacco company through its many lobbyists, significant campaign contributions and annual spending of over *SIX-BILLION DOLLARS* for public relations firms to put a better spin on their propaganda is allowed to contribute to the deaths of over *five-million people every year!* That's nearly an entire holocaust <u>every single year</u>!

By now half of the smokers out there are turning off their TVs and telling themselves they'll never vote for us because we'll take their cigarettes away. That's not the case… we understand the addictive nature of these products and will encourage the reduction of the use of tobacco by funding programs that will help... we will do everything in our power to help our citizens kick the habit once and for all. End of story… except for the fact that we plan to hold those companies liable for all injuries attributed to their products and not allow them to hide behind the veil of injurious-laws that were bought and paid for by your tax dollars through influence peddling in our halls of government.

When we speak to you about our *truth and justice* platform *we mean it!* If your company lies to the American people about the validity of your product we're not going to fine you and let you pass that cost back to us through taxes… *NO!* We're going to hold you liable and perhaps even throw you in jail, *where you belong* and not for ninety days with a little slap on the wrist. We plan on enacting laws that are

363

tough on white collar criminals, especially those who gouge us at the oil pumps or sell defective products to our military. It's going to become very expensive to lie to us, *we the people*, or cheat us in any way. We're going to revisit mandatory sentencing laws which tear our society's families apart for relatively minor crimes... especially when compared to what the wealthy have been getting away with throughout history.

Those are just some of things we plan to do. At the end of today's press conference we are going to hand out our comprehensive mission statement that will identify how we are going to achieve universal health care for *all of our citizens*.

We are going to identify how we will send every competent student through college and how all of our government backed college loans will be repaid within ten years of graduation. The days are over when a doctor can get a million dollar education and not pay back at least the bare minimum, which we have established within our guidelines. I want all of you parents to think about this for just a moment... *YOUR KIDS CAN GO TO COLLEGE IF THEY WANT TO!* All you have to do is make sure they earn it by obtaining good grades. *Our teachers are going to have a career path worth going after...* and not be asked to earn less than their importance should dictate to any intelligent society. How many minds has our country squandered through prejudice, poverty and war? How many Einstein's and Lincoln's and Martin Luther King's have been forced to live unfulfilled lives because we never recognized their potential?

And speaking of war... how much longer do we have to go on envisioning some unseen boogey-man so our war profiteers can continue to rape and pillage society's limited resources? How long will it take until we stop them from stealing our children's futures?

We're not going to be able to stop all war profiteering but we sure as Hell are going to close down the revolving doors between the military, Government and lobbyists that have been taking away our power as individuals since the end of World War II. Listen to General Dwight David Eisenhower's farewell speech as President of this great

Nation. He warned us then… and many of us saw or even experienced the results of an unchecked *Military-Industrial-Complex* with the escalation of the Viet Nam war in the sixties and seventies.

There's a reason that the defense budget continues to grow to nearly an unfathomable figure every year… and that reason is greed. Greed is more important than our children's lives… greed is more important than the future of our planet… greed is more important than the survival of our species. Well Max Dreyden and I beg to differ.

Maxwell Dreyden and I are putting our lives on the line to combat the power base that drives this nation ever farther from her vision and ever closer to a war where our weapons stagger the imagination with cruelty, effectiveness and absolute finality. Do we really need another generation of nuclear weapons? Is it really in our best interest to renege on every hard earned treaty so that we can create increasingly powerefull weapons? Does this most recent escalation of power serve to protect our tiny planet?

*Not in our vision of America!*

In *our America* we will *dismantle the war machine* that drives us into illegal conflicts and steals away our children as if they were raised just to become cannon fodder for the wealthy.

*Tell me why* we need to spend more money on our war machine than almost every other country *combined?*

*Tell me why* our department of defense's war budget continues to grow long after the cold war has ended?

*Tell me why* a half **TRILLION**, *YES! AS IN 500 BILLION DOLLARS,* is needed each and every single year to *assure our safety*… and tell me how much more is really being spent under the guise of other operations through invisible funding sources? It's time that the *Military-Industrial-Congressional-Complex* is shown for exactly what it is… and that is a *beast of war* that is only concerned with feeding it's young and not in the preservation of the Constitution of the United States or the overall well-being of our citizens, whose rights are stolen away piece by piece under the guise of *National Security!*

President Eisenhower wrote:

*"Controlled, universal disarmament is the imperative of our time. The demand for it by the hundreds of millions whose chief concern is the long future of themselves and their children will, I hope, become so universal and so insistent that no man, no government anywhere, can withstand it."*

What the world has been watching within the borders of America in recent months is not terrorism… although that's what the embedded power base would like you to believe.

How many of you go to bed thinking that a sniper is going to take your life from a mile and a half away? How many of you equate yourselves with the targets these assassins have selected? They told us who they were after and even though I was a Senator until 12:00 pm today, I slept like an innocent child because I knew that my policies and my votes spoke my true beliefs and not those imposed upon me by this tyrant or that uninvited influence. These same beliefs, some of which I have begun articulating this afternoon, will be the reason that we are now targets and this is why you all experienced the security measures we had in place for today's conference. We are not going to become martyrs if we can prevent it. We are running for public office because we understand that the system is broken almost to a point of no return. The revolution we are witnessing should not be a surprise to students of history. The vast majority of you have nothing to fear except the continuation of the status quo in government and the slow but constant erosion of your Constitutional rights.

I wish I knew the person who wrote: *"We are not put into this world to see through one another… but to see one another through."* I would like to thank that person for her sentiments and learn from her wisdom.

Who among you would not feed a needy child who appeared at your doorstep, no matter if he is white, black or purple? Who among you would send your child off to war in order to steal another nation's oil? Who among you prefers ignorance over wisdom… or blind patriotism over intelligent descent?

This room is filled with journalists but how many of you have taken the path of one of the greatest journalist who ever lived… many of you know I'm referring to Edward R. Morrow, who said:

*"We must not confuse dissent with disloyalty.*
*We will not be driven by fear into an age of unreason*
*if we remember that we are not descended from fearful men,*
*not from men who feared to write, to speak,*
*to associate and to defend causes which were,*
*for the moment, unpopular."*

How many times have our leaders tried to tell us that to speak out against them is either unpatriotic or even paramount to treason? What about our right to say what's on our minds? It's called *free speech* and yet our leaders act as if we can't use it when it comes to opposing them.

Voltaire wrote; *I may not agree with what you have to say but I shall defend to the death your right to say it!* Powerful words… coming from a man of conviction… needless to say he wasn't very poplar with the French government of his time. He also wrote: *Those who can be made to believe absurdities can be made to commit atrocities.* We can not follow political leaders blindly without the common sense use of our own convictions as a rudder. *Every single person has the potential to contribute to the well-being of all of mankind!* Who gave anyone the right to squelch that potential?

Who among you believes that your child is more valuable than your neighbors? Well me for one…" Bradford said with a chuckle trying to lighten up a bit as he took a sip of water. "No, no, not really… as much as I love and cherish my children I know they are no more or less important than those children we see starving to death because our worlds $27 trillion dollar economy can't afford to spend a mere $40 billion dollars to end world hunger every year. I don't know… maybe I'm overstepping my bounds here… maybe the world can't make it on twenty-six trillion, nine-hundred and sixty billion dollars… but I think you'll all agree that *we can* and that it would be a better world if we did.

I have only scratched the surface of our ***truth and justice platform*** and we intend to answer as many questions as possible in this meeting and in the coming weeks and months ahead. If it seems that our campaign is a little out of the ordinary then please understand that our motives are pure and simple… that against all odds we intend to fulfill our dreams and move America onto a path that we can all be proud of, a place where our neighbors welcome us warmly and not with distrust or fear, a place where humanity *in its' entirety* has a chance of over-coming greed and our thirst for power that ultimately causes us to disregard everything that we as individuals hold sacred…

In order to succeed we must first survive… and that doesn't mean just Max Dreyden and I… but all of us on this tiny blue planet that has been graced with the spark of life and set afloat amidst a sea of emptiness… like a child in the womb. What kind of parents will we be? What will we do with this gift that we've been given? What will we leave our children… the legacy of an endless war?

Einstein has already told us how World War IV is going to be fought… knowing that we are marching ever onward to a nuclear encounter he knew that mankind would ultimately be reduced to sticks and stones. I for one trust that man's opinion and will do everything in my limited power to prevent an epitaph that might read; *We had a nice run but in the end, as we were trapped inside cages of our own making, we were too greedy and too stupid to open our monkey-like hands and let go of the bombs. "* Appearing on the flat display screen behind the speakers comes a cartoon of a real-life experiment with the monkey's hand trapped inside a cage refusing to let go of a banana to free itself… it slowly morphs into a man's head atop the monkeys' body and the furry hand is now holding a nuclear bomb.

"Is this the best Uncle Sam can do? Is that to be our epitaph or are we capable of writing a better one? Together we should be rejoicing in our humanity and not fumbling backward into a more primitive state of being. The true dream of humanity isn't war… our dream begins with love and compassion for each other and for our world and all of its inhabitants. We will need your help to get there but I promise that everything we do will be for the good of our people and for the well-being of our planet. Thank you for your time and patience today, please hold your questions until Mr. Dreyden has an opportunity to speak to you. Thank you." The crowd came to its feet applauding…

It was obvious that this vital man had put his entire heart and soul into his address… it appeared as if he hadn't referred to his notes at all but had spoken instead straight from the heart. That would explain the lack of slides that had remained unused… except for one. Senator Bradford was now Candidate for President Edward Charles Bradford. He took a long drink of water and glanced over at his friend who looked fresh by comparison… he didn't notice the smile and nod from his running mate which was intended to convey that he was duly impressed by the speech.

For close to three minutes most of the crowd refused to sit down and stop applauding. They all knew what they heard was the undeniable truth and were hopeful that this leader just might be able to pull off the impossible. Those who sat back down quickly inadvertently identified themselves as either hawks or right wing neo-conservatives who were already thinking how they could spin this speech to their advantage, they could definitely use that monkey jibe as a start. The rest were happy to rejoice in the refreshing substance they had just absorbed… not so much through the ears as through the skin and the heart as a plant absorbs sunlight.

"Can I come back another time?" Quipped Maxwell Dreyden… "How do you follow that?" He answered his own question…"*YOU DON'T!* What would you all say if we just opened up the floor for questions?" And with that simple statement Dreyden had dodged the need to match the unmatchable.

369

"Oh, one thing though… in order to give my old friend a little break I would like the first two or three questions to be directed to me please. Thank you…. Barbara, go ahead you can be first." He said to one of the older journalists in the room.

"Thank you Mr. Dreyden…" she began. "How do you expect to succeed without any prior political experience?"

"Well, let's see here… If I understand politics, as described by my good friend over there, I won't know how to mix with lobbyists and military contractors or how to handle the issue of war very effectively. Well, I have been running a multi-billion dollar company for over a decade and that must account for something. I also know what it means to be honest and just and I KNOW that accounts for more than many of our political leaders are willing to admit. I know the man standing next to me as if he were my brother… and I know his heart is made out of gold… that is why I accepted his invitation to run and I will do everything I can to help us win. Yes sir, the gentleman in the fourth row with the white handkerchief in your pocket."

"Thank you Mr. Dreyden… I'm Peter Wolfe with the Times. How is it that you came out of that horrible attack unscathed?"

"This will be the only question that we will answer today concerning the assassination attempt on my life. I *want to answer it* because a good man gave his life protecting me and this is my chance to let the world know about Mr. Louis Farentino. He was a hired bodyguard with a wife and children and after the assassination of John Richard's, a short distance north of us he strongly recommended that I alternate my routines so I wouldn't be such an easy target. Now this may have seemed like a simple suggestion but his instincts were strong enough to override my… well my stubbornness and he convinced me to go into work later that morning and have breakfast with my wife instead. His sacrifice was something that my family and I will be eternally grateful for and I intend to use this second chance that I've been given to do as much good in the world as is humanly possible and every one of those deeds from this point onward will be Louis Farentino's contribution to the world and not mine."

"Spoken like a true politician…" Jason Morgan called out from the last row. "…but what about the conflict of interest with your current company and your bid for public office?"

"Thank you for that question Jason, it's one of the points I wanted to cover today. After Senator Bradford and I met and he convinced me that I would be an asset and not a hindrance to him we recognized the potential conflict of interest with my current holdings. What most people are still not aware of is that my company took a major beating when it looked like the assassins were successful. The FBI convinced me to stay out of sight and play dead long enough to help them find out who was behind the attack and I followed their recommendation to do so… much to the dismay of our stockholders who lost fortunes and my family who had to put up with me twenty-four hours a day." Dreyden said with a muffled laugh.

"Fortunately they understood the economic impact that this would have on my company and granted me permission to buy back as much of our stock as I could as it was falling through the floor. This was done with the prior approval of the SEC under the condition that I redistribute the earnings, if any, to those who were injured during the stock market's assault on our shares. That exercise was completed last Saturday and a public report is being prepared by KPMG to provide the details to the public."

"How much company stock do you still own?" A male voice shouted a bit too loudly from the first row.

"Nothing… every share of stock was either redistributed or sold when it reached 90 to 110% of its value just prior to the assassination attempt. To the degree possible the SEC allowed me to break even and the gains we did make were all transferred to our stockholders in a fair and equitable manner to reduce their losses. None of our stock-holders lost more than the same percentage of their invested value than my family did." Pointing to the second row Dreyden said; "Yes, the woman in the green dress."

"Thank you sir... I'm Pamela Hirsh from CNN. How will you be able to lead your company down a new path when you're going to be campaigning?"

"Well, as we said a few times this afternoon this is not going to be a normal campaign. The reason this isn't being conducted live is because of security precautions…"

"Does that mean you will still be actively engaged as CEO during the campaign?" Hirsh interjected.

"For the time-being, yes... I've been actively engaged with our best people rewriting our company's future. Fortunately we came out of this mess in one piece and are still strong financially. It's my responsibility that our new direction be intelligently crafted as well as kept within reasonable risk limitations. It is my intention to leave the company on a path that will make it stronger than it is now ten years down the road. I am looking into finding the best management team to fulfill that direction and when that team is in place I will resign... that should occur long before the election" Dreyden concluded. "Yes, the young man in the sixth row with the grey pinstripe suit."

"Thank you sir but my question is for Senator Bradford. Sir, what is your impression of the level of privatization that is going on? We're privatizing jails, we're trying to privatize warriors and we've even been outsourcing interrogation duties to private companies."

"Thank you for your question… it's a very important one. When the government puts out a contract to fill a bid it's supposed to go to the lowest bidder that can _**fulfill the contract specifications**_. We've all witnessed recent events where multi-billion dollar _**no-bid**_ contracts have been awarded to friends of our leaders. This is a crime done in plain view and it is an insult that we Americans endure. _**Why?**_ When government contracts are given to private companies there's a huge opportunity for services to be reduced to an absolute minimum so profits can be maximized. What often results is the lowest common denominator that is acceptable to both the contractor and the government. The contractor fulfills the obligation to provide warm bodies at the lowest price possible so the best people aren't used... that's one way the profits are kept high. Our military winds up buying parts that don't work as in the Apache helicopter scandal with Boeing.

There are certain things that do not fit neatly into any scheme of privatization... unless of course you are the schemer... like ***prisons***, which encourages the imprisonment of our population so these facilities can be filled and those profits maximized. We shouldn't incent companies to build more prisons that's absolutely ridiculous. Once these prisons exist under the private sector think of all the influence peddling that's done to make sure they stay full and profitable. What we need to do is take a look at who's in there now and who could be released back into society to lead meaningful lives.

We shouldn't privatize social security because the profiteers will strip off what they can and leave us with much less than we already have. Those should be run by ***non-profit*** professionals who are ***responsible*** for our tax dollars and not looking to get rich by cutting benefits as we've seen recently with our veterans and the substandard care that they've been given."

Bradford paused and took a long drink of water before continuing, ignoring the two dozen hands that sprung up at his momentary delay.

"Then we had the debacle in Iraq where civilian contractors were multiplying faster than rabbits and who were literally allowed to get away with murder thanks to Paul Bremer's departing edict. And let's not forget about the torture that was condoned at the highest levels within ***our*** government and the war crimes that have been perpetrated.

Those civilian interrogators were immune to prosecution from either American authorities or the new Iraqi government. Then our military personnel copied those tactics and were brought up on charges when they were found out. The media, the supposed keeper of our democratic flame, eventually got the stories out to us... but the raw truth of the matter is that these ***illegal tactics*** were instituted at the highest level of our government and the personnel that got sacrificed, by those cowards in charge, are taking the fall for following orders.

These low-level personnel are brainwashed into thinking that what they're doing by protecting their leaders is a patriotic act. Their families are disgraced and our leaders are allowed to get away with murder... *literally!* The true patriot would not take part in those illegal activities even under a direct order from a superior officer and the patriot would have the courage to stand firm, *like a rock,* to his or her convictions. The moral, self-sacrificing person is the true patriot whereas the other is degraded into a thug by those in command.

It is up to all of us to do our duty as citizens and in whatever walk of life we choose to dedicate ourselves. For all of you, here in our audience you have chosen the esteemed path of *journalist.* A true journalist cuts through the propaganda and ignores the implied threats in order to get the facts out. I have a few questions to all of you today that I'd like you to consider;

*How important is the truth to you and your employer?*

*What will you do if they try to block it from the public?*

*Is your job so important that you would be willing to go along with the power structure and knowingly remain silent and thereby culpable... or would you have the courage to stand-up and speak truth to power?*

How you answer these questions will determine whether or not you are worthy of calling yourself a journalist." Bradford concluded as he took a half step back from his podium.

"Yes, the woman with the red scarf..." Dreyden said nodding to the woman in the last row.

"Shirley Dwyer of the Washington Post... I know you're a Democrat Senator Bradford but will they support you on this platform... isn't it too progressive for them?"

"It may well be Ms. Dwyer, that has yet to be seen. Too many citizens are convinced that the Democrats and the Republicans are no more than two sides of the same coin. Heads you lose, tails you lose… it just a matter of degrees. I guess some might say that the average person prospers when the Democrats are in office and most wealthy people prosper the most when Republicans control government. All I know for absolute certainty is that the Military has never ceased to grow over the last sixty years and that someone needs to step up and say so and then do something about it. Whether we run on the Democratic ticket, which would be my desire, or are forced to run outside of the mainstream of power on an independent ticket really shouldn't matter… unfortunately we all know that it does. How many independents have been elected to office? How many to high office? How many to President? If we do run as independents it will be because we were asked to move too far away from the core values that we have begun to articulate today. If we do run on an independent ticket it will be because we no longer believe that the Democratic Party has any intention of moving away from the status quo. I believe we already know where the Republicans stand and we will do everything within the Constitution to unseat them wherever we can."

"Thank you sir, may I have a follow up question?" Dwyer asked politely.

"Go ahead…" Bradford said as he gestured with his hand.

"Do you really think you can win the Presidency on an independent ticket?

"Yes I do, with all my heart *I know we can win!* Which hole you punch on the ballot isn't going to be any different from one candidate to another… not if we've gained our senses and stopped the fraud that currently exists in our voting methods. If Americans are given a legitimate election then we will win… I have absolutely no doubt about it. Here's one more quote to consider before we end today's conference:

*"Those who cast the ballots decide nothing;
those who count the ballots decide everything."*

"Who do you think wrote that Ms. Dwyer?" Bradford asked her.

"I don't know sir... I hope it wasn't an American."

"Thankfully not, it was Josef Stalin. But what have we seen right here in *our country?* Paperless voting machines where the results *can not be verified.* Our own experts have scoffed at the vulnerability of the software used. We have seen ballots tampered with to intentionally produce erroneous results. We have seen legitimate voters removed from the final count, while others are dissuaded from voting through tactics that minimize access or provide lies telling legitimate voters that they are ineligible. But even these criminal activities pale when you take note of the fact that *we have seen the Presidency determined by the Supreme Court!* In our lifetimes!! What other period in American history would have allowed such an outrage. If anything had our Founding Fathers' stirring in their graves that insult did and if it didn't boil our blood then I think we need to examine our commitment to American ideals.

If our election process can be purified and the points of corruption removed then I guarantee you that the people will chose leaders who will bring them *prosperity without war."* Bradford concluded, taking a half step back from the podium.

Maxwell Dreyden took that opportune moment to close down the conference...

*"Thank you all for coming folks... that's it for today."* Dreyden said with a friendly wave to the crowd. He then turned the room back over to Joe Clark with a simple nod. A few moments later the two leaders left the hall without mingling while their audience continued shouting questions as they left. Instead, they rejoined two very exuberant wives who were watching from the Dreyden den.

Tim McManus remained seated in the last row observing the crowd, allowing the magnitude of what he had just witnessed to sink in. Not since Martin Luther King Jr. had he heard such a stirring speaker. *These two men **can win** on an independent ticket.* He thought to himself before enjoying the paintings he had missed earlier.